BLUE
MOTEL

edited by peter crowther

Y0-CBW-082

Blue Motel copyright © 1994 by Peter Crowther.

Introduction copyright © 1994 by Dennis Etchison.

"House of Omens" copyright © 1994 by Jessica Amanda Salmonson.

"Blue Motel" copyright © 1994 by Ian McDonald.

"The Pond" copyright © 1994 by Bentley Little.

"The Dream of Antigone" copyright © 1994 by Brian W. Aldiss.

"Susannah and the Snowbears" copyright © 1994 by Kathleen Ann Goonan.

"The Burn" copyright © 1994 by Conrad Williams.

"Quarry's Luck" copyright © 1994 by Max Allan Collins.

"The Curse" copyright © 1994 by Ed Gorman.

"Candle Magic" copyright © 1994 by Storm Constantine.

"Rosemary for Remembrance" copyright © 1994 by James Lovegrove.

"Betrayals" copyright © 1994 by Ursula K. Le Guin.

"The Reiver's Lament" copyright © 1994 by Jonathan Aycliffe.

"Isaac My Son" copyright © 1994 by Carl West and Katherine MacLean.

"The White Pirate" copyright © 1994 by Michael Moorcock.

"The Legend of Pope Joan" copyright © 1994 by David V. Barrett.

"Grandma Babka's Christmas Ginger and the Good Luck/Bad Luck Leshy" copyright © 1994 by Ken Wisman.

"All in the Telling" copyright © 1994 by Jeremy Dyson.

"Green" copyright © 1994 by Mark Morris.

All rights reserved. This book may not be reproduced, in whole or in part without the written permission of the publisher, except for the purpose of reviews.

The characters and events described in this book are fictional. Any resemblance between the characters and any person, living or dead, is purely coincidental. Because of the mature themes presented within, reader discretion is advised.

Borealis is an imprint of White Wolf Publishing.

White Wolf is committed to reducing waste in publishing. For this reason, we do not permit our covers to be "stripped" for returns, but instead require that the whole book be returned, allowing us to resell it.

White Wolf Publishing
780 Park North Boulevard, Suite 100
Clarkston, GA 30021

Printed in Canada

Also edited by Peter Crowther

NARROW HOUSES

TOUCH WOOD: Narrow Houses Volume 2

HEAVEN SENT [with Martin H. Greenberg]

TOMBS [with Edward E. Kramer]

DANTE'S DISCIPLES [with Edward E. Kramer]

Forthcoming:

DESTINATION: UNKNOWN

HEARTLANDS [with Edward E. Kramer]

CONTENTS

BLUE MOTEL

DEDICATION

Once again, for Nicky—
a few more sleepless nights, with love.

ACKNOWLEDGMENTS

Tim Holman, because everybody needs a good editor.

Kathleen Crowther,
because everyone needs a good mother.

Roger and the staff of Harrogate's Tap and Spile public
house, because everyone needs to get away from it all
once in a while.

And Oliver and Timothy Crowther, because we all need
to be reminded occasionally that the impossible often isn't.

FOREWORD

Not long after I got the go-ahead to publish a third volume of stories loosely based around a central theme of superstition, the first volume—*Narrow Houses* itself—made it to the shortlist for the Anthology category of the prestigious World Fantasy Awards. It didn't take the rosette but the nomination itself, and the many positive comments and reviews that both that first collection and its successor, *Touch Wood*, received were more than enough.

I'm delighted to be able to say that

this latest volume of the series takes our chosen theme to an almost subliminal level. Certainly there are stories which concentrate on superstitions per se—Mark Morris's "Green" and Max Allan Collins's "Quarry's Luck" are fine examples—but, for the most part, contributors have responded to my call for greater subtlety and more peripheral or tangential allegiance to the book's core theme.

Thus, this time around, we have Jeremy Dyson's engaging treatise on the universal theme of self-identification; Michael Moorcock's nautically nefarious tale which, in the great sense of Yin and Yang, postulates an oh-so-obvious converse to the old story of the Wandering Jew; and who's to say if the strange goings-on experienced by the hapless protagonist in Jonathan Aycliffe's troubled inn are fanciful or not? There are many more, all equally fascinating.

The point to all this being that, by the very nature of the definitions of the fantasy and horror genres—lesser so that of the science fiction field—there is an element of superstition intrisincally woven into the fabric of their existence. Fairies, ghosts, goblins, monsters of one kind—and, indeed, size—or another plus all manner of prices and penances to be paid...they're all the result of a certain and undeniable suspension—or adoption—of belief. And what are superstitions if not beliefs that still require some concrete proof...beliefs that only exist as a direct result of desire or need or hope?

Well if it's proof you're after, you need look no further.

Here are another seventeen stories—plus one poem and a fine introduction from Dennis Etchison—that dare to lift the moss-covered rock that lies embedded in the spongy floor of our minds and expose what lies beneath.

And, you know, if you look really closely, I think you'll agree that some of those things are still moving.

Peter Crowther
Harrogate, England
September 1994

INTRODUCTION

What sort of book is this?

From the title and cover and some of the names involved, you might conclude that it is a mystery anthology—but, as the song says, you can't judge the honey by looking at the bee.

Most mysteries are essentially reassuring, in spite of their disturbing premises, fiendishly clever plots and darkly motivated characters. They are about the violation of limits and the re-establishment of boundaries by the agents of order. Take this one, for example:

A man kills someone, and another man, a detective, decides to track down the killer and put him behind bars. The detective does this because it is his job, or because he knew the victim and has a stake in bringing the criminal to justice. Along the way he encounters many unexpected obstacles, all of which only serve to strengthen his resolve. Even at the expense of grave personal danger and perhaps devastating loss, he goes on until the killer is run to ground and justice is served.

The reason he does this is because he believes that there are, or should be, limits to human behavior; otherwise we are no better than animals. When a man's partner is murdered, someone is supposed to do something about it. In the long run it doesn't matter that the killer turns out to be the woman he loves. *Maybe I care, and maybe I'll have a few sleepless nights, but I'm sending you over.* That's the way it has to be. There is no other choice for someone with a sense of honor and decency, out of which the concept of justice arose in the first place. Solving the crime may involve a few steps outside the law, that imperfect instrument of human conscience, in order to set things right. Or it may be ironic coincidence that finally brings about a satisfactory resolution, as if God can be relied upon to mete out divine retribution as a matter of heavenly routine. *A man's got to know his limitations*, in the words of Dirty Harry Callahan. The result is always the same: the restoration of order, however temporary.

Is that what *Blue Motel* is about?

You should not be too disappointed when I tell you that the answer is a resounding *No*.

The violators in this book do not necessarily receive their just deserts. The upshot is more often an ongoing existential dilemma, suggesting that there may be no end to the cruelties described. This is more than the mordant twist that made the stories of John Collier or Roald Dahl or Alfred Hitchcock's television series so delicious. It is closer to the ethos behind David Lynch's and Mark Frost's *Twin Peaks*, a worldview that says we're quite possibly damned, or doomed to the chaos of a universe ruled by a malicious entity named Bob— or, perhaps worse, by one who is indifferent, who does not care one way or another about us at all.

There are writers here whose presence suggests that this book may have something to do with science fiction or fantasy. But this, too, only goes to prove that you can't judge the peaches by looking at the tree.

Science fiction, at least in its pure form, proposes another kind of order: namely that our existence is governed according to the rules of a clockwork universe, a nineteenth-century model of mechanical reductionism that refuses to accept as real anything not quantifiable by repeated observation and measurement. If you do not show me consensus, then it does not exist—more than that, it cannot exist, and to indulge a preoccupation with what is therefore irreal is to engage in magical thinking.

Of course the fantasists have their own whimsical

answer for this. They speak of lands and dimensions coexistent with ours, where other rules—*different* rules—apply. Whether the system is ultimately sinister or benevolent, we can all function effectively within it if we memorize the incantations, learn the names of deities that must be spoken or unspoken, and know how to read the runes. But do not forget that there are still boundaries to be guarded and maintained, because somewhere It Is Written.

These genres have something else in common, as well. They all use suspense as a primary technique, something that is not ubiquitous in non-genre fiction, the so-called "mainstream." It is a way of compelling attention and sustaining interest, and at its best is not artificial or contrived. The device arises quite naturally from some deep level of the human psyche. Perhaps it goes back to a primal curiosity about what is happening behind the closed door at the end of the hall in our childhoods, or beyond that, to the trauma about whether we were ever going to reach the end of the birth canal and come into the light; or even deeper, to our innate experience of time itself, of existence perceived linearly, one temporal increment after another, and the resultant apprehension that this lends to all lives: the nonbeing to come, or Death itself.

This is a book of stories from a related genre, but one I find altogether more interesting:

Horror.

To put it as simply as possible, these are stories about death.

Does that mean *morbid*?

Downbeat?

Depressing?

Not on your life.

If, as the song continues, you can't know a woman by looking at the mother, then you can't judge a book by looking at the cover…

Fear is an important word here, but what we fear may not be death so much as pain and suffering, and I'm gratified to see that your editor understands this. Death is not the be-all and end-all in this volume. For would it not be an insufferable arrogance, or at least a disingenuous affectation, to presume that death is undesirable? Light and darkness, being and nonbeing, form and formlessness are two sides of the same coin. You can't even have a coin without two sides. Both are necessary halves of the equation, without which there is no equation. A more correct translation of the Sanskrit word for "nothingness" might be "relativity." On the atomic level, is there any meaningful distinction between the living and the dead? And what of time—that, too, is relative, is it not? Where and what were you before you were born? Do you feel fear and dread when you think of a time before your birth, of the void out of which you came? Why, then, fear the void that is to come? What is the void but the source of the Nile, the atomic soup out of which we all arose and which we are bound to rejoin sooner or later. Is anything ever really created or lost? *So why object?* What's the big deal? What would be the point otherwise? Try to imagine playing chess with yourself. Or poker. Without someone to bluff, you would surely be bored and call it quits, and there would not even be a game.

So cheer up.

These stories are games to amuse, to disturb, to enlighten, to further confuse, to provoke as only horror stories can, by playing with this core issue, the which than which there is no whicher. They offer more than an illusion of order superimposed like a grid over the substance of our lives. They are more interesting than further endless variations on the construct of justice, cosmic or otherwise. They play with the Big One in many differing ways. Elliptically or unflinchingly, ass-backward or head-on, fearfully or humorously, with resolution or without, both plain and fancy, and all for entertainment and intellectual stimulation and the greater understanding that may follow any honest examination of such matters as life, death and eternity. It is why I write horror stories and why I read them. The end is nigh—so take heart! We are, you know, in this together.

Dennis Etchison
Los Angeles
June 1994

HOUSE

Jessica Amanda Salmonson

OF OMENS

Jessica Amanda Salmonson started writing
poetry in the 1970s as "a ploy to get lots of
little magazines for free," and her early work
tended towards the whimsical and the
heroically fantastic. More recently, however,
her poetry has matured—one need only
check out the wonderful "Lute" from
Deathrealm or "In the Looking Glass, Life
is Death," again from Deathrealm and
reprinted in last year's Year's Best
Fantasy and Horror, to realize
Salmonson now speaks with a remarkably
individual and eloquently dark voice.

But poetry isn't all she's about; a string
of novels, short story and poetry collections
and anthologies have netted her widespread

respect and several awards, including the World Fantasy Award for *Amazons!* in 1980.

"You asked for superstitions from my childhood," she writes. "Well, I was a bundle of them!" She doesn't exaggerate.

For a start, she believed that clowns were actually born that way and felt that the people she forgot to "bless" in her nightly prayers would die—unless someone else happened to bless them that night. "The list of relatives and acquaintances was very long," she adds, "their names recited obsessively with an abject fear of forgetting someone. For a while, I believed that death throughout the world was the fault of my not knowing the names of every living being or the secret of blessing them properly.

"I believed gravity could stop, so I would run from place to place, never stopping unless I was near enough to a tree or the eaves of a roof to grab hold if suddenly I began to fall upward. I made sure I could 'see' into every shadow before crossing it in case I sank into the ground, and I fretted constantly that the sun had already been extinguished, and it would take eight minutes before the last of its light would reach the earth.

"I believed that all the objects in my room had souls and, if I was unkind to any of them, they would come alive while I was sleeping and exact revenge. For a while I even became convinced all my possessions were capable of jealousy, and I struggled not to show preferences lest rejected objects began to hate me."

Come along, if you will, to Jessica's house....

A clandestine fearfulness
  lurks beneath this placidity;
Omens gather around me
  such as intellect denies.

Swallows dash about
  the chimney-pot, seeking souls;
A portrait refuses to hang straight,
  its eyes drilling into mine.
A candle gutters at midnight;
  mist shrouds the bloated moon;
An ancient oak murmurs at the bluff,
  revealing secrets to the wind.

Were these dismal hallways
  once a home?
Are these the same shadows
  where children's laughter echoed?
Were these empty rooms
  places of warmth and comfort?

Aye, these bones once were
  sheathed in pleasing flesh;
These mildewed vellums
  were a book;
This old, ill-omened house was once
  a place of laughter.

As I am enticed by the night, a
  swift awareness closes on me:
I understand the whispered secret
  of the oak, which says, "Years ago
They passed into another world,
  save one that does not know."

And so I fear swallows at the chimney-pot,
  and portraits on the wall.

BLUE MOTEL

IAN McDONALD

Ian McDonald found his literary feet with his first book, the masterful Desolation Road, and has since gone on to even greater things with the sublime King of Morning, Queen of Day and, most recently, Necroville. Alongside his longer works, he has managed to maintain an impressive parade of short stories, a graphic novel and, this year, Scissors Cut Paper Wrap Stone, a novella from Bantam. Chaga, a new SF novel set in twenty-first-century Africa, is already in the works.

As is evident from the following story, McDonald is a great sign-watcher—but there is a problem. "When you start to go out of your way to make signs happen, you can kid yourself that everything's okay," he explains. "Worse still is that if you believe in good signs, you also have to believe in bad signs…signs of divine disfavor. And because the things are so subtle, you then go through agonies trying to decide if they're for you or against you."

Which brings us nicely around to the events which befall the hapless heroine of "Blue Motel."

"It's a homage, right?" is how McDonald prefaced the letter accompanying the story. (Just as well, really, or we might not have spotted it.) "The music of Bernard Herrmann is as much a hero in the story as any other part of the Hitchcock pantheon," he continued, "so keep it in mind while you're reading."

Predestination is the name of the beast here; McDonald doesn't believe everything is preordained, but he does see some kind of pattern, even in one's acts of seeming free will. "Currently fashionable quantum theory teaches us that an infinity of possible universes can collapse out of any quantum event," he says. "What I'm concerned with is why does it always happen to be the universes with the jam-side down? Thus I believe in quantum irony: Out of all possible universes, quantum collapse is configured toward poetic justice."

In the interests of public safety, the author suggests that under no circumstances should any of the practices mentioned in this story be tried by members of the general public without the aid of a safety net. "At l e a s t ."

15

A s the saying goes, only the names are changed to protect the innocent. And, in this case, the guilty.

FRENZY

White car, black road.

Marianne Marianne, driving driving. Marianne Marianne, driving driving.

Looking in the mirror—glancing, glancing—away from the headlight dazzle of the oncoming cars—*glance*—is he there, do you see him, in the mirror, behind you, that highway cop? Did you fool him at California Charlie's, or is he still behind you, still suspicious, following, following? He was suspicious from the moment he tapped on the window and woke you up out in the desert where you'd pulled over because you couldn't drive another mile along that black highway.

Black shades, white desert.

Marianne Marianne, driving driving.

On the seat beside her, folded into a battered envelope and secured with a rubber band, fifty thousand dollars. Minus the price of a second-hand California-plate Buick.

Imaginings. Voices. California Charlie, sparky and sanforized in his shirt and dicky bow: *Hell, officer, that's*

16

the first time I ever saw the customer high-pressure the salesman.

Mr. Lavery, realtor's habitual spruceness wilting in the Phoenix city swelter: *I don't want it in the office over the weekend, Marianne. On your way home, make sure you put it in the night safe.*

Carmody, whiskey-breathed, flirtatious as only wealth can flirt, smelling of the department-store cologne his wife doubtless buys him every Christmas: *You know what I do with unhappiness? I buy it off. Fifty thousand dollars buys off a lot of unhappiness.*

Tom, damp with the post-coital honey-sweat of lunchtime meetings in cheap Phoenix hotels: *A few years more in that hole of a sports store and my father's debts will be paid off and, when the divorce comes through, we'll be together, Marianne.*

Marianne Marianne, driving driving, catches sight of the reflection of her eyes in the rearview as the first fat drops of rain burst on the windshield like crisp, juicy bugs. Hunted eyes. Guilty eyes. Are they there, Marianne, will they always be there, behind you, following, following? Not tonight. Not now, not on this long, black highway. It will be Monday before any of them notice that good, faithful Marianne, ten years' dedicated service Marianne, trustworthy Marianne, is not in for work; later still before they phone her landlady and find she has not been at home all weekend. And Lavery will leave it to the very last moment before he calls the bank to confirm his worst fears. You work for a man for ten years, you get to know him. She imagines dapper Mr. Lavery breaking the news to the Irish bluster and blow of Carmody. Again, she catches a glimpse of her eyes in the mirror. They are smiling.

She will be in another life by then.

The rain is hammering down now, so fast the wipers cannot keep up. Dark night. Black rain. Slashing wipers, squealing on the glass like the cries of black carrion birds. Blinding headlights. Marianne Marianne, can't drive further. Dazzling raindrops, tired and blinded. Driving rain, creaking wipers, rushing headlights, the money in the envelope. She must stop. Where?

There. The flickering blue neon of a motel sign, glimpsed through the slashing diagonals of rain. Tires munch wet gravel. Not much of a motel; thirteen cabins stretched in an L around the parking space. Rain cascades from faulty guttering: It's going to be a noisy night. On a rise behind the cabins looms a hulk of a house, all California Gothic verticals. Two lit upstairs windows are eyes above the devouring mouth of the porch. A silhouetted figure is a black watching pupil.

The office is unmanned. When she sounds the horn, one window-eye is extinguished and a figure comes dashing down the steps, jacket pulled over its head.

Strange boy, such a strange boy. Tall, loose-limbed, ducking and smiling, never looking you straight in the eye. Puppyish, in the sense of a puppy that has been beaten, then rewarded, then beaten again for no comprehensible reason and one day turns on the hand that rewards and beats and tears it into five dangling shreds of flesh and bone. Mother's boy.

A stuffed crow watches from the top of the filing cabinet, black glass eyes glinting.

"Have you got a vacancy?"

"Thirteen cabins, thirteen vacancies." He smiles that ducking, beaten smile, indicating the thirteen keys that hang from the "Let Us Watch Your Keys" rack. "Don't get many visitors since they moved the highway away. You must have taken a wrong turn someplace back a-ways—that's about the only way we ever get anyone. Tell you the truth, some days I don't bother turning the sign on." His hand hovers over the keys. The wooden Ma and Pa on the key rack keep their glass bead eyes strictly averted. "I'll give you cabin one; it's next to the office in case you need anything. Now, if you'll just sign the register."

"Janet Leigh. Los Angeles," she says. Long before Tom and his protracted divorce, men had always told her she looked just like the movie star. December 10, 1959. "Say, is there anywhere I can get something to eat?"

"There's a roadhouse about ten miles down the highway," says the strange boy. "But you're not really going to go out in that again, are you?" Through the open office door, rain is sheeting from the overflowing gutters. "You'd be more than welcome to have something with me up at the house; nothing grand, just milk and sandwiches, but good homely fare."

Though the office is warm, Marianne shivers as if the cold edge of a knife has been drawn across her naked thigh. She feels eyes; watching her, looking into her: the eyes of Carmody as he flirted and teased her with his thick wad of notes, the hidden eyes of the highway patrolman, the slitted eyes of California Charlie closed against the California sun, the eyes of the black stuffed crow on the filing cabinet, the bead eyes of head-scarfed Ma and pipe-smoking Pa on the key rack, the watching eyes of that old, dark house on the hill. Despite ten miles of bad road in the pouring rain, the light and warmth and company of the roadhouse seem mighty appealing.

"I think maybe I will go on to the diner after all," she says. "Thank you for your kind offer. I'll be back later, though."

The strange boy shrugs in that puppyish, cringing way of his.

"Whatever you like, Miss Leigh. I'll be up waiting for you when you get back."

Blue neon. Hammering rain.

Marianne Marianne, driving driving.

In the rearview, the blue motel sign recedes into the spatter of drops. The rain falls unrelentingly, the road stretches undeviatingly before her, the speedo needle is glued to the sixty on the dial: Nothing is

20

changed, yet Marianne is haunted by a sense of impending, of potential waiting to be realized. It is as if, instead of turning off the byroad on to the main highway, she has instead turned off the major route on to a tangle of minor roads, some of which lead her on in the way she is to go, some of which lead her back to where she has come from, and some of which lead off to unknown destinations. Though the highway goes straight ahead, she feels lost, a lone traveler in the huge dark night.

When the luminous raindrops coalesce into an orange neon farmer spastically doffing and replacing his hat to her, it seems incongruous, out of space and time, something newly invented, isolated. Secondary neons reassure her, winking pink and mauve from the wooden porch: 90 Mile Roadhouse. Eatz/Drinkz/Snax. Grills/All Day Breakfast from $1.00. Gas. Food. Ice Cold Beer. Open 25 hours. Light pours from the big, uncurtained windows. It looks like a big liner adrift on the ocean of night, far from any land.

The rain seems to be easing. Marianne switches off the frenetic slashing wipers. Ten miles. Exactly as the strange boy said.

A baker's dozen booths arranged in an L beneath the night-mirrored windows tempt her with smart chrome sugar sifters and patched naugahyde. She declines their invitation and takes a stool at the bar. There is something sad about single women in booths, like a painting she once saw, in *Harper's*, or *Vanity Fair*, or was it one of the *New Yorkers* Mr. Lavery left in the waiting area for clients? *Nighthawks at the Diner*, something like that.

At the piano at the north/northwest end of the L-shaped bar, a swarthy Middle-European-looking man in ugly horn-rim glasses squeezes odd, disquieting chords and arpeggios from the keys: uncomfortable intervals, thirds, fifths, major sevenths that circle endlessly, never reaching resolution. A jukebox blows bubbles up its neon-lit columns, awaiting its invitation to sing. Not tonight: There is strange, bleak beauty in the notes that hurry, hurry but go nowhere.

Serving You Tonight is Mona, a blousy, tired-looking woman who gives no clues to whether she is hired help or owner/proprietrix after a heavy day. Three calendars hang on the back bar: a local hardware supplier's, the gas company whose pumps stand to attention outside, and one from the Fairfax County Orange Grower's Association. Three calendars. About as good as you can reasonably expect. Four is perfection, but Marianne's never seen one. She reckons they exist only in commercial travelers' legends. Mona slides her a cup and pours coffee without a word.

The piano music spirals inward.

Tonight the 90 Mile Roadhouse has one other customer: a small fat man, perched on a stool like a Spalding Number 8 on a tee. Balding, sweating in the heat of the night. Heavy jowls. He has the look of a man for whom night is his natural element. Perhaps a commercial traveler, but for no goods Marianne can think of. Dark, minority things. He eats all the way around his fried egg, leaves it marooned in a sea of grease.

"Of course, I didn't think he'd bleed so much."

Marianne does not know what surprises her more, the words or the voice in which he speaks them. What is a fruity, oily English accent, like cold-pressed olives, doing in a place like the 90 Mile Roadhouse?

"I did that one in a crowded lift once. Fifty-six floors; fifty-five of them all to myself. I like to think I did their cardiovascular systems a service by making them walk." He stubs out the cigar he has been smoking in the yellow eye of the fried egg. Marianne suppresses a gasp. "No one with any dignity should ever have to eat a fried egg. All respect to your culinary skills, Mona." Mona grimaces and turns her attention to the cream pies beneath their transparent plastic fly covers. "It's just my idea of a conversation starter," says the fat man with the English accent. "People in all-night diners should talk. Ought to talk. Have a positive compulsion to talk, in fact. Someone has to talk the world through its limbo hours, Miss...."

"Marianne Byrd."

Handshakes are exchanged.

"Agent of chaos. The bird. The feminine principle. Flighty, mobile, untrustworthy. Peck out your eyes.

Peck off your pecker. The Harpies of Greek legend had the heads of women and the bodies of birds. Where from, bringer of chaos?"

"Phoenix," she says.

"Another bird. Where to?"

Careful, Marianne, careful, careful.

"Oh, any place. I'm not fussy. Just driving for the sake of driving."

"A bird of passage. A night bird too. No roost to lay your pretty head."

He is flirting with her. This balding, pompous slab of blubber is flirting with her.

"Oh, not really. I'm thinking of staying the night in a motel about ten miles back down the road. Quiet place, just off the highway. Can't sleep with heavy traffic roaring past my window all night."

"Good girls don't sleep in strange, off-highway motels," says the fat man. "Goodness knows what could happen to them. Horribly murdered by crazed psychopaths; knifed to death while they're taking a shower. Blood gurgling away down the plughole. Tell me, was the proprietor a man or a woman."

"A man."

"Oho. Old or young?"

"A young man. Younger than me. Not much more than a boy." Why is she telling this repellent yet strangely fascinating man these things? Compulsions in nighthawk diners.

"They're the worst. The absolute worst. I bet you if

24

you dragged the swamp nearby—because there's always a swamp nearby—you'd find the bodies of half a dozen pretty young women, just like you, who thought they'd stop the night and ended up staying a lot longer than they'd anticipated. It's their mothers. The motel proprietors' mothers, that is. Freud said it all: They want to kill their fathers and fuck their mothers. Don't pretend to get all shocked on me—Mona, coffee and the night-time special for Miss Byrd here—it's the way we're all put together, thee and me both, in here." A pudgy forefinger spirals forward to tap her forehead. "Of course, most of us never do, except for the odd juvenile motel proprietor who then realizes that he can't ever replace his father as Mother's lover, and so in a fit of jealous rage kills her too; with, say, a knife, or a necktie, or maybe a spade that's lying around somewhere. And he feels guilty: He's killed his rival and still can't have the woman he wants most. Well, you can't blame them, really, I say. Along comes this young woman, blond, pretty, wants a room for the night: Of course he's going to feel attracted to her. What red-blooded male wouldn't? But the rub is: Our motel proprietor can't allow himself to do that; it'd be betraying that first and greatest love, see? And it goes round and round in his head, the poor bastard, love, betrayal, fear, death; love, betrayal, fear, death. So he fucks them the only way he knows how. With the spade, or the necktie, or, best of all, the knife. Phallic symbol, you see. It's all in Freud, I tell you."

A sudden squall on the trailing edge of the weather front bows the windows, rattles the shingles, finds strange ways into the roadhouse and lifts the transparent lids over Mona's cream pies. The endlessly circling piano chords are suddenly chill, menacing.

"Doesn't he know any other tunes?" Marianne asks, rattled, and as she snaps out the question the music stops abruptly and the big-faced swarthy piano player spins round on his stool and he is grinning and Mona behind the counter is grinning and the strange fat man is grinning.

"You've a bitch of a sense of humor, Hitch," says Mona. "You and your stories. Mean streak wider'n a four-lane blacktop."

The fat man Hitch's jowls quiver with barely suppressed laughter.

"I'm sorry, but I don't see the joke, mister," says Marianne.

"Who says there's a joke?" says the fat man, and at that Mona and the piano player explode with laughter: tears-down-your-cheeks laughter, stitch-in-your-side laughter, piss-in-your-pants laughter. The clatter-clack of Marianne's heels on the maple floor as she storms from the bar only sends them into deeper ecstasies of laughing.

"Mind y'all have sweet dreams in your l'il ol' motel room, now," shouts Hitch in namby-pamby Scarlett O'Hara as the door of the 90 Mile Roadhouse slams. From the car Marianne can see the bodies convulsed in agonies of mirth, framed within the big picture windows.

Car starts, first pull.

In the mirror as she draws away, they are still laughing silently.

Marianne Marianne, driving driving.

The moon has sailed out from behind the storm front. The road is a silver band beneath it, gleaming with passing rain. The dashboard clock has stopped at the stroke of midnight; though she knows it is far later than that, Marianne is not tired. The night wind from the air vents is exhilarating, narcotic; each of the few cars she meets on the highway is a fellow conspirator, shiftily averting gazes in a dipping of headlight beams.

When next she awakes it will be in Pleasant City with the heavy warmth and man-smell of Tom beside her. The uncertainties she felt, the limbo of countless roads radiating from this silver highway into an infinity of possible futures are fixed now on that surety. She knows where she has come from; she knows where she is going. There is no doubt now, no possibility of turning back. Perhaps she should be thankful to that weird fat limey for putting her on to this road that only leads forward.

She feels as if she has changed destinies. In this new destiny, she drives through the night and comes with the dawn to Pleasant City and the car park behind Lewis's Sport and Leisure Store. Tom comes unwashed, unshaven, blinking to the knocking, knocking on his door wondering what the/why the hell? and she falls into his arms and never leaves them again. The divorce comes through, the debts are paid off, and they live happily ever after in Pleasant City where no one will ever find them. It is written.

Behind the wheel, Marianne smiles to her reflection in the rearview mirror as she drives down the moonlit highway, fifty thousand dollars minus the price of a California-plate Buick spilling out of her purse on the seat beside her. Behind her, the storm passes into the east. Driving, driving.

White car, white road.

SHADOW OF A DOUBT

Pleasant City is. Otherwise they wouldn't have called it that. Its industries are family-run and non-polluting. Its businesses are personal and friendly. Its doctors are amenable to antisocial hours and the vagaries of family finance; its lawyers advertise their names twice—in brass on the wall, in gilt on the window; its accountants, though members of the Fairfax County Country Club, are seldom boring. The 78s in the maltshop jukebox have not been changed since Glen Miller went MIA; the music shop sells music, by the sheet, but for those who must have plastic, you can try before you buy in any one of half a dozen soundproofed listening booths. Gumball machines stand unmolested on the sidewalks, domed heads shaded from the noonday sun by striped canvas awnings bearing the names and trades of the founding families: The features in the Cosmotheka Movie House change invariably Mondays and Thursdays (save a unique exception for *Gone With the Wind*), last continuous show 6:30 all seats fully bookable. Cinema, Presbyterian Church and porticoed City Hall face each other across the equilateral triangle of shaved turf called Liberty Park. The bandstand has been locked up since that night in 1946 when homecoming hero Rog O. Thornhill saw Japs in the undergrowth and shot out every window on the square, three ladies leaving the Presbyterian Church Whist Drive and Police Officer Gavin Elster, briefly transforming Pleasant City, CA into the hell that was forever Guadalcanal before blowing the rear two thirds of his head into the rafters. Rotting condoms drifted by the wind against the cast-iron balustrade are the only commemoration of the day Marine Sergeant Thornhill achieved his highest ever kill rate.

The houses are white-painted wood, each set back behind grass and trees, each with its *own* drive and garage. Where there are fences, they are of the Shaker pierced-picket design. These too are painted white. The people cut the grass verges and keep the streets clean.

Pleasant City, California. Population: 37,500. Elevation: 2,250. The Littlest Big City in the West. Oh yes.

The bell jingles on its curved spring as Marianne

Byrd closes the front door of Lewis Sports and Leisure Store behind her and steps into the sunlit street. At first she thought it would drive her crazy, ringing and jingling for every customer, going out and coming in, but now she no longer notices it.

Tom said she would.

Tom said she would get to know them. It will take time, people are slow in Pleasant City. He is right about that too.

So she nods to Mr. Jeffries with the broken leg in the Electric Company Office and he nods back to her: *Good morning, Marianne.* And the Robies in the Ice Cream Parlor smile and wave, though Rose, as a good Catholic, officially can't approve of the domestic set-up back of the Sports Store. Behind his lathered-up victim, Mr. Rusk the barber heliographs good morning with a silver flourish of his cut-throat, and the Balestero Brothers, who have not moved from their chairs in front of the Loomis Hardware store since before the New Deal, grin monodentally and run their eye up and down Marianne's stocking seams. Marianne doesn't mind, she quite likes the feel of the old men's eyeballs rolling all the way up to her fanny and down again. Between the Balestero Brothers sits a bright parakeet in a rusty cage. Every day they let it out to fly around Liberty Park; just as it comes to the conclusion that it is free forever, they whistle it back to its cage.

It always comes.

There is a bell on the door of Shoebridge Realty, a modern electrical one that heralds customers with a rude blast of ringing and hastens their departure with a vulgar rattle. Marianne hates the doorbell of Shoebridge's. Marianne hates most things about Shoebridge's. The arrangement of the desks, the mock-oak plastic paneling, the languishing, slightly over-watered palms—which one of the two receptionists, the tarty one or the escapee from the Carnegie Library is responsible for them?—remind her too much of another realtor's, under another sky, another time.

The magazines on the coffee table have cover paintings of melancholy midnight diners and apartments where no one looks at anyone else.

Marianne always dresses up to go to Shoebridge Realty. Best blouse, best skirt, best stockings, best shoes. High heels. Thus attired she can stand over the younger, prettier receptionist and intimidate her.

"Hello, Miss Byrd. The Lewis account, is it?"

She will not be thought a tramp, least of all by a receptionist in Shoebridge Realty.

"Hello, Jessie, yes. I'd like to make another payment."

"Certainly, Miss Byrd."

"Can I borrow your pen, please?"

"Of course."

Out back, behind the little veneered half-walls, Shoebridge is rising from his desk.

Amount in words: *one hundred and forty dollars*. In

figures: thousand hundreds tens units. Cents as written. $140.00. Lewis Sports and Leisure: Number Two Account. Authorized signature.

"Good morning, Miss Byrd, isn't it a lovely morning? Hot enough for you?"

"Real California summer, Mr. Shoebridge."

Slipping in behind the tarty receptionist, Jessie, he opens a gilt-edged ledger.

Heart pounds. Blood thunders. Far far away, birds, screaming screaming.

Shoebridge purses his lips. Eyes roll down the columns.

"Is there a problem, Mr. Shoebridge?"

"Oh, no problem, Marianne. Quite the reverse. In seven months the account has gone from being in serious arrears to five months in advance. If only all our leaseholders were this conscientious. And successful. The sports equipment business must be booming."

"Well, it is summer, Mr. Shoebridge, when young men's fancy turns to healthy pursuits." Jessie commutes a snicker to a discreet cough. "And Tom's outfitting the Pleasant City Little Leaguers this season. Shirts, shoes, masks, gloves, all with 'Sponsored by Lewis Sports and Leisure' stuck wherever we can get it to stick."

Mr. Shoebridge closes the ledger, steps back and mimes a beautiful smackeroonie, right over the bleachers, right over the Countess Cup Cakes billboard and the advertisement for Equivitol Chickfeed showing a squab carrying an enormous codfish strapped to its back, right over the A.T.&S.F. tracks into Little League Legend.

"Ten men out..." says Marianne, closing her purse.

Vrrp goes the rude doorbell behind her. Out of the corner of her eye she glimpses Miss Tarty and Miss Carnegie Library lean forward across their desks toward each other. They will be talking about her. They all talk about her, for all their smiles and waves and "good mornings," behind the closed doors and the pulled-down shutters. *Store assistant my foot; when they lock their doors and close their shutters and shut off the lights, it stops being boss and hired hand soon enough, I tell you; in that back room, that's where it all stops. Vernon Lowry actually saw into it when he was making a delivery: There's one bed. Two pillows. That's right. And her things are all over the washroom. Ah hah. He left his wife for her, you know. Soon as the D.I.V.O.R.C.E. comes through there'll be a plain gold band third finger left hand P.D.Q. You can be sure of that. Las Vegas wedding. Uh huh. Mexican divorce, soon enough, I reckon. And all those airs and graces she puts on; well, if she's so mighty fine what's she doing working in Lewis's? Ah hah, I tell you, no Yankee cracker or Southern belle ever talked like that, that's right, there's three generations of boondock white trash in there or I'm no judge of people. And the way she pushes herself forward, why, I tell you, she was standing there flirting with old Shoebridge.*

Well, let them talk. The flirting she does with the men she pays is part of the game; for all the money she has signed over their counters and into their ledgers, there is still more in the Lewis Sports and Leisure Number Two Account than they will make in their entire lives at Shoebridge Realty. Which of them, between the back-seat fumblings and the twenty-cent Tales of Torrid Romance will ever love a man so much that they will think the unthinkable, dare the undareable, do the undoable for him? Which of them will give up everything she owns, go into exile in a menial job among people who look and whisper; all out of love for a man? What do they know of love?

Marianne is smiling to herself as Tom's doorbell jingles unheard behind her.

"You look happy, honey."

"Oh, just anticipating the future, Tom. Sometimes when I think that nothing will ever change, I remind myself that those divorce papers get that little bit closer every day." Look at him, standing behind that counter with the bats and balls and shorts and shoes racked up behind him, smelling slightly of rubber, sweat and exertion. Like he does in that bed with the two pillows in the stockroom. College football muscles have not yet slackened into middle-age fat. She loves to lie back on that bed at the end of the day, light a cigarette, close her eyes and listen to the clank of weights, the small puffs and heaves of exercise, knowing that he does it for her. He wishes more than just a fit body for her and becomes morose when he cannot deliver it. What woman, given such love, would not help her man realize his dreams? "Is it all right if I'm a couple of minutes late after lunch, Tom? I want to get a couple of things."

"You don't have to ask, Marianne."

Ting goes the bell as she makes her way across the triangle to the Electric Office to put another little payment of the installment plan dream down on Mr. Jeffries's desk. And to establish her *bona fide*, a brief flirtation with the silks and satins in Wendover's Department Store.

"He'll like this," she says, running her fingers sensuously over the fabric purely to give the shop assistant something to gossip about.

Ting.

She waits until the customer has left contented with his junior baseball kit before showing Tom her goods.

"Well, what do you think?" She holds the brassiere up against her body. Suggestions of ribbed swellings. Dress to undress. "Preview of coming attractions." Forefingers jiggle the straps. Big and bouncy. Oh yes. Like he says he likes them. In his face.

Not a twitch.

Marianne shimmies behind the counter and drapes the bra over his head. Straps looped around ears; Mr. Tit Head. Twice.

Times past, less than that would have been provocation enough for him to pull down the blinds, turn the *Closed* sign outward and carry her, legs locked around his waist, arms around his shoulders, to the bed with the two pillows among the athletic supports. Today, he unhooks the straps, takes the thing off his head and lets it drop to the floor.

"Mighty fine, Marianne," he says, looking anywhere, at anything, but at her. "Always enough for something fine, something soft, something satiny and lacy for Miss Marianne Byrd."

"Tom, honey, what do you mean? What's the matter?" she asks as one by one the sounds of Pleasant City going about its business vanish into the red thunder of her bloodstream.

"Since precisely when has Lewis Sports and Leisure had a Number Two Account?"

It lies on the counter top; a paper accusation, seven inches by three. Pacific Trust Bank, Fairfax County Branch.

A paper annihilation. The sound of it is like the sudden, savage dashing of rosined bows across strings.

"Jessie called round from Shoebridge's while you were out, Marianne. Seems in your haste you forgot to sign it. 'Maybe you could, Mr. Lewis.'" He impersonates Jessie's manufactured dumb-blonde squeak. "'I'm sure the boss can sign his own Number Two Account.' And do you know what I did, Marianne? I stood there like a damn fool, and told that girl to her face that there must be some mistake, we don't have a Number Two

Account. Like a goddamn fool, I called her and Mr. Shoebridge bare-faced liars."

Tom is looking at her now. There is nothing in his eyes she can remember or recognize.

"I called the bank, Marianne. The Pacific Trust. Mr. Pemberton is the manager. But you know that, don't you? Do you know what kind of fool you feel when you have to ask about the existence of your own bank account? Very helpful, was Mr. Pemberton; very helpful people, the Pacific Trust. I should move my main account there.

"Lewis Sports and Leisure: Number Two Account. A/C No. 1034865, opened January 8, 1960, by Mrs. Marianne Byrd-Lewis, resident at 18B Main Street, Pleasant City, California. Opening balance, forty-nine thousand, two hundred and eight dollars; cash. Current balance, forty three thousand six hundred and forty dollars. Discrepancy between opening and current balances, five thousand six hundred and forty dollars."

Mrs. Kominsky from the donut shop leads her bulbous son up to the door, sees the closed sign and the business being transacted behind it. She pulls him away.

"Where?"

"To pay them off."

"I didn't ask why. I know why. I asked where. Where did it come from? Fifty thousand dollars, Marianne…" It's a fortune. It's money so much, so big that it goes beyond reality, into Ripley's Believe It Or Not Land. He is looking at her now as if she is something unbelievable, as if she is a stranger he is meeting for the first time. She supposes she is. When you live so long, so close to guilt and secrecy it works its way into you, it finds a warm, nesting space just below your liver and curls and knots and coils into a new organ; an organ of secrecy that is so much a vital part of you that, like your other organs, you no longer think about it, though your continued existence depends on its functioning. Now those tender sweetbreads and tripes have been torn out, slit open, spread on the Formica counter-top of Lewis Sports and Leisure Store.

Even so, for a moment she considers lying. Rich relatives, prematurely felled; spinster aunts enthroned in California Gothic. In the same moment she rejects them. They could only be defensive lies to confuse him and protect her, and in all the deceits and falsehoods she has spun around herself there was never any intent to hurt him, nor serve herself at his expense. Only him, only his good, only love. He deserves truth. He will have truth.

"It comes from a Mr. Carmody of Phoenix, who intended using it to buy his wife a house as an anniversary present. It was left at the office of Lavery Real Estate to be lodged in the bank's safe deposit box. I stole it." And she tells him. She tells him of the stolen lunch-hours, the snatched weekends, the pay-by-the-hour hotels and motels and the back seats of

38

cars rendez-vous-ing at remote Arizona diners and how
she had seen them stretching before her in an endless
parade of jotted telephone messages and ciphers in
diaries, that would never be more than meat on the
hoof, taken on the run because he was chained
between the clashing rocks of his dead father's debts
and his living wife's threats. She tells back to him all
those hopes and dreams of freedom, of how he said he
would do anything, anything to pay off the debts, rid
himself of his wife and be free to live again, with her.
In those motel cabins, those hotel rooms, cradled in
warm leatherette with radio playing between the seats
beneath her head, he had told her he loved her; over
and over; he loved her, he loved her, but love is more
than words, love is deeds; true love, great love will
contemplate anything for the beloved; love like that
speaks itself in the unspeakable; love like that is not a
whisper among the sweat-damp blond curls behind the
ear, but the sudden clear, cold courage to walk past the
bank with the fifty thousand dollars in your purse, walk
into your rooms, pack your things and drive out into
the darkness.

As she tells Tom all these things, the spirit seems
to go out of him. He shakes his head, mumbles no, no.

"I did it for you, Tom," Marianne says.

"I didn't ask you to!" Tom cries. "When did I ever
ask you to lie for me, cheat for me, steal for me? I don't
want that from you, I could never want that from you."
Suddenly he is pulling bills, checks, IOUs from the

cash drawer, pushing them into her hands, her purse, down the front of her dress. "Take it, take it, I don't want it, I can't have it, take it, put it back, put the whole fifty thousand back where it came from. I'll empty out my accounts, cash in an insurance policy, sell the fucking shop, that should be worth a few thousand even with its debts, but then I'm forgetting, aren't I? There are no debts: Mr. Jeffries at the Electric Company and Mr. Shoebridge at the Real Estate and Mr. Thorwald at the gas and Mr. de Winter at the insurance and Mr. Ferguson the supplier, all paid off and up to date with Mr. Fucking Carmody's fifty fucking thousand dollars!"

Weeping with rage and frustration, he sweeps the loose bills and small change off the counter into her arms. *Throws* them at her.

"I can't take it back, Tom," Marianne says. Outside, in a world from which she is insulated by the thunder of gathering inevitability, one sound penetrates: the Balestero Brothers whistling their parakeet down from the top of the bandstand to its cage. "It's been too long. Carmody'll have claimed on his insurance; he won't have it back now. He wouldn't have, anyway, you didn't meet him, Tom; he's the kind of man always has to get something, and it doesn't have to be money. So you see, I couldn't put it back." *Truth*, Marianne. You have promised yourself to tell the truth. Whatever he may damn you for, it will not be for a liar. "Even if I wanted to. But I don't want to, Tom. You know something? I said I did it for you, but that's only part of the truth. The whole truth is that I did it for me. I enjoyed stealing it. It felt good taking the money, more money than you or I could dream of, Tom. And I took it, just like that, and everyone's carefully arranged little destinies were all upset. By a little blond real estate clerk. By little me, Tom. I liked stealing it. I like having it."

"Then have it," he says, but he has lost the high ground. What had been Jehovah-righteousness is now the whining of kicked dogs; petty, petulant. "Keep it. Keep all of it." Turning his back on her, he pulls down boxes of sports shoes, sends left feet right feet, cleat soles spike soles tumbling. "Keep the whole fucking place. You paid for it, didn't you? I'm only the hired hand, the shop boy, the hired dick in the bed in the storeroom. All paid for, all earned. They were debts, yes, but they were my debts, my responsibilities. My work, my achievement, and you took them away from me. You bought me, Marianne—no, you stole me. You stole me, my hopes, my plans, my world, just like you stole that fifty thousand dollars. On a whim. Without a moment's thought or feeling. Without any regard for consequences. Name of Christ, woman, how did you ever expect to get away with it? Opening secret accounts, openly paying off debts; it was only a matter of time before someone would have told me. You might as well have gone around with *thief* tattooed on your forehead."

Because he is right; because, down there beneath her liver with the pride and the notoriety and the secrecy, coiled closer than any two bodies in a storeroom, lies a guilt that needs to name itself, to stand naked in the street so that it may be punished and thus destroy itself. Because she knows, and hates as much as loves this, she turns on him.

"I never had you for a coward, Tom. Yellow. Afraid. Tied. I gave you the chance to be free. But you can't give them up, can you? This shop, your wife, your dead father, this town, your place in it; your comfortable, familiar world. You can come with me any place on earth, live any life you choose, but that kind of freedom terrifies you, doesn't it? You don't want it, it's too much for you. You're a coward in the end."

Ting! goes the bell of Lewis Sports and Leisure Store behind him.

"Tom!"

No answer.

"I loved you, Tom!"

Not even an early afternoon shadow on the sidewalk. One by one, Marianne Byrd picks up the scattered sports shoes, puts them in the correct boxes by model and size and stacks them on the proper shelf.

Ting.

She whirls, heart flying up within her. A small, squat man, like an ambulatory toad, stands on the mat, peering around him as his eyes adjust from street glare to shop gloom.

"It really is, you know." His voice is a sixty-a-day trudge through melting blacktop. "Pleasant City," he adds, answering his own hookline.

"I'm sorry, we're closed."

"That's all right. I wasn't, ah, looking to buy anything." He advances into the store, sniffs deeply. "Ah. Sweat, liniment and warm rubber. Actually, I'm looking for someone."

"Mr. Lewis isn't in at the moment."

The squat man runs the tip of his tongue over his lips, doffs his greasy hat.

"It's not Mr. Lewis I'm looking for. I've heard that a Miss Marianne Byrd works here."

"You've found her. I'm Miss Byrd."

"Oh, that's good. My name is Antrobus; my card." A nicotine-edged rectangle of pasteboard. Pocket fluff clings to the creased corners. "I'm a private detective."

ROPE

She no longer resists the ball gag. She struggles, because he likes her to struggle when he buckles the strap hard across the back of her head, when he pulls tight the knots, when he snaps the locks and fits the little saw-toothed clamps, but she knows better than to resist, now. So she moans, and mimics that look of helpless dread he showed her in the magazines as he fastens her hands above her to the ceiling hook and straps her thighs and ankles to the special trestle he has made for her. She pretends to writhe and fight as he straddles her over the bar.

He steps back across the motel room to admire his handiwork before closing for the final refinements. The ritual is that he presses his sweating face—he is always, always sweating—close to hers and holds up the nipple clips. Her part then is to struggle, eyes wide with fear. When your mouth is contorted around a tooth-marked ball of hard rubber, you learn to do the expressive stuff with your eyes.

She hopes he will not go and buy whiskey tonight. Sometimes, when it's been a bad drive up from Phoenix, he will leave her and go out to the liquor store at the crossroads. No one need take two hours to buy a bottle of whiskey and come back. Though the pain in whatever part of her he has pulled out of true is cruel, she would rather that he never came back at all. The whiskey mocks the impotence inside him, and the impotence will work out its frustration and anger with a studded leather paddle on the soft places of her body.

Thank God, he does not look like he will need the whiskey tonight. But he'll gloat. He must gloat; it is as much part of it as the rope and the gag. He must crow his cleverness and mastery and dominance over a bound, naked, dumb woman.

He pulls the cracked leatherette lounge chair around to face her and settles deeply into it. Rolls of fat spill softly over each other. Sweat glues his body hair into sleek spines. He will sit, just watching, for several minutes without speaking.

In the next cabin, a radio is playing loudly against the stud wall. Out on the highway, cars' lights briefly illuminate the thin floral print curtain on its plastic-coated wire and pass by.

When he does begin to speak, his voice is like some long, many-legged insect emerging from the hole in his creases of facial fat.

"Did you think you were clever? Eh? Did you think you'd get clean away, that no one would ever find you, that you'd live happy ever after with that fuck-brained jock of a boyfriend? Did you? Did you?" At this point the script calls for him to slap the paddle on the arm of the chair. FX: smack of studded leather on leatherette. Her part is to frantically shake her head—depending on the degree of freedom he has allowed her, he is not beyond roping her head and tying it to the wall—and mumble into her gag things that sound like *no, no, never, Mr. Antrobus.*

"Let me tell you, girlie, no one ever gets clean away. They always leave something behind them; there's always something they forget to do, or do too well—you'd be surprised how often that one trips them up, the things that are just that teeny bit overdone. Things it takes a trained eye and mind to spot. And you were a good one, Missy Marianne; lesser than J. J. Antrobus, well, they might have lost the scent, but there's the blood of the Navajo in these veins—Great-grandpa

Antrobus fucked some squaw up on the Indian nation. Greatest trackers on God's earth, the Navajo."

The plot calls here for her to squirm in fear for her soft white flesh in the hands of the savage red man.

"You see, I reckoned straight off you'd headed west. Natural direction for anyone trying to get away. Go west, young man! So I didn't bother checking with friends or family—you might be stupid, but not that stupid. Thing is, I overestimated you. I reckoned you'd gone straight to Los Angeles, so I overshot Pleasant City and wasted a whole heap of time, and that cost a dirty dime or two—on top of what you've already cost Mr. Carmody." He points the paddle, broad as the palms of both hands, at her and she has so many times before, she tries to cringe away and roll her eyes just like Betty Page. "But something in my Navajo blood told me the trail was cold, so back I went, and with great diligence and skill, and even more expense, I started all over again."

She knows that he knows that she cannot hold herself off the knife-edge of the trestle much longer.

"And J. J. Antrobus surely hates to be shown to be wrong, girlie. But: diligence. Always diligence. And it paid off. Do you know what I found?"

She knows. She knows. God damn it, she knows.

"I found the excellent Mr. California Charlie, Used Car Dealer of Fairdale in this Sunshine State, and he had a very vivid memory of a young blonde who seemed to be in a hell of a hurry to buy a car off him.

'Hell, Antrobus, first time I ever saw the customer high-pressure the salesman.' Well, being a good citizen who knew what should be done to bad girls who take things that aren't theirs, he was only too pleased to give me the details of the car you'd bought off him."

Marianne watches with numb fascination the sweat break from Antrobus's forehead, roll down his face and drop in heavy, oleaginous spheres down the rolls of belly fat to nestle among the chrome studs of his leather shorts.

"America's greatest strength is her citizens. The free man, responsible to himself and his fellow; how can the Reds ever imagine they could beat that? It warms my old heart; so many good citizens out there. That nice boy at the motel just off the main road: 'Why yes, Mr. Antrobus, I recognize that photograph; she booked a cabin here for the night, let me see, December tenth, it was. There she is, under the name of Janet Leigh. I didn't think it was her real name—in the hospitality business you get to be able to tell when people aren't what they seem. Went up to the 90 Mile Roadhouse to get something to eat. Never came back. Always imagined something terrible had happened to her.'"

Her nipples sting where salt sweat worries at the serrations. Soon now, soon now, it will be over. In a sense it is worse than the physical pain, for Antrobus is always clever at inventing new ways to surprise her, but the tedious, misogynistic drone of his own cleverness never changes. The litany, the responses,

47

the rubrics are as invariable and holy as high mass in St. Patrick's. Now, he will rise from the chair and caress the line of her jaw with the devil's tail tip of the paddle.

"And the woman at the 90 Mile Roadhouse—well normally, I wouldn't trust a woman to remember anything right—but she surprised me, I'll admit it; every detail of the night you came in, clear as day; her, and that fat limey, and the Jewish piano-playing pisher; they all remembered the bad girl from Arizona with the guilty look. 'Ask her if she's still getting up to trouble in strange men's motels,' that fucking limey told me to tell you. Funny man, real funny. Hah fucking hah, Marianne."

According to the ritual, she has to pant and strain for the rod as if she wants it more than anything.

"And so Antrobus comes to this nice little burg called Pleasant City and, what do you know? there, right in the middle of Main Street, is the car he's been looking for, right outside Lewis Sports and Leisure Store. Of course, it's a sign from God, so in goes Antrobus, and well, I do declare! there is the bad little girl who thought that by hiding she could escape what was coming to her; a very bad little girl who got found out by Mr. James Jonah Antrobus and now has to get punished."

Stepping behind her, he yanks her off the trestle by her aching arms. With a whistle, the paddle goes up. And comes down.

✢

She was a fool to have let him into the shop that day when Tom walked out forever. She was a fool to have let him stand there sniffing the air like it was purest Chanel to him—it was, she supposes—and given him space to make his little proposition. She was a fool to have listened.

"You can have it back, take it back to him. I have lost the only man I ever loved because of it. I'll pay back what I spent; honest, I will."

The sky can only fall once. When the toad-like man had announced himself as a detective hired to find Carmody's money, she had discovered that there is a limit to pain, even a certain dim joy at the heart of it. Now it could end.

She had thought.

"Uh, uh, Missy Marianne. Too late for that. It's in the hands of the law now. And crossing state lines with it; now that was a damn fool stupid thing to do; that's a Federal offense. You done wrong, you gonna get punished for it. But J. J. Antrobus is a man who can see his way to reason where others can't. Trying to find one runaway in a big country like this, it's like that old haystack needle, lady, and maybe, in return for the right, eh, inducement? I could persuade my clients that it's a wild goose chase trying to find you."

"I can't go to jail. I can't, it would kill me."

"You won't have to go to jail if you're wise."

"How much do you want?" Out of the purse, onto the counter, the old friendly traitor: Lewis Sports and Leisure Number Two Account checkbook.

"Lady lady lady, I thought someone in your position would understand a little more about discretion, nah? Not here, Missy Marianne, not where people can see. Meet me here." He had written the name and location of a motel on the back of his business card with a silver pencil. Down on the state line, equal distances from Phoenix and Pleasant City. "Saturday. About eight? The first cabin. I've booked it, I'll be waiting for you."

He had turned to leave.

"How much? How much do you want?"

Ting, the doorbell had said.

Lewis Sports and Leisure Number Two Account had been closed, stories spread to the chattering classes of Pleasant City about Tom's sick aunt in Wisconsin, and given the state of her health she didn't really know if he'd be back, let alone when. The money had gone into an envelope and the envelope into a purse and the purse into the front seat of California Charlie's '59-plate Buick and the '59 Buick down the long black road, many hours, down to the state line and the place the detective had written on his card where the blue neon announced *rooms to let*.

She had laid the money on the dressing table in Cabin One. The veneer was coming unglued at the corners.

"How much do you want?" she had asked. "It's all there. Name your price."

"Oh, it's not money I want, Missy Marianne," Antrobus had said, sunk deep in the only armchair. "No, no, no, no, not money. I've got more money than I know what to do with. It's you, Marianne, that I want. You're my price."

He had opened his overnight case then and taken out what he called "the library" and shown her what he wanted to do with her, and how, and for how long, and when he had shown her all those women looking into the camera with expressions that all said *understand, I'm only doing this for the money*, he dug down into the bottom of the bag and brought out the things with which he wanted to do it to her.

And that was the first Saturday. Antrobus's bookings of Cabin One—next to the office, should he need anything—are the only regular money the proprietor has ever seen: The motel is isolated, off the main routes. Its small trade is mostly passing; commercial travelers, geologists, vacationers. It is custom-made for blackmail: Antrobus ensures the proprietor's silence by supplying him with photographs of the sessions. When the proprietor has finished with them, he sells them to truckers down at the Twin Oaks Tavern across the Colorado. He turns a blind eye to Antrobus's improvements to the fixtures and furnishings. The money is still in Marianne's purse. It goes everywhere with her. She never thinks about it, now.

And it is another Saturday, and Marianne is behind the wheel again, driving, driving, down to the Blue Motel on the state line.

Why put yourself through it, Marianne? Jail could be no worse. Why not this Saturday afternoon turn the car along one of those myriad different headings you sensed that night at the 90 Mile Roadhouse, take any one of them away from here and drive? The guilt will not let her. Not merely the guilt of being a thief, but the guilt of being herself, of there being something in her nature that makes men want her, need her and in the end judge her. Antrobus, Tom, Mr. Lavery; they have all sat in judgment over her. All the men she has ever known have been judges, sentencing her to give up her freedom to their desires.

She cannot drive away, not while her guilt finds a little expiation in Antrobus's pain and humiliation in the Blue Motel.

He has a new one for her. He has been working hard. It is a kind of double-ended gallows, with cross-pieces about four feet wide, one fixed to the place where the rope hangs, the other to the crosspiece at the foot. Both are fitted with rope loops. He has been thinking about it all the way up from Phoenix. She takes her clothes off and kneels in the way she has been taught as he shows her with photographs from The Library how the apparatus works.

The gag is fitted. Panting, Antrobus hauls her up. Her ankles are tied to the upper beam, her wrists to the lower. Spread-eagled upside down, Marianne Byrd hangs from the wooden gallows. Antrobus fastens a cinch around her middle, pulls it in to tie it to the main upright, arching her into an elegant, swallow-like crescent.

"Look, you're flying!" he says, proudly. Then he goes and does the gloating, looking thing in his chair.

Tonight, she knows, will be a whiskey night.

After the gloating is done, he takes the camera from his overnighter. Blue flashbulbs pop in the Blue Motel as she looks despairingly into the camera, just like Betty Page. He shoots off a complete film. Upside down, she watches him masturbate ferociously by the light from the motel neons. When he is done, he sits a long time, watching, staring, half-aroused, half-disgusted.

Definitely, a whiskey night.

"I'm going out," he says after a time, pulling on street clothes over his smeared leather shorts. He locks the door behind him. In the blue light, Marianne swings on her gallows. With the vast mass of the world balanced above her head, or so it seems, she thinks again about that other Blue Motel on its lonely highway, and how differently the world might have turned out had she turned her back on the rain, accepted that strange boy's invitation of milk and sandwiches, showered off the dust and guilt and madness and the next day gone back to well-paid anonymity.

In the car park, patrons come and go in a slamming of doors and honking of horns while in Cabin One the wooden tree creaks beneath the weight of its passenger. It is after midnight before Antrobus returns. He sits in his chair drinking from the bottle watching the California night sweat run down Marianne's body and drip from the nipple clamps to the dirty carpet. Any moment, when he is two thirds down the bottle of Wild Turkey, he will start in with the paddle and not know when to stop.

This night, he does not. The leather lies there on the arm of the chair. Antrobus sits slumped. Whiskey tears force themselves from his eyes.

"What are we going to do, Marianne?" he says gently. "It can't go on like this; weekend nights snatched at some motel miles from anywhere. It's not enough for me. I know you're grateful for what I'm helping you realize about yourself, but it has to be more, I know you understand that. I want it to be more, Marianne; and I know you want it too: a place where we can have each other, explore what we have with each other, reach new heights, explore new understandings of what we've found together."

Heart frozen by pure horror, Marianne's struggles are not feigned this time. Antrobus's knots are tight and strong.

"The money would set us up, Marianne. Buy us a little place; quiet, nice, some out of the way place where people wouldn't talk. We both know what that's like, Marianne; people, and the way they talk. We could fit it out nicely; get better stuff than this fucking junk; a place where we could make a lifetime commitment to each other, to love and serve. That's what I want, Marianne, that's what I need."

The ball gag has never let past any of her other screams. It does not fail now.

"You understand, Marianne, that I only punish you because I love you." Unbelievably, he puts the paddle back into his case and takes out a big pair of scissors. Knots pull tight under weight: He cuts the ropes and lets Marianne down. "You understand what I mean," he whispers as he lays the semi-conscious Marianne tenderly on the bed. "We'll talk, you'll see." Slipping off his leather shorts, he goes to shower off the jizz and sweat and whiskey.

Marianne understands what he means. And she understands what she has to do. The only thing she can do. She understands that every turning she had taken that she thought was a road to greater freedom was in fact a turning away from it, on to ways ever more constricting and restricting, leading here. Nowhere else than this Blue Motel. All her freedoms have been imprisonments, a narrowing down of choice to one point. The point of a pair of silver scissors.

Her hands are numb from the rope, her grip uncertain. Her bare feet are silent on the bathroom tiles. Hot water gushes jollily. She reverses her hold on the scissors to the strong, down-slashing grip. Antrobus is an ungainly black silhouette against the translucent curtain.

She pulls back the curtain. She lifts the scissors high above her head. She knows what she must do.

Yet, she hesitates a fatal moment.

Antrobus turns, sensing her shadow. His eyes bulge in disbelief. Water cascades from the hairy triangle of his genitals.

"You should put that down, girlie, you're going to cut your fingers off."

With a cry like a black bird, Marianne strikes. The tip of the scissors buries itself in the side of Antrobus's neck just above the collar bone.

He stares at the silver scissors, at the striking hand, at Marianne, at his blood spiraling down the plughole.

"Why, you."

She wrenches the scissors free and lashes at him with the open blades. Strike strike strike strike. Long bloody gashes open up in his thighs, chest, belly blubber. Antrobus reels backward against the tiled wall. Hot gushing water washes the wounds clean. Strike strike strike. Marianne pants in exertion as she slashes down with the scissors: *Die die die, just die, you fat fuck, why won't you die?* She had not realized how difficult it is to kill a man. Antrobus shields his face and

56

genitals with his hands. Marianne drives the point of the scissors into the backs of them again and again and again and again. His fingers flap uselessly before her, a blur of blood and water and flesh and terrified eyes.

The only sounds are the hiss of water and the panting of killer and victim.

Antrobus's fat body bleeds from a hundred slashes, but still he does not die. It seems to have gone on forever, the dying, but he is weakening. Marianne stabs a blade deep into Antrobus's shoulder. He lurches away, the blade snaps, leaving bloody steel embedded in his meat. His feet slip on the water and blood. He falls backward.

The sound of brass towel hook penetrating human skull is not easily forgotten. Antrobus thrashes, once.

Marianne levers his body off the hook and lets him drop into the shower tray. While he drains, she dresses, helps herself to his cigarettes and the last inch of Wild Turkey. Eight pints of blood in the average human body. Give it half an hour or so, to get it all washed away, and the piss, and the fear-shit. The water will have run cold long before then. Pity he will not be able to appreciate what it was like for her when he would bundle her up with one hundred yards of washing line, tumble her into the shower and turn the cold full on her.

She goes to look at him. His eyes are not staring at her, but at a persistent cobweb next to the extractor fan. She would not care if they were staring. For the first time, she feels free of guilt. She killed a man, she feels set free. Why should she feel guilt? There can be no guilt where there is no choice, no other way, no right road to take. No one can be held morally responsible for doing what they are fated to do. Destiny admits no guilt.

She sits on the toilet and smokes until no more blood oozes from the hundred wounds.

When it is all gone down the plughole, she pulls down the shower curtain, spreads it on the floor, and with much effort levers Antrobus out of the shower on to it. She wraps him in his polythene shroud, drags him from the bedroom and with soft blue toilet tissue cleans up, flushing the evidence in job lots of five down the john.

Careful Marianne, careful. Would not do to block the plumbing at this stage.

She grimaces at the gobbets of hair and soft gray matter clinging to the towel hook. One wipe and they are gone. Down to the drains with the rest of him.

A sudden urge to giggle takes her by surprise. Inexplicably, she wants to sit on the toilet and laugh and laugh and laugh. She cannot. She dare not. When it is all done, then will be the time for elation. Now would be foolhardy.

Twenty to one on the clock. From past experience she knows the motel won't be quiet until two. She packs Antrobus's clothes and things. The rope. The paddle. The Irving Klaw Library. She smiles at Betty

Page, forever bound. The scissors—she almost forgot. The overnighter closes *click* on them all. Marianne flicks on the radio and listens, and smokes, and watches the play of headlights across the cheap, thin curtains, and waits. She gives it twenty minutes after the click and lock of the office door before moving.

Outside, the desert night is huge and brilliant and generous. Antrobus bumps as he goes down the steps—no helping it. She ruffles the track he makes in the dusty gravel. For a moment she thinks she is not going to be able to get him into the back of his station wagon, but the sound of a truck coming down the Colorado River line lends her desperation.

Up, and in he goes.

The truck blares past, a fast-moving constellation of riding lights.

The case goes in the back with Antrobus in his plastic sheet. Marianne in the front. Keys. Keys. She forgot to get them out of the overnight case. She glances up as she fumbles, but the cabin windows stay dark.

The station wagon starts, first pull. Marianne turns out on to the main route. The night is clear. The stars have never looked so bright.

She first noticed the viewpoint back at Session Two and had memorized it in an abstracted way as the kind of place that would be nice for a picnic, if hers were the kind of life that contemplated picnics. Beyond the line of white painted stones that rather ineffectually mark the edge, the land falls sharply toward a deeply incised tributary of the Colorado. She parks the station wagon far back, almost on the highway. She does not want those stupid stones stopping it. The car is aimed clear between the graffitied picnic tables at the setting stars.

The sound of the cigar lighter springing to life is surprisingly loud in this big country. The red coil of wire ignites the glovebox garbage she has distributed on the passenger seat. The upholstery smokes, bubbles, bursts into oily flames. Marianne releases the handbrake, heaves at the door pillar to help the station wagon on its way. Tires crunch gravel.

The white stones do not even slow it up. She sees the tailgate lights flip up against the bright stars and vanish. Seconds later a soft explosion disturbs the desert night.

She does not trouble herself to look over.

Five miles back to the Blue Motel. Under such a sky, on such a night, it will be a positive pleasure. Good to walk the ache out of her muscles. Should take her an hour, an hour and a half; plenty of time to get away before the motel starts to stir.

Good thing she chose a sensible pair of heels.

NORTH BY NORTHWEST

Marianne Marianne, driving driving. Marianne Marianne, driving driving.

Even in the height of summer this land is green; softly watered by ocean fogs and sudden rains; so different, so welcoming after the deserts and drylands that have been her habitation for as long as she can remember. There is salt in the air coming to her through the open window: sea smells; kelp, ozone, iodine. The road is smooth and good driving as it dips and winds between the low, green hills, drawing her toward the ocean. All things are confirmation that this is the place for her to be: Why, at the gas station as she ate a Hershey bar, a little bird, quite oblivious of the surly teenager filling the tank, had dropped onto the hood and looked at her long and hard, first with one eye, then with the other.

It is good to have direction, to at last be going where she chooses to go. When she had driven away from the Blue Motel with the first gray light of the dawn behind her, she had not known where she wanted to go, only that it was away from the things and people that had tied her. Given freedom, she had not known what to do with it; only reveled in the gift of mobility for mobility's sake; driving, driving along the straight black highways of California. The sun had risen, and stood over her, and overtaken her, and she still had driven, driven.

Away: in a northerly direction—she could not have said why that way. Up the great central valley through orchards and farms, overtaking lumbering farm trucks and crop-sprayers on the dusty roads; driving driving.

On the seat beside her, fortysomething thousand dollars.

The sun had steered her until she could not drive any further. She had booked into a family hotel in downtown Sacramento where she had slept for fourteen hours and awoken with a feeling of *potential*, of being mistress of her own way, that she had never really known since that December Friday afternoon in Lavery Real Estate.

She breakfasted in a two-calendar diner decorated in high nauticalia—nets, glass floats that had crossed an ocean from Japan, ships in bottles—though the bay was over an hour's drive west. It was that, over her sausage and waffles, that decided her. The sea. Something west of north, to the ocean. In some coastal fishing town she could find a place to stay, a new community, and new life. Maybe buy a little business with the money. The legendary four-calendar roadhouse, perhaps. She'd have to change her name, her clothes, maybe even the color of her hair: So be it. It couldn't matter. She would be safe. She would be invisible, anonymous. Happy.

The road carries her onward. Between green hills she glimpses blue ocean.

Marianne, Marianne, driving driving, thinks about the 90 Mile Roadhouse, its three calendars and its strange freight of lives. The disquieting music of the piano player: notes hurrying hurrying, going nowhere. That strange Englishman, what had the waitress called him, Hitch? Funny she can remember that. His sad, sick stories. Had he been the oracle of free will, or the agent of predestination? Perhaps you never escape; all your running away is only running to; the long way, the way that goes right around the world to bring you back to the place where you are meant to be.

The road crests a hill, and she sees it. Behind its crescent of golden sand, nestling against the foot of the hills against the agoraphobia of the ocean: a tidy town of painted board houses and shingle roofs, webbed with telegraph poles and powerlines and other ugly attendants of civilized living. But the fishing boats seem to rest easily enough against the harbor jetty. Marianne stops the car to look longer.

The road sign announces this place to which she comes: Bodega Bay, two miles.

There seem to be a lot—an awful lot—of birds circling overhead.

B e n t l e y   L i t t l e

A former newspaper reporter and an
accomplished jazz musician, Bentley Little
won the Bram Stoker Award for best first
novel for The Revelation and has
since gone on to write more novels—
including the chilling The Mailman—
and a series of virtually unclassifiable short
stories. One of these, "The Woods Be
Dark," appeared in Touch Wood: Here's
another.

"**H**ey, hon, what's this?"

Alex looked up from the suitcase he'd been packing. April, kneeling before the box she'd found on the top shelf of the hall closet, held up what looked like a green campaign button. "Pop?" she said.

"Let me see that." He walked across the room and took the button from her hands. A powerful feeling of flashback familiarity, emotional remembrance, coursed through him as he looked at the button.

POP.

People Over Pollution.

It had been a long time since he'd thought of that acronym. A long time.

He knelt down next to April and peered into the box, seeing bumperstickers and posters, other buttons, pamphlets with green ecology sign logos.

"What is all this?" April asked.

"People Over Pollution. It was a group I belonged to when I was in college. We collected bottles and cans and newspapers for recycling. We picketed soap companies until they came up with biodegradable detergent. We urged people to boycott environmentally unsound products."

April smiled, tweaked his nose. "You troublemaking radical, you."

He ignored her and began to dig through the box, sorting through the jumbled items.

Buried beneath the bumperstickers and buttons, he

found a framed photograph: an emerald green meadow, ringed by huge darker green ponderosa pine trees. A small lake in the center of the meadowgrass, its still and perfectly clear water reflecting the cotton puff clouds and deep blue sky above.

Major flashback.

He stared at the photo, reverently touched the dusty glass. He'd forgotten all about the picture. How was that possible? He'd cut it out of an *Arizona Highways* as a teenager and had framed it because he'd known instantly upon seeing it that this was where he wanted to live. The photo had spoken to him on a gut emotional level that struck a chord deep within him. He had never been to Arizona at that point, but he'd known from the perfection presented in that scene that this was where he wanted to settle down. He would live in the meadow in a log cabin, just him and his wife, and they would awaken each morning to the sound of birdsong, to the natural light of dawn.

The girls with whom he intended to live in this paradise had changed throughout his teens—from Joan to Pam to Rachel—but the location had always remained constant.

How could he have forgotten about the photo? He'd been to Arizona countless times in the intervening years, had scouted a resort site in Tucson and another in Sedona, yet the memory of his old dream had never even suggested itself to him.

Strange.

April leaned over his shoulder, resting her head next to his. She glanced at the photo. "What's that?"

He shook his head, smiling slightly, sadly, and placed the picture back in the box. "Nothing."

That night he dreamed of the pond.

He could not remember having had the dream before, but it was somehow familiar to him, and he knew that he had experienced it in the past.

He was walking along a path, a narrow footpath through the forest, and as he walked deeper into the woods, the sky grew overcast and the bushes grew thicker. Soon it seemed as though he was walking through a tunnel. He was afraid, and he grew even more afraid as he moved forward. He wanted to turn back, to turn around, but he could not. His feet propelled him onward.

And then he was at the pond.

He stood at the path's end, trembling, chilled to the core of his being as he stared at the dirty body of water before him, at the ripples of bluish white foam that floated upon the stagnant black liquid.

The trees here, the grass, the brush, all were brown and dying. There were no other people about, no animals, not even bugs on the water. The air was still and strangely heavy. Above this spot, dark clouds blotted out all sunlight.

At the far end of the pond was an old water pump. Alex's heart beat faster. He kept his eyes averted from the rusted hunk of machinery, but he could still see out of the corner of his eye the corrosion on the old metal, the algae-covered tube snaking into the water.

More than anything else, more than the dark and twisting path, more than the horrid pond or the blighted land surrounding it, it was the pump that frightened him, its very presence causing goosebumps to ripple down the skin of his arms. There was something in the cold insistence of its position at the head of the pond, in the unnaturally biological contours of its form and the defiantly mechanical nature of its function that terrified him. He looked up at the sky, around at the trees, then forced himself to face the water pump.

The handle of the pump began slowly to turn, the squeaking sound of its movement echoing in the still air.

And he woke up screaming.

The corporation put him up at Little America in Flagstaff. The accommodations were nice, the rooms clean and well-furbished, the view beautiful. It was late May, not yet summer and not warm enough to swim, but the temperature was fair, the sky clear and cloudless, and he and April spent the better part of that first day by the pool, she reading a novel, he going over the specs.

The quiet was disturbed shortly after noon by the

loud and laughing conversation of a man and a woman. Alex looked up from his papers to see a bearded, ponytailed young man opening the iron gate to the pool area. He was wearing torn cutoff jeans, and the blond giggling girl with him had on a skimpy string bikini. The young man saw him staring and waved. "Hey, bud! How's the water?"

The girl hit his shoulder, laughing.

Alex turned back to his papers. "Asshole," he said.

April frowned. "Shhh. They'll hear you."

"I don't care."

Yelling in tandem, the couple leaped into the pool.

"Leave them alone. They're just young. You were young once, weren't you?"

That shut him up. He had been young once. And, now that he thought about it, he had at one time looked very similar to the Sixties throwback now cavorting in the pool. He'd had a beard and ponytail when he'd marched in the Earth Day parade.

What the hell had happened to him since then?

He'd sold out.

He placed the specs on the small table next to his lounge chair, took off his glasses and laid them on top of the papers. He watched the young man grab his girlfriend's breasts from behind as she squealed and swam away from him toward the deep end of the pool.

Alex leaned back, looking up into the sea blue sky. Sold out? He was a successful scout for a chain of major resorts. He hadn't sold out. He had merely taken advantage of a fortunate series of career opportunities. He told himself that he was where he wanted to be, where he should be, that he had a good life and a good job and was happy, but he was uncomfortably aware that the end result of his series of lucky breaks and career opportunities had been to provide him with a job that he would have found the height of hypocrisy in his younger, more idealistic days.

He was not the person he had been.

He found himself wondering, if he had been this age then, whether he would have supported the Vietnam War.

He had supported the war in the Persian Gulf.

He pushed these thoughts from his mind. He was just being stupid. Life was neither as simple nor as morally black and white as he had believed in his college days. That was all there was to it. He was grown up now. He was an adult. He could no longer afford the arrogant idealism of youth.

He watched the couple in the pool kiss, the lower halves of their bodies undulating in the refracted reflection of the chlorinated water, and he realized that, from their perspective, he was probably one walking cliché. A traitor to the Sixties. Yet another amoral Baby Boomer with fatally skewed priorities.

He felt a warm hand on his shoulder, turned his head to see April staring worriedly at him from her adjacent lounge chair. "Are you okay?"

"Sure," he said, nodding.

"Is it because of what I said?"

"I'm fine." Annoyed, he turned away from her. He put on his glasses, picked up his spec sheets and started reading.

He met with the realtors early the next morning, seeing them not one-by-one but all at the same time in one of Little America's conference rooms. He'd found from past experience that dealing with real estate salespeople en masse gave him a distinct advantage, firmly establishing him as the dominant partner in their relationship, saving him from the sort of high-pressure sales talk that realtors usually used on prospective clients and putting the salespeople in clear competition with one another.

It worked every time.

After his prepared talk and slideshow, he fielded a few quick questions, then scheduled times over the next three days during which he could go with the realtors individually to look at property. This time, the corporation was looking for land outside the confines of the city. Flagstaff already had plenty of hotels and motels, and Little America itself offered resort quality accommodations. To compete in this market, they had to offer something different, and it had been decided that a state-of-the-art complex in a heavily forested area outside of the city would provide just the edge that they would need.

They would also be allowed more freedom in design

and latitude in construction under county, rather than city, building regulations.

There were more sites to scout than he'd thought, more property available in the Flagstaff area than he'd been led to believe, due to a recent land swap between the Forest Service and a consortium of logging and mining companies, and he realized as he penciled in times on his calendar that he and April would probably have to skip their side trip to Oak Creek Canyon this time.

It was just as well, he supposed. Sedona and the Canyon had been awfully overcrowded and touristy the last time they'd been through.

The white Jeep bounced over the twin ruts that posed as a road through this section of forest, and Alex held on to his briefcase with one hand, the dashboard with the other. There were no seatbelts or shoulder harnesses in the vehicle, and the damned real estate agent was driving like a maniac.

The realtor yelled something at him, but over the wind and the roar of the engine he could only make out every third word or so: "We're... southern...almost...." He assumed that they were nearing the property.

Already he had a good impression of this site. Unlike some of the others, which were either too remote—with the cost of water, sewer and electrical hookups prohibitive—or too close to town, this location was secluded and easily accessible. A paved road over this dirt track would provide a beautiful scenic drive for tourists and guests.

They rounded a curve, and they were there.

At the meadow.

Alex blinked dumbly as the Jeep pulled to a stop, not sure if he was seeing what he thought he was seeing. They were at one end of a huge meadow bordered by giant ponderosas. There was a small lake toward the other end of the grass, a lake so blue that it made the sky pale by comparison.

It was the meadow whose picture he'd cut out of *Arizona Highways*.

No, that was not possible.

Was it?

He glanced around. This certainly looked like the same meadow. He thought he even recognized an old lightning-struck tree on a raised section of ground near the shore of the lake.

But the odds against something like this happening were...astronomical. Thirty years ago, an *Arizona Highways* photographer had chanced upon this spot, taken a photo which had been published in the magazine, he himself had seen the photo, cut it out, saved it and now he was in a position to buy the property for a resort chain? It was too bizarre, too coincidental, too...Twilight Zone. He had to be mistaken.

"Beautiful, isn't it?" The realtor got out of the Jeep,

stretched. "This open space here, this clearing's some thirty acres, but the entire property's eighty acres, mostly that area there beyond those trees." He pointed to the line of ponderosas south of the water. "You got yourself a small ridge that overlooks the National Forest and has a view clear to Mormon Mountain."

Alex nodded. He continued to nod as the real estate agent rambled, pretending to listen as the man led him through the high grass to the water.

Should he tell the corporation to buy the meadow?

His meadow?

Technically, his was only a preliminary recommendation, a decision that was neither binding nor final. His choice would then be scrutinized carefully by the board. The corporation's assessors, land use experts, and design technicians would go over everything with a fine-toothed comb.

Technically.

But the way it really worked was that he scouted locations, the board rubber-stamped the go-ahead and the corporation's legal eagles swooped down to see how they could pick apart the deals mapped out by the local realtors.

The fate of the meadow lay in his hands.

He stared at the reflection of the trees and the clouds, the green and white reproduced perfectly on the still, mirrored surface of the blue water.

He thought back to his POP years, and he realized, perhaps for the first time, that he had been a selfish environmentalist even in his most ecologically active days. There was no contradiction between his work now and his beliefs then. He had always wanted nature's beauty to remain unspoiled, not for its own sake—but so that he could enjoy it. He had never been one to hike out to remote wilderness areas and enjoy the unspoiled beauty. He had been a couch potato nature lover, driving through National Parks and pretty areas of the country and admiring the scenery from his car window. He had objected to the building of homes on forest land that was visible from the highway, but had not objected to the presence of the highway itself.

He'd seen nothing at all wrong with building a home in his dream meadow, although he would have fought to the death anyone else who'd tried to build there.

Now he was on the other side of the coin.

He tried to look at the situation objectively. He told himself that at least the corporation would protect the lake and the meadow, would preserve the beauty of this spot. Someone else might simply pave it over. He might not be able to build a house here and live in the wilderness with April, but he could rent a room at the resort, and the two of them could vacation here.

Along with hundreds of other people.

He glanced over at the real estate agent. "Was this spot ever in *Arizona Highways?*" he asked.

The realtor laughed. "If it wasn't, it should've been. This is one gorgeous spot. Hell, if I had enough money

I'd buy the land and build my own house here."

Alex nodded distractedly. They had reached the edge of the lake, and he crouched down, dipping his fingers in the water. The liquid felt uncomfortably warm to his touch. And slimy. Like melted Jell-O. He quickly withdrew his hand.

He stood, shaking the water from his fingers. There was a faint ringing in his ears. He looked around the meadow but found that his whole perspective had changed. The trees no longer seemed so beautiful. Rather than a miraculous example of the wonders of nature, the forest looked like a fake grove that had been inexpertly planted. The lake looked small and ill-formed, particularly in comparison with some of the pools and lagoons created for the newer resorts. The meadow, he saw now, would be perfect for either a golf course or an intra-resort park. Lighted walking paths or horse trails could be constructed through the grass and the trees. Landscaping could accentuate the meadow's natural beauty.

Accentuate natural beauty?

Something seemed wrong with that, but he could not put his finger on what it was.

"This sounds exactly like what you're looking for," the realtor said.

Alex nodded noncommittally. His gaze swept the short shoreline of the lake.

And stopped.

In the weeds on the opposite side of the water was a rusted water pump.

A chill passed through him as he stared at the pump. It was nearly identical to the one in his dream, his mind having conjured correctly even the rounded organic contours of its shape. His heart was pounding crazily, a rap rhythm instead of its usual ballad beat. He swiveled toward the realtor. The agent was staring at him and smiling. What was the expression on the man's face? Was that amusement he saw in those eyes? Was there a hint of malice in that smile?

Jesus, what the hell was wrong with him? There was nothing unusual in the real estate agent's expression. He was being paranoid.

"Should I draw up the papers?" the realtor said jokingly.

Alex forced himself to remain calm, gave the man a cool smile, did not tip his hand. "What other properties can you show me?"

While April was in the shower, he looked at himself in the full-length mirror on the back of the door. For the first time he realized that he was middle-aged. Really realized it. His gaze shifted from his thinning hair to his expanding waist to the increasing rigidity of his previously malleable features. His age was not something of which he'd been unaware—each birthday had been a ritualized reminder of his loss of youth, each New Year's Eve a prompter of the passing of time—

but he now understood emotionally what before he had comprehended only as an intellectual concept.

His best years were behind him.

He sucked in his gut, stood sideways in front of the mirror, but the effort was too much, and he let it fall. That stomach was never going to go away. He would never again have the kind of body that females would look at admiringly. The women he found attractive would no longer find him attractive.

He might die of a heart attack.

That's what had brought this on. His heart had been pounding so forcefully and for so long after he'd seen the water pump that he'd honestly been afraid it would burst. It did not seem possible that his unexercised and cholesterol-choked muscle could keep up that pace for so long a time without sustaining damage.

It had, though.

He walked across the carpeted floor of the hotel room and stared out the window at the black silhouette of the San Francisco Peaks. The mountains towered over the lights of Flagstaff but were dwarfed by the vastness of the Arizona night sky. He had two more days of scouting to do, two more days of meetings and sales pitches, but he knew that he had already made his decision.

He was going to recommend that the corporation buy the meadow.

He didn't feel as bad about the decision as he thought he would, and that concerned him a little. He stared out the window at the stars, tried to imagine what it would have been like if he really had followed his dream, not allowed himself to be deterred by practicality. Would he have been with April or someone else? Would he be living there in the meadow, by the lake, or would he have long since given up and, like most of those involved in the back-to-nature movement, joined mainstream society? Would he be where he was now anyway?

He didn't know, he wasn't sure, but he felt a vague sense of sadness and dissatisfaction as he looked into the night.

"Hon?" April called from the bathroom. "Could you bring me my panties from the suitcase?"

"Sure," he answered.

He turned away from the window and walked over to the suitcase on the floor near the bed.

He dreamed of the pond.

He walked down the narrowing, darkening path until he reached the blighted clearing, where the filthy water lay in a sickening pool. He stared at the pond, and he was afraid. There were no monsters here, no evil spirits. This was not sacred Indian land that had been unthinkingly desecrated. There were no strange creatures swimming beneath the surface of the brackish liquid.

There was only the pond itself.

And the pump.

These were the things that were scary.

Against his will, he found himself moving across the dead ground to the edge of the water. He looked across the pond at the pump and the hose protruding from its side wiggled obscenely, moving upward into the air, beckoning him.

He awoke drenched in sweat.

Two days later, he faxed his preliminary report, along with the appropriate documents and estimates, to corporate headquarters, then took April out to look at the site. He drove himself this time, using the rental car, so the going was much slower.

He parked the car at the end of the tire-tracked path and said nothing as April got out of the vehicle and looked around. She nodded appreciatively as she took in the trees, the meadow, the lake. "It's pretty," she said.

He'd been expecting something more, something like his own initial reaction when he'd first seen that photo years ago, but he realized that she had never shown that sort of enthusiasm for anything.

"It is pretty," he said, but he realized as he spoke the words that they no longer held true for him. He knew, objectively, intellectually, that this was a beautiful spot, a prime location for the resort, but he no longer felt it. He remembered the slick and slimy feel of the water on his fingers, and though his hands were dry, he wiped them on his pants.

The two of them walked through the high wispy grass to the edge of the lake. As before, the placid surface reflected perfectly the sky above and the scenery around. He let his gaze roam casually across the opposite shore, pretending to himself that he had no object, no aim, no purpose in his visual survey, but the movement of his eyes stopped when he spotted the water pump.

He glanced quickly over at April to see if she'd noticed it. She hadn't.

He looked again toward the pump. Its metal was dark, threatening in the midst of the yellow/tan stalks of the weeds, its hose draped suggestively over the small mud bank into the water. He didn't want April to see the pump, he realized. He wanted to protect her from it, to shield her eyes from the sight of that incongruous man-made object in the middle of this natural wilderness.

Was it man-made?

What kind of thought was that?

He made a big show of looking at his watch. "We'd better get back," he said. "It's getting late. We have a lot of things to do, and I have a long day tomorrow. There are a lot of loose ends to tie up."

She nodded, understanding. They turned to go, and she took his hand. "It's nice," she said as they walked back toward the car. "You found a good one."

He nodded.

❧

In his dream, he brought April to the pond. He said nothing, only pointed, like a modern-dress version of the Ghost of Christmas Yet To Come. She frowned. "Yeah? So it's an old polluted pond. What of it?"

Now he spoke: "But why is it polluted? How did it get that way? There are no factories here, no roads to this spot—"

"Who knows? Who cares?"

She obviously didn't feel it. To her, this was nothing more than a small dirty body of water. There was nothing sinister here, nothing malicious. But as he looked up at the blackness of the dead sky he knew that she was being deceived, that this was not the case.

He turned around, and she was gone, in her place a pillar of salt.

Again, he awoke sweating, though the room's air conditioner was blowing cool air toward him. He got out of bed without disturbing April and walked into the bathroom. He did not have to take a leak, did not have to get a drink of water, did not have to do anything. He simply stood before the mirror, staring at himself. His eyes were bloodshot, his lips pale. He looked sick. He gazed into his eyes and they were unfamiliar to him; he did not know what the mind behind those eyes was thinking. He leaned forward, until his nose was touching the nose behind the glass, until his eyes were an inch away from their mirrored counterparts, and suddenly he did know what that mind was thinking.

He jerked away from the mirror, almost fell backward over the toilet. He took a deep breath, licked his lips. He stood there for a moment, closed his eyes. He told himself that he was not going to do it, that he was going back to bed.

But he let himself silently out of the hotel room without waking April.

He drove to the property.

He parked farther away this time, walking the last several yards through the forest to the meadow.

The meadow.

In the moonlight, the grass looked dead, the trees old and frail and withered. But the lake, as always, appeared full and beautiful, its shiny surface gloriously reflecting the magnificent night sky.

He wasted no time but walked around the edge of the lake, his feet sinking in the mud. The opposite shore was rougher than the side with which he was familiar, the tall weeds hiding rocks and ruts, small gullies and dead sharpened branches. He stopped for a moment, crouched down, touched the water with his fingertips, but the liquid felt slimy, disgusting.

He continued walking.

He found the pump.

He stared at the oddly shaped object. It was evil, the pump. Evil not for what it did, not for what it had done, not for what it could do, but for what it was. He moved slowly forward, placed his hand on the rusted metal and felt power there, a low thrumming that vibrated against his palm, reverberated through his body. The metal was cold to his touch, but there was warmth beneath the cold, heat beneath the warmth. Part of him wanted to run away, to turn his back on the lake and the pump and get the hell out of there, but another stronger part of him enjoyed this contact with the power, reveled in the humming which vibrated against his hand.

Slowly, he reached down and pulled the lever up. The metal beneath his fingers creaked loudly in protest after the years of disuse. Yellow brackish liquid began trickling out of the pipe, growing into a stream. The liquid splashed on to the clear water of the lake and the reflection of the sky darkened, disappeared. The water near the pump began foaming, the suds blue then brown in the darkness.

He waited for a moment, then pushed the lever down again. He knelt, touched his fingers to the water. Now it felt normal to him, now it felt good.

He rose to his feet. Dimly, from the far side of the clearing, he thought he heard April call his name, but her voice was faint and indistinct and he ignored her as he began to strip. He took off his shoes, his socks, his shirt, his pants, his underwear.

He looked across the lake, but there was no sign of April. There was no one there. The last time he'd gone skinny-dipping, he thought, he'd had a beard and a ponytail.

"Pop," he said, whispered.

Naked, he dived into the water. His mouth and nostrils were filled instantly with the taste and odor of sulfur, chemicals. He opened his eyes underwater, but he could see nothing, only blackness. His head broke the surface and he gulped air. Above, the sky was dark, the moon gone, the stars faint.

The water felt cool on his skin, good.

He took a deep breath and began to swim across the lake, taking long brisk strokes toward the dark opposite shore.

THE

Brian W. Aldiss

DREAM OF ANTIGONE

In his column for The Dark Side *magazine,*
Stan Nicholls referred to Brian Aldiss as "a
national treasure," ending his review of
Aldiss's recent collection, A Tupolev
Too Far, *by saying, "How can you not*
love someone who writes a story about a
cockroach that thinks it's really Kafka?" How
indeed.

For many fans of the fantastic, Brian
Aldiss is The Guv'nor as far as British
fantasy and science fiction is concerned.

In the 1950s and '60s—alongside John
Brunner, J. G. Ballard and Michael
Moorcock—Aldiss regaled readers of the
innovative New Worlds *magazine with*
a different slant on the genre, a slant which
demonstrated a new strength in the field.

This strength was carried over into a slew of wonderful novels, beginning with The Brightfount Diaries in 1955 and culminating—so far—with this year's Somewhere East of Life, the fourth volume in the quartet which includes Life in the West (1980), Forgotten Life (1988) and Remembrance Day (1993). Along the way, we've also had Hothouse (1962), the delightful Helliconia trilogy (1982-85) and The Malacia Tapestry (1976), the latter of which I read in one unforgettable twenty-two-hour session in a hospital waiting room while my wife persuaded our first son to join the world. (It was a wonderful birth!)

Although he has no superstitions that he's aware of, Aldiss feels that the moon plays a large role in his life. "I adore that elusive coin in the sky," he says.

He also mentions his firm conviction—at the age of three or four—that he had been a wizard in a previous existence and was burnt at the stake. "And when I was a small boy," he continues, "my family moved into a haunted house in East Dereham, Norfolk. We called the ghost Bessie in an attempt to domesticate it, but for my sister and me this was a time of terror. When we went to live elsewhere, I attempted—in a mistaken fit of rationality—to ascribe a Freudian interpretation to the haunting. However, revisiting the place in the '80s, I discovered the malign presence to be still about. The local vicar eventually exorcised it. The thing disappeared with a reassuringly traditional bang—only to return in a few months. It's an ancient and horrible thing and not subjective."

Like his compatriots in the original vanguard quartet, Aldiss has repeatedly returned to mainstream fiction, embracing the contemporary and the classical with the same consummate ease that he displays when dealing with the far reaches of space. The story which follows is a fine example.

Abarred window was set high in the cell wall, like a promised glimpse of eternity. By standing on tiptoe, Joe Moon could peer out. What he saw was not eternity, but desert and bleak expanses of the inland sea—though he perceived eternity too, clear in his inner vision. Desert and sea trembled in the heat. The heat congealing in his cell made Moon mad. He stared and stared out at the dead waters as if he were looking inside his own skull.

Toward sundown, the prison warden entered the cell, bearing a jar of water, some pita bread, and a handful of fresh dates.

After setting the food down, this old and sun-dried man, as shriveled as a prune, made the announcement Moon had been expecting.

"Eight o'clock tomorrow morning," the man said. Moon had no need to ask what would happen at that time. He sank down on the bench and wiped sweat from his eyes, sighing deeply.

"Eight o'clock..." Moon repeated, trying to connect the words with reality. After a long pause, he brought himself to ask what would happen to his body.

"We'll bury it," said the warden.

If this gave Moon some comfort, he did not show it. He clutched his head, as though to save it from a general downfall.

"I brought you a book, something to read to pass the time," the warden said; this was not the first sign of sympathy he had shown the prisoner. With an effort, he pulled from the pocket of his loose garment a volume, bereft of covers, whose curled-up corners lent it a resemblance to a stale sandwich. "It's old—from last century, I believe. But it's all we've got in this place. No one reads here. I haven't read it myself."

When Moon made no move, he set the book down on the end of the bench, next to the jar and the fruit and the bread, which a beetle was already investigating.

When the warden had gone, Moon sat motionless, saying to himself over and over, "Eight o'clock tomorrow morning." He finally made a move, picking up the volume with indifference. "The only bloody book in all Central Asia, apart from the Holy Book," he said aloud, before glancing at the title. It was Sigmund Freud's *Psychopathology of Everyday Life*.

The condemned man broke into ragged laughter. He lay on the floor and laughed until he cried with misery. "Everyday? What 'everyday'?"

During his last night on earth, there in the fetid confines of his cell, Joe Moon dreamed the Dream of Antigone. His own life had been bleak, unfurnished except by blows and bruises. Although he was about to be executed as a political criminal, he still retained a buried self in which he saw himself as noble, stubborn, principled. And that buried self—because his outward life had been so mutilated, so hard and masculine—took the form of a woman, young and immortal. The woman was dark-clad Antigone of Greek story.

Dark-clad Antigone walked out from the walls of Thebes by its South Gate, into the countryside. Old women stood or squatted at their blue-painted doors, talking as the sun went down. The air was full of the music of bees, whose hives, with their painted walls, stood nearby. The women cast hostile looks at Antigone. Their conversation died as she passed by. As she walked along the path by the onion fields where she labored, a farmer driving a flock of goats passed her; it seemed to her that even the goats gave her a wide berth. She stood in the olive grove, with many kinds of flower, white, yellow, gold, and blue, petitioning the bees' attentions at her sandaled feet. Shading her eyes, Antigone gazed longingly out across the river lying congealed among its reeds, as if reflecting her mood.

She was young, raven-haired. A string of beads by the nape of her neck contained her tresses. In her face was an elfin quality more beautiful than beauty itself. Her hands and feet were coarse from her years of travel and, lately, from rough work. Her inner world was hers alone, just as she shared her body with no man.

Living had been hard for her through the fratricidal war now concluded. Young though she was, she felt herself already to have experienced as much misery as was generally an old woman's portion. She was the daughter of Jocasta and Oedipus. She thought of the sepulcher in which her father slept, finding peace at last. To herself she said, "All men should have proper burial: It's a law of God, not man."

Raspberries grew wild here. The raspberry patch, she supposed, had been tended by some man who had gone to the wars and never returned. She crammed the fruit into her mouth, making her red lips still redder. She held some of the berries in her hand as she returned to the oppressions of the city.

One of the women at the well, raggedly dressed, called abuse at her. Antigone shouted back.

"You and your damned family! My father was killed because of your kind!" they called.

For answer, Antigone spat.

"Your stupid wars, you incest-brat! My sweetheart got a spear through his chest, fighting your rotten battles!" they called.

Antigone flung a lump of donkey dung in their direction. They shouted the more. Gathering her black skirts about her thighs, she headed back to the Theban Gate. As she went, she pretended to ignore the unburied body lying mangled by the city ramparts. Yet the breeze carried to her delicate nose a scent of carrion. She held her head high as she marched past, going under the dappled shade, where gnats danced in the filtered rays of sunshine.

Above her, in the branches of the oaks, squirrels chattered and hid like disembodied spirits.

Superstitious fear brushed her mind, for dread of what they might be saying.

As she was nearing the guard at the gate, the shadow of a bird crossed her path, speeding over the parched grass. Looking up at the omen, she saw a great black crow settling into a nearby tree. It clung to a high twig and stared down upon her. "Caught!" it seemed to cry, "Caught!"

Once in the city, she hurried into her own stone house. It was no better and no bigger than anyone else's house. Inside, by the door, stood her field implement, a hoe with a cracked shaft, which Antigone had bound up with a strip of blue material torn from the hem of a garment. Troubled by the ill omen of the bird's shadow, she knelt by her altar stone to pray to the goddess Aphaia. She prepared and ate some *saganaki*, but the cheese was not of the best. Then she sat silent, hands on lap, to await the night, the time when the dead are buried—or rise up.

High above Antigone's house, in the wooden palace, sat Antigone's uncle, King Creon. He too waited, in his wooden room draped with rugs and trophies. Creon's beard was streaked white with the burden of history and the thankless task of ruling unruly Thebes. He dismissed his courtiers and sat alone by the window. The odor of the corpse by the ramparts rose up to him, together with the sound of bluebottles, angry with life. Creon kept his face free of expression. He rejected his

92

supper when Queen Eurydice brought it, but drank some dark red wine from a silver goblet.

Although her pale hand lingered momentarily on his shoulder, he shrugged it off.

Creon rested that night for no more than half a watch. His confused sleep mingled with that of the man in the condemned cell, far away in space and time. Images surfacing from bygone memory transformed snores to bugle calls, heavy gasping breaths to the sound of armed men on the march.

Into Joe Moon's troubled dreams, the dreams of a failed mercenary, came a parade of chariots, sieges, and the unceasing struggle which had afflicted him as it had Creon. Antigone's two brothers, Etiocles and Polynices, had fought each other for possession of Thebes. Etiocles had defended the city, Polynices had attacked it. Antigone had been torn by her love of them, finally to witness her brothers killing each other in battle, fighting hand to hand, only to fall and roll face downward in the trampled dirt. This was what glory had come to: flies breeding in gaping jaws, corruption, scavenging hounds.

It must have seemed to her then, in her grief, that the terrible inheritance of her father Oedipus was at last worked out, and the Furies at last placated. Moon, too, taking his pay, had reckoned himself rich enough to return home at last, to a cottage and a pair of slippers and a tabby cat.

It was not to be. Creon, taking over the war-torn

city, passed many stern laws—and one which above all affronted Antigone's sense of justice. Ceremony was commanded for the dead Etiocles. Creon himself, standing with Eurydice and Haemon, saluted the corpse of the savior of Thebes as it was drawn by soldiers to the tomb. Etiocles's body was buried with honor; Polynices' body was left to rot outside the South Gate. So Moon's body, on that final night, seemed to rot in its narrow cell, far from any consolation, barring that which was to be found in dreams.

And this was Creon's law: that anyone who attempted to bury the mutilated body of Polynices would be executed. Moon was caught by a not dissimilar law: Anyone who sided with the failed revolutionaries, as he had done, would face a firing squad.

Creon was up and about early, leaving his wife to sleep. A guard came privily to bring him disturbing news, and was summarily dealt with. Creon then bathed himself and spoke briefly with his son Haemon, who was affianced to Antigone. He settled matrimonial quarrels in the public square and presided over the court of justice. At noon, when Thebes was beginning to fall into its afternoon snooze, he went with a bodyguard to his niece's house.

The sun blazed in the street. Many houses had not been maintained and needed new thatch and tile. Creon's bodyguard was ordered to stay outside Antigone's door. The interior of Antigone's room was dark. Creon's eyes did not adjust to the change of light as rapidly as once they had done.

"Antigone, stand before me," he commanded.

She got up from her loom, bowed, and stood submissively in front of him. He was, after all, the king. How slight was Antigone against the barrel of his body: In this disproportion lay masculine power.

He spoke without preamble. "I want to examine your hands, Antigone. Show them to me."

Without protest, she brought her hands forward and held them out. Her hands were narrow and brown. The palms were hard. The fingernails were short. She wore no rings or bracelets. Creon turned them over and about as if they were stones under which he expected to find a scorpion. Beneath some nails were particles of dirt.

"You've been digging?"

"At dawn I tended my vegetable patch as usual."

"Come with me, child."

"Yes, uncle."

He walked with her slowly, down a narrow side street. The bodyguard was dismissed. Creon's arm lay across her slender shoulder in an avuncular way. Antigone did not protest. Their feet were in shadow, their faces in the full sun. Rats scampered into a gutter.

The city gate was open and he directed her through it. Then she stopped. "No, uncle, please. I don't wish to see the corpse."

"Don't be silly, girl. It's only your brother, Polynices, lying there rotting. You know that, don't you?"

He practically dragged her over to where the body lay unburied and wasps and bluebottles feasted in its interstices. Heavy scavenger birds moved reluctantly away, clucking indignantly at having to leave their spoils.

Of course she knew. The previous night, when the owl ceased to call and all nature was hushed, he had come to her bedside, he, the slain Polynices. The very manner of his coming was dreadful to her, the small sister, lying on her couch, unable to do more than raise herself on one elbow and gaze open-mouthed and pale of lip at that slow approach. The specter seemed to be lit from within with a yellowish pallor, as if made of frosted glass, and its armor likewise. Its wounds, its sickly congealed blood, only made it more dreadful, while so slowly did it advance on Antigone that a whole funeral dirge might have been sung in that time.

When the apparition spoke, words came from it without expression, and a disgusting choking scent filled the room.

"Look upon thy brother, slain by his twin, Etiocles! What misery the gods have wished upon our house, O Antigone! Do you recall a happy time when we were young and bathed together in the river? Now you are grown, you must take on a woman's role. Swear you will do that. Swear!"

And in a frail voice, she from her couch said only, "Polynices, please go away. I have dieted enough on distress."

"I cannot leave. The dawn brings my destruction. I am imprisoned." So Moon's thoughts found voice in his dream through the dead warrior.

"Polynices, you are slaughtered, and there can be no communication between us. You are a shade. Leave me, I pray. Go, make peace with your brother."

She recalled only how fierce Polynices and Etiocles had been when they were boys, and how she as a girl had been scared of Polynices, that great stone-flinger— although never so scared as she was now. But the apparition made her swear that she would bury his corpse: for until proper funeral rites were performed, he was doomed restlessly to wander the earth, disinherited.

And from pity and terror, Antigone had sworn so to do. Then the specter slowly receded into the stern silences, until there remained merely a stain in the air. After which, Antigone heard a cock crow; her neighbor in the street give vent to a furious paroxysm of coughing; ordinary nature revived, bringing back the customary nocturnal sounds, mice scuttling in the other room, the shrill of a night bird, the cry of a sentry on the sturdy ramparts of Thebes.

Putting on her wooden sandals, she had taken up her onion hoe from its corner by the door and gone quietly out into the night to do her dead brother's bidding.

All this she related now to her stern uncle, Creon,

King of Thebes, as they stood among the flies and trampled earth about the rotting body of Polynices. She withheld nothing.

He remained rooted, his dark gaze ever upon her, burdening her with that regard.

"So, Polynices came from the realm of death to lay a task on you! And did he report that there was mirth in that dark kingdom, child?"

"He made no mention of it," she said, looking into his face to try and read what was hidden there.

Creon's brow wrinkled in a frown as he made reply. "Nor is there mirth here in Thebes. I have passed a law saying that your troublesome brother's remains shall not be buried. You know the law. Those who break the law will be executed. You don't believe in ghosts, do you? That's all nonsense. Once you're dead, you're dead. You begin to stink and that's all."

"I saw what I saw in the night."

"Now then, don't be stubborn. You saw nothing, you imagined everything. It was a bad dream. We are beset by bad dreams. They are part of the inclement destiny the gods have wished upon us. Just remember, your father married my sister, Jocasta. Unbeknown to either of them, he was also her son. Thus was natural law denied. The disgrace of it.... Poor Jocasta hanged herself. She was familiar with the days when there was a matriarchy in Greece, now no more. As if all that wasn't enough, your brothers had to kill each other.

"Now by the decree you must face execution. What

say you to that, niece? How do you fancy having your head severed from that body Haemon so desires?"

Antigone looked defiant, saying in a low voice, "You are king. I am your subject. You will do what you will."

Creon growled low in his throat, a sound of pain and menace.

He walked in a circle, hands behind his back. "Only you and I know that you broke the law."

When she did not reply, Creon continued.

"So you had better behave yourself. Keep quiet, forget all about ghosts. Marry Haemon, as planned. Although he's my son, I will say he's a good lad and much in love with you. You know that?"

Antigone hung her head. Her "yes" was only a whisper, before she asked her uncle if they might leave the vicinity of the corpse. Polynices now resembled greatly her father, in having no eyes.

Creon did as she suggested, leading her to the nearest well, under a grove of acacias. Women were gathering there, pitchers on their heads. He drove them off. They feared Creon and his bloodthirsty reputation, and ran away. Creon and Antigone stood alone by the well, under the shade of the trees. When a butterfly settled on his tunic, he beat it off.

In a heavy voice, he said, "We can talk here freely. Though what I say will hardly please you."

Timidly, she said, "Uncle Creon, I like Haemon very well. I have no wish to displease him or you."

Her words seemed to anger him. Speaking in a low voice, fixing her with his dark gaze, he said, "I will repeat to you that I have passed a law saying that Polynices's remains shall not be buried. You broke the law by your feeble attempts at a funeral. Anyone who breaks the law must be executed."

"It's such a cruel law...."

"The times are cruel. I must be cruel to meet them. Hadn't you sense enough to see this would put me in a difficult position?"

They could hear dogs barking in the distant streets. "Yes," she said. "I mean no. All of nature is in harmony, uncle. Why are humans in such disharmony?"

In their hasty retreat, one of the women had left a filled pitcher standing on the wall. Creon, taking up the pitcher, began to pour its water in a slow stream down into the cool recesses of the well. The still liquid circle took the libation into its throat with ichorous gulps.

"Thus, our souls flow back into the waiting earth, never to rise again...I see no harmony in that dark drink.... A guard came to me at dawn, Antigone, all aghast. He reported seeing you, scrabbling soil and muck over what's left of Polynices. There's blood on my hands already, Antigone. It was nothing for me to silence and kill the man."

He hurled the empty pitcher into the well.

"Only you and I know what you did, Antigone. Stay in bed at night in future. Don't entertain uncouth ideas. I'm doubling the guard tonight. I protect you for

Haemon's sake, for his happiness and yours. But if you disobey the law again...." He made a derisive gesture, first opening, then clenching his upturned right hand.

Though she saw his feverish regard, Antigone responded defiantly in her smallest voice.

"I must bury my brother, uncle. That's my law."

His teeth gleamed through his beard, his eyes almost closed. "Be warned. Stay clear of man's business. Your women's business is to marry Haemon and bear him sons. I'll not spare you a second time, Antigone."

Although she trembled, she repeated, boldly enough, "I must bury my brother."

He had already turned away, to march back along the path through the parched grass toward the great wooden gates of his city. She watched his broad shoulders, moving so easily, so strongly; and in that movement saw the whole of life and the way it must go.

That night, to her terror, Polynices came again to her couch, making the same dreary progress, as if he forced his way through stone. Only the scarlet of his wounds relieved a gray appearance. That swollen mouth again moved as he spoke of his desire for burial.

Behind him strode six other warriors. Antigone could discern them only dimly. The glint of armor was their main feature. Sometimes they were not there at all, lost in the miasmas of death. Sometimes she saw their eyes, their hangdog expressions, which seemed to say, "There is no happiness in life, only duty and dejection." And it was of duty that Polynices spoke, saying, "It is your responsibility, Antigone, to see that I am given proper burial, for the honor of our family. This is the second time of asking."

His words caused a kind of booming in her ear. She flung the rug aside, to sit up on the hard couch, clutching her toes. Remembering her uncle's words, she said, "Go away, brother. Leave me. This business is not mine: It is man's business. If you are dead there is no more traffic between us. I am to marry Haemon next month."

"If you desire to free yourself of me, you must ensure that I receive a proper funeral." He lifted his bloody sword, perhaps intending to threaten, but it seemed immensely heavy, and steamed like a boiling pot when he held it vertically. "Farewell," he said.

For a long while, his ghastly white face hung there in the dark. When it faded, all that was left was a stain and a stink.

Antigone sat where she was, shivering, and soon heard dogs beginning to fight outside. The natural world was returning from its abeyance. Its ordinary sounds broke into her numb reverie. She felt able to move her limbs. She slipped on sandals and crept with her hoe out into the dark maze of streets. The pavements underfoot were often cracked and broken. Nothing had been repaired while her brothers disputed the city.

It was the dark hour before the dawn, when pale

moths were still a-flutter. Beyond the gates, a light mist hung, layered over the ground. Dark shapes slunk away. Wild dogs and foxes had been greedying at the unburied body of Polynices; heavy winged things struggled up into branches overhead. Antigone went forward with caution born of superstitious fear. She wielded her hoe like a weapon, but the scavenging animals were cowardly and faded into the thick undergrowth.

She had been at pains to dig a grave the previous night, but the ground was hard, reluctant to yield to her implement. A shallow depression was all she had managed. Into this, she had dragged Polynices, sprinkling soil over him. It had not been enough. The dogs at first light, taking a foot between their jaws, had fished the dead warrior out of his grave. Now she hardly knew what to do.

At this juncture, Joe Moon broke into his own dream and stood before Antigone in the deep deluding dusk, in the leafy shadows, at the tail end of the bosky Boeotian night.

She raised her hoe, ready to strike at him, before asking in a low voice if he were sentry or apparition.

His startlement being as great as hers, he was unable to speak for a moment, so that they held a tableau, neither moving, quite unseen, amid moths, in a silent interlude between waking and dream.

Then he found hesitant voice.

"Antigone, I am your friend. More than that, you are a part of me. You are my anima and I am dreaming you. You may not understand."

She rushed at him and sought to cleave his head open with the hoe. He seized her thin wiry arms, pressed them against her, twisted her round, and held her tightly, locked with her back against his chest.

"Hush, you little tigress! I want to help you. I need to help you. When morning comes, I shall be taken out of my cell and shot. That will be the death of you, too, in me. You see, your tale is well known, and Creon is going to have you killed in a very unpleasant way. If I can save you...."

She struggled furiously, kicking Moon's shins. "You're a crazy man! Let me go or I'll yell for the sentries."

He let her go free, throwing her hoe some distance off, saying urgently, "I'm not crazy. Let me help you do the right thing by your dead brother. I'll drag him into the woods and burn him honorably on a funeral pyre. You go to the palace and sleep with Haemon to establish an alibi. That will fool Creon. He'll think you were in Haemon's bed all night. Haemon won't give you away."

She was silent, peering up at his face. "That makes sense. Except that I mean to retain my virginity until my marriage day. But you yourself are a riddle...."

"Life's a riddle. Do we live our lives or are we lived? I don't know. In my age, we perceive ourselves as divided persons. An astonishing man called Sigmund

Freud regarded his daughter Anna as Antigone....
When the geographical world had been opened up,
Freud discovered a dark continent in each of us. And
to him, women were also an undiscovered—"

"Oh, stop talking rubbish. Are you going to help
me or not? It'll soon be light."

Moon went down on his knees. "Dear Antigone.
You can't understand. Why should you? But, you are a
valued part of me, the female part of myself I've denied
all my life. Now, on this last day of my existence—"

She clouted him over the head. "Get up! Help me
if you will, but I don't understand your speeches."

As he rose from his knees, Moon said, "Look, I
know you're a passionate person—sorry, that's a
Freudian slip—I mean a *compassionate* person. Go to
Haemon's bed now, quickly, and I will dispose of
Polynices's body for you. I promise. Go on! Run!"

In her look was a wish to trust. He felt the power
of her dark gaze upon him.

"Go!" he repeated. "Save yourself. Creon is bound
to obey a law he himself has promulgated. He's just in
that respect. He cannot spare you a second time."

"But it is the destiny of my family, and my destiny,
to suffer. What is the life of woman? Am I not merely
the fruit of those elders who came before me, men and
women burdened with guilt since time began, when
great Thebes was just a cattle market?"

"They are your archetypes, Antigone, but you can
defy them. You must defy them as you have defied
Creon. Strength is all it needs. Go, live and be happy,

marry Haemon. I swear I'll give Polynices a tremendous
funeral pyre, to set his spirit free from this earth—as I
trust mine will soon be free."

Although doubt still ruled on her face, something
in the tenor of Moon's voice convinced Antigone. She
turned and ran from him without another word,
running back to the gate of the city, her dark hair
streaming out behind her.

As if in a dream within a dream, Joe Moon went to
the poor decayed body. It had been heaved against the
city wall by the animals. A gray light filtering through
the trees allowed him to see only dimly. What in his
haste he did not notice was that Polynices's head had
been severed from its shoulders.

Taking hold of the ankles, he dragged the body
along behind him, to slither over parched grass, as he
made for the woods. There in the midst of a flowering
elder thicket, as apricot light suffused the wildwood,
he came on an old wood-cutter's hut, ruinous, with a
pile of dried logs beside it. Hurriedly pulling the wood,
Moon made a pile of it and flung Polynices's decaying
body on top. Only then, as he struck a flint and set
light to small kindling, did he notice that the skull of
the corpse was missing.

"Hell!" he exclaimed.

King Creon was up with the dawn as usual. He gave
but a glance at Eurydice's nakedness and left her

sleeping. After he had bathed his body and had had his beard curled, he went to his window and looked out beyond the city walls. Distantly through the trees, a pillar of smoke was ascending. It climbed into the still morning air and appeared almost solid, reluctant to disperse. Within its curling fumes, Creon thought he saw a woman's face displayed, with hair part obscuring her features.

He summoned his blind adviser, Tiresias. The tap of the old man's stick announced his approach.

"Tiresias, there is disaster in the royal house. Have we not had enough misery? What means that column of smoke and fire?"

Tiresias, in his whining voice, said, "What is the life of man? Something not fixed like a compass point toward good or evil. It's a weather vane that blows with the wind, that's what it is. Creon was once an enviable man, who saved his country. But now? Life without joy is no life, life with continuous burden is living death. Today, O King, the wind blows direct into your heart."

"Oh, shut your mouth, you old fool! Where in Hades is Haemon?" Without waiting for a reply, Creon marched out of the room, past the guard, and flung open the door of his son's room.

There lay Haemon, awake, looking with love into the face of Antigone, curled up next to him. The girl slept peacefully, the fringe of her lashes resting upon her rosy cheeks. One arm was curled protectively over her head, the index finger of its hand entwined with a lock of her dark hair, as if it would pluck a flower. Her defiance put from her, never had she looked more beautiful in her uncle's eye.

Haemon jumped out of bed, grabbing his naked sword as he did so.

"Get out of my room, Father!" he ordered. "Why do you enter?"

"What's Antigone doing here?" asked Creon, taken aback. "She vowed to remain chaste until her nuptial day. You have dared dishonor her?"

"She is chaste, damn you and your suspicions." The youth kept his sword at the ready. "She came to my chamber merely to seek protection, and I have not taken her maidenhood."

Creon's face grew dark with anger, but at that moment Eurydice appeared behind his shoulder, pulling a long silken gown over her shoulders, looking lascivious.

"Why are you quarreling, my husband? Must generation always interfere with generation? Leave Haemon and Antigone alone and return to bed with me. The nest is warm. The cocks are still busy crowing."

"Let them crow. I'll wring every one of their necks," said Creon. But he knew better than to argue with Eurydice, and followed her meekly enough down the corridor. As they passed Tiresias, the blind man said, tauntingly, "Those who forge the law will die on its anvil."

No sooner had he spoken than a clamor arose down

in the hall. A house servant appeared at the top of the stairs, abasing himself. When Creon challenged him, the servant spoke up hastily, wringing his hands. He reported that the guards at the South Gate had discovered the body of Polynices was missing. They waited below to report.

With an oath, Creon brushed the servant aside and ran down the stairs. In the hall of the palace, Creon's house dogs prowled and growled about the legs of two sentries. The sentries stood hesitant by the open door. A few citizens, smelling excitement, gathered behind them curiously.

One of the sentries was an older man, still upright, though his front teeth had long been knocked out. The other sentry was a mere youth, with a miniature stubble field on his chin; he had tucked a blue cornflower into his tunic pocket. Told to explain themselves, the older men declared that, as blessed light returned to the world, they had been able to see that the body of his majesty's dishonored son had been removed. They had searched and not found it. They were not to blame.

"Two little items remained where the body had lain," said the man. "We bring them here, O King, as evidence to set before you." So saying, he raised his left arm above his head. He was clutching a decomposing skull. Maggots fell to the ground and twitched about his feet.

"Polynices!" exclaimed the small crowd at the door. Their tones expressed disgust, reverence, excitement.

"What else?" demanded Creon. Though Eurydice

stifled a scream, he displayed no emotion at the horrid sight.

The older sentry then showed the second item, holding it up in his right hand. It was a hoe such as women used in the onion fields. The split at the top of its handle was bound together with a strip of blue cloth.

"That belongs to young Antigone," a woman called. "And I work beside her many a day. I know that hoe very well by sight. How many times I've told her, 'That hoe ain't no good. Get another one, Antigone, my dear,' I've said, but she's proud, she won't listen...."

"Silence!" roared the king. He began to curse the sentries and everyone else, knowing in his heart he could no longer keep secret the breaking of the law. The chill wind blew direct into his heart as prophesied. Eurydice knew it too, and Tiresias behind her. And the latter cried, "All will happen as the prophet said. Once the boulder begins to roll downhill, all who stand in its way are crushed. Such is fate."

"Yes, yes, we'll all be crushed!" screamed Eurydice. "Husband, rescind your cruel law. Immediately."

In the palace grounds, a bird called, "Caught, caught...."

The king clutched his beleaguered brow. "Those who make the law are those most subject to its command. Guards, bring Antigone hither and she shall confess her guilt."

In the general furor that followed, Joe Moon made a

second appearance within his dream. He himself was as much a specter as the ghosts from beyond the grave, having but an hour to live before he was taken out into a square courtyard and shot under a foreign flag. His appearance was as ghastly as the shade of Polynices.

Clinging feebly to the king's arm, he said, "Mighty Creon, spare a moment for introspection! Understand yourself, interpret your actions! You are helplessly acting out the inflexible male principle. Must you always dominate, whatever misery is caused thereby?"

"If I do not dominate the city, you slave, who will? Thebes needs a strong man." Mixed with Creon's royal anger was some puzzlement at this intrusion. He stood back, clutching at his beard as if for security.
Moon seized his chance to speak again.

"Then more clearly than Tiresias I will predict what will happen, for in my better days I studied the classics. By upholding your law, Creon, you will think it legitimate to entomb Antigone, your intended daughter-in-law, in a cave. There she will die. In consequence, your son Haemon, overwhelmed by sorrow, will thrust his sword into his own breast. Confronted by such misery, what will your beloved Queen Eurydice do if not bring about her own end, leaving you bereft? How will you be then, O King, O male principle?"

"I will be myself whatever befall!"—spoken in a lion's roar to alarm all present.

"And if your will fails, who then will rule Thebes?"

"Damn you, I live by my stubborn will yet," shouted

111

Creon. He struck out at Moon. But the rays of the sun
had reached the strange flag above the cell where Joe
Moon lay, his dream faltered, and his projection faded
away from Thebes forever, as light forsakes the eyes of
the dying.

In that ancient month, all happened much as Moon
said. It was a dream, yet not only a dream, but a dream
of a myth, and its end tailed away in a new fashion,
however little the dreamer could perceive the
alternatives. For in the dream, Antigone was indeed
the undying female principle, and so remained forever
living, generation after generation, like the lineaments
of a family—a big nose, say, or a cleft chin, seeing no
need to fade....

Creon indeed had Antigone bound and cast into a
cave. His soldiers tossed in with her the stinking skull
of her brother. Then the cave was sealed with a great
boulder, and the gaps plastered up with clay, so that
no light or air entered.

But the goddess Aphaia helped Haemon to escape
from Thebes. He searched until he found the cave.
Using a branch as a lever, he eased away the boulder
and unplugged the mouth of the cave. His intended
bride was still alive. When he had laved her in a brook,
her mind returned to her body. She spoke and smiled
at him.

As for King Creon in his palace: His wife, as
predicted, fell into such sorrow, imagining that both
Haemon and Antigone were dead, that she drank a

bowl of hemlock and fell down lifeless in her bathroom. Creon lived on in Thebes, ruling with a heavy hand, a lonely male principle. Law he administered; justice he never understood. As he had claimed, his will did not fail him.

Antigone and Haemon went to live simply on an island in the far Cyclades. But not all of her brother had achieved rest. They were forever haunted by the pallid vision of a rotten skull, which followed them at shoulder height. Strangely, it bore the mark as of a bullet hole which had pierced it at the temple.

Joe Moon was executed at eight o'clock in the morning, in a country and time far from Boeotia. His life-dream was over, and his dream of Antigone. He turned his head from the firing squad, and a bullet pierced it at the temple.

SUSANNAH AND THE SNOWBEARS

kathleen ann goonan

Kathleen Ann Goonan has sold stories to Interzone (the excellent "Daydots, Inc."), Asimov's (five times at last count), Amazing, Pulphouse, Tomorrow, F&SF, Omni, SF Age, Century, Omni Online, and three more to Strange Plasma. Her debut novel—Queen City Jazz, from Tor—is a New York Times Notable Book. Her second, The Bones of Time (Tor), will be out soon. If you're new to her work, then the following story should convince you to check out everything you've missed.

Goonan was born in Cincinnati, Ohio, in 1952, though she now lives in Florida. She has a degree in English as well as Montessori certification, and she taught pre-schoolers for thirteen years, mostly in a school she owned and operated herself.

As far as superstitions go, she has strong feelings about the nature of time, which she feels has never been completely explained. "Every religion copes with time in its own way," she says. "And while physicists try madly to come to grips with the problem, 'Susannah and the Snowbears' is my own explanation."

I t's been many years since Susannah first saw her Snowbears; many years and, I'm afraid, another dimension as well. That may not be correct, but that's how I think of it. If ever I returned to civilization, they would laugh at me, I'm sure, as Susannah's father did. Before he realized at the last instant that I was right.

I first became aware of Susannah's Snowbears when I was pregnant, in the year 2015. It was two years after we had finished the cabin, hidden from the Welsians in the remotest part of the Canadian Rockies.

Oh, I was young then, healthy and though not particularly beautiful, I was attractive enough, as was Susannah's father, Paul. He was tall, with a long, smooth body made muscular by the work, as was mine, of building our beautiful outlaw cabin, our place of refuge, and then filling it via helicopter with the marvelous scientific equipment which had been allotted us.

And much that had not. We took—we *stole*— immensely powerful computers, telescopes, wind- and water-powered generator set-ups, spectrometers, spare parts galore, massive backups—then stored them carefully. We had no idea where thought would take us, but we would be fully prepared. We were simply playing in the shallows of what had once been a magnificent revolution in science, and we knew it. We didn't care that we were stealing. We felt it was our duty. It was all we could do.

And the Welsians didn't know, when Paul returned the helicopter after the last transport and hiked back over a period of many months, that we had settled several hundred miles northwest of where we had been assigned.

Our cabin stood near a permanent snowfield. We had carefully ascertained the lack of a topological record of the area. After the war, when resources were so low, many obliging people turned in their parents' and grandparents' U.S. Geologic Survey Maps, but millions of quadrants were missing. We weren't afraid of such things as homers or satellite-sensitive bugs. They were possible, but we lived in such backward times, compared to what had come before, that they just weren't a part of the technological texture. No, we were safe, home free, *truly* free. We felt snug, inviolable, and it seemed as if both our minds were operating at top speed without the restraints we both had grown up with. It was heaven, a heaven of our own plan and creation.

I felt blessed, too, because I was supposed to be sterile, and I wasn't. I'm afraid that was the Snowbears' doing too; who knows. Perhaps I *was* used, but at least I had Susannah. For a while.

One afternoon I was out walking in the high meadow. It was late autumn, and cold. I sensed something, turned, and there they were.

Light-beings, solid-looking enough I suppose, yet with a golden luminosity which looked as if it would baffle touch. At first, I thought them sundogs, skipping lights on the horizon, except those only occurred in winter.

And then they came close.

I felt *regarded*, scrutinized, completely understood. There was no speech.

The communication was all one way; they took something from me, a measure of parts of me of which I had very little conscious knowledge. Genetic information. Cellular scans. Intelligence capability, though for them intelligence is quite different than for us. I *knew* what they were doing because they *let* me know, they showed me in little schematics which danced in the air, pictures tailored for human recognition.

And for a few long moments, images flashed through my mind which I'd forgotten having lived through, as they pulled memory through me as well, like thread through a needle. How the bright sun splashed through our Wels City apartment when I was a baby watching dust motes dance above my crib. I think it was still called San Francisco then. My grandparents, notorious freethinkers and rabble-rousers, being led to their execution, my parents and I forced to watch. The harsh, bitter taste of the green geneserum I was supposed to drink with all the others in my class when I was five, and how I held it in my mouth and spat it into the drinking fountain later. It was supposed to cure things, like nearsightedness, and thinking. I'm sure others did it too, encouraged like me by their parents.

I saw all this and more, too many images to mention, a whole lifetime flashed through me and was gone, spinning in spirals of light toward the beings. I could feel that they were extremely conscious, more conscious than perhaps I could imagine.

And then the baby jumped.

Later, I found it ironic that Susannah named them for the brightness of snow, not that of the sun, which figured so strongly in my own experience of them. They must have given the same sensation of blind caretaking to Susannah that I felt. The bear and the dog—the snowbear, the sundog—they were cousins of a sort. There was a canine quality of loyalty there. But loyalty to what?

I didn't know. I still don't, though all this has happened and the world has changed. It was something unearthly. Something Paul and I opened the door to, up here in the remote northern reaches where we studied the rudiments of a science once called physics. Perhaps we called them, attracted them with our particular blend of curiosity and electricity. I simply don't know.

But our new freedom had resulted in a burst of strange, new discoveries. We had been pent up all our lives, and now we were able to think, to study, to compile information which another generation might eventually find useful. Information which we did not have to bend to suit one or another ideology, not the ideology of a religion or the less visible one of a megacorporation or a country or even a philosophy or scientific theory. Truth, we thought. Blessed truth at last. Simple information. Little did we know how much we *would* change things.

Our south-facing windows had a panoramic view of endless rough ridges, an ever-changing panoply of mist, storm, and sun-washed waves of solid earth. It was beauty itself, absolute.

But Susannah, once she got old enough to know they existed, wanted the Cities.

I told Paul about the light-creatures that night in bed, as the winter stars pulsed outside our window and the small orange fire flicked shadows across the ceiling and Susannah kicked inside me.

"Oh," he laughed. "This *is* getting to you. Maybe we should go back and register the baby after all. We really need to consider the future."

"How do we know what the future will be?" I asked. I knew he was teasing, but the very thought upset me. "Governments come and go. This one could go too. If we stay here, we're ensuring that little David will be free no matter what."

"Little Susannah, you mean," he said. "You don't seem to realize she's a girl. But the time of our parents was the last free time. Even the idea of freedom has been eradicated. You're right. We might be giving this baby a really hard time if we go back now. We're prisoners here, let's face it. We're more free here than we could be anywhere else in the world, but our freedom is our prison."

I tried to consider carefully what I was about to say, but then I just blurted it all out. "I felt that when—*that*—happened, for an instant, I could see the future. Or even, maybe, an alternate Earth, one where the Welsians never came to power. It was so specific, for that instant, and so whole, a paradigm, an all-at-oneness."

"Don't go religious on me now. We're scientists, remember?"

But I lay awake long after the moon floated below the pines, thinking. The prismlike light phenomenon I'd investigated, always accompanied by a shift in the compass needle, and which I'd relayed back in my youthful idiocy when we first arrived. And those sundogs: conscious, intelligent manifestations of light.

They were the same.

Paul had set up a relay at the spot where we were supposed to be, but we knew that it wouldn't stay in good repair forever. We thought that the best thing to do would be to send out a few obscure reports, actual and supportable, and then fake our deaths. Of course, if they ever sent the helicopters out looking for us, the game would be up, and that's why at the last there was simply an enormous fire in which we supposedly perished. They could see a black spot from the air, nothing more. If they landed and kicked the debris around, it would be easy to see the fake, but it was better than nothing, and chances were excellent that no further resources would be wasted on us.

Life was wonderful. I had a painful, bloody time when Susannah was born, a little frightening too, but I was young and strong and it was quickly forgotten. She was a delightful child. I forgot about the sundogs I'd seen, put them out of my mind, probably because I was afraid, or maybe I thought with Paul that I must have been imagining things. Until one day when Susannah was three.

Her short, stocky body was wrapped in layers which made her appear even more round, and I watched her out the enormous window composed of many squares of glass while I worked on my computer. It was winter, and about twenty below, but there was no keeping the baby (she's not a *baby* any more, Paul would laugh) inside if the weather was nice. We had tramped down a portion of the snowy meadow, hollowed out the drifts, and turned them to snow castles. When the sun shone through the walls, the icy blueness was a glad ache in my throat, especially when I leaned back against a chill, smooth wall, looked out a ragged window at the sky and mountains, and held Susannah on my lap.

Now, as I watched through my window, Susannah paused at the south edge of the castle and I saw the creatures approaching across the meadow.

And then, with startling and unmistakable clarity, I was drawn into Susannah's mind.

I don't know why it happened. Maybe they allowed it to calm me, or to prevent me from rushing out and frightening Susannah. There's so much that I just must postulate, even now. My hands stopped on the keys, and it happened.

She felt no fear, for there was no threat. Only wondrous light, gorgeous humor. Though only three, she understood humor. I felt her ease of articulation as she communicated with them, a sharp contrast to her clumsy frustrating efforts to form words with her tongue and lips for Paul and me. Her thoughts were fast, surprising whole *things*, almost as tangible as objects, and I rode them as if they were my own, though I could not interject. I was always an outsider.

—Are you bears? You look like white bears, like snow. Snowbears!—

—Of course, true one. Snowbears. We are here now, just as you wanted us to be.—

She didn't understand this, but she felt a strong, instant yearning as she gazed on their bodies—bright, solid-seeming, yet bathed in a transparent glow.

She asked, —Will you give me a ride?—

How did they show mirth? Something to do with a change in the oscillation of the spectrum which surrounded them, the brilliant whiteness fanning into colors which she saw only occasionally and apprehended not only with sight, but with some other sense humans were privy to, yet did not always use.

—Here, little one. Climb aboard.—

She was lifted. Yes, they had arms. Yes, there was an odd solidity about them, though they were translucent. But that didn't puzzle her. Something else did.

—Which of you is the mother, and which of you is the father?—

Of course. I was amused. The only other pair of beings she knew were delineated in that fashion.

She felt their humorous, jostling interchange.

—Neither—, January replied, as Sparks simultaneously replied —Both—, and I knew that she had named them too.

Then Susannah was bathed in joy and light, and pictures cascaded through her vision as they had mine, but I recognized none of them, and they were too swift to recall later. She shrieked with absolute, pure happiness. As she skimmed over the snowfield on the back of Sparks, her very atoms changed, forever, in an instant, final divergence from the rest of humankind.

I felt it. A weird, sudden flip, like you see when you're titrating something and that last crucial ml drips in and it's all different. It brushed my mind like the creatures' tests on me, then rushed away into time like things do that you desperately want to forget.

They came more often after that, I know, but the times I was with them were few and rare, a gift, I guess, to calm a mother's fears. I tried to tell Paul about it and he laughed. He never saw them. Finally I gave up. I knew I wasn't crazy. In the end, it was Susannah that parted us, though we never went so far as to walk away no matter how crazy the pain got, or how little we spoke to one another, afterwards.

"Tell me about the City again," Susannah would beg as a little girl.

I would tell Wels City as if it were the myth it had always been for her.

"There were so many el-cars that they couldn't move through the streets at certain hours of the day," I always began. If I didn't, she made me start again. "They came in all colors—green, pale yellow, silver."

"What color was yours?" How well I remember her dear, eager face, pale blond hair short and wispy then, her deep brown eyes that always whispered forest to me.

"I didn't have my own. Nobody had any things like that of their own. The University gave me a pass to use one when I could prove I needed it. They were all pretty old and had to be charged often, but they were okay."

"So you had all colors." In the upper reaches of the Canadian Rockies, natural color was limited during the everlasting winters to white, blue, gray, and brown. Even in the summer, permanent snowfields were a backdrop to the wildflowers.

"Yes," I said, aware that I was bestowing richness

125

of a sort on my daughter. If we had known that I could become pregnant, perhaps we would have stolen more ROMS, the ancient ones hidden from the world by the Welsians, the ones with real information from the past. We had some, and had gone to great risk to get them. Now, I wished we had more. We couldn't risk netting on, though we pulled in sputtering, sparse shortwave via a wire we'd stretched up the side of the mountain.

"I'd like to go to Wels City," she said one night, startling us, though of course we were silly to be startled, and Paul berated me later for even telling her about all that in the first place. He would rather have had me lie, I suppose.

I remember that night well. She was six, and it was deep winter. We saved our solar batteries for emergencies, so the tiny stove we had in her room had a fire in it, and orange flames licked the fanlight on the door and threw shimmers of light across the high cedar ceiling. Susannah was wrapped in down quilts, and Paul stood over her holding a bright purple and yellow blanket he had knitted for her out of our yarn stockpile.

He stood, unable to move for a moment, then draped the blanket gently over her. He said, "You can't go to Wels City. No one even knows you're here. You're lucky and rare. You're free. They can't control what they don't know exists. Down there, you can't do what you want. Scientific information isn't used to further humanity, it's only used and distorted by the Welsians to stay in power."

"Who are the Welsians?"

"Followers of Wels."

"Who's Wels?"

"A madman," I said.

"I still want to go," she said.

Paul said, "I never want to hear that again. Ever. And no more stories about Wels City." His voice was harsh. He turned and walked out of the room and slammed the door. How well I remember Susannah's eyes—defiant, staring at the closed door. She swung that stare to me.

"I've only been telling you some of the good things, Susannah," I said. "The reason we don't live there is because." I tried to find words to describe the horror of not being able to think as you wanted, of having so much of your life controlled, of never even being sure of what was you and what was Welsian. I failed.

Of course, that wasn't the last story of Wels City. But I ceased from that point to pretty the picture for her. When she was nine, becoming desperate, I even told her about her grandparents. But by then, of course, it was far too late.

Maybe it always was.

"You can't go out today, Susannah, it's twenty below."

"Layers, Mom, layers," she said. She was already ten,

127

thin and quick; she absently twisted her long fine hair, holding it with one hand on top of her head while slipping her silk underhat on with the other. She covered it with a wool overhat, then a scarf, from the sequential hooks.

"I said no." I rose from my lab stool. I held my equations on the screen with a stroke; second nature. "Why in the world do you want to go out? Look at the pressure. Some bad weather's blowing in any time now."

"The Snowbears," said Susannah, excited. "They're coming, I know! I haven't seen them in so long. Months."

"They're not—"

"Bears," finished Susannah. "Well, what's wrong with calling them that? They're my friends. My only friends," she said, with the passion which always presaged tears. "If we could go to the City, I could have *human* friends." She whirled out into the transparent lock, and I watched her until she disappeared into the snow tunnel.

So, they were back. I didn't doubt it. Susannah always knew when they were there.

By now, she was a bright, shining child; bright in mind, I should say, though her hair, light blond, was burned almost white by the sun. She had had every advantage. Paul and I had been excellent teachers, Paul perhaps better than me. I was a grown woman and had made my own decision, but Susannah had had no choice about this exile, and it worried me. Paul chose to ignore it: Of course Susannah would stay here forever, without a mate, without ever knowing the world she was giving up. I found that absurd, and we argued about it often. We had bred curiosity and inquiry into her, nurtured it. We could not have done otherwise, I'm afraid.

When the break came, it pulled us apart.

Susannah went on a camping trip when she was twenty and didn't come back.

When the message she'd programmed into the computer came up, two weeks later, on the day she was to return, Paul was stunned.

I was not.

"You knew!" he whirled on me, his face a snarl. For an instant, I was afraid that he might hit me.

"No," I said. "I didn't know. Not really. But I expected her to leave sometime. Just not this soon." I didn't mention that my files had been repeatedly rifled during the past year, nor that I realized, now, that she had been copying maps out of the computer to assemble into a master map. One with many gaps, but she would have no difficulty finding her way to Wels City.

"What's *wrong* with you?" he shouted, this man who had gradually become a stranger (though the realization was sudden as a punch in the stomach), gray hair at his temples and a distant look in his eyes. "Aren't you worried?"

I searched my feelings and found I was not. Not really. Because I knew that Susannah had the Snowbears, and Paul did not believe in them. I had experienced them. I couldn't prove them to anyone else though; they were not mine to command. They were not repeatable phenomena.

Paul started throwing together camping gear in a frenzy.

I just sat in our old cabin room. Susannah was everywhere. A fire burned in the fireplace Paul and I had built so many years ago, and the time-patinaed pine panels shone. The bentwood furniture was covered with cushions Susannah and I had sewn two years ago. Yes, we had been very much together here. My feet nestled in a bearskin rug from before Susannah, because after her the death of animals was accompanied by hysterical grief. She'd quit eating them when she found out what she was eating but compromised on fish, always plentiful.

Paul's search yielded nothing, for she had made no secret of where she was going, and he could not go there. Death was certain, and after all, she had gone there on her own. I imagined Paul daring closer and closer to the city, then finally turning back as he realized the fruitlessness of it. I didn't blame him. He had to do something.

When he returned to the cabin, sunburned and haggard, I saw the change in his face. Yes, she was an adult. Yes, we had no right to hold her here, and could not in any case. Perhaps we could have prepared her better, though, if we had been honest about what she was going to do, what she *had* to do.

Paul took up hunting again soon after Susannah left, and for a while there was a plethora of drying skins stretched out everywhere. He abandoned all work and thought, ridiculed everything we had ever done together. "Better if we had never thought about any of this stuff," he said. "We told Susannah too much."

I just computed, theorized, experimented all the more. I pored over our old ROM texts which held Bohr, Hawking, Guth, and Feynman. I filled half a hard disk, one of the five hundred we'd brought, with equations and then, in a fit of anger, wiped it clean. I made paper, laboring with my homemade press, trying to please myself with different combinations of ingredients. Or I would put on my goggles, but I didn't make test tubes out of my solid cylinders of glass. I made bearlike creatures which glowed in the torch's blinding flame before the molten glass shifted and I lost their form.

And as I worked, I thought. What sort of light-candy, I wondered, could I leave on the doorstep to tempt the Snowbears, my only link with Susannah? I needed to understand them and tried to with every ounce of heart and mind, but there was no understanding ethereal light-beings whose physical appearance resembled bears to a three year old, who had only regarded me aloofly twenty years before, and who, as far as I knew, had spoken only to Susannah's mind, never to the ears. I couldn't come to a formula to explain them, couldn't extrapolate from any worldview an elastic mindspace to hold their reality, except one which kept occurring in my troubled dreams: Space was a door, and the door swung open, and they were there, joyous, stern, and kind. Utter hogwash, the scientist in me said, but I went on what I had until I understood them one cold day in Susannah's meadow. One appeared and came close, as close as two feet.

—Look—, he commanded. Or, after I thought about it, it was more like —Let Vision Now Exist—

So vision existed for a minute, and my pain healed.

Because in the center of the Snowbear was a sphere, and in the sphere was a three dimensional picture. Actually it was four dimensional; it moved; it had time. And the Snowbear itself—that was the fifth dimension, if one had to use those limiting terms. Somehow I knew that it was all very primitive, that the Snowbear—was it Sparks?—was taking pity on me and was trying to communicate in a fashion I could understand. Susannah was in the picture, and I saw her life in Wels City fleetingly, as she studied, dissembled, and used the Welsians at the very time they thought they were using her. Some sort of abandoned machine—an atom smasher?—I couldn't be sure—was being reactivated because of something Susannah said. A young man's face appeared for an instant. Somehow, he was important. —It is Necessary—, was the message, and —Understand—

I understood, then, because understanding was a gift they created for me. It was simple.

The Snowbears held time in their center.

I tried to tell Paul, but he only laughed in that bitter way and went back to his brooding. He was off for weeks at a time, building a weir, he said, better to trap fish, or constructing a hunting cabin on the higher slopes. We were separate, and I ached for him to feel better, but there was nothing, really, that I could do.

"When did you first see the 'Snowbears'?"

I stumbled, then sat down hard on the path where I was walking along the slope above our cabin. The tang of thawing earth in the first warm wind of spring vanished, replaced by the faint odor of an electrical short which lingered in the small booth where Susannah lay.

I listened and I looked, but I saw little through Susannah's half-lowered eyelids.

"Ever since I can remember, I've known about them." My chest contracted in pain at the sound of her words, so near.

The questioner's tone remained calm, remote.

"There must be a first memory," he persisted without inflection. "Susannah, try and see if you can picture the first time for us."

Susannah's voice, as she replied, was as remote as that of her interrogator's. Her hair, splayed out around her face as she lay on her back, tickled her cheek. Her hands, palms up, were relaxed into a curl.

"I was three. The Snowbears—"

"*Which* 'Snowbears,' Susannah?"

"It was January. January and Sparks, both of them came that time. I hardly ever saw any other ones."

"And what did they do? Did they speak to you?"

Susannah lay silently.

"Did they *speak* to you?"

There was a hint of impatience in her reply which probably caused the trance controller to check his monitors. According to them, she was still in range, still under hypnosis. She should not react with emotion. How well I knew. This was all I had escaped by fleeing here.

"I *told* you: They don't speak."

The next time they gave me Susannah, I was in bed.

She was walking up a Wels City street, high above the blue bay, on a street I remembered well from my childhood, and her legs ached. I smelled the orange she peeled in the crowded Chinese market, heard the patter of bargaining and hawking. Then someone grabbed her roughly by the arm, and I felt her mental smile: She had planned this. It was going as she had hoped.

That was all. It vanished.

My eyes opened and tracked the comforting flicker of firelight on the ceiling.

It was no dream, I knew.

Paul was gone. I rose, opened the stove door, and poked at the fire. It flared, and I stared into it, cold, very cold. Why were the Snowbears showing me this? The horror of the Welsians, of what they were and what they could do, came back to me once more, full force. Susannah's obvious control impressed me, but God, no wonder Paul wouldn't speak to me. I had allowed this. I *had*.

I pulled on my robe and lit the fire in the lab, turned on my computer, lost myself in the screen's blue glare until the morning stars appeared. I fell asleep in my chair.

Over the next two years, they granted me small glimpses of Susannah's mind like that, in miserly dribbles. Sometimes I felt that I could see the edges of their plan and tried to cobble the numbers for it, but always slid off the edges of it. I felt that perhaps my mind was too old. It was something Susannah understood, I was sure and became more sure of it as the two years she was gone passed, and that the time for *something* was drawing near. She was always in control. Always.

Because of that, I should have feared even more what

it was. Foolishly, I trusted the Snowbears and their good intent.

The cold followed me through the first lock like a live creature, wrapping itself whitely about my layers of down and silk, mingling with my breath intimately, as if it wished to leap down my throat, lay hold of my lungs and heart. A few flakes swirled in, but melted quickly from my gloves as I entered the second lock and took off my layers of clothing, hung them on sequential hooks so they would be ready to don in the correct order quickly in an emergency.

I stopped dead when hanging up my scarf. Through the glass which separated the cloak room from my work space, I saw Paul staring at the scrap of paper in his hand with a mixture of anger and disbelief on his face.

I knew that he still listened to the radio for a little while each morning. Other than that, he had gone primitive and laughed that crazy laugh of his whenever I tried to draw him into something. His face had grown thin and he looked frighteningly old to me, much older than he should.

His expression alarmed me. I went through the final door trailing my scarf and hat. "What are you doing?" I asked, thinking it very likely that he wouldn't answer. "What's wrong?"

"It can't be. It's a hoax."

"*What?*" I strode across the room and saw for myself.

It said, "Be there July 28th. Or thereabouts. I'm bringing a friend. Susannah."

"I was just listening this morning at the same time I always do," he said, "and heard this. She repeated it five times. I wrote it down."

"It's no hoax," I said. I knew instantly. I had been expecting something like this, hoping for it and dreading it at the same time.

"It *must* be," Paul said. "She wouldn't risk sending a message. Why would she? She hasn't said one word to us since she left. For all we know, she could have died."

"I told you she wasn't dead," I said, and ignored his scathing look. I was pretty good at that by now.

"I'm sick of what those damned Snowbears told you," he replied. "No, she wouldn't send a message unless…" He paused, and I understood the sad look on his face. I wished I could comfort him and was surprised at myself. I was sure I'd grown quite as cold as him.

"Not unless they've really done a job on her, you mean."

"Yes. If someone's coming, it's not her. Not any more."

I remembered the pictures, the mindriding, I hadn't told him about—though I had at first, and had been ignored—and said nothing. He continued to look at me with hostility. "If you hadn't sent in that report about the magnetic shift—"

I was amazed. "That was even before I was pregnant! When I told you about it then, it didn't bother you at all. Is that what you've been holding against me all these years?"

"*They want the Snowbears.* You're just too stubborn to admit it. That shift you reported on—"

"Fleeting though it was—"

"Right. Fleeting though it was, an anomaly like that is of the utmost importance. And Susannah is the perfect person to tell them more about it. Why won't you admit it?"

"You're telling me that you believe in the Snowbears?" I asked.

He stalked out of the room.

I sat down, feeling very weak.

God knows what might happen next.

On the appointed day, after I'd spent a happy week cleaning, getting out the old feather comforters, airing out Susannah's room, I found Paul in the living room cleaning one of his rifles.

"Just what are you planning to do with that gun?" I asked.

He inserted bullets; they made smooth sliding sounds as he pushed them in. "Nothing, I hope. Don't you remember? Today's the day Susannah—"

"I know," I said, and my voice was fierce. "Why is

my idea of an appropriate reception for our daughter so much different from yours?"

"Ellen," he said, speaking my name more gently than he had in many years, "she may not be Susannah any more. Don't you remember why we wanted to keep her here? Have you forgotten how plastic personalities are once the Welsians have some sort of use for a person?"

"She'll always be Susannah, no matter what," I rejoined angrily. "And we were wrong, dreaming, to think that we could keep another human being here forever without her permission, even if we are her parents. What kind of life would that have been?"

He clicked the rifle shut, took aim through the window. He was crazy. Fear flicked through me, tightened my stomach.

I reached over and took the rifle from his hands. He didn't resist. He just stared out the window. "Susannah is coming home," he said.

"That's right," I said gently, as I would have spoken to a child. "Susannah is coming home."

"Well," he said. "I guess we can wait and see."

"That sounds like a good idea," I said, and I hid all the firearms after that, scoured the house for more as he wandered out into the meadow and waited.

Her friend was Benjamin, I knew. As I locked away the guns, I remembered what I had seen earlier that morning, while I drank coffee.

✤

"This is Cat-Eye Falls," Susannah shouted over the roar as she scrambled out onto the slippery rocks, pink with cold. She grabbed the small towel she packed, rubbed herself vigorously, and began to climb into her clothes.

Benjamin watched from the safety of his sleeping bag. Susannah's willingness to jump into water which escaped freezing solid only because it was moving too fast to do so astounded him. And I knew that the thought occurred to him, not for the first time, that perhaps he hadn't known what he was getting into. But what difference would that have made? He'd been given no opportunity to make a choice. Any opportunity would have been meaningless anyway. He had no background in making choices.

I knew these things because I could ride his mind too. The Snowbears guided me and set me there like a child upon an elephant's back. I looked down on the workings of his mind from a great height. I was not impressed. That was their intent. I had to believe that he was too inept to do anything. I was supposed to protect him, I realized later, from Paul.

"Wakes you up," Susannah said breathlessly, sitting down beside him. She slicked back her wet hair with a brush and deftly blended it into an intricate braid, her fingers moving so fast that he couldn't follow them. "I call it Cat-Eye Falls because once I saw a wildcat standing up there at the top of the falls, watching me."

"How soon before we get there?" He wanted information, information, he'd been programmed to get *information*.

"Well, if you're so impatient, why don't you get up? The pool's free."

I smiled at what I saw. Of course, there was no Cat-Eye Falls on any map, though we used to go camping there for a week at a time during the summer. But then no one had mapped this area since the old geologic surveys. Welsians didn't care about wilderness unless it had some exploitable resource; they limited restoration to a few key cities, and when they re-opened universities they were for practical purposes only, not for the pleasure individuals might take in knowledge, but for the furtherance of Welsianism. Yet this girl had come down out of the mountains, made her way to the suburbs, and had then taken the public transport into Wels City.

I watched Benjamin go over everything again in his mind to give himself some detachment and was aware he did this several times a day because he was so completely out of his depth.

Susannah's understanding of theoretical physics, in which she quickly gained her PhD, had gained attention in high quarters. Of course, they knew who she was. The illegal offspring of the scientists sent to some vaguely remembered outpost many years ago, forgotten after they died in a fire. Her bent of interest caused an intense sifting of that data, and my goddamned twenty-year-old report, sent before communication had ceased, stood out baldly.

So they realized that her parents had been effectively isolated for years and had further broken the law by having an unregistered child with a thoroughly unapproved gene pattern. They'd never have let the two scientists go off there together had they not thought the female irrevocably sterile.

Though Susannah had been very clever at assuming a new identity, it was unclear whether naiveté or intent artfully disguised as such had allowed them to penetrate her story. Thought in the highest circles held that she was a sophisticated spy, and that a huge, unregistered group of rebels had sent her to gain technical information to help overthrow the government. Old resonators untouched for fifty years because they wasted too much energy were being restored. They'd figured heavily in her thesis; no one was sure why.

Benjamin found it hard to believe she didn't know she'd been hypnotized in the Wels fashion, which was designed to leave no trace in the subject's conscious mind (I would have too had I not known about the Snowbears); harder still to believe that she truly loved him, that it was possible for them to love each other in this maze of tangled and unclear intents. The Welsians thought she was now a part of their plan; perhaps they were wrong. Perhaps they were a part of hers. His thoughts were hard to pick out, they were like a welter of islands in a murky sea which surfaced then vanished, but I thought I could see that much. And a bit more.

He was willing to leave Wels City permanently; to become a part of whatever she was. But he mistrusted his own thoughts and motivations: Had they been planted there? And who knew what he'd find ahead? Perhaps a whole, armed society, a group of primitive rebels. But she wasn't primitive at all. On the contrary. In his opinion, she was beyond them all, tuned into something quick and sharp as light itself. He gently pulled her head down and kissed her. For the hundredth time, he felt himself lost, and glad of it. When he kissed her, he was himself, and light, like her.

Finally, the Snowbears allowed me to twist away.

I thought of how Paul and I used to be and felt tears form as I stared unseeing at the blue mountains with which we had surrounded ourselves.

"See?" Paul whirled the telescope around so I could look.

"There are two of them," I said. "She told us there would be two." For her own reasons. For the reasons of the Snowbears. Not for the reasons of the Welsians, as Benjamin evidently believed.

"There's only one reason. He's come to stake us out, to take us in. Why? Who are we hurting? Damn the Welsians. Where did you hide my rifle?"

"Can't you just wait, just wait and see?"

"See what?"

"See if she loves him," I was surprised to find myself saying quietly. "Why else would she bring someone back here?"

"If she loves him," Paul said roughly, "it's because they made her. Don't you understand? Once you let her run away, she became one of them, everything we thought we'd left behind."

I looked steadily into her eyes. "Do you really think that anyone could make her do anything she didn't want to do?"

"No," he said, and I could tell he thought it true. Susannah in her teens had possessed an inner strength and conviction which had stymied us both.

"Well, then?"

"All right," he said. "What do we have to lose, after all? Let's go meet them." His angry bravado had vanished, leaving nothing in its place except eager, obvious longing.

Benjamin's eyes darted so nervously that I wondered if, after all, he could be a robot with cameras for eyes. But I had touched his thoughts, though he was blank to me now. Damn the Snowbears!

"So tell us what you do there, in the City," said Paul, falsely jovial.

The young man looked very self-contained. It was apparent that he had a short, stiff haircut before leaving on his long trek; in the two months they had taken to come overland it had grown shaggy.

Susannah, on the other hand, was open and glowing. She looked wonderfully strong and in her prime. Her long hair was neatly braided, and she had arrived looking not in the least disheveled, but as one accustomed to traveling in style, which meant clean clothes. I imagined her scrubbing them in icy streams and letting them dry in the sun, draped like colorful autumn leaves over rocks.

"I'm in a new branch—new to you, anyway. It's a Timestudy segment. We're involved in theories about the nature of the future and past."

"And the application of your discoveries?" asked Paul.

"Well, we think that the 'future' causes waves which reach into the 'past,' much like it can be easily seen that what happens now affects the 'future.' And therefore—"

"Ambitious," I remarked, and my voice stuck in my throat as I thought of the Snowbears. "Quite ambitious. If the Welsians can even begin to put a dent in the mathematics, there have been enormous advances since—but what brings you *here*?"

I couldn't read the look he cast at Susannah.

"Susannah and I are going to get married," he said. "It's all been approved. She wanted to show me her home."

Paul and I exchanged a look. Suddenly we were one again. It felt odd. "Congratulations," I heard myself say.

I was riding again when they left, later that afternoon, a spy in the mind of my daughter. I don't think she ever knew, except at the last.

The meadow seemed a metaphor for infinity to Susannah, a complex thought transmitted whole which echoed in my own heart. The stream was still blocked by a dam of her making, and the tiny rocky pool was the right size for cooling off, nothing more.

"I planted that ten years ago," she said, pointing to the pine whose roots spidered among the silvery rocks.

Benjamin let his eyes wander over the scene; white-peaked mountains were everywhere. "Where did we come from?" he asked. He was always asking.

She just smiled at him. The sun's reflection as it sparked off ripples, which spun out as she shifted her body to admire the view, must have blinded him for an instant, because he shielded his eyes as he gazed at her.

Paul startled me by speaking. I must not have heard him as he walked out the door onto the front porch where I sat.

He said, "I just don't trust him." My vision snapped back to my own vantage point as Paul and I watched the tiny figures of Susannah and Benjamin returning up the path. But Paul was more normal than he had seemed in years, and I knew using the rifle was out of the question now.

"I don't either. But do you trust Susannah?"

Looking up, I saw tears in his eyes. "Of course I trust Susannah. More than anyone in the world."

"So you think she's still her."

"I do. She is. But why she's brought that insipid jerk up here is more than I can see."

I was trying to figure it out, myself, and was flitting into their minds more and more often, completely unashamed, gaining more control each day.

"My old clothes still fit," Susannah said excitedly. She pulled on a striped tunic she had sewn herself. Benjamin ran a finger over the unusual symbols embroidered on the cloth which fell between her breasts.

"What are these?" The Snowbears saw fit to let me know that Benjamin remembered them. They'd come through on his screen one day, fitful but indelible in their strangeness, yet obviously incomplete. He'd felt their power and importance in that one glance. The next day, he'd been assigned to "The Susannah Problem," as she was called, for the symbols were part of her thesis.

That enigmatic smile, with which he hoped he'd never lose patience.

I guess I felt a little sorry for him. He did love

Susannah. The silly young dolt thought he was prepared to fight everything for her. He just had no idea.

But then, neither did I.

One night, sitting up late with the computer, I sensed rather than saw Susannah moving in the back rooms. I was sure she was barefoot. She always had been as a child no matter how hard we had tried to threaten or persuade her to wear shoes.

"Snakes."

"They don't live up this high," she'd said airily. From the time she was old enough to pull shoes off her feet, she had.

I rose from the stool and pulled off my own shoes. Taking a deep breath, I tiptoed through the house.

I saw her, straight and thin as a pine, floating like a dim star in the moonlight down the path to the meadow.

Benjamin, however, was dressed in black, and I almost ran into him. If he hadn't been so intent on keeping to the path, which Susannah knew by heart, he might have seen me.

Susannah began to run as she reached the meadow's edge; her motions revealed imperative, desperate haste.

She reached the stone where she'd always seen them.

But when I got there, she was sobbing

uncontrollably, seated on the ground, her arms holding her legs close to her chest as she rocked back and forth.

As I hugged her she said, her voice hollow with despair, "They won't come anymore for me; they won't, they won't. I knew it was still too warm. Why did they wake me?" She refused to be comforted.

I didn't see Benjamin at all as he walked her back to the house. "Tell me what's going on," I said. "Don't we deserve to know?"

"Not yet," she said, with the old stubborn tilt of her head. "I can't tell anyone anything yet."

Paul was sitting in the living room when we got back. Susannah walked past him swiftly and closed the door to her room.

Once more, I tried to tell him about it. I had to. This time, he listened.

He didn't say anything. He just reached across and gently brushed my cheek. "I'm sorry, Ellen," he said gently. "For everything." Then he got up quickly, as if he'd said and done too much, and really, it was quite a lot, considering.

I sat on the porch and listened to the crickets in the vast, open night. I felt as open to the possibilities of life as I had twenty-six years ago, when he and I had first come up here. Had our romantic dream been broken forever, I wondered? Or could it be renewed through Susannah, who had so changed everything?

Something was still happening. As I sat there and

felt the cool night breeze on my bare arms, I was very glad.

I had missed Paul. More than I had realized.

"You look at me as if I were some kind of toad," Benjamin complained at breakfast the next morning.

"Oh, I don't think you're a toad at all," said Paul comfortably as he poured syrup on his pancakes. "I think you're much more like a vulture."

As Benjamin pushed his chair back loudly and left the kitchen, Susannah's mouth got tight.

"You don't know what you're talking about," she said angrily, and followed Benjamin.

I stood with one hand on my hip, the frying pan in the other. Then I burst out laughing. He *had* a sense of humor, once. I loved him because he could make me laugh.

After breakfast, I went into my workroom. Comforted by my winking screens, I relaxed, then began to concentrate blissfully. For years, my calculations and conclusions had simply been stored away. There was no framework for their use, no one to appreciate them. I accepted that now. Perhaps someday they would be useful. Perhaps not.

Of course, I still have all those. I just haven't had the heart to look at them.

"It's a test," explained Sparks kindly in Susannah's dream. I rode the dream, her thoughts, her mind.

I had been wrenched there from a sound sleep. Their witness. Their ever-more-willing touchstone.

"Don't take it so hard. Have faith, Susannah. We are with you."

"Why test me?" asked Susannah resentfully. "You chose me, you made me, why test me? I brought back Benjamin too, and the Welsians are all paying darned good attention; the resonators and splitters are being reactivated. They're all in a tizzy. So *why?*"

For the first time ever, Sparks appeared to be puzzled. "You did well. Your research created the necessary avenues of thought. Their old machines *are* on again; almost enough new ones are functioning too. You were not forceful, but you were effective. And yet to gain us, you must sacrifice us. Humans always test their messiahs, do they not?"

"Messiah?" asked Susannah. "I'm no messiah! Messiah to who, for what?"

"Someone must die; someone must change," said January sadly. "We wish it could be us. But you will be new. You will make everyone new."

Then she woke.

I was already far too awake.

They had spoken aloud. They had never done that before. It was still too warm for them to appear in the meadow; cold aided their transmission. And their wordspeech had been different from their thoughtspeech.

Susannah basked, in the absolute velvet dark, in the

lingering dream memory of their sonorous voices: cool, deep, and loving; many-toned. What had they said? She couldn't remember.

But *I* could, lying awake in bed. And fear caught me again.

I woke the next day determined to do something. I followed Benjamin out of the house after breakfast at practically a march. Oh, yes, I would do something at last. I must have seemed silly to them.

"How do you communicate with the Welsians?" I asked, and Benjamin jumped. He was hunched over something, standing at the edge of the meadow. His hand went into his pocket.

"What do you mean?"

"Don't give me that bull. What's that in your pocket?"

Reluctantly, Benjamin pulled it out. I wondered why it didn't occur to Benjamin to resist, or argue. Fall was turning to winter, and I'd still not figured him out. I took the smooth rectangular gray item.

"If you use it, they'll find you," warned Benjamin.

I looked at him contemptuously. "What makes you think I care? Your people are only letting you stay here anyway until they see them. Do you think you can ever figure them out?"

The Snowbears, though unsaid, hung in the air.

"What if I tell Susannah?"

"What if you do?" I asked. "If you don't, maybe I will."

He handed it over.

Paul and I examined it in the kitchen. "It's some sort of activator," Paul said. "It's set up to communicate with a mother. It's just like I said. When Susannah went down there, they pounced on her. They want to know what we've figured out up here—what *you've* figured out."

"That's right," said Susannah.

She stood in the doorway. "This isn't the only place they've appeared. There have been sightings all over the world in the past fifteen years. But only at this latitude. And give Benjamin back his sender."

"What for?" asked Paul.

"What are they, Susannah?" I asked, feeling desperate. It wasn't fair to give me so much and not all of it. But what did they care?

"I can't say," she said, and whirled and ran out of the room.

She probably didn't know much more than me.

"Where are they, Susannah?" asked the calm Welsian voice over and over. "We need an equation. You know the equation. You know it. Write it out for us." She thought it: that symbol from another dimension—of another dimension—they'd given her when small. She saw herself pulling it from her chest...giving it to them...of course, they could tell it was a threat....

"Get out of my head, damn you!"

I was startled by how loud her scream was. I heard it from the bedroom. Paul was still asleep, but I sat up in bed and felt Benjamin shake Susannah lightly by the shoulders. It took me a second to realize that she had been screaming at the Welsians, not me. Benjamin, of course, thought that *he* was to blame.

"I'm sorry, Susannah. I couldn't help it, I *can't* help it," Benjamin said, his voice pleading, almost a sob. "Don't blame me. It's not my fault."

No, mild, stupid boy, I suppose it wasn't.

Susannah took a deep breath and slipped out of bed into the frigid air. She checked the thermometer which hung outside her window with a flashlight and nodded once, sharply.

Then she lit a candle; I felt the hot match flame within her cupped hand first. She sat cross-legged in bed, pulling the covers around her shoulders. She spoke to him kindly, as if he were a child.

"Don't worry. You know next to nothing. With all their work and nosiness, they know just about zero. Do you still want to know? I'll tell you." She pulled the blanket around her more tightly. Her words frosted in the cold air, and I was frightened by my child.

"Time is a simple thing, and its laws become quite fluid during the religious ceremony of the Snowbears. They feed on time. They change time. They drink time. Benjamin, they *are* time."

She stopped. Benjamin's face was very pale in the candlelight, and my own heart seemed to have slowed.

What did she *mean*? I was there with her, but still that information was not given me. That crux was for her only.

"No," she said. "I'm sorry. It's impossible to explain. That's true—yet it's not true at all." She sighed, then looked straight at him. "It doesn't matter. There's really nothing to tell them. Use your activator. That will put this information everywhere. Everywhere in the world. Everything is ready."

She didn't even have to look to know that the aurora borealis was dancing across the sky. She watched Benjamin caress his little slab of sending devices.

"I want you to know, Susannah—"

She blew out the candle and touched him gently on the face. "It's all right. I know everything."

"NO!" I yelled, and Paul woke with a grunt, but it was too late.

It was *always* too late.

With Susannah, I felt their blessing amusement begin in her chest and ripple through her body, then spread outward through the night. Points in her body became powerful centers of exploding atoms in a precise constellatory waltz. The immense heat was actually a cool sensation as endless scenarios succeeded one another in the center of her chest, fleeting yet intense. Benjamin stared, trembling.

"Don't be afraid," she said. Her polyphonic voice touched not only his ears, but every part of his body. And mine.

It touched and illuminated every memory too, swiftly as wind before a rising storm rushes through the billion green leaves of a forest, setting each one in motion. "There is joy in time once again. The Freeing has begun," she said. "See for yourself."

And I felt what they did, at the center of the lightbeing she had suddenly become: The vitality of individuality flowed through humanity as newly made Snowbears linked thoughts and magnified one another's powers. That was merely a side effect, for I don't think they truly ever care about us, except as some sort of catalyst. "We need your energy," she said to Benjamin, pausing only for a second in the midst of her terrifying, beautiful transformation.

"*NO*," I said again, but this time within her mind, and she turned and opened toward me with as little volition as a flower when turning toward the sun, but with infinitely more beauty. She was astonished at my presence, but *knew*.

Let me go, Mother. It's what I want.

I think I could have stopped it.

I let her go.

I never could hold you, my small love.

I felt Benjamin surrender to Susannah each atom, gladly, becoming himself so clearly as he did that it seemed to last forever.

And then, it was.

It was lasting forever.

I could go down to the Cities, again, of course I could. But I am an old woman, and I prefer to stay up here, near Susannah's meadow.

The Snowbears took them all that night—Susannah, Benjamin, and even Paul, his eyes so wide and amazed as he sat up in bed and cried out her name, stricken by the immense and lovely light, the aurora borealis which danced now on the horizon more brightly than we had ever seen it, which flashed toward us at great speed. I thought they would have at least left him for me—they left other people, billions of them—but they did not. And I suppose he wouldn't have remembered, anyway.

When it was over, everything was different.

Except me.

Yes, I could go down to the Cities. They are decent once again. The change was worldwide, bloodless, after a phase of unremembered darkness complete as an eclipse of the sun. The Snowbears were kind in that. They have not always been kind. Sometimes there are bloody upheavals, revolutions, dread disease. They use humanity. Perhaps the Snowbears learn a little more each time about us and how best to use us. I don't know. But darkness and light is the pattern they weave in the mind of humanity as easily as you or I might roll over in bed at night made restless by a dream.

There are new sciences in the Cities now, free ones, real ones, but I don't care what they are, even though I see, by studying the past on my old ROMS, that this bright, happy phase may last a thousand years before the Snowbears return. I understand now how Paul felt all the time Susannah was gone, the bitterness, pain, and regret.

Sometimes I walk out to the meadow, and sometimes I think I catch a glimpse of the Snowbears there, but it is always that it is very snowy and bright, or it is only a brief parting of cloud after a week of rain.

I want them to take me too, take me to where Susannah and Paul went, because it is not fair to leave me behind like this knowing so much that others cannot comprehend or believe or remember, they can't remember; even their histories are all new. I know, I am linked into their fine nets, but I rarely explore any more. I think the Snowbears always leave some people behind, some with true memories, because they must use them as references around which to pivot, to navigate, so it doesn't change *too* much, too much to use again.

Simple ecology.

And the pivots are the crazy ones, if they dare speak. I know if I went to the Cities, I would preach. I would preach *Susannah*. "She is the one who gave you all *this*," I would say. "This lovely freedom to *think*. To be who you are. This is how it happened. Never

forget!" Over and over again. And they would laugh.
Of course they would.

But sometimes on summer days in the deep golden
grass of her meadow I am reminded of that brief, quick
ride on the back of Sparks, and I laugh at the light
still spiraling here, here in my heart. I sit on the warm
ground hugging my knees, and the mountains draw
away vast and far, each a ripple of time and, taken
together, endless.

c o n r a d   w i l l i a m s

A recipient of the British Fantasy Award for
Best Newcomer, Conrad Williams was born
in March 1969 in Warrington, Cheshire.

His work has appeared in many small
press magazines as well as in the critically
acclaimed anthologies D a r k l a n d s 2 and
S u g a r   S l e e p. More stories are due in
P a n u r g e, one of England's most
prestigious publications, and N o r t h e r n
S t o r i e s 4, which featured "The Bone
Garden." He is currently studying for an
MA degree in Creative Writing at Lancaster
University and working on his third novel.

A recipient of the British Fantasy Award
for Best Newcomer, Williams tends not to

place much faith in superstitions, although he does believe in fate. "Also, I bought a lava sculpture in Hawaii when I was twelve," he says. "The sculpture, which was of some ancient god of wisdom, accompanied me to every examination I ever sat. Needless to say, my performances in those exams were always poor.

"One superstition that has prevailed over the years is washing my hands before I sit down to write—no idea why. And I used to go out with a girl who, at my request, would kiss any envelope containing a story before I submitted it. I hope this clears up any queries editors may have regarding lipstick-smudged packages from me."

Indeed.

He flinched in the darkness when she reached for him; he could hear her feet scuffling beneath the sheets, smell perfume rising from her hair.

Adam switched on the light and stared down at the empty, creased mass of bedclothes. He fancied he could still hear the ghost of her breathing, but when he laid his hand on the mattress, it was cold. The illusion had seemed stronger this night, like a developing photograph in stages of clarity. Previously he'd sensed only a suggestion of movement, never smells or the rumor of warmth reaching toward him.

Downstairs he made hot chocolate, looking out of a kitchen window that, in daylight, afforded him a view of school fields and a forest clinging to the horizon like storm clouds. The fields had been bleached by fierce August afternoons, the hot, sweet smell of their burned grass filling his room at night. Though he couldn't yet see these things, Adam stared anyway, as if the blackness might calm him. Certainly, by the time he finished his drink, the light panic he had experienced in the bedroom had lifted, and sleep was hovering, ready to fill the vacuum. Confronted with the prospect of returning upstairs, he moved to his living room, nudging Sumo awake as he switched on the fire. The cat mewed a reproach and slunk away.

Adam rubbed at his palms as the flames grew. They reminded him of the weather these past few months: His shoulders had blistered and his fringe had been scorched blond by the sun. Kids played with molten tar in the streets, pulling it into loops like warm treacle toffee. Adam imagined what sudden rain might do to baked pavements.

A crisp tide of static burst from the radio as he plugged it in, drowning a voice that had murmured the last syllable of his name. He reduced its volume, but the voice must have come from the stereo, for only silence rushed to him from the house, save for the odd tick as the fire became hotter. Though he preferred classical music, he now steered clear of the stations which broadcast it, selecting instead a program full of chat hosted by some smoky-voiced woman to give him company until dawn came. Gladdened by her presence he relaxed, his eyes fastening on a sliver of blue between the curtains.

He thought of Monk and Debs at the office, how they'd protest when he rang in sick later. It wasn't something he particularly wanted to do, but the close weather and his current insomnia had conspired to bring him headaches, one of which he could now feel building down the left side of his face. His eye would be covered by a red net by lunchtime, the pain's pulse so pronounced that he'd see it translated to ripples in the mug of coffee he held. The dreams, or remnants of dreams—for he could never remember their content—compounded his discomfort. Each night for a week, Adam had wakened in his bed, sleepily satisfied as his wife stretched beside him until the vague echoes of his dream caught up with him. It was only then that he remembered he was a bachelor. Why he should be indulging in wishful thinking he couldn't fathom. He had never judged himself lonely—alone yes, but not isolated, brooding. His circle of friends was wide—he never wanted for company—but his celibacy was of his own choosing; it had nothing to do with being incompatible. Perhaps his partnered dreams were filled with arguments, moments of spite dredged from the deep waters of his youth.

Those times had been tear-filled for him, listening from the half mask of his blanket as his parents' voices lashed each other. He'd known a burning knot that grew in his stomach, tightening with each muffled scream of hate, each curse. Once there'd even been a slap and an ensuing silence that did more for his dread than any amount of invective. He'd promised himself a life without wives, growing to believe that being born alone was the sign—for anyone willing to recognize it—that life was meant to continue so. No matter how sweet the fruit of love might initially be, ripening and decay must follow.

He washed down a couple of pills and dressed in his running gear hoping a little fresh air might cleanse him. Outside, the night's color was weakening, with dawn already an ochre stain threatening the rooftops. He'd be back before its promise of light was fully realized. He set off at a swift pace to get his blood keen before settling into a measured stride that took him down by the allotments at the foot of his road. To his left, beyond rows of frazzled cabbage, the woods stole back their shape from the night, ready for another onslaught from the sun. Light swirls of dust twisted between stunted vegetables like ghosts dancing on graves. Despite the cool morning air, Adam's mouth became rapidly spitless, perhaps because of the sight of so much parched land. It was as if the color green had never existed. The people he saw were mostly silhouettes in windows, backlit by fires or lamps, though he jogged past one man clenching a plastic bag between his feet. The man watched him from behind a caul of orange. It took a moment for him to realize the man was raising a flame to his cigarette, but by that time Adam had rounded a corner and was heading toward Dallam, its houses bunched between tracts of land that on one side cradled the brook and, on the other, the gasworks. Beyond that lay the dual carriageway connecting the motorway to town.

Adam hoped that by the time he returned he would be whipped enough to catch up on some sleep, though the pain killers had yet to make inroads to his headache. If anything, the pain had intensified, now lacing his hairline and jaw, pummeling an eyeball as effectively as a hastily swallowed cold drink. Trying to ignore the discomfort, Adam turned his mind to Carol, who had been his last girlfriend.

Curiously, she appeared as a series of snapshots clipped from memory—none of them impressing him with importance, which made him feel guilty. They had gone together for two years; it seemed selfish that all he could muster were a few petty images of their shared time—she pulling off her sweater and getting an earring caught in the wool; running after an old man who'd dropped his wallet; catching fruit Polos tossed to her open mouth from across the room. Unremarkable all, leading him to think their relationship had been foolish and wasted. The one crucial memory had been of their last exchange when he told her he didn't want them to live together. She'd assumed too much; assumptions ought never to be made, he thought, as he chased the night sky, a stitch beginning to contest the throb in his head.

Once home, he slouched over his front gate sucking air into his lungs. He looked up and saw a light go off in his bedroom though he didn't recall leaving it on. He let himself into the house, moving slowly in the dark, listening for footsteps. None of the rooms showed any sign of intruders yet the lightbulb by his bed felt warm. He switched it back on to prove it hadn't died, then perched on his bed wondering if the electricity flow in the house was faulty.

Adam took a long shower and, as the water drained him of tension, his mind relaxed, offering further rationale for what had happened. His fingers had been chilled by the run—that's why the bulb felt recently used. Also, his headache might have fashioned popping lights in his skull; one of which he could have mistaken for something more sinister. Or it could have been a doused light from over the road reflected in his window.

The rash that had arrived on his palms last week was developing, becoming more distinct every day. Now there were soft weals traveling the pads of flesh on a parallel with his life lines. If he put his hands together, miming an open book, the weals made a V shape across them. He dried himself carefully and splashed disinfectant on his hands, wincing at how raw they felt. He tried to recollect how the contagion had found him. There had been no nettles he could think of, or scratches that might have caused infection. And unless he had suddenly become allergic to Sumo, no reasonable cause occurred to him. When first he had visited the surgery, the doctor had guessed at prickly heat; certainly the weather encouraged it, and Adam had gone away reassured. But surely that didn't involve swellings of this kind? If they failed to improve by tomorrow he would seek a second opinion.

He dressed the weals lightly, flexing his hands to ensure some give in the bandages. The pain surprised him; hadn't he made a drink this morning without its distraction?

Minutes before nine, he called the office. Debs answered around a mouthful of toast, cheering him instantly. Though he now had a bona fide excuse for absence, he wondered if being at work might bring the tonic he needed.

"It's Adam," he said. "Guess what."

"Monk's going to go up the wall you know."

"I know, but he can cope. I've a bad head and my hands look like they've been washed in acid."

He heard her swallow before taking another bite of breakfast.

"Will you be in tomorrow? It's stock taking, don't forget, and there's no way we'll get it done on our own."

"Promise. Even if my hands fall off in the night."

She sighed. "Okay, but don't blame me if you get an earful from Monk later on."

He hung up, and silence fell, wreathing him like smoke. The thought of spending his day in the house made him uncomfortable, though he'd done it often before. He could measure the heat outside as it increased purely by watching the people that walked by the windows. Early morning had produced a light sweater, a cardigan, even a man in a coat. Now, approaching eleven, boys in shorts, girls wearing halter tops and cut-offs were the order of the day. The heat was accumulating inside too until by noon, it settled over him, stealing the air from his lungs and gluing his fringe to his forehead. Eyes closed, he drifted in and out of sleep, the tattoo of pain in head and hands keeping perfect time. The dryness in his throat became so acute that he began to gag, though the sound seemed disassociated from him. When he came to, the proximity of the walls sprang back as though startled by his eyes. The sounds continued, clearly not his own.

They were coming from upstairs. It sounded as though someone were strangling.

He took the stairs two at a time, pausing on the landing as Sumo strolled out of the bedroom. They looked at each other as the cat casually licked at a paw. The sounds had stopped.

"Fur balls again, Sumo?" Adam asked, crouching. The cat ignored him. "Go on, cough again. Show Daddy." Sumo yawned and collapsed on his back, offering a white tummy which Adam stroked.

He made lunch for them both, but the heat had spoiled their appetites. Ensuring Sumo's water bowl was full, Adam pocketed his keys and went out, heartened to find it was slightly cooler than indoors. By the time he had reached the park, a film of sweat covered him, painting a patch on the chest of his tee-shirt.

The park wasn't as full as he had expected. He felt as though he'd brought part of the house with him; its mood, its claustrophobia. Where he believed he'd find freshness, he'd stumbled on more still, stale land. The houses across from him shimmered in bands of molten brick. A brown smell of canal. Horns bleated on distant roads as drivers were poached in their cars. Everywhere: the sun. It shone so intensely in the blanched sky that Adam couldn't even begin to guess where it might be. An impure heat it shed, drenching him as eagerly as rain. Licking his lips, Adam could taste the air's heavy flavor as well as his own salt.

Further along the path, where greensward swept

down to a rapidly dwindling pond, benches were clustered beneath trees. He perched on an iron armrest and looked down to the water. A figure strolled its perimeter, plucked by haze to nonsense: an elongated blur of white and pink. He sought an expression in the blond curve of hair, but ripples from the pond had infected her substance. The lower half of her body was sucked into a seamless metallic union with the water. The subsequent impression he gathered was that she glided, rather than stepped, an illusion furthered by heat vapors that clung to her, softening her body's angularity to an extent that she resembled liquid. Slowly, her shape diminished as she moved away from the pond's farthest bank. She seemed to be sinking into the gray strips of mirage, and Adam was reminded of carnival mirrors chopping sections from his body until he was a face with feet. Threatening to vanish completely, the girl turned his way, the pink suggestion of her face eliciting his gasp. He made to call the name that had pricked some dim part of his memory, yet he'd forgotten it just as swiftly. By the time he reached the pond she'd gone.

Back home, he prepared vegetables for that evening's meal, trying to come to terms with what he had seen. Glasses of red wine helped, assuaging his headache and offering a comfortably softened point of focus—something medicine had not been able to do. He guessed the suspicion that he knew her had arisen from a projection on the woman from a part of his past, though he couldn't imagine why he had reacted that way. He felt he knew her. He also felt she was completely alien to him. The unease created a chill pocket that enclosed him, manifesting itself in the flashback of waking moments when his dreams lay restless beside him.

Pans filled, he took the bottle to his living room, where he dug out some old photograph albums to satisfy his maudlin pangs. Since moving from his parents' house some years before, Adam turned frequently to these pictures, searching for some aspect of family that might cheer him. There was no doubt he got on better with his mother and father now he no longer lived in the same building, but his link with them felt weakened. Visiting them was like visiting friends. He would now sit in the living room and discuss the economy where once he would have snatched crusts of bread from the kitchen and go up to play records in his bedroom. Those things he missed. Trivialities like Mum calling him in for dinner—he doubted he'd hear that again. The photographs helped rekindle the better moods of those times, helped to camouflage the nasty truth. His parents would love to see him married, despite their own failure, yet Adam thought it would distance them even further from him for then, though he would still be their son, he would be somebody else's primary responsibility. Growing up, he thought, flicking the pages, was all about wrenching yourself away from people who would die for you.

He turned a page and happened upon a picture of himself, perhaps six months old, gazing dozily from his mother's arms. His eyes were blue then—weren't all babies' eyes blue? His grandmother was fond of saying that the color you were born with belonged to the body you owned in a previous incarnation. It would fade as your new body forgot about its past. Adam's eyes were hazel now.

The house closed in around him.

Even with the television on, Adam couldn't shake off the heaviness of the air. It felt gravid with meaning, like skies primed for a snowfall. When the night came, offering another stifling layer, Adam closed the curtains and switched on all the lights. He stared at the food waiting to be cooked. Rather than inspire his appetite, the wine had dulled it. He climbed the stairs into an area of palpable cold. Presumably the landing had been protected from the afternoon's heat.

In the sanctity of his room, he peeled the stained bandages gingerly from his hands. The swellings had lessened, though now the weals had grown a pattern, a series of raised obliques, as though a length of hemp had bitten into his flesh. He dabbed ointment, bitterly relishing the bright sting. His grandmother had always said that if a cut stopped hurting, you should worry.

He left the blinds raised and opened a window to combat his room's humidity. Pulling back the sheets, the moment of shock he felt as the darkness came for him fretted his heart. He listened to its rush as the moon made a negative of the rooftop view.

He drifted, thinking of rain and the walk he would take in it as it washed the world. Outside, a hum rose into the sky as if the buildings were relaxing in the brief respite from summer. The lazy blink of Adam's eyes became more pronounced; his dreams hovered, sensing his arrival. He felt the duvet twitch beside him as a frost spread across the window rapid as breath. On the cusp of sleep, he saw the beautiful woman by the pond look at him, her head tilted to one side. The tilt did not seem natural. Next to him, someone started to breathe. It sounded strained, hoarse. He saw the glitter of her eyes, the pattern at her throat which matched that on his hands. As he felt her cold body move over him, he wondered if he might once have been married after all, many years ago.

QUARRY'S LUCK

max allan collins

Max Allan Collins is the author of some thirty novels in the suspense field. His historical thriller, True Detective, introducing Chicago P.I. Nate Heller, won the Private Eye Writers of America Shamus Award for the best novel of 1983; Heller's most recent outing, Stolen Away, won the same award for 1993.

Collins also has three contemporary suspense series—Nolan, Quarry and Mallory: a thief, a hit man and a mystery writer, in that order—and he is the author of the best-selling novel, Dick Tracy, based on the film on which he was a consultant. His short story, "Deadly Allies," *has been nominated by the Mystery Writers of America for an Edgar Award.*

His acclaimed series of historical thrillers about Eliot Ness continues with Murder by the Numbers *and, together with his research associate George Hagenauer, Collins has recently completed* Chicago Mob Wars, *a boxed set of trading cards from Kitchen Sink Press that marks the first ever accurate non-fiction account of the Untouchables.*

He scripted the internationally syndicated comic strip Dick Tracy *from 1977-1993, and, with artist Terry Beatty, he is creator of* Ms. Tree, *the DC comic book character which is now in development as a television series. He has also scripted DC's* Batman *and has written an Edgar-nominated critical study of Mickey Spillane and a history/review of TV detectives. And* still *he finds time to review movies for* Mystery Scene *and rattle off the occasional short story.*

Collins lives in Muscatine, Iowa, with his wife—writer Barbara Collins—and their son, Nathan. The Collinses have had other successful collaborations, too—notably the excellent short story "Cat Got Your Tongue" for Gorman and Greenberg's 1992 collection, Cat Crimes III.

Collins's primary fear is vertigo—"undoubtedly caused by seeing Hitchcock's film of the same name at the impressionable age of ten," he says. "I don't really have any superstitions, though I do believe in luck: I've seen too many careers benefit from it— and too many flounder for the lack of it—to feel otherwise. But, like Quarry, I believe in making my own."

Once upon a time, I killed people for a living.

Now, as I sit in my living quarters looking out at Sylvan Lake, its gently rippling gray-blue surface alive with sunlight, the scent and sight of pines soothing me, I seldom think of those years. With the exception of the occasional memoirs I've penned, I have never been very reflective. What's done is done. What's over is over.

But occasionally someone or something I see stirs a memory. In the summer, when Sylvan Lodge (of which I've been manager for several years now) is hopping with guests, I now and then see a cute blue-eyed blond college girl, and I think of Linda, my late wife. I'd retired from the contract murder profession, lounging in a cottage on a lake not unlike this one, when my past had come looking for me and Linda became a casualty.

What I'd learned from that was two things: The past is not something disconnected from the present—you can't write off old debts or old enemies (whereas, oddly, friends you can completely forget); and not to enter into long-term relationships.

Linda hadn't been a very smart human being, but she was pleasant company and she loved me, and I wouldn't want to cause somebody like her to die again. You know—an innocent.

After all, when I was taking contracts through the man I knew as the Broker, I was dispatching the guilty.

I had no idea what these people were guilty of, but it stood to reason that they were guilty of something, or somebody wouldn't have decided they should be dead.

A paid assassin isn't a killer, really. He's a weapon. Someone has already decided someone else is going to die, before the paid assassin is even in the picture, let alone on the scene. A paid assassin is no more a killer than a nine millimeter automatic or a bludgeon. Somebody has to pick up a weapon, to use it.

Anyway, that was my rationalization back in the '70s, when I was a human weapon for hire. I never took pleasure from the job—just money. And when the time came, I got out of it.

So, a few years ago, after Linda's death, and after I killed the fuckers responsible, I did not allow myself to get pulled back into that profession. I was too old, too tired, my reflexes were not all that good. A friend I ran into, by chance, needed my only other expertise—I had operated a small resort in Wisconsin with Linda—and I now manage Sylvan Lodge.

Something I saw recently—something quite outrageous really, even considering that I have in my time witnessed human behavior of the vilest sort—stirred a distant memory.

The indoor swimming pool with hot tub is a short jog across the road from my two-room apartment in the central lodge building (don't feel sorry for me: It's a bedroom and spacious living room with kitchenette, plus two baths, with a deck looking out on my storybook view of the lake). We close the pool room at 10:00 P.M., and sometimes I take the keys over and open the place up for a solitary midnight swim.

I was doing that—actually, I'd finished my swim and was letting the hot tub's jet streams have at my chronically sore lower back—when somebody came knocking at the glass doors.

It was a male figure—portly—and a female figure—slender, shapely—both wrapped in towels. That was all I could see of them through the glass; the lights were off outside.

Sighing, I climbed out of the hot tub, wrapped a towel around myself, and unlocked the glass door and slid it open just enough to deal with these two.

"We want a swim!" the man said. He was probably fifty-five, with a booze-mottled face and a brown toupee that squatted on his round head like a slumbering gopher.

Next to him, the blonde of twenty-something, with huge blue eyes and huge big boobs (her towel, thankfully, was tied around her waist), stood almost behind the man. She looked meek. Even embarrassed.

"Mr. Davis," I said, cordial enough, "it's after hours."

"Fuck that! *You're* in here, aren't you?"

"I'm the manager. I sneak a little time in for myself, after closing, after the guests have had their fun."

He put his hand on my bare chest. "Well, *we're* guests, and we want to have some fun, too!"

His breath was ninety proof.

I removed his hand, bending the fingers back a little in the process.

He winced and started to say something, but I said, "I'm sorry. It's the lodge policy. My apologies to you and your wife."

Bloodshot eyes widened in the face, and he began to say something but stopped short. He tucked his tail between his legs (and his towel) and took the girl by the arm, roughly, saying, "Come on, baby. We don't need this horseshit."

The blonde looked back at me and gave me a crinkly little chagrined grin, and I smiled back at her, locked the glass door, and climbed back in the hot tub to cool off.

"Asshole," I said. It echoed in the high-ceilinged steamy room. "Fucking asshole!" I said louder, just because I could, and the echo was enjoyable.

He hadn't tucked towel 'tween his legs because I'd bent his fingers back: He'd done it because I mentioned his wife, who we both knew the little blond bimbo wasn't.

That was because (and here's the outrageous part) he'd been here last month—to this very same resort— with another very attractive blonde, but one about forty, maybe forty-five, who was indeed, and in fact, his lawful wedded wife.

We had guys who came to Sylvan Lodge with their families; we had guys who came with just their wives; and we had guys who came with what used to be called

179

in olden times their mistresses. But we seldom had a son of a bitch so fucking bold as to bring his wife one week, and his mistress the next, to the same goddamn motel, which is what Sylvan Lodge, after all, let's face it, is a glorified version of.

As I enjoyed the jet stream on my low back, I smiled and then frowned, as the memory stirred.... Christ, I'd forgotten about that! You'd think that Sylvan Lodge itself would've jogged my memory. But it hadn't.

Even though the memory in question was of one of my earliest jobs, which took place at a resort not terribly unlike this one....

We met off Interstate 80, at a truck stop outside of the Quad Cities. It was late—almost midnight—a hot, muggy June night; my black T-shirt was sticking to me. My blue jeans, too.

The Broker had taken a booth at the back; the restaurant wasn't particularly busy, except for an area designated for truckers. But it had the war-zone look of a rush hour just past; it was a blindingly white but not terribly clean-looking place, and the jukebox— wailing "I Shot the Sheriff" at the moment— combatted the clatter of dishes being abused.

Sitting with the Broker was an oval-faced, bright-eyed kid of about twenty-three (which at the time was about my age, too) who wore a Doobie Brothers T-shirt and had shoulder-length brown hair. Mine was cut short—not soldier-cut, but businessman short.

"Quarry," the Broker said, in his melodious baritone; he gestured with an open hand. "How good to see you. Sit down." His smile was faint under the wispy mustache, but there was a fatherly air to his manner.

He was trying to look casual in a yellow Banlon shirt and golf slacks; he had white, styled hair and a long face that managed to look both fleshy and largely unlined. He was a solid-looking man, fairly tall—he looked like a captain of industry, which he was in a way. I took him for fifty, but that was just a guess.

"This is Adam," the Broker said.

"How are you doin', man?" Adam said, and grinned, and half rose; he seemed a little nervous, and in the process—before I'd even had a chance to decide whether to take the hand he offered or not—overturned a salt shaker, which sent him into a minor tizzy.

"Damn!" Adam said, forgetting about the handshake. "I hate fuckin' bad luck!" He tossed some salt over either shoulder, then grinned at me and said, "I'm afraid I'm one superstitious motherfucker."

"Well, you know what Stevie Wonder says," I said.

He squinted. "No, what?"

Sucker.

"Nothing," I said, sliding in.

A twentyish waitress with a nice shape, a hair net and two pounds of acne took my order, which was for

181

a Coke; the Broker already had coffee and the kid a bottle of Mountain Dew and a glass.

When she went away, I said, "Well, Broker. Got some work for me? I drove hundreds of miles in a fucking gas shortage, so you sure as shit better have."

Adam seemed a little stunned to hear the Broker spoken to so disrespectfully, but the Broker was used to my attitude and merely smiled and patted the air with a benedictory palm.

"I wouldn't waste your time otherwise, Quarry. This will pay handsomely. Ten thousand for the two of you."

Five grand was good money; three was pretty standard. Money was worth more then. You could buy a Snickers bar for ten cents. Or was it fifteen? I forget.

But I was still a little irritated.

"The two of us?" I said. "Adam, here, isn't my better half on this one, is he?"

"Yes he is," the Broker said. He had his hands folded now, prayerfully. His baritone was calming. Or was meant to be.

Adam was frowning, playing nervously with a silver skull ring on the little finger of his left hand. "I don't like your fuckin' attitude, man...."

The way he tried to work menace into his voice would have been amusing if I'd given a shit.

"I don't like your fuckin' hippie hair," I said.

"What?" He leaned forward, furious, and knocked his water glass over; it spun on its side and fell off my

182

edge of the booth and we heard it shatter. A few eyes looked our way.

Adam's tiny bright eyes were wide. "Fuck," he said.

"Seven years bad luck, dipshit," I said.

"That's just mirrors!"

"I think it's any kind of glass. Isn't that right, Broker?"

The Broker was frowning a little. "Quarry." He sounded so disappointed in me.

"Hair like that attracts attention," I said. "You go in for a hit, you got to be the invisible man."

"These days everybody wears their hair like this," the kid said defensively.

"In Greenwich Village, maybe. But in America, if you want to disappear, you look like a businessman or a college student."

That made him laugh. "You ever see a college student lately, asshole?"

"I mean the kind who belongs to a fraternity. You want to go around killing people, you need to look clean-cut."

Adam's mouth had dropped open; he had crooked lower teeth. He pointed at me with a thumb and turned to look at the Broker, indignant. "Is this guy for real?"

"Yes indeed," the Broker said. "He's also the best active agent I have."

By "active," the Broker meant (in his own personal jargon) that I was the half of a hit team that took out the target; the "passive" half was the lookout person, the back-up.

"And he's right," the Broker said, "about your hair."

"Far as that's concerned," I said, "we look pretty goddamn conspicuous right here—me looking collegiate, you looking like the prez of a country club, and junior here like a road show Mick Jagger."

Adam looked half bewildered, half outraged.

"You may have a point," the Broker allowed me.

"On the other hand," I said, "people probably think we're fags waiting for a fourth."

"You're unbelievable," Adam said, shaking his greasy Beatle mop. "I don't want to work with this son of a bitch."

"Stay calm," the Broker said. "I'm not proposing a partnership, not unless this should happen to work out beyond all of our wildest expectations."

"I tend to agree with Adam, here," I said. "We're not made for each other."

"The question is," the Broker said, "are you made for ten thousand dollars?"

Adam and I thought about that.

"I have a job that needs to go down, very soon," he said, "and very quickly. You're the only two men available right now. And I know neither of you wants to disappoint me."

Half of ten grand did sound good to me. I had a lake-front lot in Wisconsin where I could put up this nifty little A-frame prefab, if I could put a few more thousand together....

"I'm in," I said, "if he cuts his hair."

The Broker looked at Adam, who scowled and nodded.

"You're both going to like this," the Broker said, sitting forward, withdrawing a travel brochure from his back pocket.

"A resort?" I asked.

"Near Chicago. A wooded area. There's a man-made lake, two indoor swimming pools and one outdoor, an 'old town' gift shop area, several restaurants, bowling alley, tennis courts, horse-back riding...."

"If they have archery," I said, "maybe we could arrange a little accident."

That made the Broker chuckle. "You're not far off the mark. We need either an accident, or a robbery. It's an insurance situation."

The Broker would tell us no more than that: Part of his function was to shield the client from us, and us from the client, for that matter. He was sort of a combination agent and buffer; he could tell us only this much: The target was going down so that someone could collect insurance. The double indemnity kind that comes from accidental death, and of course getting killed by thieves counts in that regard.

"This is him," the Broker said, carefully showing us

185

a photograph of a thin, handsome, tanned man of possibly sixty with black hair that was probably dyed; he wore dark sunglasses and tennis togs and had an arm around a dark-haired woman of about forty, a tanned slim busty woman also in dark glasses and tennis togs.

"Who's the babe?" Adam said.

"The wife," the Broker said.

The client.

"The client?" Adam asked.

"I didn't say that," Broker said edgily, "and you mustn't ask stupid questions. Your target is this man—Baxter Bennedict."

"I hope his wife isn't named Bunny," I said.

The Broker chuckled again, but Adam didn't see the joke.

"Close. Her name is Bernice, actually."

I groaned. "One more 'B' and I'll kill 'em *both*—for free."

The Broker took out a silver cigarette case. "Actually, that's going to be one of the...delicate aspects of this job."

"How so?" I asked.

He offered me a cigarette from the case and I waved it off; he offered one to Adam, and he took it.

The Broker said, "They'll be on vacation. Together, at the Wistful Wagon Lodge. She's not to be harmed. You must wait and watch until you can get him alone."

"And then make it look like an accident," I said.

"Or a robbery. Correct." The Broker struck a match,

lighted his cigarette. He tried to light Adam's, but Adam gestured no, frantically.

"Two on a match," he said. Then got a lighter out and lit himself up.

"Two on a match?" I asked.

"Haven't you ever heard that?" the kid asked, almost wild-eyed. "Two on a match. It's unlucky!"

"*Three* on a match is unlucky," I said.

Adam squinted at me. "Are you superstitious, too?"

I looked hard at the Broker, who merely shrugged.

"I gotta pee," the kid said suddenly, and had the Broker let him slide out. Standing, he wasn't very big: probably five seven. Skinny. His jeans were tattered.

When we were alone, I said, "What are you doing, hooking me up with that dumb-ass jerk?"

"Give him a chance. He was in Vietnam. Like you. He's not completely inexperienced."

"Most of the guys I knew in Vietnam were stoned twenty-four hours a day. That's not what I'm looking for in a partner."

"He's just a little green. You'll season him."

"I'll ice him if he fucks up. Understood?"

The Broker shrugged. "Understood."

When Adam came back, the Broker let him in and said, "The hardest part is, you have a window of only four days."

"That's bad," I said, frowning. "I like to maintain a surveillance, get a pattern down...."

Broker shrugged again. "It's a different situation.

They're on vacation. They won't have much of a pattern."

"Great."

Now the Broker frowned. "Why in hell do you think it pays so well? Think of it as hazardous duty pay."

Adam sneered and said, "What's the matter, Quarry? Didn't you never take no fuckin' risks?"

"I think I'm about to," I said.

"It'll go well," the Broker said.

"Knock on wood," the kid said, and rapped on the table.

"That's Formica," I said.

The Wistful Wagon Lodge sprawled out over numerous wooded acres, just off the outskirts of Wistful Vista, Illinois. According to the Broker's brochure, back in the late '40s, the hamlet had taken the name of Fibber McGee and Molly's fictional hometown, for purposes of attracting tourists; apparently one of the secondary stars of the radio show had been born nearby. This marketing ploy had been just in time for television making radio passé, and the little farm community's only remaining sign of having at all successfully tapped into the tourist trade was the Wistful Wagon Lodge itself.

A cobblestone drive wound through the scattering of log cabins, and several larger buildings—including the main lodge where the check-in and restaurants were—were similarly rustic structures, but of gray weathered wood. Trees clustered everywhere, turning warm sunlight into cool pools of shade; wood-burned signs showed the way to this building or that path, and decorative wagon wheels, often with flower beds in and around them, were scattered about as if some long-ago pioneer mishap had been beautified by nature and time. Of course that wasn't the case: This was the hokey hand of man.

We arrived separately, Adam and I, each having reserved rooms in advance, each paying cash up front upon registration; no credit cards. We each had log-cabin cottages, not terribly close to one another.

As the back-up and surveillance man, Adam went in early. The target and his wife were taking a long weekend—arriving Thursday, leaving Monday. I didn't arrive until Saturday morning.

I went to Adam's cabin and knocked, but got no answer. Which just meant he was trailing Mr. and Mrs. Target around the grounds. After I dropped my stuff off at my own cabin, I wandered, trying to get the general layout of the place, checking out the lodge itself, where about half of the rooms were, as well as two restaurants. Everything had a pine smell, which was partially the many trees, and partially Pinesol. Wistful Wagon was Hollywood rustic—there was a dated quality about it, from the cowboy/cowgirl attire of the waiters and waitresses in the Wistful Chuckwagon Café to the wood-and-leather furnishings to the barnwood-framed Remington prints.

I got myself some lunch and traded smiles with a giggly tableful of college girls who were on a weekend scouting expedition of their own. *Good*, I thought. *If I can connect with one of them tonight, that'll provide nice cover.*

As I was finishing up, my cowgirl waitress, a curly-haired blonde pushing thirty who was pretty cute herself, said, "Looks like you might get lucky tonight."

She was refilling my coffee cup.

"With them or with you?" I asked.

She had big washed-out blue eyes and heavy eye make-up, more '60s than '70s. She was wearing a 1950s style cowboy hat cinched under her chin. "I'm not supposed to fraternize with the guests."

"How did you know I was a fraternity man?"

She laughed a little; her chin crinkled. Her face was kind of round and she was a little pudgy, nicely so in the bosom.

"Wild stab," she said. "Anyway, there's an open dance in the ballroom. Off the Wagontrain Dining Room? Country swing band. You'll like it."

"You inviting me?"

"No," she said; she narrowed her eyes and cocked her head, her expression one of mild scolding. "Those little girls'll be there, and plenty of others. You won't have any trouble finding what you want."

"I bet I will."

"Why's that?"

"I was hoping for a girl wearing cowboy boots like yours."

"Oh, there'll be girls in cowboys boots there tonight."

"I meant, just cowboy boots."

She laughed at that, shook her head; under her Dale Evans hat, her blond curls bounced off her shoulders.

She went away and let me finish my coffee, and I smiled at the college girls some more, but when I paid for my check, at the register, it was my plump little cowgirl again.

"I work late tonight," she said.

"How late?"

"I get off at midnight," she said.

"That's only the first time," I said.

"First time what?"

"That you'll get off tonight."

She liked that. Times were different, then. The only way you could die from fucking was if a husband or boyfriend caught you at it. She told me where to meet her, later.

I strolled back up a winding path to my cabin. A few groups of college girls and college guys, not paired off together yet, were buzzing around; some couples in their twenties up into their sixties were walking, often hand-in-hand, around the sun-dappled, lushly shaded grounds. The sound of a gentle breeze in the trees made a faint shimmering music. Getting laid here was no trick.

I got my swim trunks on and grabbed a towel and headed for the nearest pool, which was the outdoor one. That's where I found Adam.

He did look like a college frat rat, with his shorter hair; skinny pale body reddening, he was sitting in a deck chair, sipping a Coke, in sunglasses and racing trunks, chatting with a couple of bikinied college cuties, also in sunglasses.

"Bill?" I said.

"Jim?" he said, taking off his sunglasses to get a better look at me. He grinned, extended his hand. I took it, shook it, as he stood. "I haven't seen you since spring break!"

We'd agreed to be old high-school buddies from Peoria who had gone to separate colleges; I was attending the University of Iowa, he was at Michigan. We avoided using Illinois schools because Illinois kids were who we'd most likely run into here.

Adam introduced me to the girls—I don't remember their names, but one was a busty brunette, Veronica, the other a flat-chested blonde, Betty. The sound of splashing and running screaming kids—though this was a couples hideaway, there was a share of families here, as well—kept the conversation to a blessed minimum. The girls were nursing majors. We were engineering majors. We all liked Creedence Clearwater. We all hoped Nixon would get the book thrown at him. We were all going to the dance tonight.

Across the way, Baxter Bennedict was sitting in a

deck chair under an umbrella reading *Jaws*. Every page or so, he'd sip his martini; every ten pages or so, he'd wave a waitress in cowgirl vest and white plastic hot pants over for another one. His wife was swimming, her dark arms cutting the water like knives. It seemed methodical, an exercise work-out in the midst of a pool filled with water babies of various ages.

When she pulled herself out of the water, her suit a stark, startling white against her almost burned black skin, she revealed a slender, rather tall figure; tight ass, high, full breasts. Her rather lined leathery face was the only tip-off to her age, and that had the blessing of a model's beauty to get it by.

She pulled off a white swim cap and unfurled a mane of dark, blond-tipped hair. Toweling herself off, she bent to kiss her husband on the cheek, but he only scowled at her. She stretched out on her colorful beach towel beside him, to further blacken herself.

"Oooo," said Veronica. "What's that ring?"

"That's my lucky ring," Adam said.

That fucking skull ring of his! Had he been dumb enough to wear that? Yes.

"Bought that at a Grateful Dead concert, didn't you, Bill?" I asked.

"Uh, yeah," he said.

"Ick," said Betty. "I don't like the Dead. Their hair is greasy. They're so...druggie."

"Drugs aren't so bad," Veronica said boldly, thrusting out her admirably thrustworthy bosom.

"Bill and I had our wild days back in high school," I said. "You shoulda seen our hair—down to our asses, right, Bill?"

"Right."

"But we don't do that anymore," I said. "Kinda put that behind us."

"Well I for one don't approve of drugs," Betty said.

"Don't blame you," I said.

"Except for grass, of course," she said.

"Of course."

"And coke. Scientific studies prove coke isn't bad for you."

"Well, you're in nursing," I said. "You'd know."

We made informal dates with the girls for the dance, and I wandered off with "Bill" to his cabin.

"The skull ring was a nice touch," I said.

He frowned at me. "Fuck you—it's my lucky ring!"

A black gardener on a rider mower rumbled by us.

"Now we're really in trouble," I said.

He looked genuinely concerned. "What do you mean?"

"A black cat crossed our path."

In Adam's cabin, I sat on the brown, fake-leather sofa while he sat on the nubby yellow bedspread and spread his hands.

"They actually do have a sorta pattern," he said, "vacation or not."

Adam had arrived on Wednesday; the Bennedicts

had arrived Thursday around 2:00 P.M., which was check-in time.

"They drink and swim all afternoon," Adam said, "and they go dining and dancing—and drinking—in the evening."

"What about mornings?"

"Tennis. He doesn't start drinking till lunch."

"Doesn't she drink?"

"Not as much. He's an asshole. We're doing the world a favor, here."

"How do you mean?"

He shrugged; he looked very different in his short hair. "He's kind of abusive. He don't yell at her, but just looking at them, you can see him glaring at her all the time, real ugly. Saying things that hurt her."

"She doesn't stand up to him?"

He shook his head, no. "They're very one-sided arguments. He either sits there and ignores her or he's giving her foul looks and it looks like he's chewing her out or something."

"Sounds like a sweet guy."

"After the drinking and dining and dancing, they head to the bar. Both nights so far, she's gone off to bed around eleven and he's stayed and shut the joint down."

"Good. That means he's alone when he walks back to their cabin."

Adam nodded. "But this place is crawlin' with people."

"Not at two in the morning. Most of these people are sleeping or fucking by then."

"Maybe so. He's got a fancy watch, some heavy gold jewelry."

"Well that's very good. Now we got ourselves a motive."

"But *she's* the one with jewels." He whistled. "You should see the rocks hanging off that dame."

"Well, we aren't interested in those."

"What about the stuff you steal off him? Just toss it somewhere?"

"Hell no! The Broker'll have it fenced for us. A little extra dough for our trouble."

He grinned. "Great. This is easy money. Vacation with pay."

"Don't ever think that…don't ever let your guard down."

"I know that," he said defensively.

"It's unlucky to think that way," I said, and knocked on wood. Real wood.

We met up with Betty and Veronica at the dance; I took Betty because Adam was into knockers and Veronica had them. Betty was pleasant company, but I wasn't listening to her babble. I was keeping an eye on the Bennedicts, who were seated at a corner table under a buffalo head.

He really was an asshole. You could tell, by the way he sneered at her and spit sentences out at her, that he'd spent a lifetime—or at least a marriage—making her miserable. His hatred for her was something you could see as well as sense, like steam over asphalt. She was taking it placidly. Cool as Cher while Sonny prattled on.

But I had a hunch she usually took it more personally. Right now she could be placid: She knew the son of a bitch was going to die this weekend.

"Did you ever do Lauderdale?" Betty was saying. "I got so drunk there...."

The band was playing "Crazy," and a decent girl singer was doing a respectable Patsy Cline. What a great song.

I said, "I won a chug-a-lug contest at Boonie's in '72."

Betty was impressed. "Were you even in college then?"

"No. I had a hell of a fake ID, though."

"Bitchen!"

Around eleven, the band took a break and we walked the girls to their cabins, hand in hand, like high school sweethearts. Gas lanterns on poles scorched the night orangely; a half-moon threw some silvery light on us, too. Adam disappeared around the side of the cabin with Veronica and I stood and watched Betty beam at me and rock girlishly on her heels. She smelled of perfume and beer, which mingled with the scent of pines; it was more pleasant than it sounds.

She was making with the dimples. "You're so nice."

"Well thanks."

"And I'm a good judge of character."

"I bet you are."

Then she put her arms around me and pressed her slim frame to me and put her tongue halfway down my throat.

She pulled herself away and smiled coquettishly and said, "That's all you get tonight. See you tomorrow."

As if on cue, Veronica appeared with her lipstick mussed up and her sweater askew.

"Good night, boys," Veronica said, and they slipped inside, giggling like the school girls they were.

"Fuck," Adam said, scowling. "All I got was a little bare tit."

"Not so little."

"I thought I was gonna get laid."

I shrugged. "Instead you got screwed."

We walked. We passed a cabin that was getting some remodeling and repairs; I'd noticed it earlier. A ladder was leaned up against the side, for some re-roofing. Adam made a wide circle around the ladder. I walked under it just to watch him squirm.

When I fell back in step with him, he said, "You gonna do the hit tonight?"

"No."

"Bar closes at midnight on Sundays. Gonna do it then?"

"Yes."

He sighed. "Good."

We walked, and it was the place where one path went toward my cabin, and another toward his.

"Well," he said, "maybe I'll get lucky tomorrow night."

"No pick-ups the night of the hit. I need back-up more than either of us needs an alibi, or an easy fuck, either."

"Oh. Of course. You're right. Sorry. 'Night.'"

"Night, Bill."

Then I went back and picked up the waitress cowgirl and took her to my cabin; she had some dope in her purse, and I smoked a little with her, just to be nice, and apologized for not having a rubber, and she said, Don't sweat it, pardner, I'm on the pill, and she rode me in her cowboy boots until my dick said yahoo.

The next morning I had breakfast in the café with Adam, and he seemed preoccupied as I ate my scrambled eggs and bacon, and he poked at his French toast.

"Bill," I said. "What's wrong?"

"I'm worried."

"What about?"

We were seated in a rough-wood booth and had plenty of privacy; we kept our voices down. Our conversation, after all, wasn't really proper breakfast conversation.

"I don't think you should hit him like that."

"Like what?"

He frowned. "On his way back to his cabin after the bar closes."

"Oh? Why?"

"He might not be drunk enough. Bar closes early Sunday night, remember?"

"Jesus," I said. "The fucker starts drinking at noon. What more do you want?"

"But there could be people around."

"At midnight?"

"It's a resort. People get romantic at resorts. Moonlight strolls..."

"You got a better idea?"

He nodded. "Do it in his room. Take the wife's jewels and it's a robbery got out of hand. In and out. No fuss, no muss."

"Are you high? What about the wife?"

"She won't be there."

He started gesturing, earnestly. "She gets worried about him, see. It's midnight, and she goes looking for him. While she's gone, he gets back, flops on the bed, you come in, bing bang boom."

I just looked at him. "Are you psychic now? How do we know she'll do that?"

He swallowed; took a nibble at a forkful of syrup-dripping French toast. Smiled kind of nervously.

"She told me so," he said.

❧

We were walking now. The sun was filtering through the trees, and birds were chirping, and the sounds of children laughing wafted through the air.

"Are you fucking nuts? Making contact with the client?"

"Quarry—she contacted me! I swear!"

"Then *she's* fucking nuts. Jesus!" I sat on a bench by a flower bed. "It's off. I'm calling the Broker. It's over."

"Listen to me! Listen. She was waiting for me at my cabin last night. After we struck out with the college girls? She was fuckin' waitin' for me! She told me she knew who I was."

"How did she know that?"

"She said she saw me watching them. She figured it out. She guessed."

"And, of course, you confirmed her suspicions."

He swallowed. "Yeah."

"You dumb-ass dickhead. Who said it first?"

"Who said what first?"

"Who mentioned 'killing.' Who mentioned 'murder.'"

His cheek twitched. "Well...me, I guess. She kept saying she knew why I was here. And then she said, I'm why you're here. I hired you."

"And you copped to it. God. I'm on the next bus."

"Quarry! Listen...it's better this way. This is much better."

"What did she do, fuck you?"

He blanched; looked at his feet.

"Oh God," I said. "You did get lucky last night. Fuck. You fucked the client. Did you tell her there were two of us?"

"No."

"She's seen us together."

"I told her you're just a guy I latched on to here to look less conspicuous."

"Did she buy it?"

"Why shouldn't she? I say we scrap Plan A and move to Plan B. It's better."

"Plan B being...?"

"Quarry, she's going to leave the door unlocked. She'll wait for him to get back from the bar, and when he's asleep, she'll unlock the door, go out and pretend to be looking for him, and come back and find him dead, and her jewels gone. Help-police-I-been-robbed-my-husband's-been-shot. You know."

"She's being pretty fucking helpful, you ask me."

His face clenched like a fist. "The bastard has beat her for years. And he's got a girlfriend a third his age. He's been threatening to divorce her, and since they signed a pre-marital agreement, she gets jackshit, if they divorce. The bastard."

"Quite a sob story."

"I told you: We're doing the world a favor. And now she's doing us one. Why shoot him right out in the open, when we can walk in his room and do it? You got to stick this out, Quarry. Shit, man, it's five grand a piece, and change!"

I thought about it.

"Quarry?"

I'd been thinking a long time.

"Okay," I said. "Give her the high sign. We'll do it her way."

The Bar W Bar was a cozy rustic room decorated with framed photos of movie cowboys from Ken Maynard to John Wayne, from Audie Murphy to the Man with No Name. On a brown mock-leather stool up at the bar, Baxter Bennedict sat, a thin handsome drunk in a pale blue polyester sport coat and pale yellow Banlon sport shirt, gulping martinis and telling anyone who'd listen his sad story.

I didn't sit near enough to be part of the conversation, but I could hear him.

"Milking me fucking dry," he was saying. "You'd think with sixteen goddamn locations, I'd be sitting pretty. I was the first guy in the Chicago area to offer a paint job under thirty dollars—$29.95! That's a good fucking deal—isn't it?"

The bartender—a young fellow in a buckskin vest, polishing a glass—nodded sympathetically.

"Now this competition. Killing me. What the fuck kind of paint job can you get for $19.99? Will you answer me that one? And now that bitch has the nerve…"

Now he was muttering. The bartender began to move away, but Baxter started in again.

"She wants me to sell! My life's work. Started from nothing. And she wants me to sell! Pitiful fucking money they offered. Pitiful…"

"Last call, Mr. Bennedict," the bartender said. Then he repeated it, louder, without the "Mr. Bennedict." The place was only moderately busy. A few couples. A solitary drinker or two. The Wistful Wagon Lodge had emptied out, largely, this afternoon—even Betty and Veronica were gone. Sunday. People had to go to work tomorrow. Except, of course, for those who owned their own businesses, like Baxter here.

Or had unusual professions, like mine.

I waited until the slender figure had stumbled halfway home before I approached him. No one was around. The nearest cabin was dark.

"Mr. Bennedict," I said.

"Yeah?" He turned, trying to focus his bleary eyes.

"I couldn't help but hear what you said. I think I have a solution for your problems."

"Yeah?" He grinned. "And what the hell would that be?"

He walked, on the unsteadiest of legs, up to me.

I showed him the nine millimeter with its bulky sound suppresser. It probably looked like a ray gun to him.

"Fuck! What is this, a fucking hold-up?"

"Yes. Keep your voice down or it'll turn into a fucking homicide. Got me?"

That turned him sober. "Got you. What do you want?"

"What do you think? Your watch and your rings."

He smirked disgustedly and removed them; handed them over.

"Now your sport coat."

"My what?"

"Your sport coat. I just can't get enough polyester."

He snorted a laugh. "You're out of your gourd, pal."

He slipped off the sport coat and handed it out toward me with two fingers; he was weaving a little, smirking drunkenly.

I took the coat with my left hand, and the silenced nine millimeter went *thup thup thup*; three small, brilliant blossoms of red appeared on his light yellow Banlon. He was dead before he had time to think about it.

I dragged his body behind a clump of trees and left him there, his worries behind him.

I watched from behind a tree as Bernice Bennedict slipped out of their cabin; she was wearing a dark halter top and dark slacks that almost blended with her burnt-black skin, making a wraith of her. She had a big white handbag on a shoulder strap. She was so dark the white bag seemed to float in space as she headed toward the lodge.

Only she stopped and found her own tree to duck behind.

I smiled to myself.

Then, wearing the pale blue polyester sport coat, I entered their cabin, through the door she'd left open. The room was completely dark, but for some minor filtering in of light through curtained windows. Quickly, I arranged some pillows under sheets and covers, to create the impression of a person in the bed.

And I called Adam's cabin.

"Hey, Bill," I said. "It's Jim."

His voice was breathless. "Is it done?"

"No. I got cornered coming out of the bar by that waitress I was out with last night. She latched on to me—she's in my john."

"What, are you in your room?"

"Yeah. I saw Bennedict leave the bar at midnight, and his wife passed us, heading for the lodge, just minutes ago. You've got a clear shot at him."

"What? Me? I'm the fucking lookout!"

"Tonight's the night, and we go to Plan C."

"I didn't know there *was* a Plan C."

"Listen, asshole—it was you who wanted to switch plans. You've got a piece, don't you?"

"Of course…"

"Well you're elected. Go!"

And I hung up.

I stood in the doorway of the bathroom, which faced the bed. I sure as hell didn't turn any lights on, although my left hand hovered by the switch. The nine millimeter with the silencer was heavy in my right hand. But I didn't mind.

Adam came in quickly and didn't do too bad a job of it: four silenced slugs. He should have checked the body—it never occurred to him he'd just slaughtered a bunch of pillows—but if somebody had been in that bed, they'd have been dead.

He went to the dresser where he knew the jewels would be, and was picking up the jewelry box when the door opened and she came in, the little revolver already in her hand.

Before she could fire, I turned on the bathroom light and said, "If I don't hear the gun hit the floor immediately, you're fucking dead."

She was just a black shape, except for the white handbag; but I saw the flash of silver as the gun bounced to the carpeted floor.

"What...?" Adam was saying. It was too dark to see any expression, but he was obviously as confused as he was spooked.

"Shut the door, lady," I said, "and turn on the lights."

She did.

She really was a beautiful woman, or had been, dark eyes and scarlet-painted mouth in that finely carved model's face, but it was just a leathery mask to me.

"What..." Adam said. He looked shocked as hell, which made sense; the gun was in his waistband, the jewelry box in his hands.

"You didn't know there were two of us, did you, Mrs. Bennedict?"

She was sneering faintly; she shook her head, no.

"You see, kid," I told Adam, "she wanted her husband hit, but she wanted the hit man dead, too. Cleaner. Tidier. Right?"

"Fuck you," she said.

"I'm not much for sloppy seconds, thanks. Bet you got a nice legal license for that little purse pea-shooter of yours, don't you? Perfect protection for when you stumble in on an intruder who's just killed your loving husband. Who *is* dead, by the way. Somebody'll run across him in the morning, probably."

"You bitch!" Adam said. He raised his own gun, which was a .380 Browning with a home-made suppresser.

"Don't you know it's bad luck to kill a woman?" I said.

She was frozen, one eye twitching.

Adam was trembling. He swallowed; nodded. "Okay," he said, lowering the gun. "Okay."

"Go," I told him.

She stepped aside as he slipped out the door, shutting it behind him.

"Thank you," she said, and I shot her twice in the chest.

I slipped the bulky silenced automatic in my waistband; grabbed the jewel box off the dresser.

"I make my own luck," I told her, but she didn't hear me, as I stepped over her.

I never worked with Adam again. I think he was disturbed, when he read the papers and realized I'd iced the woman after all. Maybe he got out of the business. Or maybe he wound up dead in a ditch, his lucky skull ring still on his little finger. The Broker never said, and I was never interested enough to ask.

Now, years later, lounging in the hot tub at Sylvan Lodge, I look back on my actions and wonder how I could ever have been so young, and so rash.

Killing the woman was understandable. She'd double-crossed us; she would've killed us both without batting a false lash.

But sleeping with that cowgirl waitress, on the job. Smoking dope. Not using a rubber.

I was really pushing my luck that time.

THE
CURSE

E D   G o r m a n

Whether he's working in crime, suspense, mystery, horror or western genres, Ed Gorman is one of the finest short story writers in America, a fact I've shared with various readers of various magazines in a string of reviews and articles over the past couple of years. Unfortunately, there's precious little of his work available in the UK, although last year's Shadow Games appeared here first, in paperback from Blake, and The Autumn Dead (Allison & Busby, 1987), which introduced private eye Jack Dwyer, can still be found in selective bargain bins. And believe me, bargains don't come any sweeter.

His twenty-two story collection,

Prisoners, *the debut release from Richard Chizmar's excellent CD imprint, can be found in specialty crime bookstores, and Hollywood Pictures has recently optioned his novella,* "Moonchasers." *Of* The Marilyn Tapes, *his new novel scheduled for release in late 1994, Joe Gores says,* "A dumdum between the eyes…(it will) blow the back of your skull off."

Adding to the notes he supplied with his story, "Long Time till Morning Comes," *for* Narrow Houses, *Gorman considers himself every kind of hypochondriac there is.*

"If somebody says, 'You look a little pale, Ed,' within twenty minutes I'm driving myself to the hospital. This was particularly bad when I was growing up. Older kids would tell me all sorts of rotten things that were going to happen to me and I always believed them. Come to think of it, the first time I made out my will I was six years old."

With "The Curse," *Gorman is in a similarly playful mood. At least for a while.*

It's not a very manly thing to admit, being dumped four different times in that three-year period. Four different women, serious women, good women, decent women, had taken turns casting me off, and always for the same reason: I was just too god damned possessive. And I was well aware of it. That was the hell of it. The harder I tried to control my jealousy, the worse it became. Got so bad, in fact, that Susan—icy blond Susan who always became giggly sentimental Susan after a few sips of wine and a few tokes of good Mexican grass—not only kicked me out of her apartment (I was a failing lawyer just as I was a failing lover) but got a restraining order barring me from a) following her, b) phoning her, and c) (and most humiliating of all) even writing her.

Susan was the fourth, and after her it all sort of went to shit, several long months of binge drinking and living off the kindness of strangers and getting dropped as a junior partner from my country club law firm…and ending up as a junior, junior partner for a firm that chased ambulances and advertised on TV as "The Poor Man's Friend." We did everything except show them how to trick up a whiplash case, and we probably would have done that, but we could never be sure that our client wasn't actually a spy from the state bar examiner's office…a spy eager to lift our right to practice law.

Also during this time, I broke out in a kind of retro-acne (who got acne at age thirty-eight?), failed on several highly embarrassing occasions to mount an erection at the proper moment, and began suffering honest-to-God alcoholic blackouts.

Then one day, I woke up in a strange white room glowing with almost blinding light. At first, I thought I'd gone to meet our cosmic maker—then I settled for the assumption that I was in a hospital room of some kind. And then I saw the alligator. A long scaly slimy one working its slithery insidious way across the floor to my bed. I screamed until I was hoarse and until I could no longer find the strength to twist and writhe against the leather straps that held me down.

A nurse came bearing a hypodermic needle. I shouted at her to be careful of the alligator. But she only smiled and said, "Delirium tremens, Mr. Calloway. Delirium tremens."

And then I was in a different room, one no less white, one no less glowing, but now the straps were gone and I could sit up at will, and instead of the nurse, Amy was there, beautiful, gentle Amy, the second woman who'd dumped me over these past few years, and she was saying that she wanted us to try again, that now that I wasn't drinking....

I held her in my arms, fragile as spring flowers, and kissed her deeply and truly and wonderfully, recalling now how sweet her breath always was and how tender her small sweet breasts felt against my chest....

A few weeks later, Amy got me a job at the prestigious firm where she worked....

"I just don't want to do it any more, David."

"God, Amy, we've only been going out for four months."

"Yes, and what a four months. Following me, opening my mail, picking up the bedroom phone and listening whenever I get a call—and Michael thinks you're the one who's been sending him those threatening notes."

"Good old Michael."

"I don't want to hear your sarcasm about him any more. I know he's sort of a—well, he can be a prick, I mean, I have to admit that—but at least he doesn't try to keep me a prisoner."

"And, unlike me, he makes a lot of money."

"David, you don't—"

"And also unlike me, he drives a nice new sports car and flies to Aspen to ski every other weekend and—"

"And unlike you, he doesn't believe that old Jamaican men can actually put hexes on each other."

"And that means what, exactly? That I'm crazy, I suppose?"

"It means you should start seeing your old shrink again. I mean, David, you really *believe* that if you aren't nice to that filthy old man—"

She shook her wonderful blond head.

"David, please, for my sake if not yours, get some help, all right?"

By now, the health food restaurant was starting to empty from the noon traffic, giving the eavesdropping busboy, who was pretending to be wiping off tables, every opportunity to hear clearly what we were saying.

There's something exciting about overhearing lovers argue. Makes you feel so lucky and superior.

I thought of changing the subject, of not giving the busboy his full measure of titillation, but then I decided I didn't care any longer. I was losing Amy, and I didn't care about much else at all.

"For your information, Amy, I've checked on four different people who hassled that old Jamaican. And you know what happened to them?"

"Oh, God, David, and you wonder why I want to break it off? If you're not skulking around after me, you're telling me that the old Jamaican has the power to kill people with his mind."

"He does, Amy. He really does."

She shook her elegant head. "Oh, David, don't you see how fucking crazy this is?"

Amy never used the F word unless she was truly exasperated. She'd been truly exasperated a lot lately.

"I'm sorry, I shouldn't have said, you know, the F word."

"You're thirty-six, Amy. You have every right to say the F word."

She smiled sadly. "Not according to my staunch

Methodist mother. She heard me say it to my sister last Christmas and was just shocked."

"I like your mother. I like your family. I want to be a part of it someday—as soon as you'll marry me."

"And what do I get for a wedding present—does the old Jamaican move in with us?"

The busboy smirked.

Oh, he'd deny it. Say, Hey, man, I wasn't even listening, I was jes doin' my work, you know?

But he'd be lying.

Because he did smirk. And I saw him. Honest.

Amy started pushing out of our booth, slender and professional in her blue Paolo Gucci silk suit and glowing white ruffled blouse, ever the competent lawyer and the subtly erotic young woman. God, I hated Michael at that moment. I could see him making love with her; and worse, I could hear the sounds of pleasure and satisfaction she made in response. The old panic, the old grinding sense of loss, came to me just then and I looked out the window at the lunch-hour professionals hurrying back to their jobs...and I felt totally alien from them. A different species from a different planet.

"You all right?" she said. I had to give Amy her kindness. She was through with me but she didn't enjoy the spectacle of my suffering.

"Yeah, I'm all right. Thanks."

There, in full view of the busboy, who was smirking

again, his fox-like white face just now ducking behind a post...Amy leaned over and kissed me.

"I'm sorry it didn't work out, David."

"So am I. I really love you, Amy."

"You'll meet somebody else."

"Not like you."

"That's what you said after Linda dumped you. Then you met Jane." She looked exasperated again but not exasperated enough to use the F word. "You just have to relax with women, David. Just kind of hang out with them and let them have their own lives and you have your own life, too. You're just too possessive. It's that simple." A smile. "You really will meet somebody soon, David. You're a damned good-looking guy and a lot of fun when you're not—Well, you know." Another brief dry kiss. "And by the way, I've convinced Michael not to fire you."

"Fire me? For what?"

"For what? Are you kidding, David? For bursting into the conference room when he and I were preparing a brief and starting to shout and—"

"I thought you two were—You know what I thought."

She sighed, shook her head. "David, we're lawyers. Professionals. We don't hop up on the conference room table in the middle of the afternoon and have sex."

"A lot of lawyers do."

"Well, we're not a lot of lawyers. There were clients

in the outer office, Michael's clients, when you did that and—Well Michael was pissed. Really pissed. It took me most of the night to talk him out of firing you."

"Yeah," I said, unable to stop myself, "and I bet I know what it took to finally persuade him."

"You asshole! I save your job and you say that to me! I wish I'd never gotten you this job!"

She gave the busboy a big dramatic finish. She slapped me hard across the face.

I trailed her all the way back to the office, stuttering and stammering and apologizing.

Michael said, "Shut the door, David."

I shut the door. Came over and sat down on the supplicant side of his desk. Even his most powerful clients were his supplicants. There was just an air about Michael that made you feel automatically inferior. Even Napoleon probably would have kissed his ass a little. It was the Yale degree and the hard handsome face and the big muscular football body and the slight sneer he seemed to have for everything and everybody, as if nothing was ever quite up to his expectations. If he had met God in person, Michael would probably have been a little disappointed.

The office itself complemented Michael's self-image perfectly—Persian rugs and antique Chippendale consoles and a grandfather clock he was eager to tell you had once tolled the hour in the House of Lords.

"You're a whining, incompetent fuck-up, David."

"Thank you."

"I just wanted you to know what I thought of you."

"I appreciate it," I said.

"And there's one more thing I want you to know. Everybody else on the staff knows it, so you should know it, too. The only reason I'm not throwing your scrawny ass out on the street is because Amy has begged me not to."

"I see."

"You see, but you don't give a damn, do you? You'll stay here anyway, knowing that everybody's snickering behind your back and whispering about what a pathetic fuck-up you are."

"Nobody else will hire me."

The sneer. The $2,000 custom-tailored blue suit, the $175 haircut—and the priceless sneer. Very effective combination. He said, "Life must be pretty simple when you don't have any pride."

Only now were his words beginning to hurt me. At first there'd been a certain novelty to his arrogance. But now his words were a mirror into which I was forced to look.

He had a gift for cruelty, our Michael. At the entrance to the park where staffers often ate lunch, he one day spat on a homeless man who blocked his path. Another time he slapped an admittedly shrill but very sad AIDS demonstrator who accidentally brushed up against him. He performed both acts with relish and boasted afterward that ours would be a better world if only more people treated "scumbags" that way. Only when he talked about his son from his first marriage did you see any humanity in Michael, and that wasn't sufficient to balance off against his zeal for meanness.

"And I want you to give up your office to that new junior partner," he said.

"Where will I do my work?"

"Well, first of all, the nature of your 'work' has changed. You're no longer an attorney, you're an assistant in the law library. And secondly, you'll be in that back office with the rest of the ladies."

"I suppose my pay'll be cut?"

The sneer again. He sat up to his desk, perfect jaw propped on his perfect fist. "Oh, no, David, you miss the point. If I cut your pay, you'd quit for sure. But if I don't cut your pay, you'll have to put up with all the humiliation. There isn't a law firm in this state that would hire a fucking soak like you for the money I'm paying you."

"You cocksucker."

"Am I supposed to be impressed, David? Is calling me a cocksucker your way of telling me that you're going to quit?"

I said nothing.

"I didn't think so." He nodded to the far end of his baronial mahogany office. He had enough leather chairs in here to seat the entire U.S. Supreme Court. "Now trot your ass back with the other ladies."

What can I tell you? Even with his generous

salary—and it was generous—I was two months arrears in my rent, and the bank was about to take back my car. My debts from drinking days took all the money I had.

No way I could quit, even if he flogged me every day in front of the entire staff.

"Cocksucker," I said, and stood up.

"Give my love to the girls," he said, and then picked up the phone. He made it a point to call somebody important every twenty minutes or so. As much as he liked to impress others, he liked to impress himself even more.

By the middle of the following day, I'd moved my materials to the large room in the back where the word processors and the law library were located. The women there tried to be sympathetic but I could tell they didn't have much respect for me. When I'd ask one of them a question, she'd look just over my shoulder and smile at one of her friends. Smirking, I guess you'd call it. The way the busboy had smirked in the restaurant. The way Michael smirked all the time.

Even worse, as I was hauling an armload of my books and papers to the back, Amy came up and said, "You really should quit, David. For your own dignity. You'd really be better off starving."

Easy for her to say.

By noon, I needed an escape.

I bought a chili dog from beneath a street vendor's

striped canvas umbrella and then drifted over to the park.

At the entrance closest to the law office there sit, on either side, two huge lions painted an enamel black. They look ancient as Egypt and imposing as Russia. Just behind the one on the left sits the old Jamaican homeless man. I'd never learned his name. He just appeared, like a suddenly sprung Jack-in-the-Box, shambling toward you, bald ebony head bobbing, hard gnarled hand out, palm up, into which you are supposed to drop money.

After I learned his secret, what he does to people who anger him, I always gave him money. One crisp new dollar each and every time I entered the park.

He was there today, worn gray overcoat despite the hot October day, flapping black buckle boots instead of shoes, and a face that looked like a head pygmies had shrunk to half-size—ebony, gleaming with sweat, old as midnight, pitiless in its gaze that somehow managed to be both stupid and terrifying at the same time. As usual, beneath the topcoat, he wore a lurid filthy purple shirt and a necklace of yellow beads.

"You good mon, you good mon," he said again and again, as if he had been programmed to say only those three words. And looked at you from glistening dark eyes that gleamed with a secret only they knew, some profound, urgent secret that you were too white and too young and too naive and too soft to understand at all.

I laid my dollar in the palm of his hand.

This brought me close enough to hold my breath. His body odors were indescribable—two parts dirty flesh to one part clinging feces to two parts rotted food.

"Good mon, good mon," he said again, nodding, already lining up his next customer, a jaunty young man in a sailor suit.

I went on into the park and ate my lunch, far enough away so that I could no longer smell the man, but close enough, and at an angle, so that I could still see him work.

And work he did.

He must have hit up a dozen people as I sat there finishing my chili dog and wishing I hadn't quit smoking. The two most enjoyable cigarettes a smoker ever has are after food and after sex.

Not everybody gave him money.

A few pushed past, scowling at him as they scowled at all homeless people, and for a few breathless seconds, I wondered if he was going to give them The Eye.

That's how I thought of it.

He gave it only rarely, and it was something you really had to earn. Most people who refused him got only a scowl. But there were some—well, if you jostled him or insulted him or laughed at him...you got The Eye.

He'd kind of cock his head to the right and fix you in his dark and gnarly gaze for a moment and then—I swear this is true—a tiny glow appeared in the iris of each eye and...

Well, when you eat in the same park, you get used to seeing certain faces and when you suddenly don't see them any more...

You wouldn't see them around and you'd ask their friends about them and then they'd tell you about the terrible accidents that had befallen them.

That's what I'd tried to explain to Amy, who'd dismissed it as more of my paranoid ravings (she'd spent twenty minutes with my shrink in the hospital, and he'd told her that I had paranoid tendencies—which made me wonder just what else he'd told her). But I'd seen him give four different people The Eye and I'd seen what had happened to them.

The man who laughed at him one day—electrocuted.

The woman who cursed him—cancer.

The woman who called him a dirty name—plane crash.

The man who pushed him—heart attack.

I'd seen each of them do these things; seen him give them The Eye; and then heard, soon thereafter, about their fates. I spent a long afternoon at the library reading about voodoo, finally understanding at least one of the old man's often-shouted words—"Legba! Legba!" he'd cry, calling to one of voodoo's most important deities, one who gave the old Jamaican great powers as a sorcerer.

If I hadn't been so recently in the bughouse, imagining snap-jawed alligators in my room, I might have gone to the police with my theory. But all they'd have to do was check into my background a bit and find—

"Bet he outlives us all," my friend the accountant said. He reminds me of the loud, irritating next door neighbor that sitcom heroes always had in the fifties and sixties, right down to his golf sweater and his red socks with his blue slacks and white-and-black saddle shoes. He wore a fraternity ring the size of a baseball.

He sat next to me on the park bench.

"Probably got every disease there is, probably sleeps in an alley most nights, probably hasn't seen a doctor in thirty years, but I bet the bastard is here a long time after we're gone."

"You're probably right," I said.

"They make me sick," he said, his fleshy face becoming a mask of displeasure. "Bastards probably make more panhandling than you and I do working and paying taxes."

"Maybe so."

"I wish that boss of yours could've pushed through that petition with city hall. But with those god damned liberal faggots—" He paused, nodded. "Hey! Is that Grade-A prime beef or what?"

She was young and she was devastatingly beautiful and this was a city park on a warm autumn day that was so perfect it almost made you giddy.

And made her look even younger, lovelier.

"Is that a pair of tits or what?"

He didn't even know how to speak of her, let alone appreciate her. She had a face that was melancholy in its beauty; and wrists and ankles of heartbreaking, coltish grace; and an aura of gentleness I wanted to hide inside, like shade on a hot day.

"Not much of an ass, though," my friend the poet was saying. "Myself, I like a little meat on the ass." Then, he cackled. Not laughed, cackled. "That old fucker is hittin' her up, that Jamaican or whatever he is." Another cackle. "Man, I sure wish that boss of yours coulda gotten rid of all of them."

And it was then, the second time he said it, that I realized how I was going to rid the world of one Michael Malone.

I stood up and said, "Well, I'd better head back."

"Following that sweet little piece of ass is what you're gonna do," the accountant said. "Right?"

I didn't want to disappoint him. "Right."

On the way out of the park I did something I'd never done before. I tipped the old man a second crisp new dollar bill.

He looked at me in that slow, sly way of his and I had the sense that he knew exactly what I had in mind for Michael Malone.

I knocked. On the other side of the door, he snarled. At least that's what it sounded like. I peeked in.

"What the fuck do *you* want? Whatever it is, just tell my secretary."

"I wanted to invite you to lunch."

The smirk. "Hey, David, you don't have to kiss my ass. I mean, I'm not a glutton. Putting you back with the women is plenty of humiliation for me. Honest."

"I just thought we needed to talk."

This was the day after my demotion. "Talk about what? Believe it or not, David, I've got a lot of work to do. Even if you don't."

"About my quitting."

A laugh. "You mean, you're not going to keep on taking my bullshit?"

"I guess not."

"Well, hell, David, that's *worth* a lunch. Seeing a guy find his balls again. It's kind of touching, actually." The smirk. "You going to tell me off? Tell me what a selfish, egotistical shit I am?"

"Probably."

"Good. I love that kind of stuff." The smile. "Tell you what, we'll go to Rodman's and I'll pick up the tab."

"I'd rather go to the park."

"No wonder chicks are always dumping you. You get a chance to have a free lunch at the nicest place in the city, and you'd rather go over and sit on a park bench that pigeons have been shitting on."

"I'll stop back around noon."

For just a moment there, he dropped his bully-boy

pose and stared at me curiously. "*What the hell's really going on here, David?*" his eyes said.

But then he slid back into character. "After we're done eating, can we sing some campfire songs?"

"Look at that asshole."

We were approaching the entrance to the park, Michael Malone and I, when a singularly scruffy homeless man appeared from behind a large bush, zipping up his pants.

"He probably took a dump behind there, too, and didn't even wipe his ass."

"They get pretty disgusting," I said. Hard as I tried to be compassionate about the homeless, some of them did make me sick occasionally. I got tired of them using the city as one big toilet.

"You know what death squads are?" Michael said.

"You mean the ones in El Salvador?"

"Right. At night the cops go in and they haul out all the bad elements and kill them and then bury them out in the country so that nobody can find them. That's what we need to do with homeless people in this country."

"I agree with you that some of these people belong in prison or in mental hospitals, and some of them are just too lazy to work, but death squads..."

And that's when I saw him.

The old Jamaican. Leathery brown face. Sinister

dark eyes. Filthy spittle running down the side of his mouth.

I'd been careful to keep Michael on the inside, to the left, the side which the old man always worked.

We were within a few feet of him now.

He'd step toward us.

And Michael, being Michael, would say something nasty to him.

And that's when I'd give Michael a little nudge, right into the old man.

And then Michael would really get angry, having had to actually brush against one of the unclean this way.

And he'd start calling the old man names.

And the old man, being the old man, would have had enough, and he'd hex Michael.

His eyes would narrow. And he'd do that little trick with his glowing irises. And he'd say a few voodoo words in Jamaican.

And a few days later, Michael would be dead of an accident. Good old Michael.

Three feet separated us now.

The Jamaican was closing in to ask for money.

A sneer was already appearing on Michael's face as he realized that he was about to be hit up for money.

Two feet now.

The Jamaican closing in fast.

And then Michael saw her.

Don't ask me her name.

Maybe Michael didn't even *know* her name.

But he recognized her and she recognized him and they started waving and walking toward each other.

This happened when Michael was less than a single foot from the grasp of the Jamaican.

Michael turned to the right suddenly and started walking away.

Leaving me there to stare into the eyes of the Jamaican, to hand him my usual crisp new dollar bill, and to wonder if Michael didn't have some kind of radar that kept him from great harm.

He'd been so close to the old man.

This frigging close.

And then—

"You ever read what's in hot dogs?" Michael said, fifteen minutes later.

"I guess not."

"They throw in tongue and lips and eyes. Shit like that."

"No wonder they taste so good."

"You shouldn't eat crap like this. Bad for you."

"I didn't see you turn it down."

"Two, three times a year max, I eat crap like this. Holy shit."

"What?"

"You see that chick?"

"I thought you were in love with Amy."

"You're really a shithead, you know that?"

"I don't like you any better, you arrogant prick." Pause. "I'm quitting."

"Good."

But already his attention was wandering, and who could blame him? A nice green park on a nice warm autumn day with two or three dozen nice warm women all eating their lunches in the park? Who could concentrate on anything but them?

"I'm going to say something that will probably strike you as very corny, Michael."

"And that would be what?"

"That would be—I want you to be faithful to Amy."

"I was wrong about you. You really do have balls."

"I care about her."

"I'm touched."

"The way you sleep around, you could kill her. AIDS is really spreading, Michael."

He stood up.

We'd been here nearly half an hour, fighting our way through three different attempts at chit-chat, and finally getting to the real point.

"I'm going back," he said.

"I'm serious. About Amy."

"Is that supposed to scare me?"

"No. It's supposed to make you think—about her."

The smirk. "You're such a fucking candy-ass, David, and the pathetic thing is you don't even know it."

He led the way back toward the park entrance, blessing the prettiest of the young ladies with his *bon vivant* smile. The especially pretty ones, he even gave a nod. How nice of him.

My opportunity was passing and I knew it.

Here came the lions flanking the entrance. Here came the old Jamaican, panhandling with shabby fervor.

We were going to walk right back to the office.

Right past the old man.

Right into Michael's wonderful future.

When we were two feet from the Jamaican, I realized that I had only one chance left.

The old man's back was to us. He was cajoling some change from a middle-aged woman who looked slightly afraid of him.

Michael, predictably, was surveying the landscape for sight of new ladies on whom to settle the largesse of his smile.

He was looking at an exceptionally fetching redhead who was talking to the blond woman next to her on the park bench when I nudged Michael.

"What?"

"God, did you see that?"

"See what?"

"That old bastard there. The Jamaican."

"What about him?"

"He spit on that woman."

"You're shitting me?"

"Spit right in her face."

"That cocksucker!"

No cannon could have fired him more truly at a target. Michael went directly for the old man, whose back was still to us as the middle-aged woman hurried back down the sidewalk.

Michael grabbed the old Jamaican by the collar of his filthy gray overcoat, spun him around, snatched him by his lapels and then hurled him into one of the stone lions.

The old man hit with such force that he catapulted off the lion and pitched face-first to the ground.

A small crowd had gathered, shouting at Michael to leave him alone.

"He spit on that woman!" Michael explained to an angry cop who had just strolled, all crisp blue uniform and imposing nightstick, upon the scene. "Tell him, David. He spit on her, didn't he?"

But I wasn't interested in either Michael or the cop.

All I cared about was the old guy, who was picking himself up with angry dignity.

His gaze never left Michael.

The irises exploded with little neutron bombs of rage.

Talk about your hexing.

This was hexing that had never been known to mankind before.

He gibbered in Jamaican, but even though I didn't understand the exact words, I certainly divined the intent.

My good friend Michael here was in deep, deep shit.

"You all right, fella?" the cop said to the old guy, making it clear that he didn't like having to defend the rights of homeless creeps.

The Jamaican said nothing.

Just stared.

With his crazed dark eyes.

At Michael.

For the first time, Michael took note of that gaze, of all that anger and malice, and he looked upset, if not downright frightened.

"Let's get out of here," he said, and then, barely at a perceptible level, "That old fucker gives me the creeps."

He didn't speak until we were very near the office. "You wouldn't be bullshitting me, would you?"

"What's that supposed to mean?"

"He really spit on her?"

"Far as I could tell. I mean, from the angle where I was standing, it sure *looked* like he spit on her."

We had reached the office parking lot, where his new red Maserati was parked. He rubbed up against it like a lonely dog against a new human leg.

He was still shaken, sweating much more than the seventy-three degree heat warranted.

"You see that old fucker stare at me?"

"Kinda spooky guy, isn't he?" I said.

He looked at me hard. "He really spit on that woman?"

"Far as I could tell he did, Michael. From the angle where I was standing, I mean."

"You're pathetic."

"Does that mean you want to come over tonight and make love?"

"You trick Michael into assaulting that old Jamaican guy. And now I suppose you think something terrible's going to happen to him."

I said nothing.

I had been sitting alone in the darkness of my living room for more than two hours, playing over and over some of the old tapes I associated with Amy—a little Boz Scaggs, the romantic stuff he did; and Kenny G. She liked him; I didn't, but now I was learning to like him because he made her lovely face so vivid in my mind.

"Well, for your information, David, Michael and I are planning to get married in two months—December 10. And I wouldn't worry about what to get us for our wedding because you won't be invited." She clucked, the way she would cluck years later, when she was a society matron. Whether Amy knew it or not, that was her destiny.

But as for now...in the gloom, teenagers roaring past three floors below on the sweet warm autumn night...in the gloom she sounded angry and frantic and betrayed.

"God, David, when he told me what you did—you know, lying to him about the old man spitting on that woman—I realized just how far you're gone. You need help, David. Serious, serious help. Michael's going to be fine and we're going to get married and have a great life and you—you can just fuck off!"

The F word.

She slammed down the phone.

Leaving me to the silence.

I wanted to be one of those teenage boys in the hot cars with the blasting radios and my arm around a sweet young chick.

Have it all ahead of me, young manhood, endless sexual adventure, a sense of almost giddy hope as I naively contemplated my future. Hell, at eighteen I'd truly believed that if I couldn't conquer the entire world, I could at least steal a few continents.

After a long time, I went through the dark apartment to my bedroom in the back where, months earlier, Amy had forgotten and left a blouse hanging in my closet.

Every once in a while, when my loss started to overwhelm me, I'd go back there and hold the blouse to me as if we were dancing, and then I'd put my nose to the shoulder and smell the sweet perfume she'd worn, and for a time a kind of exquisite melancholy would sunder me and I would dance around the room with the blouse until tears filled my eyes and a shuddering passed through my entire body.

I called her back, but when she answered, I hung up immediately, having no idea what to say.

Michael died on a rainy Thursday morning.

A very common kind of accident really.

Stepping out of the shower.

Heel of the foot snagging a slippery bar of soap.

Hands grasping for purchase on the edge of the shower.

But too late.

At least, this was how Amy later reconstructed that terrible morning for the police and then the medical examiner and then the District Attorney.

Freak accident.

Case closed.

"Are you happy?"

"Who is this?"

Darkness.

No traffic below in the street.

A distant train rumbling through midnight.

I'd had three joints before tumbling into my lonely bed. Now, trying to struggle awake, I was disoriented.

"You know who this is."

"Amy?"

"You're smart, David. I mean, to be perfectly honest, I always thought you were kind of dumb. But you're not. You're very crafty. You knew that the old Jamaican bastard could actually hex people."

"Amy, I've been trying to tell you that for over a year. But you wouldn't believe me."

"And you know what you also knew?"

"Amy, please, listen I—"

"You also knew I couldn't go to the police. I'd be a laughing stock. 'The man I loved was killed because this old Jamaican dude put a hex on him.' The word would get out. All over. Every time I walked into a court room, the judge would smile at me and shake her head and think, 'There's that pathetic young attorney who believes in hexes.' You really are smart, David. You got away with killing somebody—and nobody can prove it. But you're not that smart, David. Oh, no. Because I'm going to get you. That I promise you. I'm going to figure out some way to do it, David, no matter how long it takes. Do you understand me?"

She was shrieking.

"DO YOU UNDERSTAND ME?"

"Yes, Amy, I understand you."

"You fucker," she said. "You fucker!"

And then she slammed the phone.

You know the funny thing?

Two weeks after Michael's death, I went back to work at his law firm. Tom Regison, Michael's partner, was forced to take on Michael's caseload, at least temporarily, and he needed somebody who was at least somewhat familiar with his cases, which just happened to be the cases Michael had assigned me to when I'd first started working here.

Amy was not nice.

Region had obviously warned her in advance that I was coming back temporarily. By the time I got there, Amy had really practiced up on her scowls and her glares and her cold poisonous glances. I was treated to all three every time we happened to pass each other in the hallways.

After a few days of eating in a restaurant, I bought a chili dog and went back to my usual place in the park. Indian summer was dying with great reluctance, leaf smoke an exhilarating aroma across the small rolling hills of the city park.

The old man paid me no special attention.

I gave him a dollar each way—I'd come to think of it as essentially a toll-road situation—and he gave me a few of his completely incomprehensible mumblings.

"You good mon, you good mon," he'd say. As usual, those were the only words of his I could understand at all.

I tried a little flirting, something I'd always been pretty good at actually, pick-up lines tumbling successfully from my tongue—but nobody was interested. Over the course of four or five lunches in the park, I must have hit on every good-looking woman there, bearing a wedding ring or not, but it was a long litany of No Sales.

I knew better than to approach Amy. Not now. She'd need at least a year to begin forgetting. Then I hoped that she'd see that things had turned out for the best...that she and I would be together. For life.

I had patience.

Work saved me. I got caught up in a few of the cases, in the intellectual and legal challenges they offered. I worked nights. I worked Saturdays. I even worked a few Sundays.

A few weeks later, exhausted from another long morning in the office, I grabbed my suit coat and headed for the park. The last of autumn's burnished leaves were falling from the trees now; at night you could smell winter creeping down from Canada. I needed a long lunch break to regain my stamina. Those chili dogs contain some mighty good nutrition.

I was a quarter block from the park entrance when I saw two burly men in police officer blue yanking the Jamaican away from his post between the lions.

I had no idea what was going on, only that a small crowd was gathering, only that the Jamaican was screaming curses at his captors in—well, I suppose it was Jamaican.

He was twisting and turning violently, trying to escape their clutches, when he looked back over his shoulder and saw me.

Silver spittle began to foam immediately in the corner of his mouth; his eyes flared with that familiar glow. "Legba curse you! Legba curse you!" he cried at me.

I was terrified.

He was giving me The Eye—the same Eye that had killed Michael—but why?

I started walking toward him—confused and genuinely startled that he was screaming at me—when I saw a white legal document float from the hand of one of the officers trying to grasp the old bastard.

I reached down and picked it up and recognized what it was immediately—a formal legal complaint from the City Attorney. I scanned the five lines on the front of the tri-fold and saw that the old man was being charged with Criminal Trespass, the law most often used against homeless people since vagrancy was declared unconstitutional by the Supreme Court.

All right, he was being thrown out of the park—but why blame me for it?

Then I opened the tri-fold and saw whose name was on the complaint.

One David Calloway.

Me.

By the time I saw my name, the two police officers were putting the old man in the back seat of a squad car and hauling him away.

I ran up to the back window, knowing I couldn't pound on it without getting myself arrested, but catching the old man's attention by waving at him.

"I didn't do it! I didn't call in this complaint! I swear I didn't!"

But all he did was sit there in his purple shirt and yellow beaded necklace and leathery black skin.

And give me The Eye.

Not just any eye.

The Eye.

The fucking Eye.

The police cruiser pulled away from the curb.

I must have run half a block behind the cruiser, waving the complaint in the air, screeching that I didn't do it! I didn't do it!

But the old man wasn't even looking at me now.

He'd done his work.

Now it was just a matter of time.

The call came that night. Late.

"I saw you in the park today," Amy said. "Picking up that complaint. Seeing your name on it. Pretty cool on my part if I say so."

"Amy, god damn, do you have any idea what you've done to me?"

"The same thing you did to Michael."

"But, Amy—"

"I thought of shooting you. And then I thought of poisoning you and then I thought of setting you on fire. But that would mean I'd have to go to prison. And this is so much easier. Just letting that old Jamaican do my work for me."

"I thought you hated him."

"That's the funny thing, David. All of a sudden I've got kind of a soft spot in my heart for him."

And then she hung up.

It's been six days now.

Six unimaginably long days.

I won't leave the house.

Why make it easy for him?

A car could hit me. A tree could fall on me. A mugger could shoot me.

What I'm hoping is that there's kind of a time limit on this deal. You know, maybe if Legba doesn't nail you right away—well, maybe the whole thing expires.

That's why I'm in bed now.

And not moving except to tip-toe very, very carefully into the bathroom to pee.

I'm not even eating anything. Just like that sneaky fucking Legba to have me choke on it.

Six days.

Figure I'll give it eight or nine to be safe.

Then I'll give Amy a call and tell her how sorry I am for being such a shit and all. She won't forgive me right away, but eventually she will.

Don't you think?

Huh? Don't you think so?

CANDLE MAGIC

storm constantine

In a relatively short time, Storm Constantine has established herself as one of the major new voices in fantastic literature.

The recently released novel, Calenture, has topped off a nine-book history which began with the noted Wraeththu trilogy, and she has still found the time to write some thirty short stories while managing to produce training course material for computer programs, fit in the occasional stint as finance officer for a local voluntary organization, and manage a band called Empyrean. She also provides writing and computer services to "a few other bands." "All in all," she says, "I'm too busy...but who's complaining?"

Constantine was a very superstitious child, highly imaginative and hyper-aware of omens, for which she devised a whole series of "weird little rituals to repel bad luck." "I couldn't look at this one tree," she recalls, "though I can't remember why. But I would run, shielding my eyes, until I had reached a particular stretch of the street where I knew I would be safe. Maybe one day I'll go back and check out the tree.

"I'm better now. Since I got into quantum physics, I guess I think I can probably influence things myself. I still see a significance in things, but I suppose it's just observation; like storing data."

It's getting a little dark, don't you think? Time to light a candle...

The candle was already lit when Felicia came home with the intention of enjoying her Friday afternoon off in peace. She hadn't realized her flat-mate, Emma, was off work as well. A scorching day, too hot for May, and Emma was sitting on the floor lighting candles.

"Oh, you're here," Emma said, looking up. She sounded as disappointed as Felicia to find she'd have company for the day. The air in the room was thick with pungent fruity incense.

"Hmm. Had time in lieu. What are you doing?" Felicia went to open the windows.

Emma glanced at the candle. "Thinking…"

"Thinking…" Felicia nodded. There was a suppressed excitement in Emma's expression she was familiar with. "Anyone I know?"

Emma smiled secretively. "You know what's going on…."

Felicia shook her head and dragged her handbag, which was more like a satchel, over to the sofa. She slumped down and delved for her cigarettes in the depths of the bag. "I don't think either of us knows what's going on," she said, lighting up and inhaling with gusto.

Emma laughed again. "Poor Fliss, you're just too practical!"

Felicia disliked the implication in Emma's words. She knew Emma often thought her a dull, unimaginative creature. She took a deep breath. "Look, Em, I'm a friend, so I have to say it: You're obsessed!" She waved her arm emphatically, scattering cigarette ash over the sofa and Emma's lap.

Emma brushed the gray powder from her curled legs as if without thinking. Her expression had soured. "So grateful for your support!"

"Em, *please!*" Felicia groped behind the sofa for an ashtray. "What am I supposed to think?" She laughed nervously. "Next, it'll be eye of newt and wing of bat; you're crazy!"

Emma drew up her knees gracefully, pushing back her auburn hair. She reached toward the single blue candle standing in a congealing pool of wax on the coffee table. Her fingers were a fan against the flame. "It can be done," she murmured.

A week previously, Emma had announced that she was in love. Felicia had known Emma for a long time and recognized immediately that her friend had fallen victim to yet another of the intense romantic fantasies to which she seemed particularly vulnerable in the spring. Outside the window, even in the heart of the city, there was a thrumming vitality to the air. It was possible to feel the thrust of growth, and to be carried with it. Emma's imagination certainly seemed drawn to greater extravagances. Felicia was used to this ritual behavior. Sometimes she became impatient with it, at other times she was prepared to be understanding. For all Emma's peculiar habits, she and Felicia got on together well, and Felicia had shared accommodations with too many people to undervalue that fact. Still, she and Emma were very different. Felicia had been in love three times in her life, and had once been engaged, but all her affairs had ended in infidelities and unpleasant scenes. Now, she was being cautious and kept her few suitors at arm's length, allowing them the occasional privilege of her company in a restaurant or club, and even more rarely the odd night of sex in the flat. To Emma, however, love seemed to mean spending endless hours alone, locked in desperate reverie, a condition encouraged by periodic sightings of the object of her desires. It seemed almost like a sickness, a ravaging fever that burned her out. Actual relationships had occasionally sprung from her obsessions, but they had possessed the life-span of a plucked poppy. Felicia doubted Emma had ever been out with anyone who she wasn't obsessed with. Any other man who had the temerity to approach her was rebuffed instantly. Since Felicia and Emma had lived together in the flat—nearly four years now—Felicia had seen several beautiful young men go in and out of Emma's room, and a couple of those had wanted to become permanent fixtures. It had always been Emma who'd sent them packing. Felicia had even been out for a drink with one of them afterwards, to listen to his woeful rantings of unrequited love. Once Emma had decided she no longer liked them, they might as well not exist for her. Still, until the moment they cut their own throats with an unwise remark or behavior Emma found disappointing, her regard for them was merciless in its intensity. No wonder they felt so bewildered once they'd been rejected. Felicia often felt very sorry for them, but she stood by her friend's determination not to stick with a relationship she was not happy with.

"You'll never learn, will you!" Felicia said, shaking her head, the remark softened by a smile.

Emma refused to be drawn into a sisterly spirit. She frowned. "I know what you're thinking. 'Not this again.' I don't expect you to understand, but..." She hesitated. "This time, it's different." Before Felicia could respond, Emma uncurled from the floor and began to prowl about the room.

Felicia didn't know what to say, wary of encouraging Emma's fixations, but nervous of upsetting her too much. Emma was touching things in a slow, deliberate manner; her beads hanging across the mirror, her crystal in its nest of velvet on the sideboard, her own throat. She and Felicia were the same age—twenty-seven—although Felicia always felt so much older than Emma.

"Perhaps we should talk about it," Felicia said, aware that her voice sounded too shrill. Even though she'd opened the windows, the air in the room was hot; hot and damp and dark. The flat only got the sun in the morning. Later, there might be thunder.

"Talk? There is little to say. I know what I want."

Emma turned and smiled a cat's smile, lifting her thick hair in both hands. It appeared to be a studied pose, but Felicia had never quite convinced herself that Emma struck her regular dramatic postures consciously.

"Then, why bother telling me about it at all?"

Emma shrugged. "I thought it best to, in case anything happened."

"What do you mean by that?" Felicia became aware of tension across her forehead, a frown forming. Perhaps it was caused by the humid atmosphere. "Sometimes, you frighten me, Em." She stubbed out her cigarette with swift, sharp prods. "What you need is a good time. Less mooning around, more real life."

Emma ignored the advice. "There's nothing to be afraid of. I *will* have him, Fliss...."

Felicia shook her head and gestured at the candle. "And is that what this is all about? Sitting here being witchy and dreaming dreams? Oh, Em, I can't decide whether you want to be the Lady of Shalott or Cleopatra!"

"You always laugh," Emma said nonchalantly, apparently unembarrassed. She came back to squat before the coffee table, her pale hand hovering over the candle flame, her eyes intent. "This candle, it is exactly the right color...." Her voice sounded portentous and full of intent.

Felicia sighed. Emma's mystical leanings occasionally bothered her; mostly, they could be ignored. "It's just a candle," she said, and then jumped up too quickly from the sofa. Emma's image seemed to vibrate before her eyes. She rubbed her face, finding her upper lip wet. "Can't bear this heat! Want a drink?"

Emma shook her head. "I'm okay, thanks."

Left alone in the room, Emma cupped her hands around the flame. She took a deep breath, held it, breathed out slowly. "Listen to me…" she said to the flame. "Help me…." She closed her eyes and threw back her head, clasping her crossed ankles. The image of The Man was difficult to conjure because she was distracted by the sound of Felicia humming loudly to herself in the small kitchen off the sitting-room. She couldn't visualize his face properly. Traffic outside, the sound of children across the street as they played in the school playground; the clatter from builders working on the house next door: all mundane intrusions.

"I believe in what I want," she whispered fervently, "And to believe is to *make* it true."

"What did you say?" Felicia's voice asked from the doorway.

At night, alone with the moon, it was easier for Emma to direct her thoughts. Arms by her side or across her chest, it didn't matter, she visualized. Felicia had argued: "Okay, so he's good-looking, but that doesn't mean he's a nice person." Felicia *would* say something like that. She was attracted to men who were like herself; dependable and direct, scrubbed and neatly dressed.

Emma undressed in the dark and spread out her Tarot cards face down on the rugs in the pale light that came in through the shivering, gauzy curtains. Silvery incense smoke filled the room with the scent of jasmine. She picked a card and held it to her chest for a while, without looking at it. Then, she examined picture. It was The Moon—signifying secrecy and delusion. No, Emma thought. It is mystery and magic. She scooped the cards up into their silk wrap and lit herself a cigarette, leaning back against the end of her bed. She felt the flat was aware of her, its walls listening to the beat of her heart, her thoughts. Felicia was out with all her secretary friends, drinking in wine bars, no doubt being chatted up by dull men. Emma always felt the flat manifested a different personality when she was in it alone. People like Felicia, for all their good intentions, killed any subtle atmosphere that did not fit into their narrow view of reality. Their presence suffocated mystery. They were like rotor-scythes plowing through an overgrown garden, restoring order to something that had been precious and beautiful in its wilderness. Tonight, Emma felt powerful, and it burned within her like hate. If she stood up, her head would brush the ceiling. Her heart was projecting a net of luminous beams, each of which pulsed like a star at its tip.

She couldn't remember where she had first seen The Man. She was aware Felicia privately scorned what she saw as Emma's regular crushes on people, but Emma couldn't convey to her friend how, this time, the invasion of her thoughts had been not only unwelcome, but somehow threatening. She was torn two ways by the yelping dogs of Resentment and Yearning. The last time she'd fallen in love had been devastating. The man had shattered all her dreams by being not only insensitive and coarse, but unintelligent. He'd confessed he'd not read a book since childhood, and the mirror of Emma's hopes had cracked from side to side. He had been beautiful, but the beauty had been a scale on his skin, easily scratched off. Since then, Emma had vowed not to fall into the same emotional state again. She would retain her common sense and snuff out any mad desires before they took hold of her. She was too old now for childish passions. Felicia was always saying she should go for personality rather than looks in a man, but for Emma the two had to be intertwined. She had very precise standards. Still, this did not mean the right person wasn't waiting for her somewhere. She must not make another mistake. Surely the intensity of her feelings now meant she might have found her soul-mate at last?

Felicia did not know to what extent the current infatuation had affected Emma because Emma had kept the details quiet. She could not confess to how she had become a fevered, feral thing, spending whole evenings following The Man from bar to bar, skulking in shadows, awed and sickened by what she saw as his unbearable loveliness. His face looked intelligent, his bearing was aloof yet intriguing. He was like a well-bred animal: graceful and aware of his own beauty without seeming arrogant. All this, Emma had discerned from a distance. For some reason, she could not employ her usual tactics and approach him. It was not fear of rejection exactly, but perhaps a fear of being disappointed again. She'd seen him looking at her sometimes.

"Where have you been?" Felicia would say when Emma came in late alone.

"Out." A shrug.

"Who with?"

Emma would lie. "Pat, Alison...you know." She didn't want Felicia to know she'd been on her own. Solitude was part of the condition. The pain conjured by the aching desire for The Man was companioned by an exquisite melancholy. She had to be alone, in order to surrender herself to the daydreams that filled her mind. At work, it was easy because she could fantasize as she was hunched over her drawing-board. Since she seemed so busy, nobody would bother her. In her mind, she lived out a hundred scenarios of actually speaking to The Man, different ways in which they could meet. She knew the best nights for locating him: Saturdays, Sundays, and occasionally on Wednesdays. He always seemed to be with people, but she couldn't remember their faces. She didn't know any of them. They were nobodies, eclipsed by his flame. At night, she dreamed of cards falling like leaves, twisting before her face, but she could never see their symbols. During the day, she would sometimes get angry with herself and say aloud, beneath her breath, "This is stupid! I'm going to forget it. It's pathetic!" And she would straighten her spine, empty her mind of wandering thoughts, apply herself to a mundane task, and imagine the yearning had gone. But then the night would come again and that strange magic would, stirring within her, and she would say to herself, "I have to see him," and find herself on the street, pulling on her jacket, her face hot, walking quickly.

Sometimes, she couldn't find him, and then she'd become a demented thing, knocking back drinks too swiftly, going into places that, normally, she'd never dare enter alone. It was as if he *knew*. At the end of the evening, almost out of her mind, she would catch a glimpse of him; his tawny hair, his dark eyes, and that would be enough. Then she could go home again and light the candles. Sometimes, she wondered whether she really had seen him or not.

On Saturday, Felicia thought Emma looked listless and depressed. The fizzing euphoria, so typical of her infatuations, was absent. Could it really be different this time? She knew so little about Emma's latest crush. She resolved to be sympathetic, and made them a pot of tea so they could sit down to a chat. "How many times have you spoken to this man?" she began, intent on building a dossier of facts about him.

Emma's eyes skittered away from Felicia's own. Felicia made a mental note.

"Well...once. He passed me in the pub. Put his hand on my arm."

"Is that all?" Felicia tried to keep her voice low. "What did he say?"

"He said 'excuse me.'"

Felicia took a sip of tea to smother an involuntary smile. Then she put down her mug. "Emma...how can I say this? You can't be in love with someone you don't know."

Emma jumped up angrily. "Then it isn't love! Something else!" She clawed her hair.

The outburst surprised Felicia. "What else?"

Emma stared at her fiercely with eyes that seemed to burn within. "I've been looking for something," she said quickly, "looking for years. Now I think I've found it. I have to have him, Fliss. We have to have each other. I know it's right. I feel it. I..."

"Hold on!" Felicia held up her hands. "Does he ever look at you, make any signal he's interested in you?"

Emma swung around and began to play with her beads hanging over the mirror. "Of course he does."

"Then perhaps you should simply make the first move. Go up to him. Speak. It can't be that difficult. Pat or Ally would be with you."

Emma was silent.

"Shall we go out together tonight?" Felicia suggested brightly. "We haven't been out together for weeks! You've been seeing so much of Pat and..."

"I need some of his hair!" Emma interrupted hotly. "Then it would work better. I'd have a focus. I need to bring him to me."

"Emma," Felicia began carefully, "if you got close enough to him to pull his hair out, you could also say hello...."

Emma suddenly threw back her head and laughed loudly, causing Felicia to wince visibly. She saw something ancient standing there, something primeval yet essentially female. Emma thought Felicia lacked imagination, but she did not.

Although Felicia hadn't seen The Man, Emma had described him in such detail, she felt she'd recognize him if she saw him. Tall, long hair, and, like Emma, a lover of the colors black and purple. Emma had found paintings in books with which to illustrate her descriptions. "His nose is like this, his mouth like this...." Felicia indulgently paid attention, inwardly rather appalled that a woman of Emma's age could act so immaturely. This man might as well be a famous musician or a film star, seeing as Emma had built up her love for him on appearances alone. Still, Felicia comforted herself that Emma would soon tire of this paragon, once she got to know him. So far, all her infatuations had burned themselves out quickly, once the objects of desire proved themselves to be disappointingly human and therefore unworthy of Emma's attention. Thus, in Felicia's opinion, Emma must introduce herself to this new idol as soon as possible. What Emma expected from a man was, in Felicia's opinion, virtually supernatural, and nobody could live up to that.

"Emma, tonight, you are going to speak to your fancy man, even if I have to drag you over to him myself!"

"Perhaps you're right," said Emma.

Felicia sighed. How could a grown woman be such a child?

Emma dressed herself in a long black dress that swirled like smoke around her ankles and wore her rich, dark red hair loose down her back, almost as if it were a symbol of her own power. Felicia dressed in a short dress that hugged her figure and shouted at the night in tropical colors. Both wore jackets—Emma leather, and Felicia something expensive in cashmere she'd picked up in town. She and Emma walked along an avenue that was fragrant with spring, an unlikely-looking pair of companions. Above them, the moon rose full and heavy. Felicia chattered on aimlessly about people at work, mostly because she could think of nothing else to say. Inside, she felt quite nervous.

Emma appeared serene, nodding vaguely at Felicia's remarks, a slight smile on her face. She was imagining that a black panther walked on either side of her, and her hands were touching each one lightly between the ears.

They went from bar to bar, drinking, Felicia talking, an occasional friend pausing to chat; the evening stretched before them. Emma looked feverish, as if she were about to go into battle, and her eyes were never still, scanning faces. Looking at her friend's strained expression and darting eyes, Felicia thought, "I don't really know this woman; she is a stranger." And bought them both another drink.

Emma raised her glass, smiled. "The elixir of life!" she said.

It was late, nearly closing time in the bar that had an extension until two, when Emma eventually spotted The Man. She hissed and grabbed Felicia's arm savagely. "There!"

Bodies milled around them, obstructing sight. There was high laughter, the offense of conflicting perfumes.

Felicia peered. "Where?" Her face had gone shiny. She was beginning to grin back at the shaved-neck office boys lurking at the boundary of her and Emma's space.

"Over there."

Felicia giggled and stood up. "Right, this is it. Come on!"

Emma pulled her back down on to her stool. "No!" For a moment, she sat silent, her head bowed, and then she looked up. "I'll go alone. I have to." She swallowed the last of her drink, stood up and smiled shakily. "Well, this is it! Now or never!"

Felicia raised her glass. "Good hunting, then!"

Felicia let herself into the flat alone. All the rooms were in darkness. Felicia didn't like the way the flat felt when it was dark. She turned on lights everywhere and picked up the remains of Emma's candle, which was nothing more than a blue puddle in an old saucer on the coffee table. Kicking off her shoes, Felicia padded into the kitchen and turned on the kettle. She felt light-headed, but not drunk. The night had been fun. Pity Emma had walked out on her. Hardly a sensible thing to do. No woman should walk the streets alone in the early hours of the morning. Luckily, Felicia had had enough cash left to get a cab.

The kettle thumped and groaned to itself. Felicia put instant coffee and sugar into a mug. There was a click, followed by a disgruntled whine as the kettle switched itself off. As she picked it up, Felicia became aware of the intense silence of the flat beyond the kitchen. It seemed as if time had stopped.

Then the sounds came.

It was like flapping, something huge and dark, flapping. Felicia ran out into the living-room, convinced an owl, or some other large bird, had got in and was rampaging round the flat. The noises stopped the instant she walked into the room. For a moment, there was silence, and then she heard a muffled crash from the hallway, followed by an abrupt mew or stifled cry. Felicia stood in the living-room doorway, perplexed, the kettle still held in one hand. The hall beyond looked endless. Emma's door was closed.

"Em!" Felicia called. The silence had come back, that thick silence she hated. The walls seemed vigilant, waiting. Felicia crept forward.

Suddenly, a great sound, a trumpeting, like a siren going off blasted right through her. She realized it was a scream. Rapid, frantic sounds, like something beating itself against the door, came from Emma's room. Then, again, silence.

"Em!" Felicia ran to the door, but was reluctant to open it, afraid. She knocked on it loudly. "Em, are you all right?" She put her ear against the door. She thought she could hear Emma's voice. No words, just inarticulate sound; distress.

Are you brave? Felicia asked herself. Is someone in there with her? Is someone hurting her? She gripped the kettle more firmly and put her hand on the door handle. She expected the door to be locked, but it wasn't.

Emma was alone, sitting awkwardly on the floor beneath the window, which was slightly open. The lamps were off, but the street-lights outside shone right into the room. Emma's possessions, which she treasured so highly, had been strewn about the room, as if in fury. And over everything were shining droplets of a dark liquid: the walls, the floor, the bed. Near Emma, by the window, a large, dark puddle covered the carpet. Felicia's gorge rose; at first she thought it was blood. But the smell in the room, the overwhelming stink of burnt wax, of a hundred candles recently extinguished, quickly advised her sensible mind otherwise. Still, she was aghast. "Em, what's happened?" She glanced around herself, afraid some man would leap from the shadows.

Emma stared at her without expression. Her feet were bare; spattered with droplets of wax. It looked as if she'd been scratched.

Felicia advanced cautiously into the room, stepping over the mess. Emma owned over a dozen Tarot packs, and they seemed to have been scattered at random around the room. Many of the cards were torn. "What the hell have you done? Em...Em?" Felicia put down the kettle and squatted beside her friend. She attempted to pull Emma into a comforting embrace, but Emma struggled away.

"Get off me!" Her voice was unnaturally gruff. She seemed to have no whites to her eyes.

Felicia felt nauseous. The smell rising from the huge puddle of congealing wax at Emma's feet was too cloying; sweet, but somehow meaty as well. Some cheap scented candles? No, surely not. How many would Emma have had to burn to produce such a pool? There were feathers stuck in it: feathers and unidentifiable dark lumps. Felicia looked away. She did not want to think about it. "Emma, where did you get to? You shouldn't have come home alone. Why are you upset? What did he say? Wasn't he interested?"

Emma blinked slowly and crawled along the wall on hands and knees. Then she squatted with her knees up by her ears, her mouth stretched into a grin. There was a dark oily crust around her nostrils, as if she'd been bleeding wax. "I went to him. I spoke...."

"What did he say?"

Emma sighed, her head rolling from side to side. "Everything. Everything that I wanted to hear."

"Then why did you walk out like that?"

"We walked out together...."

Felicia stood up, brushed down her dress. "Emma, don't lie! I saw you. You went out of that place like a hurricane! In fact, you knocked one girl's drink all over her. I thought he'd told you where to go!"

Emma threw back her head. It looked as if she was laughing, but there was no sound. "We were together," she said, in the same dull, low voice. "We are together now, and he is with me always."

"Emma...Emma!"

Emma had clasped her knees, and began to rock gently. She sang an insistent refrain: "Together, forever, together, forever...."

Outside, the moon hung low in the sky like a bag of blood, mottled with cloud.

ROSEMARY

James Lovegrove

FOR REMEMBRANCE

James Lovegrove is a firm believer in in-depth
background research, and in order to create
a convincing period feel for "Rosemary for
Remembrance" he sat down and watched a
whole episode of Dad's Army on the
television. Such a busy work schedule would
seem to leave him little time for writing, but
he is, in fact, currently working on a number
of projects including a musical, a novel, a
comic, a comic novel and possibly even a
novel comic.

Having a story ("The Landlady's Dog")
in the first volume of Narrow Houses
was an auspicious event for James in that all
the wishes he expressed in his biographical

details then have since come true. This time, therefore, he would like to be a millionaire, make it illegal for people to drive while wearing hats, and have Joan Cusack leave her home number on his answering machine.

At nine o'clock every morning, in scorching sunshine, in freezing rain, in sickness and in health, Rosemary would go down to the old brick bus shelter.

In the sixteen years since the routes had changed no buses had plied this street, but still Rosemary walked down to the shelter every day and sat or stood peering out along the long straight stretch of road, waiting for a certain green bus to draw up and a certain man to disembark. In winter she would be there in her overcoat and the odd woolen hat she had knitted for herself (it resembled nothing so much as a tea-cosy), stamping her felt boots and clapping her mittened hands. In summer, wearing sandals and a plain cotton dress, she would sit where the sunlight reached in through the doorway, inching herself in one direction along the bench as the sun rolled in the other direction across the sky. She never brought a book or a newspaper with her, occupying herself solely with the act of waiting. And after a day of waiting she would go home again. And every day for fifty-two years she did this—even after the buses stopped coming, the buses she had never once climbed aboard.

People called her mad, and Rosemary would have been the first to admit that this wasn't exactly *normal* behavior. But she was not mad. Oh no. She knew that the bus she was waiting for would come eventually, and on that bus would be the man she loved. She was perfectly clear about that. She had been perfectly clear about that for fifty-two years. And when children streaking by on their bicycles caught sight of her lurking in the shelter and screamed "Mad Rosemary! Mad Rosemary!" she would grimly shake her head (her heart was too callused to be wounded by the words of babies). No, not mad. Not unless believing a promise was a form of madness.

There had once been a line of shops on the opposite side of the road from the shelter—an ironmonger's, a greengrocer's, a bakery—but when the first big supermarket opened in the city center, the shops had died, one by one. Rosemary had watched as the Closing Down signs were replaced by For Sale signs and then by broken glass and then boards, to which children had quickly added signatures and obscene slogans. And finally, in a long deafening month of demolition, the shops had been erased altogether, and now there was just a patch of hummocky wasteland littered with oil-drums and tin cans and rotting lengths of wood and broken chunks of brick and breeze-blocks and nettles and foxgloves and the occasional poppy. From this minor apocalypse Rosemary's bus shelter had somehow been spared. Perhaps it was too small, too insignificant. Beneath the demolishers' notice.

The loss of the row of shops had brought with it a gain, for it had revealed a view of the city beyond—rooftops and factories, railyards and copper-green steeples—a view which had entranced Rosemary and which had not staled with familiarity but had over the years become a part of her inner landscape, so deeply ingrained in her imagination that she could lie in bed at night and conjure it up, perfect down to the smallest detail. Rosemary had seen the rise and fall of tower-blocks and the rise again of shopping centers and multi-story car parks and eight-screen cinemas. Over the years she had watched the skyline fluctuate like a sea in slow motion. The city was never still. It was restless and ever-changing—something that could only be perceived by the eyes of a constant, faithful observer.

And each day at dusk, when the bus had not come, Rosemary would sigh and brush the dust from her skirt and say, "Maybe tomorrow." And home she would go to the small, neat, scrupulously clean flat the council had appointed her, and there she would peck at a bird-sized meal before turning in for the night. And the last thing she said before she fell asleep every night, her private prayer, was: "Maybe tomorrow."

And so it was for fifty-two years, until the day tomorrow came.

∞

It was a gusty November evening. Tramps had used the shelter the night before, and Rosemary had to huddle in the doorway, her face out in the wind, to keep the smells of urine and cider from her nose. Black-bellied clouds flowed overhead, and there was a taste of rain in the air. Grit swirled along the pavement, and sheets of newspaper turned intermittent cartwheels in the roadway. Rosemary had endured colder weather than this, but still the wind reached fingers through her flesh and twanged her bones like harp-strings. She had never yet missed a day at the bus stop through illness, although there had been many mornings when she would rather have stayed indoors and in bed, when opening the door to her flat and walking down the stairs had been a mental as well as physical effort. One of these bitter days might see her sicken for something serious. Sometimes she could feel an ache deep within her, like iron, like knives. What if she should be laid up in bed the day the bus came? What if she failed to keep her half of the bargain? Please God, no.

She shivered painfully. Then, over in the wasteland on the other side of the road, a flutter of black caught her eye.

It was a magpie, resplendent in piebald livery. Perched on an outcrop of rubble, it was cocking its head this way and that, the sapphire glints in its plumage sparkling with each twist and turn.

Rosemary watched the magpie, waiting, listening. The bird did nothing, merely stood and eyed the unpromising sky. Then a second magpie arrived, swirling down on splayed, gust-buffeted wings, to land beside the first. The two birds ignored one another for a while on their rubble island, with just a contemptuous flicking of tails to show that either acknowledged the other's existence at all. Then one opened its beak and let out a cry—*ak-ak-ak-ak-ak!*— to which the other replied in kind, and their chatter whooped and skirled in the wind. All at once, as if on a prearranged cue, both birds took flight, allowing the wind to lift them and carry them away and away until they were no more than dots on the horizon, twin specks circling one another into oblivion.

Rosemary smiled gently to herself. Smiled knowingly. Perhaps today, after all...

Now another sound drew her attention.

It came from the west, and at first it seemed to be the noise of an airplane swooping in low to the airport that lay a mile or so out of town, beyond the ring road. Sometimes the prevailing wind blew sudden demented bursts of reverse jet-thrust clean across the city, the distant brays of gargantuan beasts.

But this wasn't an airplane. The sound was too precise, too near.

She had been fooled before, had let her heart leap with hope only to plummet when what she could have sworn was the diesel engine of a bus turned out to be that of a lorry or a taxi or a goods van. Nevertheless, bearing the magpies in mind, Rosemary listened intently, canting her head and squinting. And hoping. Dear God, hoping.

There was nothing.

Then there was something that shimmered into existence at the end of the road as though from a desert heat-haze: a green rectangle, growing larger, coming closer, gaining size and solidity.

Suddenly trembling from head to foot, from scalp to corns, Rosemary clutched the wooden frame of the doorway. Yellow teeth crawled out to bite her lower lip. Straining her old eyes, she made out small darker rectangles within the green rectangle; now what looked like a downturned drooping chrome-plated mouth; now two white eyes. It took her a moment to identify these as the windows, radiator grille and headlights of an old green bus. Now she could read the number on the front of the bus, although it wasn't any number she recognized. It looked like an eight on its side. The destination board below was blank.

And she could hardly bear to believe it, and yet there it was, plain as day, trundling toward her. The bus she had waited fifty-two years to meet. Fifty-two years! Here it was. At last. Good Lord, shouldn't she be happy? Delighted? Delirious? After all this time? Instead, she was only apprehensive.

The bus approached at a furious pace, racing the clouds. When it was less than fifty yards away and showed no sign of slowing, Rosemary was gripped by a sudden panic. What if it didn't stop? What if she had waited all these years only to have the reason for that wait whoosh past, leaving her waving and begging vainly in its wake?

She stuck out her hand.

The bus loomed.

She gesticulated.

The bus drew level with her.

She yelled, "STOP!!!"

And with a momentous groan the bus jammed on its brakes and, wheels locking, tires screaming on the tarmac, white smoke billowing out from under its wheel-arches, shuddered to a halt, lurching forward on its suspension so violently its body seemed in danger of breaking free of its chassis and skidding on down the road.

Rocking back on its axles, the bus came to rest. The tire-smoke drifted on.

Ten seconds ticked by, ten seconds in which Rosemary had time to note the long narrow poster advertising Craven "A" cigarettes and the fine film of dirt that clung to the bus's bodywork like a second skin. Then, dimly through the smeary windows, she saw the silhouette of a man rise to his feet and make his way down the aisle. He seemed to be the bus's only passenger. He exchanged a word with the driver, whom Rosemary could not make out at all, just a shadowy man-shape hunched over his steering wheel, and then with a pneumatic hiss the doors of the bus concertinaed open. The man stepped out. The doors closed behind him.

He stood before her.

"Hello, love," he said.

Rosemary hesitated, then said, "George," breathlessly, like a schoolgirl, like a giddy little schoolgirl.

George braved a smile. "How are you?"

"I'm…"

Whatever she might have been going to say was lost—mercifully, perhaps—in the growl and churn of the bus's engine starting up.

Exhaust pipe spouting black fumes, the bus lumbered off, and Rosemary looked worriedly back at George, who was still struggling to make that awkward smile fit.

"Don't panic," he said. "It'll be back."

When it occurred to her to look for the bus again, it had disappeared from view, the sound of its engine mingling with the wind and fading.

The wind dragged a strand of George's hair across his face, and Rosemary reached up to push it back into place. Her hand, brushing his skin, felt its coolness.

She said, "I hoped…I mean, I *thought* you'd look older. I don't know why. I thought you might at least have aged along with me."

"You look fine," he said. Irrelevantly, she thought.

"No, that's not it at all. It just doesn't seem fair that I should have dried up and wrinkled and my fingers have grown gnarled—I've even sprouted a mustache, for heaven's sake!—and you've stayed, well...perfect."

He touched *his* mustache self-consciously, as if by wearing it he had inadvertently insulted her. "There are certain rules...."

"I'm not blaming you," she said. "I'm happy to see you, George, honestly I am. It's been quite a wait." And with that, and a light laugh, she dismissed fifty-two patient, interminable years.

"You didn't have to wait."

"Yes, I did. What else was I supposed to do? Marry?"

"I wouldn't have minded."

"And who was I to have married?"

"There was that Blakeney chap, what was his first name? Christopher?"

"Charlie. Charlie Blakeney."

"That's the one. He was sweet on you, wasn't he? And he had money. He'd have made a good husband."

"I didn't want a good husband, George, I wanted you."

George raised an eyebrow in an immaculate arch, and the smile settled more comfortably on his face. "Oh, you're a one, Rosemary. How I've missed your sense of humor. You wouldn't believe how boring it is where—"

"No," she interrupted, cupping her hands over her

ears, "I don't want to hear about it. I don't want to know anything about it."

"I'm sorry. How about we just kiss?"

"I don't want you to kiss me either. It'd be revolting for you."

"I've so missed kissing you."

"You're looking at me. Don't you *see* me? Don't you see what I am? I'm an old woman, George! I'm old enough to be your grandmother!"

"That's not what I see. Are you cold?"

"No."

"You shivered. Shall we take cover?" He gestured at the shelter, taking her arm to guide her in. She stood her ground.

"No, not there."

"Is there somewhere else we could go?"

"How long have we got?"

"A while. Enough time."

"Oh well, in that case…There's a café at the end of the road."

"May I?" George crooked his elbow, and Rosemary slotted her hand through, and like that, like a grandmother and her grandson out for a quiet evening stroll, they set off down the road.

∞

She was eighteen and a shop-girl when George waltzed

into her life at a tea-dance at the Hotel Grand; he was twenty and a bank clerk. When he first asked her if he might have the honor, she refused, bending down and pretending to adjust the seam of her best (her only) nylons. He insisted, she refused again, at which point Maureen nudged her in the ribs, hard, and whispered in her ear that she would have to be doolally to let *this* fish slip through the net. He was devilishly handsome, Maureen added. And he was, and that was what worried Rosemary. Why should so handsome a man pick so plain a girl as she, not least when there were a dozen prettier among those lined up along the wall? Might he be doing it for a bet?

Nevertheless, she accepted George's third request. It meant something, that he had asked three times. She let him take her hand and lead her out on the floor, and as the band warbled through a glutinously slow version of "My Blue Heaven," a muted tenor saxophone carrying the melody, she let him draw her around the ballroom until they were directly below the large crystal chandelier. There, beneath that glittering manmade constellation, he asked her name and told her his, and then they moved off again into the slowly spiraling flow of dancing couples.

He danced well, but that was only to be expected for a man of his polish and sophistication. He led confidently and Rosemary was content to follow, fitting her slingback steps around those of his brogues. She found she was liking the feel of his dry hands and the rasp of his serge trousers against the front of her legs, and just when she was on the verge of enjoying herself, the dance ended, there was applause, and all the band rose to their feet to hipsway through a faster, jazzier number. George broke contact, stepped back and said, "Only slow dances for me."

"Oh?"

"You can lose yourself in a slow dance," he explained. "You can drift out of time, and it seems that the dance will never end. The fast ones just make time pass more quickly, and we're given so little time, so few years to live, it seems a shame to hurry things along."

A few moments later, Rosemary was making her way through the cavorting crowd back to Maureen, who grabbed her and said, "Well?"

"Well what?"

Maureen rolled her eyes. "Am I talking to a simpleton? Did he ask you out, Rosie? Are you going to see him again?"

"Yes," said Rosemary vaguely. "Yes, we're going to the pictures. Tomorrow evening."

It was a good year for the pictures. Rosemary was especially looking forward to *The Wizard of Oz*, about which she had heard so much, but as it hadn't yet reached this corner of the world, she was quite happy to settle for *Wuthering Heights*. George was late arriving at the cinema, and it occurred to her that she was being stood up, and just as she was steeling herself to go home, nonchalantly around the corner he sauntered. He took the Capstan from his lips, ground it out beneath his heel, then pecked her on the cheek. "Shall we go in?"

Now that he was here, she was glad he had been late. She had been hoping to miss the newsreel. He wasn't quite late enough, though, and the few minutes of Pathé they did catch left Rosemary feeling sick and dizzy as the knowledge of what was coming tightened its coils inside her. Not even the Porky Pig short could completely dispel her sense of dread. George smoked his Capstans all the way through the main feature, adding to the wreaths of cigarette mist that floated above the audience's heads into which the projector shed ghost-images—phantoms of Laurence Olivier and Merle Oberon flitting across a spectral moor—before the true images finally collided with the screen. Toward the end of the film, George took Rosemary's hand in his, enclosing her fingers in smooth dryness. She couldn't be sure through the blur of her own tears, but she had a pretty good idea that he was crying too.

He was an unusual man, she thought. He looked like a dashing gay blade—and she had met enough of those to know what a waste of time they were, mentioning no names, Charlie Blakeney—but he had an intelligence and a subtlety, an intrinsic shyness, an inner smile, that you couldn't help but love. Love? Had she just thought the word "love"? Silly thing! Warm to. That was what she had meant to think. Or like. You couldn't help but like. Yes.

They walked out into the August evening. The entire western sky from zenith to horizon was filled with milky orange light, as though reflecting the glare of a vast furnace burning over the edge of the world.

"I must be getting home," she said. "My parents…"

"I understand. May I see you again?"

She laughed in surprise. "Of course."

"This weekend," he said. "What are you doing this weekend?"

∞

There was not much life in the café. An indolent chef tended chips in a bubbling deep-fat fryer, every so often giving the basket handle a good shake, the peak of his culinary expertise. A sleepy waitress lounged on the counter watching a game show on a black-and-white portable. The only other patrons apart from Rosemary and George were a pair of gray-headed old men stirring their tea and studying the sports pages. Even the flies circling around the ultraviolet light on the wall seemed in no hurry to close in and meet their deaths on the electrified grille.

"Yes?" the waitress called over to them as they settled down at a table.

"Nothing for me," George told Rosemary.

"Just coffee for me," Rosemary told the waitress, who repeated the order sardonically (it was hardly stretching her service skills to fetch a cup of coffee). "I shouldn't," Rosemary confided to George, "what with my bladder, but then this is a special occasion."

George was carefully laying the salt and pepper cruets, the sugar cellar and the plastic tomato-shaped ketchup dispenser to one side of the table so that there was nothing except a couple of feet of checked, chipped Formica between him and Rosemary. She in turn removed her tea-cosy hat and her mittens.

"It's not exactly a Joe Lyons," he remarked.

"There aren't any of those any more." She lowered her voice. "This is the best we can do."

"I know. I have been keeping up on current events."

"Can you do that?"

"I thought you didn't want to know anything about it," he said with a teasing grin. "I distinctly heard you say…"

"Yes, sorry, you're right. But you can't blame me for being curious. I'll find out soon enough, won't I?"

He nodded somewhat sadly. "Don't get your hopes up."

"We'll be together, though, won't we?"

"Yes," he said.

"That's all I've ever wanted."

"It can get frightfully dull."

"Then we'll liven it up."

"There are rules."

"You make it sound so stuffy. That's not like you."

"I'm simply preparing you. I don't want you to be disappointed."

The waitress slapped the coffee down on the table and looked at George. He shrugged. "Sorry, I've no money on me."

Rosemary fumbled for her purse.

The arrangement was that they should meet near her house that Sunday, not actually *at* her house, because she didn't think she was ready for him to meet her parents quite yet, but by the railings of the church a couple of streets away, and then they would take the bus out into the countryside. She was to prepare a picnic, he would bring a rug and something to drink. Her mother was wise to the game, but for her father's sake they pretended that Rosemary was going on a jaunt with Maureen, and Maureen helped cement the alibi by coming round the evening before on the pretext of making plans. Maureen giggled a lot and dropped the unsubtlest hints, but Rosemary's father did not cotton on; at least, he gave no indication of cottoning on. He merely told the girls to enjoy themselves, be careful and watch out for strange men.

This sent Maureen into gales of laughter. Rosemary was not amused.

George was late, naturally. He didn't seem to be aware that he had no sense of time. He wore a watch and wound it regularly, but it was no more than a sartorial adornment, like a tie or a collar-stud. Rosemary didn't criticize. It was one of those faults that could only be corrected with constant dedicated attention, in months, not minutes. And she didn't want him to think her a nag. She merely said, "We've missed one bus already."

"Then we shall catch the next one," he replied.

They walked to the bus shelter and waited for the noon bus. The day was hectic but warm, and Rosemary regretted her tweed skirt. They talked idly, and Rosemary made him laugh with a story about a difficult customer she had had yesterday, a woman who was clearly a size 14 but who insisted on trying out nothing larger than a 10 and then complaining that it was too tight around the bust and waist. When Rosemary had had the temerity to suggest a garment with a little more room in it perhaps, the woman had rounded on her and given her a good ear-bashing. *Are you calling me fat?* she had roared. *Are you saying I'm blooming well fat?* Rosemary could laugh about it now, but at the time she had been quite upset.

"The perils of honesty," George said.

The bus came, and George bought two day-return

tickets to a small village ten miles west of town. Half an hour later they alighted at the village green and stood there swaying slightly beneath the oppressive weight of the sun. Ducks preened themselves beside a standing pond and from somewhere there came the sound of a hammer striking an anvil, tolling like a bell.

George spent a moment or two in consultation of his map, then shouldered the knapsack that contained the picnic and two bottles of stout, pointed to the hills, said, "This-a-way," and set off at a brisk pace. Cradling the rolled-up rug in her arms, Rosemary followed.

They soon left the village behind, taking a bridlepath until it met a chalk track that curved upward into the flank of a hill, then following this. Blackberry bushes sprung about on either side, their fruit mellow red and tightly budded. Trees drooped their branches in the young couple's hair, and in the cool recesses of shade, flies and gnats swarmed. A dragonfly kept pace with them for a while, supporting itself on a blur of air, until some urgent errand saw it dart away with a wink of electric blue. George took a clinical delight in each and every manifestation of nature, even a spongy cluster of horse droppings; it made a welcome change from the vicissitudes of life behind the teller's window, he claimed. Rosemary agreed. She loved the smell of fresh air.

She didn't want to appear weak, and she kept pace with him as best she could, but eventually, when they were about halfway up the hill, she had to beg for a rest. George glanced around and decided this was as good a place as any to stop for lunch, and they laid out the rug on a sloping patch of grass beside the track and ate potted-beef-and-tomato sandwiches and apples and shared a bar of softening chocolate with the entire valley spread out at their feet. George uncapped the beer bottles with a rock, and Rosemary drank just enough of hers so that she wouldn't get tipsy and, when George wasn't looking, poured the rest away.

Gazing across to the next ridge of hills, pale with distance, lilac in the haze, she suddenly said, "Do you think we're really going to go to war?"

"I think there's a pretty good chance," said George after a moment's thought, "now that Mr. Hitler and Uncle Joe have joined hands. It all depends. You can't predict these things. We've sworn to protect Poland and that's good. It's important that we show that we're prepared to fight. If we don't do that, we might as well let them walk in and hoist the Swastika over Buckingham Palace tomorrow."

"Can't we talk with them? Bargain? Negotiate?"

"We can. We have. We should keep on doing so, and we should hope for the best but prepare for the worst."

"But so many people will die."

"Come on, old girl," said George, leaping lithely to his feet and extending a hand. "Let's not think about that. Not today. Let's think about it when it happens."

They gathered up their things and began the slow steady climb to the top.

For the next four weeks, and then even after war was declared, they spent their Sundays this way, taking the bus to some remote unpopulated area and losing themselves in the vastness of the land. They would find trails and byways not marked on the map and follow them to their conclusion, which was more often than not a dead end or a gate leading to farmland and signposted *KEEP OUT*. They had a none-too-perilous encounter with an angry bull, and passed one whole afternoon lying in long grass watching a plowman and team reduce a fallow field to a corded rectangle of dark brown earth. Conversation as they walked was unforced and easy, and when they were out of breath or had run out of things to say, they carried on in companionable silence, the subtle background sigh of the countryside filling in the vacancies. It never rained on their Sundays.

The inevitable meeting with Rosemary's parents went well. George and her father discovered a mutual love of Will Hay, and one whole course of the meal was taken up with improvised quickfire music-hall repartee which left the men red-faced and helpless with laughter and Rosemary and her mother nonplussed but quietly smiling. After George went home, her father's seal of approval was characteristically terse: "Nice fellow. You can bring him round again."

George's parents lived in London, so the obligation

did not have to be reciprocated, at least not yet, and Rosemary was relieved. She doubted she would have made as good an impression on George's parents as he had on hers, for she behaved awkwardly in the company of strangers, and she was hardly the sort of girl she imagined George's mother had in mind for her son. She had few illusions about that. Looking in the mirror at her little nose and drab brown eyes and narrow lips, Rosemary wondered again what George had first seen in her at the tea-dance, what had drawn him—heart in mouth, or so he claimed—all the way across the ballroom floor. What *was* it? What quality did she possess that was invisible to everyone except him? Was he playing some sort of game with her? She knew there was a certain kind of man who liked to string a dull plain girl along while romancing a whole chorus-line of glittering beauties behind her back, returning to the dull plain girl whenever one of the glittering beauties rejected him because the dull plain girl was always there, the dull plain girl would inevitably be waiting for him; but they were a vicious breed, such men, a terrier breed. Charlie Blakeney was one. Although he had taken Rosemary out on a number of occasions and had once asked her to marry him, Maureen had told her that he kept a gaggle of dolly-birds on the go, flitting from one to the next. Besides, he was flash with his money, and flash men only wanted one thing from a girl.

George was not like that at all. He would never betray her like that.

∞

She picked the coffee up and sipped at it loudly. George stared at her, just curiously, with a slight flicker of amusement in his eyes. There were aimless laughs and shouts from the portable television. She set the coffee down again, not sure she had even tasted it.

At last she said, "Does it hurt?"

"Does it still hurt?"

"No, I mean in general. When it happens. Does it hurt everyone?"

George sighed. "To be honest, love, I wouldn't know. I know it hurt *me*, but that's because it took about a day, after the wound, a day lying in a bed in the field hospital with this heaviness in my chest, this feeling of wrongness, and blood filling my throat, and…"

She held up her hands, wincing. "Please. I can't bear it."

"I thought you wanted to know."

"In general. No details."

"It's different from person to person, that's all I can tell you. Some slip peacefully away, no struggle. Others linger."

"I'm prepared for it to hurt. I don't mind a bit of

pain. Especially if I know there's an end to it and something beyond."

"There's an end," George assured her.

Night had drifted down outside, and Rosemary caught sight of herself in the window, and the other diners and the waitress and the chef, all pale ghosts in the darkened glass. Of George in that black mirror-café there was no sign, yet there he was sitting right in front of her. She wondered if anyone else would notice that her companion cast no reflection.

There were all kinds of pain.

There was pain the day George volunteered. He came round to her house as soon as the bank closed, and even as she stood at the top of the stairs while her mother opened the front door, Rosemary knew, because his face was calm, the self-control more in evidence than ever before, and because a recruiting office had opened up on the high street yesterday afternoon. Before he could even say, "Hello, Mrs. Thomas," to her mother, Rosemary had turned and fled to her room.

His knock was quiet and polite. He had never been in her bedroom before. "Love? Love?" He opened the door softly. He looked for her on the bed but she wasn't there: She was standing at the window with her arms folded and her head held high, gazing out at the rows of roofs that rolled away and grew fainter in the thick autumnal twilight. He came to her and took her waist in his hands and turned her gently round to face him. He was surprised to see tears. He simply had not prepared himself for tears. He reached for his handkerchief, this being the appropriate thing to do, and she let him dab it around her eyes. If it made him feel better.

"I can't explain it," he said, leading her to the bed and sitting her down and sitting himself down beside her. "I can't expect you to understand."

"Why? Am I stupid or something?"

"It had to be done." Not *I had to do it*. It had to be done. "I saw that poster in the window, and it was as if it was calling out to me."

"But I thought you were dead against it, all the fighting and such. I thought you said we should negotiate."

"Of course, but it's too late for that now. It's been tried and it's failed. I said we should hope for the best but prepare for the worst, and the worst has happened. I can't simply ignore it now. I have to show how I feel."

"So much of being a man is about show," she said, half to herself. She thought she hated him then, but that hate was just a darker love.

"It would have happened anyway," he said, as if this was some compensation. "This war isn't going to be won overnight, and sooner or later they're going to have to start calling people up. I'm young, I'm healthy, and being a bank clerk is hardly vital to the nation's interests. It would only have been a matter of time."

"So when do you leave?"

"A fortnight tomorrow."

"Where are you going?"

"A camp down on the coast. After that, who knows? But I'll write to you. I'll write every day. If that's what you want."

It wasn't what she wanted but, all things being equal, it was the best she could hope for.

And there was pain that final fortnight: a long drawn-out ache of loss that tainted everything Rosemary did, made her dreary work days drearier, fragmented her sleep into short naps that lengthened the night, and, on evenings out with George, required her to wear a mask of jollity from beginning to end. He for his part gamely struggled to be himself and keep her amused at all times, and she smiled whenever possible, and both of them avoided the subject that they had to avoid, but the anticipation of their parting lurked behind their laughter, dogged them along the gas-lit streets, trailed them into restaurants and clubs, and squatted at their feet sighing quietly throughout their goodnight kisses on the front doorstep of her parents' house. It was as if the sadness to come had cast its shadow back through time, and the closer they came to the day George had to leave, the deeper and broader and thicker that shadow grew.

And there was a special kind of pain the very last Sunday they shared together.

As usual—even after only a couple of months, the habit had worn itself comfortably smooth into their lives—they packed up a picnic and took the bus out into the countryside, to walk and lose and find themselves. It was the first day that really felt like autumn. The air smelled of brown leaves and bonfires and had that cold tang that would not really disappear now until spring. Trees slumped (the effort of summer having finally taken its toll) and, with the harvest in, the fields were turned and empty and expectant. Rooks like priests and inland gulls like white-coated doctors ministered to the broken earth, dragging out worms and grubs. In two days' time, George would be on the train to the coast.

They picked their way through the subsiding landscape, he with his knapsack, she with her rolled blanket. They found a spot to eat their picnic on the wrinkled slope of a hill. Rosemary drank all of her bottle of stout, pouring none away, and then said, "You will be careful, won't you? When you get out there."

"Careful? As in dodge bullets? As in hold back while everyone else is charging forward? I can't be careful, old girl, I can only be lucky."

"You sound brave."

"I'm scared helpless. I don't want to die any more than you do."

"Then don't die!" It seemed a ridiculous thing to say, but through a mist of sorrow and anger and beer, it made perfect sense to her. You could choose not to die in the same way that you could choose not to live. It wasn't a question of bullets or grenades or shells or gas. It was a question of belief.

"I'll try," George said, taking her hand and patting it. "I'll do my level best. When it's over, I'll come back for you, and we'll…"

"Yes?"

That was when he would have asked her to marry him, on that cool green hillside on that brisk afternoon. Why didn't he? What stopped him? What thought came to him holding a grim finger to its lips? A foreboding? Fear of tempting providence? Or was it merely the fear of making a promise he did not know for certain that he could keep? That was most likely it. And when he turned away, Rosemary could tell what he was thinking. She had seen it in his face. He was thinking, *Well, there'll be time enough for that later, when I come back and there's a future again. There'll be time for plans and schemes and dreams. There'll always be time.*

"We'll see," is what he said eventually.

It was then that a magpie swooped down, landing with uncharacteristic boldness less than five yards away from them, and stood gazing at them both with eyes that were filled with deep dark glittering avian knowledge, and then it seemed to come to a decision and it opened its beak and it cried: *ak-ak-ak-ak-ak! ak-ak! ak-ak-ak-ak-ak!*

And Rosemary, remembering something her mother used to say when she was little, that the chattering of magpies signified a death, felt a coldness steal over her.

And there was a unique pain in the bus shelter that night.

The city was silent and dark, and inside the bus shelter was darker still, and on the slats of the wooden bench, awkwardly, Rosemary gave herself to George.

During the clumsy overtures, as they shuffled into position, clothing rustling about them, he asked her in a choked whisper if it was safe, wasn't there some risk if he…? And she hushed him and said it was safe, she had seen to it that it was safe, perfectly safe.

It was only the whitest shade of a lie. Maureen, being well versed in such matters, had given Rosemary sound advice on choosing her moment, striking when the iron was, so to speak, cooling, and Rosemary had listened carefully because she wanted nothing more to come from this moment than a memory.

And the memory was made of this: of George's quickening gasps, of his fingernails digging through her jersey into the flesh of her back, of the terror of being caught, of his final cry, of her relief as she climbed off that no one had chanced along. But above all the memory was of the initial exquisite lancing between her legs. That pain fixed the memory into place like a pin through a butterfly.

And there was more pain when it came to accompanying George on the bus down to the railway station and saying goodbye to him there, but this pain was mitigated by the fact that she had been preparing herself for it for over a fortnight. It was like the pain of an injection, worse in the anticipation than the execution. Surrounded by clouds of steam and other couples parting, it was also a pain shared and therefore lessened. The two of them simply clutched one another, just as the other couples were clutching, and their kisses were no different from anyone else's kisses, just a pair of lips pressing a pair of lips, and then the train's whistle screeched impatiently and George clambered up into the carriage and had to go. He waved to her all the way down the platform. He waved until he dissolved in steam.

∞

"We're closing now," the waitress informed them without a hint of apology. "You'd better be off." The two old men with the sports pages, being regulars here, knowing the form, had left a few minutes ago.

"It's all right," said Rosemary. "We were just going anyway. We've got a bus to catch."

George rose to help her to her feet. She did not refuse his hand. Her hip bones were a little stiff.

"Come on," said the waitress, holding open the door. "I haven't got all bloody evening."

"You're frightfully rude," George said, and the waitress puckered her mouth as though she had just swallowed a sour grape.

"Out," she said.

They went out into the night, and just as the waitress was about to close the door behind them George turned and said, "January, eleven years from now."

The waitress scowled. "You what?"

"Ovarian cancer."

The waitress's expression brightened, and she returned a contemptuous grin. "Wrong. Pisces, *actually*."

George just smiled, and it was only after he and Rosemary had walked well out of earshot that she asked him what all that had been about.

"She won't even think about it until the time comes, and then she'll remember," he said. He looked satisfied.

"Oh," said Rosemary, understanding. "Wasn't that a bit mean? I must say I don't recall you ever being cruel like that. Not even to be kind."

"I can't help having changed, love. Just the waiting itself wore me down. The boredom was enough to turn the sweetest nature bitter. From time to time, I screamed for release."

"And isn't there release?"

"Only for those allowed to take it."

"And weren't you?"

George halted to look at her. "Don't you see?"

She shook her head.

"I made a promise." He said it as if it were the most obvious thing in the world. "I made a promise to you. And you held me to it by waiting."

"Oh my God." Her hand flew to her whiskery mouth.

"By waiting, all day, every day," he said with a confirming nod.

"Oh my good God, I never thought...It never occurred...I never realized...."

"Of course you didn't, old girl."

"Fifty-two years," she said with a sigh, a wisp of breath in the wind. "If I'd known..."

"I don't hold it against you. If I hold it against anyone, it's whoever made up the rules of the game and then refused to explain them to us."

"How can I say I'm sorry?"

"Don't."

"All that time..."

"It wasn't so bad," he said, in the same airy dismissive tone that she had said, *It's been quite a wait*, just after he had stepped off the bus. "For either of us. Was it?"

"But at least I had a life."

"Did you?" he asked matter-of-factly. "Did you really? How different was your existence from mine? Not much. You weren't living, you were just going through the motions, that's all. At least I didn't have to pretend that."

"I never realized," she said again.

"That's the tragedy of it," he said. "Neither of us did."

His letters from the camp were filled with amusing little episodes that happened during training, jokes at the expense of the RSM, thumbnail sketches of his comrades and cheerfully blithe descriptions of the privations and hardships of military life—cleaning the latrines on a frosty morning, the greasy food doled out in the mess, being shouted at from dawn till dusk, and the sheer daily fatigue that, come bedtime, made a camp bed seem as soft and welcoming as a king-sized divan. He always signed off on an optimistic note. "Everyone keeps telling us to keep our chins up," one letter ended, "but I know you'll be doing that anyway, old girl, so all I can say is keep yours higher than the rest of them. I remain, yours affectionately, G."

She tried, for his sake, and her mother and Maureen rallied round. Her mother kept her busy around the house. She had taken on piecework and engaged Rosemary to spend a couple of hours each evening mending trousers and reattaching buttons, their needles darting while her father read the paper by the sighing grate. Maureen, meanwhile, became a surrogate George, dragging Rosemary out to the pictures and tea-dances. Her father, for his part, was not unaware of the situation and did his best to keep his daughter entertained at mealtimes with solo Will Hay routines, although these, being so closely associated in her mind with George, caused her as much pain as they did pleasure. And she wrote to George almost daily, matching him anecdote for anecdote, keeping him informed about funny and finicky customers, giving small critiques of films she had seen but he could not see because there were no cinemas near the camp, and trying to show him that she was getting on with her life as normal, as he wanted, while still making it clear that things were not the same. The closest she came to saying she missed him was mentioning their Sunday day-trips, which was the one role of George's that Maureen could not and would not fill. "When you come back," she wrote, "we shall each buy a bicycle or perhaps even a tandem(!) and pedal our way further and further out of town. We shall form our very own cycling club and we shall go when we like and where we like."

In George's last letter from the camp the levity was still there, but caged between the lines there was agony and, as the letter progressed, the agony seeped out through the bars.

"Basic training is complete," he wrote, "and I am now a fully-fledged Private in the King's army, or so I am told, although I don't feel any different, I just feel like a bank teller in a uniform with big boots and a gun. Nothing else here has changed, either. The food is still awful and the weather is still rotten, and the Sergeant Major is still both. The wind from the sea smells foul, like bad fish. I long for the still sweet air of home. (Ho ho!)

"But here's the bad news, old girl. (But as you turned nineteen last week, perhaps I should be calling you 'young woman' instead!) We've been given our marching orders. It's time to up sticks and go. Britannia calls, England expects and all that. We'll be shipping out in four days' time. What do you know? Action! So soon! As for where we're going, I'm not at liberty to say, *malheureusement*, but rest assured I will be keeping an eye out for myself. I won't forget what you said about not dying. Why would I be so stupid as to get myself killed when there's so much to live for?

"In the past I haven't promised you anything, Rosemary. This is not because I had no promises to make but because I did not want to make a promise I couldn't keep. I realize now that this was a mistake, now when it is almost—but still not!—too late to rectify the error. I realize that my notion of honesty was misguided. I believed that if I said anything to you that contained the smallest hint of a lie, it would somehow hurt you, damage you in some way, that you were a tender fragile creature to whom it was better to say nothing than say something untrue. But little lies are necessary, useful things, as necessary and useful as— if you pardon the slightly crude analogy—manure is to a rose.

"It doesn't matter if a promise is made that cannot be kept as long as it is made with *every intention* of being kept. I particularly regret not promising that I would come home safe and well, and I make that promise now, here, on paper, in black ink. Lacking the witness of your own eyes, I will call on God instead.

"I promise that I will come home. I promise that I will come home to you, Rosemary. Come what may, I will be back. One day, when the fighting's done, I will take the bus from the station and you will meet me at the shelter where you gave me my first glimpse of the truth about necessary lies, and there I will make another promise to you, the promise I should have made on that hillside that cold Sunday afternoon, that we will be together. Always.

"I don't know when you'll get another letter from me again, love. I will write, but I can't vouch for the postal system. It's bad enough here. Imagine what it's going to be like abroad.

"My fondest regards to your parents and to Maureen—and to you, old girl, the promise.

"Yours affectionately, G."

The next letter she received, three months later, was not from George but from his mother. It began:

"Dear Rosemary Thomas,

"As a precaution, my son gave me your address before he left, and although we have not met, I am not ignorant of the regard in which he held you, and so I feel it is only right and fair that you, after his close relatives, should be the first to be informed…"

They were near the bus shelter now. From a distance, with its tiled roof and sturdy walls, it looked like a tiny house, a single tiny house at the side of an uncommonly wide road; or perhaps, amid all that wasteground desolation, a solitary mausoleum in a gone-to-seed graveyard.

The wind pounded at their backs, urging them on, but George was in no hurry and Rosemary was certainly in no hurry. These were her last few steps on this earth. She savored them. She savored the taste of the city air in her mouth, the sight of the city's gray-sea skyline, the sound of the wind batting at her ears, the slap of her coat-tails around her legs, the pressure of George's hand on her arm, the sensation of her body still working, her muscles still propelling her, her bones still obliging, her heart still thumping, the blood still rolling through her veins and the breath still heaving in and out of her lungs. She cherished the little life left to her, the last possession she had to her name, even as she prepared herself to surrender it up.

At the entrance, they stopped.

"What do we do?" she asked.

"We just sit."

"Will it be long?"

"Not long."

The wino reek inside wasn't so bad, once she had resigned herself to it. George seemed not to notice. Used, discarded containers of one kind or another littered the floor: crisp packets, condoms, fish-and-chip newspaper. Crudely scrawled messages of love and hate on the walls, with their numerals and misspellings, were so many incomprehensible hieroglyphs.

George heard the bus first, when the rumble of its engine was still beyond the threshold of normal human hearing. He put his cool dry hand on Rosemary's.

"Here it comes," he said. "Don't be scared."

"I'm not scared."

"Good girl."

At that moment she felt a slight discomfort, a little like a twinge of trapped wind, but it quickly passed, and then she could hear it too: the distant grind of cogs meshing, teeth gnashing, gears and gear-shafts, wheels turning, coming closer, combustion, a thousand tiny fiery detonations per second, approaching, the low steady thrum of rubber tread on tarmac, the wheeze of exhaust, getting nearer now and nearer and nearer still, the churning engine, the thunderous engine, growing in size and might until the noise drowned all others and was the only noise in the whole world, an immense, engulfing roar of motion and travel and revolution and repetition, and at last the bus appeared in the entrance to the shelter, sliding across the doorway and filling the frame with dusty green and rectangles of glass, and came to a halt with a hiss of hydraulics and a sigh of pneumatics.

"Now," said George kindly. "Are you ready?"

"Of course."

They stood up and stepped out.

Clouds of fumes purled around the bus, and great shudders passed through it, the pulsing vibrations of the idling motor, rattling the windows.

The doors concertinaed open. Rosemary peered up at the dark driver within. He was smiling whitely, brightly.

"All aboard," he said.

She turned to George. "There's no pain," she said. This was almost a revelation. "There's no pain at all."

BETRAYALS

ursula k. le guin

Ursula Le Guin (née Kroeber) was born in 1929 in Berkeley, California, to anthropologist-father Alfred and writer-mother Theodora, author of I s h i . She went to Radcliffe College and did graduate work at Columbia University before marrying Charles Le Guin, a historian, in Paris in 1953. They have lived in Portland, Oregon, since 1958 and have three children and two grandchildren.

Le Guin has written for as long as she can remember, starting with poetry and, in the 1960s, moving on to short stories and novels. She continues to write both poetry and prose and in a number of fields, including realistic fiction, science fiction, fantasy, young children's books, young adults' books, screenplays, essays, verbal texts for musicians, and voice texts for performance or recording. Her current tally is more than eighty short stories—many collected into four volumes—plus two collections of essays, eight books for children, five volumes of poetry and sixteen novels. Among the honors her writing has received are a National Book Award, five Hugo Awards, four Nebula Awards, the Kafka Award, a Pushcart Prize and the Howard Vursell Award of the American Academy of Arts and Letters.

Her occupations, she says, are writing, reading, housework and teaching. She is a feminist, a conservationist, and a Western American, passionately involved with West Coast literature, landscape, and life.

When asked about superstitions, Le Guin had this to say: "The characters of this story are trying to follow what we call a superstition, which I borrowed for them from India.

"After the years of youth and the years as householders and citizens, the Hindus and the Buddhists tell us, people do well to turn their back on work, family and all relationships and material things, choosing to live alone in poverty and to trust the charity of strangers as they turn their attention from this life to the next.

"The root of the word 'superstition' means something left behind, a remnant...of belief, I suppose. Though this seems merely a custom, it is, in fact, a remnant of a religious attitude that we long ago turned away from: the belief that life may be lived in a sacred manner; that old age has its own important work, needful to society; and that it takes your whole life to make your soul."

"On the planet O there has not been a war for five thousand years," she read, "and on Gethen there has never been a war." She stopped reading, to rest her eyes and because she was trying to train herself to read slowly, not gobble words down in chunks the way Tikuli gulped his food. "There has never been a war." In her mind the words stood clear and bright, surrounded by and sinking into an infinite, dark, soft incredulity. What would that world be, a world without war? It would be the real world. Peace was the true life, the life of working and learning and bringing up children to work and learn. War, which devoured work, learning, and children, was the denial of reality. But my people, she thought, know only how to deny. Born in the dark shadow of power, we set peace outside our world, a guiding and unattainable light. All we know to do is fight. Any peace one of us can make in our life is only a denial that the war is going on, a shadow of the shadow, a doubled unbelief.

So as the cloud-shadows swept over the marshes and with the page of the book open on her lap, she sighed and closed her eyes, thinking, "I am a liar." Then she opened her eyes and read more about the other worlds, the far realities.

Tikuli, sleeping curled up around his tail in the weak sunshine, sighed as if imitating her, and scratched a dreamflea. Gubu was out in the reeds, hunting; she could not see him, but now and then the plume of a reed quivered, and once a marsh hen flew up cackling in indignation.

Absorbed in a description of the peculiar social customs of the Ithsh, she did not see Wada till he was at the gate, letting himself in. "Oh, you're here already," she said, taken by surprise and feeling unready, incompetent, old, as she always felt with other people. Alone, she only felt old when she was overtired or ill. Maybe living alone was the right thing for her after all. "Come on in," she said, getting up and dropping her book and picking it up and feeling her back hair where the knot was coming loose. "I'll just get my bag and be off, then."

"No hurry," the young man said in his soft voice. "Eyid won't be here for a while yet."

Very kind of you to tell me I don't have to hurry to leave my own house, Yoss thought, but said nothing, obedient to the insufferable, adorable selfishness of the young. She went in and got her shopping bag, reknotted her hair, tied a scarf over it, and came out onto the little open porch. Wada had sat down in her chair; he jumped up when she came out. He was a shy boy, the gentler, she thought, of the two lovers. "Have fun," she said with a smile, knowing she embarrassed him. "I'll be back in a couple of hours—before sunset." She went down to her gate, let herself out, and set off the way Wada had come, along the path up to the winding wooden causeway across the marshes to the village.

She would not meet Eyid on the way. Eyid would be coming from the north on one of the bog-paths, having left the village at a different time and in a different direction than Wada, so that nobody would notice that for a few hours every week or so the two young people were gone at the same time. They were madly in love, had been in love for three years, and would have been long since married if Wada's father and Eyid's father's brother hadn't quarreled over a piece of property and set up a feud between the families that had so far stopped short of bloodshed, but put marriage out of the question. The land was valuable; the families, though poor, each aspired to be leaders of the village. Nothing would heal the grudge. The whole village took sides in it. Eyid and Wada had nowhere to go, no skills to keep them from the terrible poverty of the cities, no family in another village who might take them in. Their passion was trapped in the hatred of the old. Yoss had come on them, a year ago now, in each other's arms on the cold ground of an island in the marshes—blundering onto them as once she had blundered onto a pair of fendeer fawns holding utterly still in the nest of grass where the doe had left them. This pair had been as frightened, as beautiful and vulnerable as the fawns, and they had begged her "not to tell" so humbly, what could she do? They were shivering with cold, Eyid's bare legs were muddy, they clung to each other like children. "Come to my house," she said sternly. "For mercy sake!" She stalked off.

Timidly, they followed her. "I will be back in an hour or so," she said when she had got them indoors, into her one room with the bed-alcove right beside the chimney. "Don't get things muddy!"

That time she had roamed the paths keeping watch, in case anybody was out looking for them. Nowadays she mostly went in to the village while "the fawns" were in her house having their sweet hour.

They were too ignorant to think of any way to thank her; Wada, a peat-cutter, might have supplied her fire without anyone being suspicious, but they never left so much as a flower, though Eyid always made up the bed very neat and tight. Perhaps indeed they were not very grateful. Why should they be? She gave them only what was their due: a bed, an hour of pleasure, a moment of peace. It wasn't their fault, or her virtue, that nobody else would give it to them.

Her errand today took her into Eyid's uncle's shop. He was the village sweets-seller. All the holy abstinence she had intended when she came here two years ago, the single bowl of unflavored grain, the draft of pure water, she'd given that up in no time. She got diarrhea from a cereal diet, and the water of the marshes was undrinkable. She ate every fresh vegetable she could buy or grow, drank wine or bottled water or fruit juice from the city, and kept a large supply of sweets—dried fruits, raisins, sugar-brittle, even the cakes Eyid's mother and aunts made, fat disks with a nutmeat squashed on to the top, dry, greasy, tasteless, but curiously satisfying. She bought a bagful of them and a brown wheel of sugar-brittle, and gossiped with the aunts, dark, darting-eyed little women who had been at old Iad's wake last night and wanted to talk about it. "Those people"—Wada's family, indicated by a glance, a shrug, a sneer—had misbehaved as usual, got drunk, picked fights, boasted, got sick and vomited all over the place, greedy upstart louts that they were. When she stopped by the newsstand to pick up a paper (another vow long since broken; she had been going to read only the *Arkamye* and learn it by heart), Wada's mother was there, and she heard how "those people"— Eyid's family—had boasted and picked fights and vomited all over the place at the wake last night. She did not merely hear; she asked for details, she drew the gossip out; she loved it.

What a fool, she thought, starting slowly home on the causeway path, what a fool I was to think I could ever drink water and be silent! I'll never, never be able to let anything go, anything at all. I'll never be free, never be worthy of freedom. Even old age can't make me let go. Even losing Safnan can't make me let go.

Before the Five Armies they stood.

Holding up his sword, Enar said to Kamye:

My hands hold your death, my Lord!

Kamye answered: Brother, it is your death they hold.

She knew those lines, anyway. Everybody knew those lines. And so then Enar dropped his sword, because he was a hero and a holy man, the Lord's younger brother. But I can't drop my death. I'll hold it to the end, I'll cherish it, hate it, eat it, drink it, listen to it, give it my bed, mourn it, everything but let it go.

She looked up out of her thoughts into the afternoon on the marshes: the sky a cloudless misty blue, reflected in one distant curving channel of water, and the sunlight golden over the dun levels of the reedbeds and among the stems of the reeds. The rare, soft west wind blew. A perfect day. The beauty of the world, the beauty of the world! A sword in my hand, turned against me. Why do you make beauty to kill us, my Lord?

She trudged on, pulling her headscarf tighter with a little dissatisfied jerk. At this rate she would soon be wandering around the marshes shouting aloud, like Abberkam.

And there he was, the thought had summoned him: lurching along in the blind way he had as if he never saw anything but his thoughts, striking at the roadway with his big stick as if he was killing a snake. Long gray hair blowing around his face. He wasn't shouting, he only shouted at night, and not for a long time now, but he was talking, she saw his lips move; then he saw her and shut his mouth and drew himself into himself, wary as a wild animal. They approached each other on the narrow causeway path, not another human being in all the wilderness of reeds and mud and water and wind.

"Good evening, Chief Abberkam," Yoss said when there were only a few paces between them. What a big man he was, she never could believe how tall and broad and heavy he was till she saw him again, his dark skin still smooth as a young man's but his head stooped and his hair gray and wild. A huge hook nose and the mistrustful, unseeing eyes. He muttered some kind of greeting, hardly slowing his gait.

The mischief was in Yoss today, she was sick of her own thoughts and sorrows and shortcomings. She stopped, so that he had to stop or else run right into her, and said, "Were you at the wake last night?"

He stared down at her; she felt he was getting her into focus, or part of her; he finally said, "Wake?"

"They buried old Iad last night. All the men got drunk, and it's a mercy the feud didn't finally break out."

"Feud?" he repeated in his deep voice.

Maybe he wasn't capable of focusing any more, but she was driven to talk to him, to get through to him. "The Dewis and Kamanners. They're quarreling over that arable island just north of the village. And the two poor children, they want to get married, and their fathers threaten to kill them if they look at each other. What idiocy! Why don't they divide the island and marry the children and let their children share it? It'll come to blood one of these days, I think."

"To blood," the Chief said, repeating again like a half-wit, and then slowly, in that great, deep voice, the voice she had heard crying out in agony in the night across the marshes, "Those men. Those shopkeepers. They won't kill. But they won't share. If it's property, they won't let go. Never."

She saw again the lifted sword.

"Ah," she said with a shudder. "So then the children must wait...till the old people die...."

"Too late," he said. His eyes met hers for one instant, keen and strange; then he pushed back his hair impatiently, growled something by way of goodbye, and started on so abruptly that she almost crouched aside to make way for him. That's how a chief walks, she thought wryly, as she went on. Big, wide, taking up space, stamping the earth down. And this, this is how an old woman walks, narrowly, narrowly.

There was a strange noise behind her—gunshots, she thought, for old city usages stay in the nerves— and she turned sharp round. Abberkam had stopped and was coughing explosively, tremendously, his big frame hunched around the spasms that nearly wracked him off his feet. Yoss knew that kind of coughing. The Ekumen was supposed to have medicine for it, but she'd left the city before any of it came. She went to Abberkam, and when the paroxysm was over and he stood gasping, gray-faced, she said, "That's berlot: Are you getting over it or are you getting it?"

He shook his head.

She waited.

While she waited she thought, what do I care if he's

sick or not? Does he care? He came here to die. I heard him howling out on the marshes in the dark, last winter. Howling in agony. Eaten out with shame, like a man with cancer who's been all eaten out by the cancer but can't die.

"It's all right," he said, hoarse, angry, wanting her only to get away from him; and she nodded and went on her way. Let him die. How could he want to live knowing what he'd lost, his power, his honor, and what he'd done? Lied, betrayed his supporters, embezzled. The perfect politician. Big Chief Abberkam, hero of the World Party, who had destroyed the World Party by his greed and folly.

She glanced back once. He was moving very slowly or perhaps had stopped, she was not sure. She went on, taking the right-hand way where the causeway forked, going down onto the bog-path that led to her little house.

Five hundred years ago these marshlands had been a vast, rich agricultural valley, one of the first to be irrigated and cultivated by the Werelians when they colonized Yeowe and brought their serfs and slaves to work there. Too well irrigated, too well cultivated; fertilizing chemicals and salts of the soil had accumulated till nothing would grow, and the Bosses went elsewhere for their profit. The banks of the irrigation canals slumped here and there and the waters of the river wandered free again, pooling and meandering, slowly washing the lands clean. The reeds grew, miles and miles of reeds bowing a little under the wind, under the cloud-shadows and the wings of long-legged birds. Here and there on an island of rockier soil a few fields and a village remained, a few sharecroppers left behind, people living there because they had nowhere else to go. And all through the marshes there were lonely houses.

Growing old, the people of Werel and Yeowe might turn to silence, as their religion recommended them to do: When their children were grown, when they had done their work as householder and citizen, when as their body weakened their soul might make itself strong, they left their life behind and came empty-handed to lonely places. Even on the Plantations, the Bosses had let old slaves go out into the wilderness, go free. Here in the North, freedmen from the cities had come out to the marshlands and lived as recluses in the lonely houses. Now, since the Liberation, even women came.

Some of the houses were derelict, and any soulmaker might claim them; most, like Yoss's thatched cabin, were owned by villagers who maintained them and gave them to a recluse rent-free as a religious duty, a means of enriching the soul. Yoss liked knowing that she was a source of spiritual profit to her landlord, a grasping widower whose account with Providence was probably otherwise all on the debit side. She liked to feel useful. She took it for another sign of her incapacity to let the world go, as the Lord Kamye bade her do. *You are no longer useful*, he had told her in a hundred ways, over and over, since she was sixty; but she would not listen. She left the noisy world and came out to the marshes, but she let the world go on chattering and gossiping and singing and crying in her ears. She would not hear the low voice of the Lord.

Eyid and Wada were gone when she got home; the bed was made up very tight, and the foxdog Tikuli was sleeping on it, curled up around his tail. Gubu the spotted cat was prancing around asking about dinner. She picked him up and petted his silken, speckled back while he nuzzled under her ear, making his steady roo-roo-roo of pleasure and affection; then she fed him. Tikuli took no notice, which was odd. Tikuli was sleeping too much. She sat on the bed and scratched the roots of his stiff, red-furred ears. He woke and yawned and looked at her with soft amber eyes, his red plume of tail stirring. "Aren't you hungry?" she asked him. I will eat to please you, Tikuli answered, getting down off the bed rather stiffly. "Oh, Tikuli, you're getting old," Yoss said, and the sword stirred in her heart. Her daughter Safnan had given her Tikuli, a tiny red cub, a scurry of paws and plume-tail—how long ago? Eight years. A long time. A lifetime for a foxdog.

More than a lifetime for Safnan. More than a lifetime for her children, Yoss's grandchildren, Enkamma and Uye.

If I am alive, they are dead, Yoss thought, as she always thought; if they are alive, I am dead. They went on the ship that goes like light; they are translated into the light. When they return into life, when they step off the ship on the world called Hain, it will be eighty years from the day they left, and I will be dead, long dead; I am dead. They left me and I am dead. Let them be alive, Lord, sweet Lord, let them be alive, I will be dead. I came here to be dead. For them. I cannot, I cannot let them be dead for me.

Tikuli's cold nose touched her hand. She looked intently at him. The amber of his eyes was dimmed, bluish. She stroked his head, scratched the roots of his ears, silent.

He ate a few bites to please her, and climbed back up onto the bed. She made her own dinner, soup and rewarmed soda cakes, and ate it, not tasting it. She washed the three dishes she had used, made up the fire, and sat by it trying to read her book slowly, while Tikuli slept on the bed and Gubu lay on the hearth gazing into the fire with round golden eyes, going roo-roo-roo very softly. Once he sat up and made his battlecall, "Hoooo!" at some noise he heard out in the marshes and stalked about a bit; then he settled down again to staring and roo-ing. Later, when the fire was out and the house utterly dark in the starless darkness, he joined Yoss and Tikuli in the warm bed, where earlier the young lovers had had their brief, sharp joy.

She found she was thinking about Abberkam the next couple of days as she worked in her little vegetable garden, cleaning it up for the winter. When the Chief first came, the villagers had been all abuzz with excitement about his living in a house that belonged to the headman of their village. Disgraced, dishonored, he was still a very famous man. An elected Chief of the Heyend, one of the principal Tribes of Yeowe, he had led a great movement for what he called Racial Freedom. Even some of the villagers had embraced the main principle of the World Party: No one was to live on Yeowe but its own people. No Werelians, the hated ancestral colonizers, the Bosses and Owners. The Liberation had ended slavery; and in the last few years the diplomats of the Ekumen had negotiated an end to Werel's economic power over its former colony-planet. Most of the former Bosses and Owners, even those whose families had lived on Yeowe for centuries, had already withdrawn to Werel, the Old World, next inward to the sun. They must all go, said the World Party. Go and not return as traders or visitors, never again pollute the soil and soul of Yeowe. Nor would any other foreigner, any other Power. The Aliens of the Ekumen had helped Yeowe free itself; now they too must go. There was no place for them here. "This is our world. Here we will make our souls in the image of Kamye the Swordsman," Abberkam had said over and over, and that image, the curved sword, was the symbol of the World Party.

And blood had been shed, of course. No Werelian could feel safe after the massacres in the East and South; but even after all the Werelians were gone, the fighting went on. Always, always, the young men were ready to rush out and kill whoever the old men told them to kill, each other, their parents, wives, children; always there was a war to be fought in the name of Peace, Freedom, Justice, the Lord. Newly freed tribes fought over land, the city chiefs fought for power. All Yoss had worked for, setting up public education in the capital, had come to pieces in the last ten years, as the city disintegrated in one ward-war after another.

In all fairness, she thought, despite his waving Kamye's sword, Abberkam in leading the World Party had tried to avoid war, and had partly succeeded. His preference was for the winning of power by policy and persuasion, and he was a master of it. He had come very near success. The curved sword was everywhere, the rallies cheering his speeches were immense. ABBERKAM AND RACIAL FREEDOM! said huge posters stretched across the city avenues. He was certain to win the first free election ever held on Yeowe, to be Chief of the World Council. And then, nothing much at first, the rumors. The defections; his son's suicide. His wife's accusations of debauchery and gross luxury. The proof that he had embezzled great sums of money given to his party for relief of districts left in poverty by the withdrawal of Werelian capital. The revelation of the secret plan to assassinate the Envoy of the Ekumen and put the blame on Abberkam's old friend and supporter Demeye.... That was what brought him down. A chief could indulge himself sexually, misuse power, grow rich off his people and be admired for it, but a chief who betrayed a companion was not forgiven. It was, Yoss thought, the code of the slave.

Mobs of his own supporters turned against him, attacking the old Werelian Residency, which he had taken over. Supporters of the Ekumen joined with forces still loyal to him to defend him and restore order to the capital city. After days of street warfare, hundreds of men killed fighting and thousands more in riots around the continent, Abberkam surrendered. The Ekumen supported a provisional government in declaring amnesty. Their people walked him through the bloodstained, bombed-out streets in absolute silence. People watched, people who had trusted him, people who had revered him, people who had hated him, watched him walk past in silence, guarded by the foreigners, the Aliens he had tried to drive from their world.

She had read about it in the paper. She had been living in the marshes for over a year then. "Serve him right," she had thought, and not much more. Whether the Ekumen was a true ally or a new set of Owners in disguise, she didn't know, but she liked to see any chief go down. Werelian Bosses, strutting tribal headmen, or ranting demagogues, let them taste dirt. She'd eaten enough of their dirt in her life.

When, a few months later, they told her in the village that Abberkam was coming to the marshlands as a recluse, a soulmaker, she had been surprised and for a moment ashamed at having assumed his talk had all been empty rhetoric. Was he a religious man, then?—Through all the luxury, the orgies, the thefts, the powermongering, the murders? No! Since he'd lost his money and power, he'd stay in view by making a spectacle of his poverty and piety. He was utterly shameless. She was surprised at the bitterness of her indignation. The first time she saw him she felt like spitting at the big, thick-toed, sandaled feet, which were all she saw of him; she refused to look at his face.

But then in the winter she had heard the howling out on the marshes, at night, in the freezing wind. Tikuli and Gubu had pricked an ear but been unfrightened by the awful noise. That led her after a minute to recognize it as a human voice—a man shouting aloud, drunk? mad?—howling, beseeching, so that she had got up to go to him, despite her terror; but he was not calling out for human aid. "Lord, my Lord, Kamye!" he shouted, and looking out her door she saw him up on the causeway, a shadow against the pale night clouds, striding and tearing at his hair and crying like an animal, like a soul in pain.

After that night, she did not judge him. They were equals. When she next met him she looked him in the face and spoke, forcing him to speak to her.

It was not often; he lived in true seclusion. No one came across the marshes to see him. People in the village often enriched their soul by giving her food, harvest surplus, left-overs, sometimes at the holy days a dish cooked for her; but she saw no one take anything out to Abberkam's house. Maybe they had offered and he was too proud to take. Maybe they were afraid to offer.

She dug up her root-bed with the miserable short-handled spade Em Dewi had given her, and thought about Abberkam howling, and about the way he had coughed. Safnan had nearly died of the berlot when she was four. Yoss had heard that terrible cough for weeks. Had Abberkam been going to the village to get medicine, the other day? Had he got there, or turned back?

She put on her shawl, for the wind had turned cold again, the autumn was getting on, and went up to the causeway and took the right-hand turn.

Abberkam's house was of wood, riding a raft of tree-trunks sunk in the peaty water of the marsh. Such houses were very old, going back centuries, to when there had been trees growing in the valley. It had been a farmhouse and was much larger than her hut, a rambling, dark place, the roof in ill repair; some windows boarded over, planks on the porch loose as she stepped up on it. She said his name, then said it again louder. The wind whined in the reeds. She knocked, waited, pushed the heavy door open. It was dark indoors. She was in a kind of vestibule. She heard him talking in the next room. "Never down to the adit, in the intent, take it out, take it out," the deep, hoarse voice said, and then he coughed. She opened the door; she had to let her eyes adjust to the darkness for a minute before she could see where she was. It was the old front room of the house. The windows were shuttered, the fire dead. There was a sideboard, a table, a couch, but a bed stood near the fireplace. The tangled covers had slid to the floor, and Abberkam was naked on the bed, writhing and raving in fever. "Oh, Lord!" Yoss said. That huge, black, sweat-oiled breast and belly whorled with gray hair, those powerful arms and groping hands, how was she going to get near him?

She managed it, growing less timid and cautious as she found him weak in his fever and, when he was lucid, obedient to her requests. She got him covered up, piled up all the blankets he had and a rug from the floor of an unused room on top; she built up the fire as hot as she could make it; and after a couple of hours he began to sweat, water pouring out of him till the sheets and mattress were soaked. "You are immoderate," she railed at him in the depths of the night, shoving and hauling at him, making him stagger over to the decrepit couch and lie there wrapped in the rug so she could get his bedding dry at the fire. He shivered and coughed, and she brewed up the herbals she had brought, and drank the scalding tea along with him. He fell asleep suddenly and slept like death, not wakened even by the cough that racked him. She fell asleep as suddenly and woke to find herself lying on bare hearthstones, the fire dying, the day white in the windows.

Abberkam lay like a mountain range under the rug, which she saw now to be filthy; his breath wheezed but was deep and regular. She got up piece by piece, all ache and pain, made up the fire and got warm, made tea, investigated the pantry. It was stocked with essentials; evidently the Chief ordered in supplies from Veo, the nearest town of any size. She made herself a good breakfast, and when Abberkam roused, got some more herbal tea into him. The fever had broken. The danger now was water in the lungs, she thought; they had warned her about that with Safnan, and this was a man of sixty. If he stopped coughing, that would be a danger sign. She made him lie propped up. "Cough," she told him.

"Hurts," he growled.

"You have to," she said, and he coughed, hak-hak.

"More!" she ordered, and he coughed till his body was shaken with the spasms.

"Good," she said. "Now sleep." He slept.

Tikuli, Gubu would be starving! She fled home, fed her pets, petted them, changed her underclothes, sat down in her own chair by her own fireside for half an hour with Gubu going roo-roo under her ear. Then she went back across the marshes to the Chief's house.

She got his bed dried out by nightfall and moved him back into it. She stayed that night, but left him in the morning, saying, "I'll be back in the evening."

He was silent, still very sick, indifferent to his own plight or hers.

The next day he was clearly better: The cough was phlegmy and rough, a good cough; she remembered well when Safnan had finally begun coughing a good cough. He was fully awake from time to time, and when she brought him the bottle she had made serve as a bedpan, he took it from her and turned away from her to piss in it. Modesty, a good sign in a Chief, she thought. She felt pleased with him and with herself. She had been useful. "I'm going to leave you tonight; don't let the covers slip off. I'll be back in the morning," she told him, contented with herself, her decisiveness, her unanswerability.

But when she got home in the clear, cold evening, Tikuli was curled up in a corner of the room where he had never slept before. He would not eat and crept back to his corner when she tried to move him, pet him, make him sleep on the bed. Let me be, he said, looking away from her, turning his eyes away, tucking his dry, black, sharp nose into the curve of his foreleg. Let me be, he said patiently, let me die, that is what I am doing now.

She slept, because she was very tired. Gubu stayed out in the marshes all night. In the morning Tikuli was just the same, curled up on the floor in the place where he had never slept, waiting.

"I have to go," she told him, "I'll be back soon— very soon. Wait for me, Tikuli."

He said nothing, gazing away from her with dim amber eyes. It was not her he waited for.

She strode across the marshes, dry-eyed, angry, useless. Abberkam was much the same as he had been; she fed him some grain-pap, looked to his needs, and said, "I can't stay. My dog is sick, I have to go back."

"Dog," the big man said in his rumble of voice.

"A foxdog. My daughter gave him to me." Why was she explaining, excusing herself? She left; when she got home, Tikuli was where she had left him. She did some mending, cooked up some food she thought Abberkam might eat, tried to read the book about the Worlds of the Ekumen, about the world that had no war, where it was always winter, where people were both men and women. In the middle of the afternoon she thought she must go back to Abberkam and was just getting up when Tikuli too stood up. He walked very slowly over to her. She sat down again in her chair and stooped to pick him up, but he put his sharp muzzle into her hand, sighed, and lay down with his head on his paws. He sighed again.

She sat and wept aloud for a while, not long; then she got up and got the gardening spade and went outdoors. She made the grave at the corner of the stone chimney, in a sunny nook. When she went in and picked Tikuli up she thought with a thrill like terror, "He is not dead!" He was dead, only he was not cold yet; the thick red fur kept the body's warmth in. She wrapped him in her blue scarf and took him in her arms, carried him to his grave, still feeling that faint warmth through the cloth, and the light rigidity of the body, like a wooden statue. She filled the grave and set a stone that had fallen from the chimney on it. She could not say anything, but she had an image in her mind like a prayer, of Tikuli running in the sunlight somewhere.

She put out food on the porch for Gubu, who had kept out of the house all day, and set off up the causeway. It was a silent, overcast evening. The reeds stood gray and the pools had a leaden gleam.

Abberkam was sitting up in bed, certainly better, perhaps with a touch of fever but nothing serious; he was hungry, a good sign. When she brought him his tray he said, "The dog, it's all right?"

"No," she said and turned away, able only after a minute to say, "dead."

"In the Lord's hands," said the hoarse, deep voice, and she saw Tikuli in the sunlight again, in some presence, some kind presence like the sunlight.

"Yes," she said. "Thank you." Her lips quivered and her throat closed up. She kept seeing the design on her blue scarf, leaves printed in a darker blue. She made herself busy. Presently she came back to see to the fire and sat down beside it. She felt very tired.

"Before the Lord Kamye took up the sword, he was a herdsman," Abberkam said. "And they called him Lord of the Beasts, and Deer-Herd, because when he went into the forest he came among the deer, and lions also walked with him among the deer, offering no harm. None were afraid."

He spoke so quietly that it was a while before she realized he was saying lines from the *Arkamye*.

She put another block of peat on the fire and sat down again.

"Tell me where you come from, Chief Abberkam," she said.

"Gebba Plantation."

"In the east?"

He nodded.

"What was it like?"

The fire smoldered, making its pungent smoke. The night was intensely silent. When she first came out here from the city, the silence had wakened her, night after night.

"What was it like," he said almost in a whisper. Like most people of their race, the dark iris filled his eyes, but she saw the white flash as he glanced over at her. "Sixty years ago," he said. "We lived in the Plantation barracks. The canebrakes; some of us worked there, cut cane, worked in the mill. Most of the women, the little children. Most men and the boys over nine or ten went down the mines. Some of the girls too, they wanted them small, to work some of the shafts a man couldn't get into. I was big. They sent me down the mines when I was eight years old."

"What was it like?"

"Dark," he said. Again she saw the flash of his eyes.

"I look back and think how did we live? How did we stay living in that place? The air down the mine was so thick with the dust that it was black. Black air. Your lantern light didn't go five feet into that air. There was water in most of the workings, up to a man's knees. There was one shaft where a soft-coal face had caught fire and was burning, so the whole system was full of smoke. They went on working it because the lodes ran behind that coke. We wore masks, filters. They didn't do much good. We breathed the smoke. I always wheeze some like I do now. It's not just the berlot. It's the old smoke. My father died of the black lung. All the men did. Forty, forty-five years old, they died. The Bosses gave your family money when the father died. A bonus. Some men thought that made it worthwhile dying."

"How did you get out?"

"My mother," he said. "She was a Chief's daughter from the village. She taught me. She taught me religion and freedom."

He has said that before, Yoss thought. It has become his stock answer, his standard myth.

"How? What did she say?"

A pause. "She taught me the Holy Word," Abberkam said. "And she said to me, 'You and your brother, you are the true people, you are the Lord's people, his servants, his warriors, his lions: Only you. Lord Kamye came with us from the Old World and he is ours now, he lives among us.' She named us

Abberkam, Tongue of the Lord, and Domerkam, Arm of the Lord. To speak the truth and fight to be free."

"What became of your brother?" Yoss asked after a time.

"Killed at Nadami," Abberkam said, and again both were silent for a while.

Nadami had been the first great battle of the Uprising which finally brought the Liberation to Yeowe. If the revolutionaries had continued to work together against the plantation owners and the exportation cartels, they might have driven the Werelians offworld then, forty years ago. But the Uprising had splintered into tribal rivalries, chiefs vying for power in the newly freed territories, bargaining with the Bosses to consolidate their gains. Thirty years of war and destruction, and nothing gained. Only the arrival of the Envoys of the Ekumen had finally done what the revolutionaries set out to do at Nadami.

"Your brother was lucky," said Yoss.

Then she looked across at the Chief wondering how he would take this challenge. His big, dark face had a softened look in the firelight. His gray, coarse hair had escaped from the loose braid she had made of it to keep it from his eyes and straggled around his face. He said slowly and softly, "He was my younger brother. He was Enar on the Field of the Five Armies."

Oh, so then you're the Lord Kamye himself? Yoss retorted in her mind, moved, indignant, cynical. What an ego!—But, to be sure, there was another implication. Enar had taken up his sword to kill his Elder Brother on that battlefield, to keep him from becoming Lord of the World. And Kamye had told him that the sword he held was his own death; that there is no lordship and no freedom in life, only in the letting go of life, of longing, of desire. Enar had laid down his sword and gone into the wilderness, into the silence, saying only, "Brother, I am thou." And Kamye had taken up that sword to fight the Armies of Desolation, knowing there is no victory.

So who was he, this man? this big fellow? this sick old man, this little boy down in the mines in the dark, this bully, thief, and liar who thought he could speak for the Lord?

"We're talking too much," Yoss said, though neither of them had said a word for five minutes. She poured a cup of tea for him and set the kettle off the fire, where she had kept it simmering to keep the air moist. She took up her shawl. He watched her with that same soft look in his face, an expression almost of confusion.

"It was freedom I wanted," he said. "Our freedom."

His conscience was none of her concern. "Keep warm," she said.

"You're going out now?"

"I can't get lost on the causeway."

It was a strange walk, though, for she had no lantern, and the night was very black. She thought, feeling her way along the causeway, of that black air he had told her of down in the mines, swallowing light. She thought of Abberkam's black, heavy body. She thought how seldom she had walked alone at night. When she was a child on Banni Plantation, the workers were forbidden to leave the barracks after dark; after the Liberation, when she lived in the city, women never went anywhere alone at night. There were no police in the working quarters, no streetlights; district warlords sent their gangs out raiding; even in daylight you had to look out, try to stay in the crowd, always be sure there was a street you could escape by.

She grew anxious that she would miss her turning, but her eyes had grown used to the dark by the time she came to it, and she could even make out the blot of her house down in the formlessness of the reedbeds. The Aliens had poor night vision, she had heard. They had little eyes, little dots with white all round them, like a scared calf. She didn't like their eyes, though she liked the colors of their skin, mostly dark brown or ruddy brown or tan, warmer than her people's blue-brown, or black-blue like her and Abberkam. Cyanid skins, the Aliens said politely, and ocular adaptation to the radiation spectrum of the Werelian System sun.

Gubu danced about her on the pathway down, silent, tickling her legs with his tail. "Look out," she scolded him, "I'm going to walk on you." She was grateful to him, picked him up as soon as they were indoors. No dignified and joyous greeting from Tikuli, not this night, not ever. Roo-roo-roo, Gubu went under her ear, listen to me, I'm here, life goes on, where's dinner?

The Chief got a touch of pneumonia after all, and she went into the village to call the clinic in Veo. They sent out a practitioner, who said he was doing fine, just keep him sitting up and coughing, the herbal teas were fine, just keep an eye on him, that's right, and went away, thanks very much. So she spent her afternoons with him. The house without Tikuli seemed very drab, the late autumn days seemed very cold, and anyhow what else did she have to do? She liked the big, dark raft-house. She wasn't going to clean house for the Chief or any man who didn't do it for himself, but she poked about in it, in rooms Abberkam evidently hadn't used or even looked at. She found one upstairs, with long low windows all along the west wall, that she liked. She swept it out and cleaned the windows with their small, greenish panes. When he was asleep she would go up to that room and sit on a ragged wool rug, its only furnishing. The fireplace had been sealed up with loose bricks, but heat came up it from the peat fire burning below, and with her back against the warm bricks and the sunlight slanting in, she was warm. She felt a peacefulness there that seemed to belong to the room, the shape of its air, the greenish, wavery glass of the windows. There she would sit in silence, unoccupied, content, as she had never sat in her own house.

The Chief was slow to get his strength back. Often

he was sullen, dour, the uncouth man she had first thought him, sunk in a stupor of self-centered shame and rage. Other days he was ready to talk; even to listen, sometimes.

"I've been reading a book about the worlds of the Ekumen," Yoss said, waiting for their bean-cakes to be ready to turn and fry on the other side. For the last several days she had made and eaten dinner with him in the late afternoon, washed up, and gone home before dark. "It's very interesting. There isn't any question that we're descended from the people of Hain, all of us. Us and the Aliens too. Even our animals have the same ancestors."

"So they say," he grunted.

"It isn't a matter of who says it," she said. "Anybody who will look at the evidence sees it; it's a genetic fact. That you don't like it doesn't alter it."

"What is a 'fact' a million years old?" he said. "What has it to do with you, with me, with us? This is our world. We are ourselves. We have nothing to do with them."

"We do now," she said rather bluntly, flipping the bean-cakes.

"Not if I had had my way," he said.

She laughed. "You don't give up, do you?"

"No," he said.

After they were eating, he in bed with his tray, she at a stool on the hearth, she went on, with a sense of teasing a bull, daring the avalanche to fall; for all he was still sick and weak, there was that menace in him, his size, not of body only. "Is that what it was all about, really?" she asked. "The World Party. Having the planet for ourselves, no aliens? Just that?"

"Yes," he said, the dark rumble.

"Why? The Ekumen has so much to share with us. They broke the Werelian hold over us. They're on our side."

"We were brought to this world as slaves," he said, "but it is our world to find our own way in. Kamye came with us, the Herdsman, the Bondsman, Kamye of the Sword. This is his world. Our earth. No one can give it to us. We don't need to share other peoples' knowledge or follow their gods. This is where we live, this earth. This is where we die to rejoin the Lord."

After a while she said, "I have a daughter, and a grandson and granddaughter. They left this world four years ago. They're on a ship that is going to Hain. All these years I live till I die are like a few minutes, an hour to them. They'll be there in eighty years—seventy-six years, now. On that other earth. They'll live and die there. Not here."

"Were you willing for them to go?"

"It was her choice."

"Not yours."

"I don't live her life."

"But you grieve," he said.

The silence between them was heavy.

"It is wrong, wrong, wrong!" he said, his voice

strong and loud. "We had our own destiny, our own way to the Lord, and they've taken it from us—we're slaves again! The wise Aliens, the scientists with all their great knowledge and inventions, our Ancestors, they say they are—Do this! they say, and we do it. Do that! and we do it. Take your children on the wonderful ship and fly to our wonderful worlds! And the children are taken, and they'll never come home. Never know their home. Never know who they are. Never know whose hands might have held them."

He was orating; for all she knew it was a speech he had made once or a hundred times, ranting and magnificent; there were tears in his eyes. There were tears in her eyes also. She would not let him use her, play on her, have power over her.

"If I agreed with you," she said, "still, still, why did you cheat, Abberkam? You lied to your own people, you stole!"

"Never," he said. "Everything I did, always, every breath I took, was for the World Party. Yes, I spent money, all the money I could get, what was it for except the cause? Yes, I threatened the Envoy, I wanted to drive him and all the rest of them off this world! Yes, I lied to them, because they want to control us, to own us, and I will do anything to save my people from slavery—anything!"

He beat his great fists on the mound of his knees, and gasped for breath, sobbing.

"And there is nothing I can do, O Kamye!" he cried, and hid his face in his arms.

She sat silent, sick at heart.

After a long time he wiped his hands over his face, like a child, wiping the coarse, straggling hair back, rubbing his eyes and nose. He picked up the tray and set it on his knees, picked up the fork, cut a piece of bean-cake, put it in his mouth, chewed, swallowed. If he can, I can, Yoss thought, and did the same. They finished their dinner. She got up and came to take his tray. "I'm sorry," she said.

"It was gone then," he said very quietly. He looked up at her directly, seeing her, as she felt he seldom did.

She stood, not understanding, waiting.

"It was gone then. Years before. What I believed at Nadami. That all we needed was to drive them out and we would be free. We lost our way within a year, two years. I knew it was a lie. What did it matter if I lied more?"

She understood only that he was deeply upset and probably somewhat mad, and that she had been wrong to goad him. They were both old, both defeated, they had both lost their child. Why did she want to hurt him? She put her hand on his hand for a moment, in silence, before she picked up his tray.

As she washed up the dishes in the scullery, he called her, "Come here, please!" He had never done so before, and she hurried into the room.

"Who were you?" he asked.

She stood staring.

"Before you came here," he said impatiently.

"I married, worked in shops," she said. "After the Liberation, I went to the college. I administered the teaching of science in the schools. I brought up my daughter."

"What is your name?"

"Yoss. Seddewi Tribe, from Banni."

He nodded, and after a moment more she went back to the scullery. He didn't even know my name, she thought.

Every day she made him get up, walk a little, sit in a chair; he was obedient, but it tired him. The next afternoon she made him walk about a good while, and when he got back to bed he closed his eyes at once. She slipped up the rickety stairs to the west-window room and sat there a long time in perfect peace.

She had him sit up in the chair while she made their dinner. She talked to cheer him up, for he never complained at her demands, but he looked gloomy and bleak, and she blamed herself for upsetting him yesterday. Were they not both here to leave all that behind them, all their mistakes and failures as well as their loves and victories? She told him about Wada and Eyid, spinning out the story of the star-crossed lovers, who were, in fact, in bed in her house that afternoon. "I didn't use to have anywhere to go when they came," she said. "It could be rather inconvenient, cold days like today. I'd have to hang around the shops in the village. This is better, I must say, I like this house."

He only grunted, but she felt he was listening intently, almost that he was trying to understand, like a foreigner who did not know the language.

"You don't care about the house, do you?" she said, and laughed, serving up their soup. "You're honest, at least. Here I am pretending to be holy, to be making my soul, and I get fond of things, attached to them, I love things." She sat down by the fire to eat her soup. "There's a beautiful room upstairs," she said, "the front corner room, looking west. Something good happened in that room, lovers lived there once, maybe. I like to look out at the marshes from there."

When she made ready to go he asked, "Will they be gone?"

"The fawns? Oh yes. Long since. Back to their hateful families. I suppose if they could marry, they'd soon be just as hateful. They're very ignorant. How can they help it? The village is narrow-minded, they're so poor. But they cling to their love for each other, as if they knew it…it was their truth…."

"'Hold fast to the noble thing,'" Abberkam said. She knew the quotation.

"Would you like me to read to you?" she asked. "I have the *Arkamye*, I could bring it."

He shook his head, with a sudden, broad smile. "No need," he said. "I know it."

"All of it?"

He nodded.

"I meant to learn it—part of it anyway—when I came here," she said, awed. "But I never did. There never seems to be time. Did you learn it here?"

"Long ago. In the jail, in Gebba City," he said. "Plenty of time there…These days, I lie here and say it to myself." His smile lingered as he looked up at her. "It gives me company in your absence."

She stood wordless.

"Your presence is sweet to me," he said.

She wrapped herself in her shawl and hurried out with scarcely a word of goodbye.

She walked home in a crowd of confused, conflicted feelings. What a monster the man was! He had been flirting with her: There was no doubt about it. Coming on to her, was more like it. Lying in bed like a great felled ox, with his wheezing and his gray hair! That soft, deep voice, that smile, he knew the uses of that smile, he knew how to keep it rare. He knew how to get round a woman, he'd got round a thousand if the stories were true, round them and into them and out again, here's a little semen to remember your Chief by, and byebye, baby. Lord!

So, why had she taken it into her head to tell him about Eyid and Wada being in her bed? Stupid woman, she told herself, striding into the mean East wind that scoured the graying reeds. Stupid, stupid, old, old woman.

Gubu came to meet her, dancing and batting with soft paws at her legs and hands, waving his short, end-knotted, black-spotted tail. She had left the door unlatched for him, and he could push it open. It was ajar. Feathers of some kind of small bird were strewn all over the room and there was a little blood and a bit of entrail on the hearthrug. "Monster," she told him. "Murder outside!" He danced his battle dance and cried Hoo! Hoo! He slept all night curled up in the small of her back, obligingly getting up, stepping over her, and curling up on the other side each time she turned over.

She turned over frequently, imagining or dreaming the weight and heat of a massive body, the weight of hands on her breasts, the tug of lips at her nipples, sucking life.

She shortened her visits to Abberkam. He was able to get up, see to his needs, get his own breakfast; she kept his peatbox by the chimney filled and his larder supplied, and she now brought him dinner but did not stay to eat it with him. He was mostly grave and silent, and she watched her tongue. They were wary with each other. She missed her hours upstairs in the western room; but that was done with, a kind of dream, a sweetness gone.

Eyid came to Yoss's house alone one afternoon, sullen-faced. "I guess I won't come back out here," she said.

"What's wrong?"

The girl shrugged.

"Are they watching you?"

"No. I don't know. I might, you know. I might get stuffed." She used the old slave word for pregnant.

"You used the contraceptives, didn't you?" She had bought them for the pair in Veo, a good supply.

Eyid nodded vaguely. "I guess it's wrong," she said, pursing her mouth.

"Making love? Using contraceptives?"

"I guess it's wrong," the girl repeated, with a quick, vengeful glance.

"All right," Yoss said.

Eyid turned away.

"Goodbye, Eyid."

Without speaking, Eyid went off by the bog-path.

"Hold fast to the noble thing," Yoss thought, bitterly.

She went round the house to Tikuli's grave, but it was too cold to stand outside for long, a still, aching, midwinter cold. She went in and shut the door. The room seemed small and dark and low. The dull peat fire smoked and smoldered. It made no noise burning. There was no noise outside the house. The wind was down, the ice-bound reeds were still.

I want some wood, I want a wood fire, Yoss thought. A flame leaping and crackling, a story-telling fire, like we used to have in the longhouse on the Plantation.

The next day she went off one of the bog-paths to

a ruined house half a mile away and pulled some loose boards off the fallen-in porch. She had a roaring blaze in her fireplace that night. She took to going to the ruined house once or more daily, and built up a sizable woodpile next to the stacked peat in the nook on the other side of the chimney from her bed-nook. She was no longer going to Abberkam's house, he was recovered, and she wanted a goal to walk to. She had no way to cut the longer boards, and so shoved them into the fireplace a bit at a time; that way one would last all the evening. She sat by the bright fire and tried to learn the First Book of the *Arkamye*. Gubu lay on the hearthstone sometimes watching the flames and whispering roo, roo, sometimes asleep. He hated so to go out into the icy reeds that she made him a little dirt-box in the scullery, and he used it very neatly.

The deep cold continued, the worst winter she had known on the marshes. Fierce drafts led her to cracks in the wood walls she had not known about; she had no rags to stuff them with and used mud and wadded reeds. If she let the fire go out, the little house grew icy within an hour. The peat fire, banked, got her through the nights. In the daytime, she often put on a piece of wood for the flare, the brightness, the company of it.

She had to go into the village. She had put off going for days, hoping that the cold might relent, and had run out of practically everything. It was colder than ever. The peat blocks now on the fire were earthy and burned poorly, smoldering, so she put a piece of wood in with them to keep the fire lively and the house warm. She wrapped every jacket and shawl she had around her and set off with her sack. Gubu blinked at her from the hearth. "Lazy lout," she told him. "Wise beast."

The cold was frightening. If I slipped on the ice and broke a leg, no one might come by for days, she thought. I'd lie here and be frozen dead in a few hours. Well, well, well, I'm in the Lord's hands, and dead in a few years one way or the other. Only dear Lord let me get to the village and get warm!

She got there, and spent a good while at the sweet-shop stove catching up on gossip, and at the news vendor's woodstove, reading old newspapers about a new war in the eastern province. Eyid's aunts and Wada's father, mother, and aunts all asked her how the Chief was. They also all told her to go by her landlord's house. Kebi had something for her. He had a packet of cheap nasty tea for her. Perfectly willing to let him enrich his soul, she thanked him for the tea. He asked her about Abberkam. The Chief had been ill? He was better now? He pried; she replied indifferently. It's easy to live in silence, she thought; what I could not do is live with these voices.

She was loath to leave the warm room, but her bag was heavier than she liked to carry, and the icy spots on the road would be hard to see as the light failed. She took her leave and set off across the village again and up onto the causeway. It was later than she had thought. The sun was quite low, hiding behind one bar of cloud in an otherwise stark sky, as if grudging even a half-hour's warmth and brightness. She wanted to get home to her fire and stepped right along.

Keeping her eyes on the way ahead for fear of ice, at first she only heard the voice. She knew it, and she thought, Abberkam has gone mad again! For he was running towards her, shouting. She stopped, afraid of him, but it was her name he was shouting. "Yoss! Yoss! It's all right!" he shouted, coming up right on her, a huge wild man, all dirty, muddy, ice and mud in his gray hair, his hands black, his clothes black, and she could see the whites all round his eyes.

"Get back!" she said, "get away, get away from me!"

"It's all right," he said, "but the house, but the house—"

"What house?"

"Your house, it burned. I saw it, I was coming to the village, I saw the smoke down in the marsh—"

He went on, but Yoss stood paralyzed, unhearing. She had shut the door, let the latch fall. She never locked it, but she had let the latch fall, and Gubu would not be able to get out. He was in the house. Locked in: the bright, desperate eyes: the little voice crying—

She started forward. Abberkam blocked her way.

"Let me get by," she said. "I have to get by." She set down her bag and began to run.

Her arm was caught, she was stopped as if by a seawave, swung right round. The huge body and voice were all around her. "It's all right, the kit is all right, it's in my house," he was saying. "Listen, listen to me, Yoss! The house burned. The kit is all right."

"What happened?" she said, shouting, furious. "Let me go! I don't understand! What happened?"

"Please, please be quiet," he begged her, releasing her. "We'll go by there. You'll see it. There isn't much to see."

Very shakily, she walked along with him while he told her what had happened. "But how did it start?" she said. "How could it?"

"A spark; you left the fire burning? Of course, of course you did, it's cold. But there were stones out of the chimney, I could see that. Sparks, if there was any wood on the fire—maybe a floorboard caught—the thatch, maybe. Then it would all go, in this dry weather, everything dried out, no rain. Oh my Lord, my sweet Lord, I thought you were in there. I thought you were in the house. I saw the fire, I was up on the causeway—then I was down at the door of the house, I don't know how, did I fly, I don't know—I pushed, it was latched, I pushed it in, and I saw the whole back wall and ceiling burning, blazing. There was so much smoke, I couldn't tell if you were there, I went in, the little animal was hiding in a corner—I thought how you cried when the other one died, I tried to catch it, and it went out the door like a flash, and I saw no one

was there and made for the door, and the roof fell in."
He laughed, wild, triumphant. "Hit me on the head,
see?" He stooped, but she was still not tall enough to
see the top of his head. "I saw your bucket and tried
to throw water on the front wall, to save something,
then I saw that was crazy, it was all on fire, nothing
left. And I went up the path, and the little animal,
your pet, was waiting there, all shaking. It let me pick
it up, and I didn't know what to do with it, so I ran
back to my house and left it there. I shut the door. It's
safe there. Then I thought you must be in the village,
so I came back to find you."

They had come to the turn-off. She went to the side
of the causeway and looked down. A smear of smoke,
a huddle of black. Black sticks. Ice. She shook all over
and felt so sick she had to crouch down, swallowing
cold saliva. The sky and the reeds went from left to
right, spinning, in her eyes; she could not stop them
spinning.

"Come, come on now, it's all right. Come on with
me." She was aware of the voice, the hands and arms,
a large warmth supporting her. She walked along with
her eyes shut. After a while she could open them and
look down at the road, carefully.

"Oh, my bag—I left it—It's all I have," she said
suddenly with a kind of laugh, turning around and
nearly falling over because the turn started the
spinning again.

"I have it here. Come on, it's just a short way now."

He carried the bag oddly, in the crook of his arm. The other arm was around her, helping her stand up and walk. They came to his house, the dark raft-house. It faced a tremendous orange and yellow sky, with pink streaks going up the sky from where the sun had set; the sun's hair, they used to call that, when she was a child. They turned from the glory, entering the dark house.

"Gubu?" she said.

It took a while to find him. He was cowering under the couch. She had to haul him out, he would not come to her. His fur was full of dust and came out in her hands as she stroked it. There was a little foam on his mouth, and he shivered and was silent in her arms. She stroked and stroked the silvery, speckled back, the spotted sides, the silken white belly-fur. He closed his eyes finally; but the instant she moved a little, he leapt and ran back under the couch.

She sat and said, "I'm sorry, I'm sorry, Gubu, I'm sorry."

Hearing her speak, the Chief came back into the room. He had been in the scullery. He held his wet hands in front of him and she wondered why he didn't dry them. "Is he all right?" he asked.

"It'll take a while," she said. "The fire. And a strange house. They're...cats are territorial. Don't like strange places."

She could not arrange her thoughts or words, they came in pieces, unattached.

"That is a cat, then?"

"A spotted cat, yes."

"Those pet animals, they belonged to the Bosses, they were in the Bosses' houses," he said. "We never had any around."

She thought it was an accusation. "They came from Werel with the Bosses," she said, "yes. So did we." After the sharp words were out she thought that maybe what he had said was an apology for ignorance.

He still stood there holding out his hands stiffly. "I'm sorry," he said. "I need some kind of bandage, I think."

She focused slowly on his hands.

"You burned them," she said.

"Not much. I don't know when."

"Let me see." He came nearer and turned the big hands palm up: a fierce red blistered bar across the bluish inner skin of the fingers of one and a raw bloody wound in the base of the thumb of the other.

"I didn't notice till I was washing," he said. "It didn't hurt."

"Let me see your head," she said, remembering; and he knelt and presented her a matted shaggy sooty object with a red and black burn right across the top of it. "Oh, Lord," she said.

His big nose and eyes appeared under the gray tangle, close to her, looking up at her, anxious. "I know the roof fell onto me," he said, and she began to laugh.

"It would take more than a roof falling onto you!"

she said. "Have you got anything—any clean cloths—I know I left some clean dishtowels in the scullery closet—Any disinfectant?"

She talked as she cleaned the head-wound. "I don't know anything about burns except try to keep them clean and leave them open and dry. We should call the clinic in Veo. I can go into the village, tomorrow."

"I thought you were a doctor or a nurse," he said.

"I'm a school administrator!"

"You looked after me."

"I knew what you had. I don't know anything about burns. I'll go into the village and call. Not tonight, though."

"Not tonight," he agreed. He flexed his hands, wincing. "I was going to make us dinner," he said. "I didn't know there was anything wrong with my hands. I don't know when it happened."

"When you rescued Gubu," Yoss said in a matter-of-fact voice, and then began crying. "Show me what you were going to eat, I'll put it on," she said through tears.

"I'm sorry about your things," he said.

"Nothing mattered. I'm wearing almost all my clothes," she said, weeping. "There wasn't anything. Hardly any food there even. Only the *Arkamye*. And my books about the worlds." She thought of the pages blackening and curling as the fire read them. "A friend sent me that from the city; she keeps sending me books, she never approved of me coming here, pretending to drink water and be silent. She was right, too, I should go back, I should never have come. What a liar I am, what a fool! Stealing wood! Stealing wood so I could have a nice fire! So I could be warm and cheerful! So I set the house on fire, so everything's gone, ruined, Kebi's house, my poor little cat, your hands, it's my fault. I forgot about sparks from wood fires, the chimney was built for peat fires, I forgot. I forgot everything, my mind betrays me, my memory lies, I lie. I dishonor my Lord, pretending to turn to him when I can't turn to him, when I can't let go the world. So I burn it! So the sword cuts your hands." She took his hands in hers and bent her head over them. "Tears are disinfectant," she said. "Oh I'm sorry, I am sorry!"

His big, burned hands rested in hers. He leaned forward and kissed her hair, caressing it with his lips and cheek. "I will say you the *Arkamye*," he said. "Be still now. We need to eat something. You feel very cold. I think you have some shock, maybe. You sit there. I can put a pot on to heat, anyhow."

She obeyed. He was right, she felt very cold. She huddled closer to the fire. "Gubu?" she whispered. "Gubu, it's all right. Come on, come on, little one." But nothing moved under the couch.

Abberkam stood by her, offering her something: a glass: It was wine, red wine.

"You have wine?" she said, startled.

"Mostly I drink water and am silent," he said. "Sometimes I drink wine and talk. Take it."

351

She took it humbly. "I wasn't shocked," she said.

"Nothing shocks a city woman," he said gravely. "Now I need you to open up this jar."

"How did you get the wine open?" she asked as she unscrewed the lid of a jar of fish stew.

"It was already open," he said, deep-voiced, imperturbable.

They sat across the hearth from each other to eat, helping themselves from the pot hung on the firehook. She held bits of fish down low so they could be seen from under the couch and whispered to Gubu, but he would not come out.

"When he's very hungry, he will," she said. She was tired of the teary quaver in her voice, the knot in her throat, the sense of shame. "Thank you for the food," she said. "I feel better."

She got up and washed the pot and the spoons; she had told him not to get his hands wet, and he did not offer to help her, but sat on by the fire, motionless, like a great dark lump of stone.

"I'll go upstairs," she said when she was done. "Maybe I can get hold of Gubu and take him with me. Let me have a blanket or two."

He nodded. "They're up there. I lit the fire," he said. She did not know what he meant; she had knelt to peer under the couch. She knew as she did so that she was grotesque, an old woman bundled up in shawls with her rear end in the air, whispering, "Gubu, Gubu!" to a piece of furniture. But there was a little scrabbling, and then Gubu came straight into her hands. He clung to her shoulder with his nose hidden under her ear. She sat up on her heels and looked at Abberkam, radiant. "Here he is!" she said. She got to her feet with some difficulty, and said, "Goodnight."

"Goodnight, Yoss," he said.

She dared not try to carry the oil lamp and made her way up the stairs in the dark, holding Gubu close with both hands till she was in the west room and had shut the door. Then she stood staring. Abberkam had unsealed the fireplace, and some time this evening he had lighted the peat laid ready in it; the ruddy glow flickered in the long, low windows black with night, and the scent of it was sweet. A bedstead that had been in another unused room now stood in this one, made up, with mattress blankets and a new white wool rug thrown over it. A jug and basin stood on the shelf by the chimney. The old rug she had used to sit on had been beaten and scrubbed and lay clean and threadbare on the hearth.

Gubu pushed at her arms; she set him down, and he ran straight under the bed. He would be all right there. She poured a little water from the jug into the basin and set it on the hearth in case he was thirsty. He could use the ashes for his box. Everything we need is here, she thought, still looking with a sense of bewilderment at the shadowy room, the soft light that struck the windows from within.

She went out, closing the door behind her, and

went downstairs. Abberkam sat still by the fire. His eyes flashed at her. She did not know what to say.

"You liked that room," he said.

She nodded.

"You said maybe it was a lovers' room once. I thought maybe it was a lovers' room to be."

After a while she said, "Maybe."

"Not tonight," he said, with a low rumble: a laugh, she realized. She had seen him smile once, now she had heard him laugh.

"No. Not tonight," she said stiffly.

"I need my hands," he said, "I need everything, for that, for you."

She said nothing, watching him.

"Sit down, Yoss, please," he said. She sat down in the hearthseat facing him.

"When I was ill, I thought about these things," he said, always a touch of the orator in his voice. "I betrayed my cause, I lied and stole in its name because I could not admit I had lost faith in it. I feared the Aliens because I feared their gods. So many gods! I feared that they would diminish my Lord. Diminish him!" He was silent for a minute, and drew breath; she could hear the deep rasp in his chest. "I betrayed my wife many times, many times. Her, other women, myself. I did not hold to the one noble thing." He opened up his hands, wincing a little, looking at the burns across them. "I think you did," he said.

After a while she said, "I only stayed with my

husband a few years. It wasn't a good marriage. I had some other men. What does it matter, now?"

"That's not what I mean," he said. "I mean that you did not betray your men, your child, yourself. All right, all that's past. You say, what does it matter now, nothing matters. But you give me this chance even now, this beautiful chance, to me, to hold you, hold you fast."

She said nothing.

"I came here in shame," he said, "and you honored me."

"Why not? Who am I to judge you?"

"'Brother, I am thou.'"

She looked at him in terror, one glance, then looked into the fire. The peat burned low and warm, sending up one faint curl of smoke. She thought of the warmth, the darkness of his body.

"Would there be any peace between us?" she said at last.

"Do you need peace?"

After a while she smiled a little.

"I will do my best," he said. "Stay in this house a while."

She nodded.

THE

Jonathan Aycliffe

REIVER'S LAMENT

With Naomi's Room, Jonathan Aycliffe produced one of the best traditional ghost stories since the halcyon days of M. R. James. He then went on to follow it up with a second, the equally unnerving Whispers in the Dark, and then completed the hat-trick last year with The Vanishment. Not bad for a side-line, because Aycliffe is, in fact, Daniel Easterman, who already has a string of best-selling thrillers such as The Last Assassin, The Seventh Sanctuary and Brotherhood of the Tomb.

Easterman was born in 1949 in Belfast, where an early interest in Egyptology led to a wider passion for oriental matters, a passion which was consolidated by his conversion, aged seventeen, to an Iranian religious movement known as Baha'ism.

After studying English at Trinity College, Dublin, Easterman moved to Scotland and Edinburgh University, where he finished a second degree in Persian and Arabic. In 1975, he started his doctoral studies at King's College, Cambridge, and married his wife, Beth, also an English graduate. In 1980, back in the UK, Easterman made a formal break with the Baha'i religion, adopting the secularist position he still retains. Between 1981 and 1986, he taught Arabic and Islamic studies at Newcastle University before taking up writing full-time.

Right from the beginning, Easterman took a committed stand on the defense of Salman Rushdie. "No one," said a reviewer, "has explored the intellectual and moral dilemmas posed by the Rushdie affair with more subtlety." During 1993, Easterman was a judge for the Catherine Cookson Award and served on the adjudication panel for the Ian St. James Awards. He collects teapots (and fine teas), enjoys the cinema, hates traveling, and is addicted to good chocolate.

Not surprisingly, Easterman is "a hard-nosed rationalist"— or, at least, that's how he likes to think of himself. "I'm very skeptical about religious and occult beliefs, astrology, reincarnation, New Age ideas and so on," he says, before adding, "but as anyone who has read my novels will know, I am deeply conscious of the importance of the irrational as a factor in human life. Even scientists often adopt an irrational position in defense of pure science just as secularists adopt an irrational stance about secularism."

Thus, he does not believe in ghosts but is easily "spooked" by old houses and graveyards. "Much of this is undoubtedly childhood fears carried into adulthood," he says, "although I think ghosts represent much more than that: they represent memories, regrets, remorse, inability to come to terms with the past, the presence of our own past in our present, or the simple sense of continuity with people now dead.

"I am perpetually puzzled by one curious thing. There are three ghost-story writers closely attached to King's College: M. R. James, A. N. L. Munby, and myself. All three of us were, in some measure, bibliographers and antiquarians, and all three of us have published serious studies in that area. But however much I ponder on this, I can never quite work out what significance, if any, to attribute to it."

Look—there's a pub up ahead: Fancy a drink?

Eglingham, Ellingham, and Edlingham are three villages that form a long, flat triangle to the west, north-west, and south-west of Alnwick, in the heart of Northumberland. In all three cases, as in so many place-names throughout the county, the "g" preceding the "h" is soft. Eglinjum, Ellinjum, and Edlinjum. Outsiders, searching for one or another of them, not infrequently misread the signposts and stray a few miles in the wrong direction. You can see them, if you know where to look, from the ninety-foot-high Brislee Tower, built by Robert Adam for the first Duke of Northumberland, to which, it is said, he would climb in order to survey all his estates. From the ground it is much less easy.

It was just such a mistake that brought me to Edlingham one Christmas Eve several years ago. Snow had started to fall that morning, and by the time I left Newcastle it had thickened into a small blizzard. When I left the A1 at Alnwick, the side roads were growing steadily more treacherous. All around, the countryside was white. It raised my spirits to be surrounded by such whiteness, as though the snow and the cold were somehow guarantors of Christmas cheer. For a while, the snow lightened, and I began to enjoy my adventure in the wilderness.

I had been invited to spend Christmas with friends in Eglingham, the largest and prettiest of the three villages. John and Frances had abandoned London for life in the north earlier that year, and I had not yet had an opportunity to visit them in their new home. Like most southerners, I regarded the journey as one to be undertaken only under the greatest duress. I had broken my trip at Newcastle in order to stay with other friends in Jesmond, and had spent most of the day with them, leaving for Eglingham later than intended.

The Volvo handled well enough in the snow, but heavy flakes had started to fall again, and I was growing nervous to be driving through the dark in such conditions. The thought of spending the night trapped in a drift between nowhere and nowhere was not remotely cozy. It was, I think, my anxiety to reach John and Frances's as quickly as possible and to relax with them in front of the log fire so lovingly described in their letters that made me miss my way.

Just past the turn-off to the B6347, there is an old signpost and a turning that is more like a fork. The sign was on the far side of the road, obscured by darkness and snow. I was certain that the pointer to the left said "Eglingham." I turned left accordingly into a much narrower road that went down between leafless trees, all the time straining ahead of me to catch sight of the first sign of a light that would signal the outskirts of the village.

Outside, it was pitch dark. Thick snowflakes churned through the beam of my full headlamps, held momentarily in light as they rushed the last inches to the ground. I could see no lights ahead and felt the fear in me grow that I might, after all, have lost my way. I did not dare to stop nor try to turn in that narrow, snow-choked road; otherwise I would have driven back to the signpost. If I had done... Well, it's better not to think of that. What was done was done.

I had very little choice, really. Not knowing the roads or the overall layout of the district, I could not guess what options, if any, lay open to me. The map I had bought for the trip was quite inadequate. It was Eglingham or nothing now, I thought. Except that I was not driving towards Eglingham.

Once or twice, where the road dipped steeply, snow had piled itself up in concentrated pockets that were difficult to pass. I looked anxiously at the fuel gauge: the petrol tank was lower than I had thought. The situation was not yet perilous, but if I was really lost, then it might still turn so. I kept a steady speed, peering through the snow-clotted windscreen into the night. By now I would have settled for a shepherd's hut if there had been one.

Then, as though by a miracle, a light appeared ahead, followed within moments by a second and a third. I breathed a sigh of relief. Wherever I was, I thought, I was going to stay put.

There was no name-plate at the entrance to the village, or, if there was, it was well hidden by night and snow. It was less a village than a clustering of farm-houses that formed an unlit street of sorts. There were perhaps a dozen houses in all. It was much smaller than I had anticipated. For the first time, I began to suspect that I might not be in Eglingham after all.

I slowed down and stopped just before the last

house. When I looked back, I could see a few lights in the cottage windows, a handful of shadows cast on the road, the continuing fall of snow. There were no Christmas decorations in any of the windows, no fairy lights, no trees. A bleak place it looked, gloomy, isolated, and without the cheer of the season.

Above the door of one house hung an inn sign. I reversed through the tracks I had left until the car was level with it. I could just make out the lettering on the sign: "The Reiver's Lament." The illustration above the words was too much in shadow for me to tell what it showed.

I parked as close to the curb as possible and switched off my engine. Silence rushed in, as thick and heavy as the snow. I looked ahead and then back, and noticed that no other cars had been parked in the short street. For no clear reason, this made the village seem more cut off than before, a white place, desolate, sad and cold.

Stepping out of the car, I was immediately plunged into the bitter night air. It rushed about me like high water, icy and unpitying. My feet sank into several inches of freezing snow. I had not come prepared for this. Shivering, I stumbled to the door of the pub. Now that I was close up, the house appeared dingy and insalubrious. The wood of the door was rough and without polish. I found a latch and, pressing it down, pushed the door open.

I found myself at once in a gloomy square room filled with tobacco smoke. At one end stood a long wooden counter, and behind it shelves on which green and brown bottles had been lined up without apparent order. It was not the cheeriest of pub lounges. There was no television, no pin-ball machine, no dart-board, no juke box. The wooden floor was lightly sprinkled with sawdust. In London or New York, a fortune would have been spent in creating such an "authentic" effect.

Round a coal fire in the center sat a group of men, their ages ranging, as near as I could tell, from the mid-forties to what in one case looked like minutes short of the grave.

They all looked round at me as I blundered in. I felt self-conscious, standing there sprinkled with snow in a jacket and trousers and wet shoes, the archetypal town-dweller out of his depth in the unforgiving countryside. How unforgiving I did not then know.

I walked to the bar, watched all the way, acutely conscious of my wet feet leaving dark traces on the wooden floor. There was no one behind the counter. One of the men at the fire called out in a loud voice.

"George! You've got a customer."

"Thank you," I said, but the man had already turned back to his mates. They still watched me, as though afraid I might run off with the small change. A door next to the bar opened and through it came a man whom I took to be the landlord. He was dressed in a grimy white shirt over which he wore an even dirtier apron. His face was surly, divided unevenly by a soft reddish mustache over thin lips. His skin was freckled and coarse, with open pores. Unhealthy, porous, winter pale. He looked to be in his mid-fifties, lost and frightened behind watery eyes.

"Can I get you something?" he asked.

A flat voice, neither polite nor insulting. Holding everything back.

"I seem to have got lost in the snow," I said. "I've driven over from Newcastle tonight."

"Oh, aye?"

"The snow came on more heavily than I anticipated. I'm not from the region. Everything went well till Alnwick or so. After that the road got harder to follow."

"Lost, you say?"

"I'm looking for a house belonging to friends of mine who moved here earlier this year. Maybe you know them. John and Frances Barrington. If you could just show me the way to their house…"

He looked blankly at me, shaking his head slowly.

"There's no one round here by that name," he said.

"This is Eglingham, isn't it?"

He did not answer at once. He just looked at me through those watery eyes, as though trying to reach a decision as to what might be done with a dumb creature from the snow like me.

"You've missed your way," he said at last. "Eglingham's a fair step from here, ten mile or more."

"Where am I, then?"

"You're in Edlingham. The signs sent you astray, I don't doubt. That happens from time to time."

"But...I've got to be there tonight. I promised to spend Christmas with them."

He shook his head again.

"You'll not make it to Eglingham now," he said. "Roads will be closed by now. Doubt if you'd get two mile."

"But I've got to be there," I repeated. "They're expecting me."

"Expectation won't get you there any quicker."

I turned and glanced at a window nearby. Though I could see it only dimly, the snow was still there, swirling past as thickly as ever. On reflection, I realized that the landlord was right. I was stuck for the night at least.

"I'd best let my friends know," I said. "Is there a telephone I can use?"

The landlord shook his head for the third time.

"All the lines are down," he said. "Sometimes they stay for days at a time. There's not likely to be anyone out here till after Christmas."

On further reflection, I saw that there was little need to phone. John and Frances would surely guess what had happened. They knew I had got as far as Newcastle, they knew how the weather had turned and how difficult the roads were.

"I have nowhere to stay," I said. "Is there a hotel of any sort near the village?"

Someone behind me laughed slyly under his breath. I looked round and caught sight of faces still turned toward me. As though they were sizing me up.

"There's nowhere in or near Edlingham," the landlord said. "We don't have many people passing through. No casual visitors."

"But I can't just spend the night in the car. There's barely enough petrol to last till morning. I'll freeze."

The landlord frowned, as though coming to a difficult decision. He glanced at the men behind me, as though expecting comment of some kind; but no one spoke. I looked round. Their eyes were turned away from me now, fixed on the fire or the floor. Someone picked up a poker and roused the coals to a sudden flame. Another cleared his throat. One picked up a glass of beer and sipped from it slowly and deliberately. But no one looked at me. It was as though I had grown invisible or been snatched suddenly away. As if the men by the fire and I inhabited different rooms.

I looked back at the landlord.

"We have a small room here," he said. "We sometimes let it out to travelers. It isn't much. But you'll not freeze to death. It's five pounds for the night. Breakfast's another pound."

I accepted his offer gratefully. It would be a miserable night, I had no doubt, and a dull enough wakening on Christmas morning. It was not how I had planned to start the day: a one-pound breakfast and snow piled against the door. Looking about me, I realized for the first time that the room in which I stood had not so much as a sprig of holly in it, or a branch of mistletoe.

"Will my car be all right in the street?" I asked.

"There'll be no more traffic through here tonight," the landlord said. "Maybe not for days now. Leave your car be."

"I'll be wanting to leave first thing tomorrow," I said. "Is there anywhere in the village I can get some petrol?"

He shrugged.

"No doubt Tom Harbottle will be able to oblige you. He usually keeps some by. But I don't see as you'll be on your way tomorrow, nor for a while after that. This bad spell isn't likely to break before New Year. You could be here a week or more."

I looked at him aghast. The thought of spending a week in this hole was scarcely bearable.

"I'll show you to your room," he said. "If you want anything from your car, you'd best bring it in before the snow gets any higher."

I did as he suggested. All the items I needed for the night were already in the overnight bag I had packed for my stay in Newcastle. I retrieved it from the boot and locked the car. Snow had already crept up as far as the hubcaps.

When I returned to the inn, I was met, not by my cheerless host, but by a thin woman of medium height and startling looks whom I assumed to be his wife. She had long straggling hair, knobby elbows, and an unfortunate leer that she evidently took for a smile. Her face seemed uneven, as though pressed in slightly from one side, but to such a degree that the distortion thus produced was scarcely perceptible. Every time I caught sight of her, I was left with the vague impression that something was wrong.

"This way," she said. She spoke in a tired, colorless voice. I thought she seemed nervous about something.

She led me through a narrow door I had not noticed previously, up a flight of steep stairs. It was cold out here, away from the fire. The only light came from bare bulbs on the landings. Embossed wallpaper painted a dirty brown; a threadbare stair carpet as far as the top floor, then unvarnished wooden treads; a smell like old, faded perfume; our feet, hollow on the stairs, as we climbed to the top.

We came at last to a little landing with three doors. The woman opened the first on my left.

"In here," she said, standing to one side in order to let me pass. As I did so, her hand reached inside for a light switch. A dim bulb came to life behind a dusty shade.

It was a small, ill-proportioned room, decorated long ago and left to grow old. In one corner stood an iron bedstead. There was a straight-backed wooden chair, some hooks on the bare wall, and a patchwork rug on the floor beside an old gas fire.

The landlady came forward and bent down to the fire. She drew a box of matches from her apron pocket.

"Seeing as it's Christmas," she said, "and it's snowing out, you can have a bit of warmth. Usually, we'd charge extra. But since it's Christmas…"

It was the first anyone had so much as mentioned the time of year. She struck a match and got the fire going. It was as cheery as it was going to get in here, I thought.

"The bathroom's the door at the end of the landing," she said. "You can have a bath in the morning if you want. Breakfast's at eight if you feel hungry. Seeing as it's Christmas, you can have a lie-in till half-past if you like. Will you need anything more tonight?"

I shook my head. All I wanted to do by now was to get my head on a pillow and try to snatch some sleep.

"No thanks," I said. "I'll try to sleep. Perhaps you could wake me in the morning in time for breakfast. Would you mind?"

"No, that's all right. I'll be up at six, same as usual. I'll give you a knock."

She turned to go. At the door, she hesitated, then turned back.

"You may hear...noises," she said. "In the night. I'd pay no heed to them. We come and go sometimes. It being Christmas."

"I'm sure I'll sleep through it all," I said.

"That's right," she said. "Best to get some sleep."

I thought she seemed troubled, though whether on my account or her own I could not tell.

"I'll be all right," I said. "My friends will guess what's happened tonight."

She nodded and went out, closing the door behind her. I sat down on the bed and looked round me. It was as bleak and unadorned a room as I had ever been in. Unlovely, damp, cramped, and little used, it sat at the top of this curiously quiet house, waiting—for months at a time, perhaps—for a traveler to come and give it a little life and a little purpose. The walls were stark, bare plaster painted slate gray.

Notwithstanding the fire—my landlady's Christmas gift to a stranger—the room was abysmally cold. I could not yet face the thought of undressing. The unaired bed was certain to be cold and damp. I thought that, if the room warmed up sufficiently, I might just sit in my overcoat—which I had made a point of bringing in from the car—and get through the night as best I could.

I got up and went to the window. It gave out onto a rear yard, lighted partially by a window on the ground floor. Farther than that, I could not see. I imagined dark fields full of winter trees, their branches naked in the blizzard. And birds and animals huddled against slow death in unlit hedgerows. The snow fell more heavily than ever. I watched it with mounting despair, filled with thoughts of growing helplessness and unease. All I wanted was for morning to come and the snow to disperse enough to open up my road home.

A little at a time, the room was growing warmer. I sat for a while in front of the fire, finding some sort of consolation in it. What I could not understand was why I felt such a need to be consoled. I was upset, naturally, at having lost my way and, in all likelihood, missed spending Christmas with close friends. And I was depressed by the thought that I might have to spend more than a single night here, cut off from everything, while the world outside went on with its festivities. But none of that should have darkened my spirits as profoundly as this. I felt waves of real despair wash over me, despair so fierce I had to fight it off almost physically. Was it just self-pity grown out of proportion, or was it something else? Thinking back, it seemed that I had begun to feel this way from the very moment I set foot in the Reiver's Lament. As though the place itself carried spores of despair that settled and grew in the undefended spirit.

Displeased with myself for such ridiculous conjectures, I lay down on the bed, propped up against the pillows, and wrapped my overcoat round me. There is something sinister about snow, the way it falls without a sound. Rain it is possible to measure against the loudness with which it strikes roofs and windows. But snow piles up all round you unheard and unsuspected until you wake and look out and find yourself in a whiteness unthinkable but a short time earlier. I lay with my eyes closed, imagining the snow taking hold of everything. Time passed and the silence carried on, uninterrupted, and by degrees I fell into an uncomfortable sleep.

I woke with a start, soaked in sweat, as if I had a fever. The room had grown impossibly hot, and in my clothes and coat I felt as though I were being slowly baked. Shuffling the coat from my shoulders, I swung round, clutching my head. The heat had made it ache, and my throat was dry and catching. I glanced at my wristwatch: It was after three o'clock.

A little unsteadily, I got to my feet. It was stifling.

I turned the fire down as low as it would go, knowing I had no matches with which to relight it should it go out, then crossed to the window and opened it. It had stopped snowing. The clouds had vanished, leaving an enormous moon low in the sky. As far as I could see, deep snow lay on the fields. Nothing moved. The air was as cold as ice. I remained there for a while, breathing the air and cooling down. The feeling of depression had not left me. My heart was racing. I needed to go to the bathroom. Closing the window, I stepped to the door. As I neared it, I paused. I could hear something outside. Footsteps coming up the stairs, furtively. More than one person, several perhaps. They reached the landing. I did not understand why, but my feeling of unease began to deepen. I sensed that something terrible was happening, something no one wanted me to know about. I had a deep reluctance to go out onto the landing. No, not a reluctance—a loathing.

They started to talk in low voices, barely more than whispers. I could not make out the words, only the intonation and the variation between speakers. Two men and two women, I guessed. Subdued voices, furtive and guilty like the footsteps.

There was a keyhole in the door. I bent down and pressed my eye against it. The landing was in darkness. But I could sense them, standing there in the dark.

Suddenly, the whispering stopped. I heard the door to the room next to me open. A light went on, spilling out onto the landing, though not brightly. I could see no one. I heard more footsteps, then the door closed and the light vanished.

The room had grown very cold. Not gradually, not from the cool air I had let inside, but all at once, as though dipped in ice water. I sensed that the entire house had turned to ice. I went to the bed and found my overcoat and put it on.

A muffled cry came from next door. A horrible, strangled cry, human yet bestial. It made me want to retch. The next moment, it was followed by a sickening thud, as though someone had taken a heavy stick and brought it down on something soft but not quite yielding. That was followed by a louder cry, horrendous and quite pitiful. And that by a second blow. The cries and blows went on for a long time. A very long time. I shook each time a blow landed. The cries grew weaker and then ceased altogether, but the thuds continued without remittance. And then they too fell silent.

I did not move once throughout it all. Nothing on earth could have brought me to venture out there, to open my door, to cross the small landing, to enter the next room. I stood there shivering, fixed to the spot, listening, hearing everything, unable to stop listening. It was not physical fear that held me back, it was an instinctive horror of something immaterial.

The door to the next room opened. The footsteps, louder now, crossed the landing and started down the stairs. There were no voices. Gradually, the footsteps faded and I was left alone in the silence. The temperature in my room had risen again.

I knew I could not stand there for the rest of the night. Tossing my overcoat onto the bed, I steeled myself and opened the door. The landing was dark. I found a light switch to the left of the door and flicked it down. A bright light came on. The landing was just as I had seen it earlier. The door to the next room was closed.

I had come this far, I had to go the rest of the way. My hand was shaking as I reached for the knob and turned it.

The light switch did not operate. I let the door swing wide open until the light from the landing fell directly into the room. It was quite unfurnished. But not empty. It was in here, everything I had felt, inhabiting the room like a presence that could not be conjured away. On the plain floorboards, dark, misshapen stains lay like water-lilies on an unmoving pond.

I heard a sound behind me. George and his wife were standing at the top of the stairs, watching me.

"You shouldn't be out here," George said. "Not tonight." His voice was strained, like that of someone afraid of words for what they may uncover.

"You should get back to bed," his wife said. I had not been told her name. It scarcely mattered. "You'll catch your death of cold out here."

"I heard something," I said.

"Go back to bed," she said. "It's nearly morning. It was only noises. Best ignored. Best not to talk about them."

I scrutinized their faces, sensed the fear. I would get nothing out of them. I nodded and went back to my room to wait for morning. Sleep did not come again. I sat alone, listening for sounds that were not there. Just before dawn, I went to the window. It had started to snow again.

The next morning, I left immediately after breakfast. Only George had been downstairs, and he had remained surly and monosyllabic for as long as I was there.

The Volvo could not be moved. George took me to the end of the street, to the house of a neighbor with a Land Rover. They agreed to drive me to Eglingham if they could get through. I took a few things with me and left the rest in the car.

John and Frances were not surprised by my late arrival. But when I told John where I had spent the night, I thought he looked at me a little oddly. We passed a quiet day, though I fear I was not the guest they had planned for. There were a few others, local people with whom they had made friends, for lunch. Afterwards, it was just the three of us.

"I'm not good company, I'm afraid," I said at yet another lull in the conversation. "Being stranded in the countryside hasn't done much for my spirits."

John looked at me hard, then nodded.

"No," he said. "Listen, Frances and I have some calls to make. Presents for people in the village. Why don't you stay in here by the fire? You look as though you could do with a rest."

He got up and went to the bookcase. After a little search, he took down a small volume and flicked through it.

"Here," he said, "you might like to give this a look over while we're out."

It was a slim book, printed in 1967 by a small press in Newcastle, and entitled *Border Ways and Byways*.

"You'll find the Reiver's Lament on page seventy-six," said John. He glanced at me with a look that came close to pity, then went out, shutting the door behind him.

I did not open the book at once. Perhaps I feared what I might find. And when I opened it, I did not turn at once to the page John had indicated. I skimmed through it, reading a passage here and a paragraph there, entirely at random, without understanding a single word. My mind was still filled with thoughts of what I had heard the night before. It would be many months before I could get that sound out of my head. Even now, in winter, when it snows and everything around me is dipped in silence, I hear it again. And I wonder if my friend did right to give me that book to read.

I turned at last to page seventy-six. There was an entry on Edlingham, and in it a bold-type passage of over two pages on the Reiver's Lament and its unfortunate history. The distant past need not concern us here. It is to more recent events that I wish to draw to your attention.

In the 1930s and '40s, the inn was owned by people called Dickinson. I believe George, the landlord of my acquaintance, was their grandson. They had three sons, the eldest of whom, Reginald, went missing in the closing months of the war in Europe. His mother died soon after that, and his father's death followed in about a year.

The inn passed to Reginald's next brother, Bertie, in partnership with the youngest, William. Bertie and William had great plans to expand the business, to take advantage of the boom they could see coming.

But their hopes were rudely dashed in the winter of 1947. On Christmas Eve, when the family were all gathered together for the festival, there was a knock at the door. Reginald Dickinson had come back. It is unclear where he had been and what had happened to him; but it seems that, within a short time of his arrival, he had already made it clear that he and a young Frenchwoman he planned to bring to Northumberland would take over the family business. Bertie and William would have nothing.

They had given up everything to make the inn a success. Now, faced with the threat of ruin, they decided to act quickly. No one else had seen Reginald arrive in Edlingham. If they did away with him, no one would be any the wiser. After Reginald had gone to bed in his old room at the top of the house, they sat and talked over their plan. No one would volunteer to carry out the deed, and finally they decided it should be a joint action.

In the middle of the night, they climbed the stairs and entered Reginald's room, carrying heavy sticks. It was a cold night, with heavy snow outside. Reginald was half asleep when they came to him. It is not recorded who struck the first blow. But one after the other, two men and two women, they cudgeled him slowly to death. It had to be slow, so no one afterwards could say which blow had killed him. They had sworn to share the guilt, even as they planned to share the business.

There is little to add. Reginald's French girlfriend arrived after the snow thawed and set afoot inquiries that led to the arrest of the brothers and their wives. The truth came out, and they were condemned to death. They were hanged in the summer of 1948, on successive days, at Durham prison. And local superstition has it that, every Christmas Eve, they are condemned to return to the Reiver's Lament and to re-enact their crime. But, after all, the border country is full of superstitions.

ISAAC

carl west and katherine maclean

MY SON

Carl West and Katherine MacLean are married and live together in a handbuilt house on twenty acres of Maine woods, surrounded by beautiful, tiny, granite swimming pools. They paint, sculpt and write, do carpentry, build greenhouses, cut trees and move the landscape around in wheel barrows, and occasionally they sell something.

The idea for the following story came from a Maine ex-Marine back from the Vietnam war with a job in Portland. He explained over coffee how he had returned home to a Micmak town in the north woods and found his girl and his best friend had married when he was listed missing in action. His parents had sold his clothes and books and guns and traps and trapping rights.

"He was rescued from murdering them

all by passing out drunk in the woods on top of spilled wine bottles," MacLean adds. "While unconscious, he talked with an old man who gave him fatherly advice and seemed totally real. The fatherly voice took all the pain and anger from him, and he woke up under a giant pine, under a pile of pine needles, feeling newly clean inside and changed forever. Later, he heard it was called a Grandfather Tree.

"Mycelium mat of the kind that feeds pine roots really seems to have some relation to neural fibers of the dendrites of the brain, and they die at 106 degrees," she explains. "More and more cellular life is being found to be a symbiotic fusion of originally separate beings. The mycelium-neuron suspicion is in scientific literature that was brought to our attention by Christopher Mason, my son. I worked it into a plot that Carl changed and wrote."

Katherine MacLean is the author of numerous short stories and novels that have been translated into twenty languages. She was the recipient of the 1971 Nebula Award for her novella "The Missing Man." The Diploids (1962), a collection of some of her stories from the 1950s—including the wonderful "A Pyramid In The Desert"—proved a major distraction to the editor of this book, then thirteen, when he should have been applying grammatical Band-Aids to splintered syntax. (My apologies and thanks, therefore, albeit belated, to Alan Jones, my long-suffering English master at Leeds Grammar School, who would often ask me where I thought such behavior [reading paperbacks during lessons] would get me. Here's the answer.)

Carl West has taught art and is a former police officer who has lived and traveled through Central America and the South Pacific. He has co-authored one novel with MacLean—Dark Wing—and now divides his time between his farm and writing science fiction. Right now, they are both working on their own new books as well as collaborating on a third science fiction novel.

Whoever thinks that only big is beautiful, begin here....

379

All day long they climbed, the boy lagging behind him, the two working higher and higher, past the houses, past the roads, through sloped meadows, circling brush and brambles, resting in thin forests. The boy lagged and wandered and asked the same questions over and over in a dull mumble.

The father remembered the happy, almost singing voice of his son before the fever, the clever words, now stopped. Tears stung his eyes. He stopped and shared soda and sandwiches with the boy, and watched him for signs of improvement.

It had been a long year of waiting and watching, the two away from schools, out of doors, the child regaining health and grace, the father losing money, getting behind on his research. He had talked with old locals who remembered what medicine men had done for the brain damaged, the spirit-lost. Their stories had agreed.

Above, projecting from a distant white line of granite ledge towered the green-black spike of a huge hemlock evergreen, "Grandfather Tree." They were closer now, but the climb was steep. He turned aside to find an easier slope. The boy was tired. The whining repetition of the boy's voice was a dull pain in his ears.

The late afternoon sun sent long lengthening shadows and pools of cooling dark. He turned back to one and took the boy's arm. "Let's rest, then I'll carry both packs if you collect some firewood on the way."

The boy looked up dully and mumbled, "Straps hurt," and did not take off his straps. The father had to repeat twice before the boy understood and dropped his pack.

Later, his father shouldered both packs and trudged more slowly up the trail, while his boy ran ahead, gathering wood, cracking dead branches off trees with a silent grace that was different from the enthusiasm and exclamations of discovery of the years before the fever.

"Healthy," his father said. "Animal," his silent observation added and he ground his teeth against anger. The city doctors had said there was no hope. On the trails through Maine and Canadian forests, collecting botanical specimens, bringing his son, old Indians had looked at the boy and remembered that the spirit lost to a fever or blow on the head could sometimes be brought back by offerings to a grandfather tree that seemed a bad dream.

Under the great tree there was a wide spread of rounded ground, like a thick rug cushioned with fallen pine needles two feet deep. While the boy built a fireplace on the windswept granite ledge, his father carried one of his flakes of white granite up to the shade of the great tree and dug a groove. He lifted the bedding of pine needles and folded it back like layers of blankets until it turned damp and dark and showed the magic silver threads.

He was reassured by the sight of the mold. Trying not to break any of the silver web, he dug deeper until small tree roots stopped his fingers. It was deep enough. He smoothed it neatly into a body-sized trench, picked up the rock and called his son.

Afterward, he replaced the brown, damp layers with their silken white threads, tucking them in around the damaged bloody head and over the kerchief he had draped over the blank child's face, covering the motionless body, hoarsely singing the old native chants, and mixing it with calling on a god he no longer believed.

He sat beside the grave and remembered. He taught botany. A young native American studying at his college had come to his office and asked him about "ghost trees." He had confessed he had been blessed with advice and peace from a ghost tree after drunkenly trying to commit suicide beneath it, puking and spilling wine and drinking and leaking blood from crashing through brush and trying to cut his veins with a broken wine bottle, howling his rage against an unjust world until he passed out. He woke two days later under a huge old pine, feeling at peace, clearly remembering long talks with an old man who was a pine tree. The new peace of mind had lasted and become permanent. Afterward, the old men of his village had told him the tree was called Grandfather.

The botanist had tried to find the biggest hemlock

hanging over the Indian student's home village. It was dark under the great old tree. He felt a presence over him and looked up, but it was not an old man, it was the dark branches of the tree. The last purple clouds of sunset were fading in the west and he could no longer see his son's grave.

In the dark he stumbled and crashed downhill toward the ghostly glimmer of white rock ledge and fell by the two backpacks and the unused pile of firewood and lay waiting. After many hours he turned on an electric lamp and opened a book on growing spruce trees. It opened to a folded page.

"The long threads of mycelium mesh substitute for the shorter root threads of the tree and bring nourishment to an evergreen from a much wider expanse, often from a radius of fifty feet around an old isolated tree. In exchange for sugar and possibly aromatic terpenes in the sap sent down from the green top, the mat interfaces with the tree root and sends up minerals and dissolved nitrogen nutrients. The mat also recognizes the taste of certain diseases and virus infections that strike trees and provides appropriate antibiotics such as the mold provides for itself. It is notable that Larch, Pines, Spruce and Hemlock growing on almost pure rock but with a thick mycelium mat inhabiting the surrounding mulch are conspicuously taller and straighter, and have often lived and grown well beyond the lifespan of evergreens rooted in the normal soil of bottomland.

"We recommend that researchers look for the best mycelium samples below the fastest-growing pines in the most barren ground. It is worth noting that the samples of white mycelium threads collected must be kept in a cool damp medium in the dark and never exposed to a temperature higher than 105.5 Fahrenheit. It has been pointed out that 105.5 to 106 is the critical death or dysfunction temperature of the neurons of the human brain and this coincidence has launched speculation among the proponents of the chimera theory of evolution that cells are symbiotic associations of different organisms, that a case can be argued that nerves had originally been mycelia...."

He stopped reading. This book had misled him into this terrifying act. He put his head in his hands. Thoughts whispered: If the silver threads insert themselves into tree roots to feed and heal the tree in exchange for sugar water with terpenes and aromatics... Exchange...aromatics...alcohol...wine. Greeks...libations. The story of the student's leaking blood and bottles of spilled wine lying around him as he slept....

The father rose and carried bottles and cans up through the dark and poured all the remaining wine and all the boy's sodas around the brown earth blanket of his grave, and dissolved sugar in water and poured that too.

In the late morning he returned down the

mountains, praying loudly and incoherently and not looking behind him. The boy followed, carrying both their packs and asking often, in a clear educated voice, "What's the matter, Dad? Tell me, what's the matter?"

But his father was afraid.

m i c h a e l   m o o r c o c k

OR, TALES OF
A   DEAD
MAN'S CHEST
IN   WHICH
WE   ARE
APPRISED OF
UNGUESSED-
AT HORROR

Michael Moorcock was born in London in
1939 and says he spent most of World War
II in a paradise of bomb sites and dog-fights.
He's spent most of his time since then
writing.

Although he is probably best known
within the genre for his Eternal Champion
saga, a complex and seemingly unending
forty- or fifty-book sequence comprising
several series and a hapless central
protagonist doomed to inhabit myriad
identities always fighting on the side of
Order, he is equally revered by the so-called
literary establishment for a string of
ambitious and immensely readable tomes,
including Byzantium Endures,
The Brothel in Rosenstrasse
and the Whitbread Prize-shortlisted
Mother London. His work with
New Worlds—first as a contributor
and, more importantly, as the magazine's
editor—is acknowledged as the single most
influential force on the improving standards
and widening ambitions of the genre.

Politically an active pro-feminist,
Moorcock has campaigned against both

censorship and pornography. He is all for abolishing the Obscene Publications Act and introducing an Act which empowers those who have been harmed by pornography to take action against it. A regular contributor of political, scientific and literary articles to the likes of The Observer, The Daily Telegraph, The New Statesman, The Los Angeles Times, the late lamented Punch and even Woman's Journal, Moorcock has also published a travel book (Letters From Hollywood), books on literary criticism (such as Wizardy and Wild Romance) and, with Colin Greenland, Death Is No Obstacle, a book about literary technique.

A film of his Jerry Cornelius book, The Final Programme, was produced in 1973, and Moorcock also co-wrote "The Land That Time Forgot" with Jim Cawthorn. His legendary rock and roll performances are featured on many records by the band Hawkwind, and he has also recorded with his own band, The Deep Fix.

"As for superstitions," he writes, "mine are mostly very conventional and derive from my mother, who is very superstitious. She has something very like second sight, and so, as a boy, I was inclined to take her warnings seriously.

"I do all the usual things—touching wood, throwing salt over my left shoulder and so on—but my experience has shown that, fingers crossed, seven years' bad luck does not necessarily follow the breaking of a mirror: but I still believe it's best not to tempt fate.

"My mother believes that if you drop a knife and pick it up yourself then bad luck will follow. If nobody has visited her for a few days, the carpet can be littered with silverware."

Moorcock regards the superstitions by which we are manipulated by governments to be afraid or pugnacious or greedy as the ones to fear and reject. "I said in Mother London," he says, "that we survive by means of our myths and our superstitions. But we are also destroyed by them. We have to be careful about the ones we elect to follow. The current bunch of political superstitions—right and left, if those terms still mean anything—are beginning to look pretty scary to me."

INTRODUCTION

We visit Las Cascadas again, learning a little more of Begg Mansions and Sporting Club Square. Our main tale concerns Captain Horace Quelch, the infamous White Pirate and self-advertised "Last Christian Corsair on the Barbary Shore," and his oddly suited paramour, the Rose, a famous adventuress—How they first met, serving by some fluke an identical cause, while running guns into Africa. Yet this is not our central theme, which addresses the mystery of Quelch's unadvertised cargo, known from Port o' Spain to Ghana's Corsair Coast as "The Dead Man's Chest," and carrying with it an enormous weight of legend and myth…

CHAPTER ONE
The Rover's Return

One night, a trim schooner came into Las Cascadas Bay, dropping her anchor and her bilges to the vociferous disgust of the port's residents crowding their buff-coloured terraces and lush balconies to peer down on dark emerald-blue waters at that pale gold ship drifting in moonlight as if she had just sailed in from fairyland.

The schooner was, the rumour ran, crewed entirely by beautiful women. Don Harold Palimpest had seen them through his glass—and he could read a book on the moon with that powerful tool.

An official visitor to the island republic, Captain Albert Begg, R.N., was paying a courtesy call to the British Honourary Consul, Don Victor Dust, whom he had discovered to be a man of enormous literary education and enthusiasm, with a tolerant knowledge of life to match Begg's own, making Don Victor the best company Begg had experienced in his years of seven oceans, five continents and a hundred secret missions. They sat smoking on Dust's balcony, facing directly across the bay which was warmed, even at midnight, by lights from the bars and restaurants along the harbour and the almost-full moon shining directly overhead. From here they could watch the newcomer and speculate about her in the luxury of their reclining chairs.

Captain Begg opined that the schooner was too clean for a trader and her canvas too tidy for a private yacht. He thought she could be a youth-training vessel out of Gibraltar who had lost her signals, since she flew none; but he admired whoever had built her, and he doubted if he'd seen a fore-and-aft topsail rig so sweet in all his years at sea, and sweetly kept too. He pointed to fiery brass and blinding paint, reflecting the town dreaming in velvet on three sides of the bay.

Then Captain Begg smiled, for a flag ascended her mainmast just as the schooner swung girlishly, to reveal on her rounded stern the legend *Hope Dempsey*, *Casablanca*, painted in English and idiosyncratic but skilful Arabic.

And Captain Begg stood up, raising his glass.

Captain Horace Quelch had come back early to the islands, risking by a defiant week his amnesty, not due to begin until the first of November. It could be his last challenge, to show he had sold only his liberty to Laforgue the Pirate Chaser, never his spirit—and gambling that Count Estaban, the republic's governor, would turn a blind eye to a Cross of St. George now standing straight as a Spaniard's spine at his topgallant.

"Here's to the last Christian pirate," said Captain Begg, and Don Victor was bound to join him in his toast.

Don Victor guessed that Count Estaban, a great diplomat, would choose to ignore Quelch's affront, rather than try to arrest the pirate and succeed only in chasing him back to open seas where, from Aden to Zarzamora, he could continue his clever and ruthless trade. For Quelch was the only pirate Laforgue had ever been forced to strike a bargain with.

Now, even as the muezzin began their exquisite calls to prayer from Las Cascadas's etiolated spires, the strains of a defiant gramophone came up to those who still took an interest in the schooner. A tune popular during and after the Great War of 1915, a guitar, an accordion and various oddly shaped rhythm-sticks, a Latin dance.

Captain Begg, yearning for Don Harold's glass, thought he saw against a porthole's oil-lit yellow the shadows of his old friends, Captain Quelch and Colonel Pyat, performing the tango with the grace everyone had so admired when, in their glory days, they had all been comradely adversaries on the routes between Alexandria and New Orleans.

Next morning, when he went down to the port to buy his bread and his *Al País*, Begg heard that Captain Quelch was only awaiting a passenger and would be leaving again on the afternoon tide. Whereupon Captain Begg, anxious not to miss this opportunity, hired a boatman in the harbour and was rowed out to the *Hope Dempsey*, to be greeted enthusiastically by Horace Quelch, who had last served with Begg on Albanian minesweepers during the War of the Balkan Secession.

"I hope I'm not disturbing you, old boy." Begg embraced his old rival.

Horace Quelch kissed the navy man on both bearded cheeks. "My dear Albert! I am forever *a vostro beneplacito* for you! What brings you to Don Estaban's little fiefdom?"

Captain Begg explained that he was on an official visit. He admired the ship. He marvelled at her smartness.

"I have the best crew in the world," explained Quelch modestly.

The two old seadogs spent a comfortable couple of hours together in Quelch's bookish, almost fussy, cabin and caught up on mutual pals—pirates or King's Navy, it hardly mattered from their distance—and their successes, failures or resolutions of other sorts. Half a bottle of superb Armagnac was also consumed, together with four Castro cigars, to make the future look hopeful to them again and their past nothing lost, merely a confirmation that it was still satisfying and rewarding to steer a course that always had at least a few unexpected currents in it.

Thus rejuvenated, Captain Begg made it to his dinghy, with many further expressions of affection and declarations of the most profound comradeship, also faith in the years to come, and passed out, to be carried tenderly back to shore by one of Captain Quelch's own crew.

Albert Begg would say: "I never did see his passenger go aboard, though I found out later, of course, who it was." He would offer as authority for his own report the fact that Quelch's passenger was a distant relative on his uncle's side.

CHAPTER TWO

in which captain Quelch's expectations
are thoroughly defeated but not
entirely disappointed

Captain Quelch was deeply satisfied that society was about to repay its debt to him in the person of Count von Bek, whose agent had offered half a million gold ryads for a comfortable passage with some small cargo to Essouira which, in those days, was a port famous for the piety of its citizens and the briskness of its African arms trade. Knowing he could out-run anyone from Laforgue down, Quelch saw the job as an easy one. He felt his Kentish farm become reality when he accepted the offer, which would also be excellent cover for him to unload an embarrassing quantity of long boxes containing what had been in their day the best Martini repeating carbines ever smuggled to the Rif. "Now you can get more per gun from some fat Casablanca merchant who wants one to hang over his marble mantel and lie about how he took it from a grateful legionnaire who had begged for and received his mercy at the Battle of Ouarzazate, than you once got for a whole case! It's easy money, old boy. But is it sporting? The profit's huge and nobody shoots you if the goods should prove faulty. *Caveat emptor*, indeed! It's a turning world, isn't it, my dear Count!" He chatted man-to-man with his mysterious passenger who murmured responses from within a great weather-cloak but did not seem ready for conversation. Quelch displayed the interior of the luxurious little saloon and departed with almost religious courtesy as he accepted his first quarter million in a velvet purse of intricate Berber ornament, and said that the Count was welcome on the bridge whenever the Count was so disposed; meanwhile the cargo luggage was being carefully stowed, as directed. After securing his gold, Quelch went to give particular attention to the usual collection of massive cabin trunks without which no German nobleman was able to travel a mile or two to an overnight ball, and a longer, narrower box, tightly wrapped in dark, blood-red cloth bound with long braids of glistening silver and gold, a baroque jewelled crucifix burning upon the upper surface.

Quelch judged this last to be a family relic, being brought under some archaic vow to a North African resting place, where an ancestor had once lost his heart to a local Fatima. Doubtless the Count was that unfortunate relative chosen to supervise the digging up of the elderly romantic's corpse (no matter what its condition) as soon as the yearning ancestor's hated spouse was safely gone from this world to reconciliation in the next.

The fad for disinterment and exotic reburial had been popular for over fifty years and showed no sign of disappearing. Quelch put it all down to cheap yellowback novels by E. Mayne Hull and Pierre Loti, not to mention those interminable Frances Day musical comedies, forever touring *The Desert Song* about the Levant and Magrib and still depressingly popular with German and British residents.

When the anchors were up and his exquisite schooner blossoming under full sail, flaunting all the laws of the sea, pushing hard toward Tripoli, his passenger appeared in the wheelhouse revealing herself as the famous adventuress Countess Rose von Bek, whereupon Captain Quelch dryly advised her to take the ship's boat and row like hell for Las Cascadas because his crew was as fine a bunch of hand-picked oriental nancy-boys as you could wish to find ashore or afloat.

"But they don't like women much. They reckon, my dear Countess, that women bring bad luck. They threw a pretty little thing of fourteen overboard only a month or two back. They have a strict code, don't you know, and take a firm moral line against anyone who transgresses it. Her boyfriend had a longer, more conspicuous and altogether grislier finish. A sore little bottom by the end of the day, what? Proper punishment for any naughty nipper. In their book, at any rate. And mine, really."

The Rose ignored this teasing. She recognised Quelch's kind and knew his measure, but she took the precaution of having the crew assembled for a few minutes. Addressing them in their own languages she informed them that they were fools intent on ensuring their destruction if they burdened their souls with superstition. They were drowning, she said, in their own shit, their own ignorance. They would never be free or fulfil their dreams unless they educated themselves and learned to behave as civilised men. Then she informed them that she was paying a large sum for her passage; thus, for the duration of her time aboard, she would be their commander.

The laskars looked once to Quelch, who turned his shrugging back on them; then they knelt as a man to offer her their hearts and their lives.

"Bad luck for whom, Horace?" she asked, sideways at him.

And he was bound to grin and tip his dirty cap to her. At which the Rose immediately fell under his charm, experiencing a powerful sensation, mixed lust and profound recognition. She had lost her heart to the old pirate. A tiny gasp escaped her perfect lips.

CHAPTER THREE
In which a famous Angel is Discussed

In the old days, Quelch would always spend his
Christmas break with Albert and Caroline Begg. It was
Albert Begg who had given him a taste for the sea and
helped him find the courage to trade places and
professions with his twin brother, the salty Maurice.

While a guest at Sporting Club Square, Quelch
would accompany his host round the gardens every
evening. The square was at its best in the late autumn
with its windows' yellow light softening the glowing
terracotta touched by a setting orange sun. The great
London trees were still red and golden brown, not yet
in full fall, and beyond them were the stately
silhouettes of those uniquely ordered buildings, each
mansion block a different architectural conceit, a
wedding cake in Buckingham brick, and then a pink
aura, a light blue sky.

Once, stopping beside his favourite bed of late
dahlias, Captain Begg had asked Quelch, then a rather
timid housemaster, if he had ever heard of the Nation
of Angels, a supernatural world in which ideal versions
of ourselves wage war against evil? Quelch admitted
that he had not. He only knew, he said, of one
legendary angel, the Rose of Sporting Club Square
herself, who was said to be a particular guardian of the
Beggs.

Captain Begg had smiled at this. "But one has to

be a true innocent to see her, I'm told, so I've no chance and you neither, old chum."

Ironically, in those days, Quelch really did have a chance, but his own romantic sensibilities had led him away from innocence until here he was, the most feared old swaggerer on either side of the Tideless Sea.

Now, as he admitted the extent of his fascination with the Rose, he recalled that legend vividly. He believed in his bones that the famous Angel was with him on board. What was worse, he had fallen in love with her. But worse still, she was attracted to him. He was conquered. He was terrified.

For the first few otherwise agreeable days, while the schooner turned and steered on secret currents, moved by winds known only to Quelch and his crew, the Rose and Captain Quelch kept as wide a distance as possible as each wrestled with chaotic emotions. The third day, at dinner, they declared their madness and accepted it.

Contrary to the captain's predictions, the crew became deeply sentimental and were greatly moved by the union, celebrating it by giving extra pride to their duties and cheering the couple whenever they appeared together on deck. So the rest of the voyage was spent in a kind of ecstacy; with Essouira reached, the rifles sold cheaply and carelessly and the Countess's chief errand put in abeyance once she had delivered the cabin trunks (full of modern Mausers) to her partner 'Rabaq Bey. She then returned her attention to the enchanting Captain Quelch who wished to sail with her to his old stronghold and show her its beauty and his treasure.

CHAPTER FOUR
in which our Lovers are roused from their glamour by a monstrous manifestation

Castella de Las Piños: For years, this Spanish-style fortified village, with its outrageously baroque Gaudi castle, had never fallen to an enemy gun and rarely seen so much as an enemy mast. The return of their popular chief and his bride was welcomed with considerable festivity by the citizens, some of whom had even served a season or two of their own with the Rose, when she had belonged to the Brotherhood of the Coast, called the Barbary Vixen by her enemies or the Red Angel by her admirers. Here was a fitting spouse for their captain; a goddess to adore. Her sword, Swift Thorn, she now sported on her hip, and Quelch was both amused and besotted by her dash, her graceful choreography.

Barnaby Slyte, elected Mayor of Las Piños, offered the general sentiment when he spoke on the quayside and hoped the master and mistress had come to settle down for a while.

"That's for Fate to decide, good old Slyte," says Captain Quelch, clapping his portly bo'sun on the back. "But I have a feeling I'll be sticking my feet up for a while, at least."

Then, with the townsfolk behind them, as colourful a mob of lace-trimmed butchers and their doxies as ever graced a pirate fortress, Quelch took her up the winding street to his Moorish gateway, rival to the Alhambra, and then into the castle, a filigree fantasy in four-foot granite blocks and carved marble, to order the place emptied so that he might take her privately to his vaults stacked with the loot of three continents, to make Monte Cristo's wealth seem modest. It had been accumulated, Quelch boasted, wholly through ransoming fat daughters of the Tripoli Merchants, every one of whom was returned to her father with her innocence intact.

"Still blood money, Horace," she insisted, continuing an ongoing argument. "Earned by the employment of terror and force."

"Well," says Captain Quelch, "true enough, my dear Rose, but it's a complicated world, and not every one of those charming little ladies was pleased to be restored. I get their letters. To this day." He bowed to her, deeply, his back toward his mounds of treasure, and he picked up a gorgeous Egyptian necklace, gold and turquoise and rubies, offering it on the flat of his hand.

He was too much of a gentleman to show his disappointment when she refused the gift. After all, he told himself, it was this prim quality which he so admired in her. He blamed his public school education, but he was helpless before its endless power.

Lost Pines, as the English called it, was famous for

the tall evergreens which framed its elegant white
domes and towers, as orderly and neat a port as any
on the Magribi coast. Her huge population of cats kept
the streets clean as the houses, and the whole town
was touched by a pleasant scent of sage and rosemary.

As well as the Mausers, which had made her a good
profit, even at that low price, the Rose had also carried
four kilos of Meng and Ecker's #1 Special Mixture,
which was currently banned in Morocco, where the
State had the monopoly, and thus worth a fortune on
the red market. She had been planning to move up the
coast to Tafouelt, the walled city of the Blue Men, and
trade her M&E with the Tuareg for their silver and
their ivory. An ounce or two of this was broken out
and placed in Horace Quelch's ornate brass hookah,
which dominated the centre of his leather-panelled
private smoking room, painted in the Persian mode and
full of luscious Leighton paintings and Crane tiles, part
of the Lipton salvage when the millionaire grocer's
yacht was found abandoned on Fever Sound in 1919.

The lovers shared their memories and elaborated
upon each other's dreams, aiming for a state of visual
and spiritual consciousness neither had experienced
since their early days but which now seemed achievable
again. They were almost successful and the memory was
sweet reward enough. They indulged those elegiac
tastes to which the visionary romantic is prone, when
denied melodrama or at very least a doomed love affair,
and they wept once or twice for a lost idyll, but mostly
they remembered their age and station and kept

enough humour in reserve to remind them that this was almost certainly no more than a pleasant lull in a lifetime of exotic action.

Sure enough, after a couple of weeks, the couple was aroused from some intricately comfortable embrace by the news that the *Hope Dempsey* was missing from the harbour, her crew with her. Could it be that Quelch's hand-picked homophiles had betrayed him, after all?

The Rose, sickened by this sudden return of common sense, raised an exquisite hand to her perfect lips and spoke in an appalled whisper. "Oh, no! The cargo!"

"Just your mysterious box, Countess." Her lover was unmoved by his vessel's high value but knew that a hull as clean and responsive as that only came under your feet once in a lifetime. He was determined to pursue and recapture his beloved schooner.

The Rose was quickly persuaded of her own self-interest, and together they called for a crew from amongst the townsfolk, to take the cumbersome old ocean-going dhow, *Scheherazade*, in pursuit of the stolen schooner.

CHAPTER FIVE
In which The Rose Reveals something About an undying Ancestor

Their eager, if rusty, complement gradually remembered how to coax the best out of a sluggish vessel, and the *Scheherazade* was soon making good speed through the outlying islands, the course of the *Hope Dempsey* reported from watch-towers set up to warn of unfamiliar ships in the pirate domain.

The Rose and Captain Quelch studied maps in the charthouse. They found the course a little baffling. "Why should they be setting into the Cameroon Bite, a place avoided by even the most daring pilots and sporting sailors?" asks Quelch, taking a tidy measurement.

"Because they no longer care if they live or die," the Rose told him. "They serve another master now."

"What more do you know?" he demanded, laying down his rule.

"Only that there is something alive in your hold, Captain."

"An animal?"

"If you like. I would describe it as a creature which has lost all reason, all humanity, yet which was once everything a man might wish to be."

"You mean you had a living *man* in that box you brought aboard, Rose?"

"Not living in any sense you mean, Horace. This poor monster is cursed with longevity, yet can never know happiness. For centuries he has wandered the world, desperate for death, seeking, he says, the one human being who can save him and bring him rest. I have listened to him, dreaming within his prison—a prison his relatives constructed for him, enjoining me to grant him the peace he sought. Oh, make no mistake, Horace, he is active and very powerful—able to put a score of people under his spell at once. He has profound knowledge of every oriental and occidental science. He recognises no morality in the ordinary meaning of the term. He is fearless because he has feared everything and been destroyed by nothing. He exists only to feed his bizarre cravings and is utterly without compassion. He is dedicated I believe, to destroying what little order this civilisation of ours had tried to erect against Chaos and Old Night. I was told he would remain dormant for at least six months, long enough to do what I had to do. He has gathered power, even as he slept! I feared as much, but I quieted myself, indulged myself."

"But what does this mean, my dear?" he wished to know.

"It means, Horace, that we have a monster loose amongst us. I was entrusted with the mission of taking him to the far Sahara and burying him at the abandoned Oasis of the Ouled Nail, which was poisoned with radium and is now avoided by nomads and caravans alike. You are not bound to help me recapture the creature, Horace. This is a task for which I should be entirely responsible."

But Quelch was resolute. "He has my ship, Rose, my dear. And my crew? Don't you think he's put some sort of 'fluence on those obedient laskars? A monster indeed! You must tell me more of his story when it's politic. Meanwhile, I was equally lax and am equally bound to aid you in this matter."

The Rose admitted that she could think of no better

ally in such an enterprise. They smoked what remained of their M&E then retired to their bunk to await some revelation.

"He was known as Manfred, Count of Crete and Lebanon. He married a great-grandmother of the von Beks. There was no issue."

"So he is not even a blood relative!" said Quelch.

"Many people believe him to be Jewish," she said, "though he denies this vehemently...."

"But that's a well-known story," said Quelch, slowly, savouring his recollections. "Browning did a poem on the subject. And so did Austin. My favourite's always Wheldrake. I knew him before the War, when he was living in Putney. He'd walk across the bridge at the same time that I was going out. I was in digs there, in one of those old rooming houses overlooking the Thames, all massive buttresses and gothic turrets, with rowing sheds on either side. Mrs. Ottoman ran it and also served teas on her terrace during the summer for the boating parties and oarsmen who made Ottoman's the favourite stopping place below Hammersmith and one of the most popular on the entire river, from Oxford to Greenwich. Wheldrake went there out of season, breaking his walk to enjoy a half-pint of beer before returning home to The Cedars. It was there that he signed my copy of *Bernice Beati* for me—before the police seized pretty much the whole edition from his printers. I became something of a protégé of his, I suppose. I used to be proud of that, but fashions change, don't they? *Cave quid dicis, quando, et cui*, eh? My mistake was always to be too outspoken. My patron became unfashionable, my own literary career was nipped in the bud and I was forced to take a job as housemaster at an obscure school on the Kent coast where I was forever plagued by fat boys, practical jokers and pious young heroes who, thank God, were mostly wiped out at the Battle of Buchenwald. Wasn't the Count of Crete mixed up with some scandal during the Second Empire? Some terrible financial thing in which thousands of ordinary people were ruined?"

"Who wasn't?" She had hardly listened to his anecdote.

"But why would he be taking my ship to the Cameroon Bite and how has he seduced my laskars? Their sense of self-preservation is their greatest virtue."

"You could say the same about Count Manfred," she murmured and then was unwilling to continue the conversation.

CHAPTER SIX
In which captain Albert Begg finds Himself once Again Involved with His old friend Alfred

Begg was on his way back to Gibraltar when he received the news over the Morse that the *Hope Dempsey* had broken her parole and was heaving into forbidden waters, some kind of Arab craft pursuing her—both ships weaving a bafflingly irregular course.

Captain Begg had orders to make for waters off the Cameroon Bite and observe the movements of the vessels, reporting back to Georgetown at regular intervals.

This was familiar stuff, Begg would tell his future listeners, since most of my service life was in Naval Intelligence, which is a wonderful niche for a chap who loves languages and has a passion for fiction. A comfortable berth in my time and probably still is— though you miss being able to tune in the Savoy Orpheans on the radio. Moreover my curiosity was whetted by my old friend's mysterious behaviour. I had it in mind to be of help to him, if that were possible within the broad terms of what we perceived (in that idiosyncratic arm of our service) as our duty.

Needless to say (Begg continued) I was not going to expose either my ship or my crew to danger and had no intention of venturing into the Bite itself. The Rose, brave as she is, has only sailed into the Biloxi Fault, never through the Lavender Haze. I had no special qualities as a sailor and, as an observer, was not expected to do anything but let the second officer run things. My job was to study the movements of a pirate on broken parole but not to engage him. If in danger I should have the presence of mind to signal for help in good time. We had a nine-inch Bofors and an old Gatling for armament, sufficient for a fighting chance against a Zeppelin or a heavily armed fishing boat, but useless against modern aircraft. Still, we weren't likely to encounter anything very sophisticated—not that a gun would be proof against—so we ran up the usual signals and laid off below that appalling horizon....

But such terrors were all in the past, of course, Begg hastened to warn his listeners, some of whom were small children at the family home in Begg Mansions and were beginning to look alarmed. Albert Begg realised it was as if someone had told him, when he was their age, that King Kong was still abroad and might come round the corner at any moment, walking down Olympia Avenue to tear the roof off the building and pluck them out like toy soldiers. "No more a threat than old King Kong," he said, to reassure them.

At this, the children became baffled. King Kong was no longer part of their mythology. Even the wild realities of thirty years ago seemed a little too fanciful for present tastes.

"Such uncertainties are abolished now and good riddance to them, I say. I am ready to enjoy the security and predictability achieved under this current triumph of Law and hang the obvious consequences. But you should study a little, my children, the experience of the past, because already in my short lifetime I see the same kind of people making the same mistakes, resulting in the same awful consequences for society at large. Avoid prescriptive politics, my dears, at all costs. They are un-English, whether they come from Left or Right. They are always wrong, always bad. And those who provide the prescriptions all too rarely suffer the consequences of their outrageous, egotistical follies. And there is nothing more time-wasting than a clash of prescriptions in parliament. It is the business of parliament to interpret the popular will, not patronise its voters!"

Whereupon he stopped himself and offered the children a grave apology. Turning to the adults he suggested, through some harmless code, he make a pretty little ending for the children and tell the true tale later. The parents agreed to this, so he obliged.

The children were treated to a tale of monsters vanquished and were sent to bed, bearing with them that comfortable thrill of a demon confronted and overpowered. But their parents made themselves more comfortable by the fire with full glasses and their attention upon the old salt, who never failed to enjoy the effects of his own retailings, but he avoided any further political excursions.

The sky (he went on) was alive with sinuous funnels of gas—browns and blacks and greys—through which a hellish sun burned murky rays and the sea was agitated, neurotic. There was no soothing rhythm to the waters of the Cameroon Bite. You have seen the pictures, I am sure, but you could never imagine the experience of being there, even at so great a distance.

We had recently had our optics renewed and could get some pretty good sightings. Soon we had made out the *Hope Dempsey* under full sail, steering an irregular but rapid course that was roughly north-west. Behind her, making impressive speed, came an ordinary trading dhow, by some means following almost exactly in the schooner's wake.

The mystery was that the Lavender Haze lay off to their starboard and their course lay away from it. So they were not, after all, planning to enter the Haze. And what of the vampire—or whatever it was—which now commanded the *Hope Dempsey*? But I race ahead of my tale....

Two days later, pretty much due north of the Haze, when the ships had disappeared from view and not been sighted by us for twenty-four hours, we picked up the outlines of a small sailing dinghy, its canvas in rags, making desperate speed, by another queer route, toward us.

I gave the order to move in a little closer and shorten the distance between us.

I had a feeling we were picking up survivors.

CHAPTER SEVEN
In the shadow of the Haze

"I really wasn't prepared for anything radical," said the Rose, handing Quelch's spyglass back to him.

"There's always a price to pay for these idylls, in my experience," Quelch told her. "It's in the nature of our game, dear Rose. But I must admit I expected a more natural conclusion to our affair. I suppose this way is at least dramatic. Good theatre, perhaps, but hard on old bones."

"I've never known a sailor more stuffed with superstitions and discredited opinion," she said. "You can make a game of this, Horace, as much as you wish. But if we do not find Count Manfred, there will be the most catastrophic consequences, not least for my father and the entire Lombardian government!"

Impressed by her tone, Quelch assured her that it was not important whether he took her seriously—though indeed the case did seem serious—since he would soon have the wheel of the *Hope Dempsey* firmly under his two hands, her crew disciplined and about their ordinary business and everything ship-shape, as it was when they first anchored in Lost Pines Bay. "It's in my self-interest, Rose."

The Rose accepted this for the time being, knowing that her lover was not a thorough-going exponent of enlightened self-interest. The ex-pirate was bearing it in mind to learn more of that valuable box and its wormy occupant. He knew that people had killed to get it. What kind of creature was capable of controlling his laskars from within a coffin? If he could find out more, he knew that such information might bring a handsome profit from the Romans, the Greeks or any other friendly government wanting to be privy to Lombardy's particular secrets.

"Our first task is to engage them," she reminded him, "and there is still too much distance between us."

Then she proposed a plan whereby she took the wheel and used a skill or two of her own.

To his credit, Quelch had every faith in her and

congratulated her when her superior navigation got them a mile or two closer to the wandering *Hope Dempsey*. And then he understood their course.

"Only one island remained above water after the upheaval," he said. "It's known as Duke's Island by the English and Isla de Juifes by the Portuguese and Arcadians. It's said to conceal a vast treasure buried since the time of Christ by Joseph of Arimathea and it has an underground castle ruled by an undying lord mourning the loss of his abducted daughter and hating all living creatures as much as he hated himself! Could your Count Manfred have left Duke's Island and now be returning?"

"If that were the case and this journey at his instigation," declared the Rose, "then why should I have been charged with the task of burying him in that radium dump at Oasis Ouled Näil? No, Captain Quelch, it is my ancestor's happy adaptability, his desire to refuse the fact of death at any price, which motivates this voyage. I would swear to it. He knows so much. I am not at all sure who or what he will find at the Isla de Juifes! But I do not think it will be himself."

She looked away toward the gathering coils and gassy knots which passed, faint shadows, within the icy depths of the Lavender Haze. She felt almost defeated.

CHAPTER EIGHT
Addressing the Jungle

"These days," Begg continued, "it is impossible to understand the terror in which the Haze was held. It had appeared overnight, and while no ship that had sailed into it had ever returned, occasionally it spewed something out which had no business breathing ordinary mortal air and moving beneath an ordinary mortal sun. The thing had spawned an entire industry in almanacs and geomancies, not to mention religious and scientific cults.

"We still have some of those cults hanging on in spite of all their evidence having been banished to whatever part of the astral plane it originally sprang from. My only regret was that the cults were not sent back to limbo with the object of their faith. But you can imagine the awful fear of the Haze which must have filled the Rose and Captain Quelch, for all their wide experience of the world. Only madness and agony lay within. And death of course."

He explained how, by combining their considerable sailing skills, they managed to steer the lumbering *Scheherazade* into the little hidden harbour of Duke's Island and find the *Hope Dempsey*, an affronted aristocrat but none the worse for her experience, recently abandoned, her crew deep in a sleep that looked sorcerous, while the oblong box from the hold lay with its lid torn off and a swathe of red cloth draped over ropes of gold and silver hiding a jewelled crucifix, perhaps some sort of device adopted by the occupant as a means of identification. Its meaning puzzled Captain Quelch. Was this a secret of the Lombardian royal family's? Only an aristocrat would abandon such a valuable piece without a thought. He made no move toward it but followed the Rose to the main deck.

"There," she said, "you have your ship and your crew again, Captain, and none the worse for wear, I'd guess. As soon as those boys wake up they'll be ready to follow you to hell and back, mark my words. You can sail on now. Only leave me the dhow, the box and a couple of your laskars, so I can get away from here when my duty is done."

"Well, madam," says Quelch after a little thought, "my curiosity has me now and won't let me go until it's satisfied. I'd be obliged if you'd let me join your expedition to the interior. I could be of help. I am something of an expert with the revolver." And privately he considered the potential political import of whatever secret the old Count carried and which could so embarrass Rose von Bek's Irish father, the engineer O'Bean, or cause trepidation in the House of Lombardy.

Touched, but not entirely convinced, the Rose accepted his help. After taking refreshment aboard the schooner, they headed a small expedition up into the jungle while Bo'sun Slyte, sweat running like mountain rivers down the soft geography of his upper body, took charge of the hands and gave orders to revive the laskars, if that were possible.

Barnaby Slyte waited four days before he allowed himself to suspect that his captain and the rest weren't returning. Only now were the laskars beginning to awake, and they spoke sluggishly in pidgin about a "berry bad, berry, berry bad debil fella belong deepdown nogood." But they could offer no further description of the sea-thief who had commanded them from a rope-bound coffin deep within the hold.

All that Slyte learned, Begg said, increased his sense that his master and mistress were leading their men against some creature of demonic malice, whose psychic powers were impossibly advanced.

Meanwhile, Barnaby Slyte was confounded. He feared it was his duty to lead an expedition up the trail through the jungle to the castle, to learn of his captain's fate.

He was not to know that Quelch's messenger, a distant cousin, had been bitten by a cobra and collapsed on the road, which the natives called the Sacred Trail of Death and which they travelled only when their time had come.

CHAPTER NINE
A confusion of wanderers

Protected by local superstition, Quelch, the Rose and their party reached the top of the wooded hill without serious incident and stood beside a deep moat staring up at a massive Gothic castle, evidently of late-Victorian or even Edwardian restoration, combining modern comfort with archaic grandeur. Captain Quelch noted the excellent pointing.

"Rather reassuring." He gave his attention to the cylinders of his twin Colts, rubbing the barrels on his sleeve to shine them up a bit. He replaced the pistols in his belt. "Are we ready, Countess?"

The Rose drew her slender sword, Swift Thorn, and led the way across the unguarded drawbridge into the castle's barbican which had none of the depressing Norman severity on which it was modelled, but had been laid out in a series of geometric flower-beds, full of every variety of seasonal blooms and shrubs. There was a settled, domestic air to the place, even though it was deserted.

Receiving no response to their echoing halloos, they entered the door of the main keep. The interior was as cheerful and well lighted and the papered walls showed a preference for William Morris and the arts and crafts movement, particularly the Scottish school. Captain Quelch recognised many original paintings which he had thought lost.

At length they entered a warm, book-lined, oak-beamed hall, twinkling with polished brass and copper, in which a hearty fire blazed. The furniture was largely Eastlake, of a somewhat heavy, ecclesiastical style, perfectly in tune with the revived romanticism of the castle. Wine, spirits and beer were arranged on the hospitable sideboards. Two massive leather easy chairs stood either side of the fire and on an elbow table next to one sat a book (*Don Estaban and Duke Rupoldo* by Carlisle), an empty Galley glass and a jar of mints; there was a footstool before this chair, the indentations showing that it had been recently used. The farthest walls were lined with glass-fronted bookshelves containing a conspicuous array of disparate bindings and titles, representing all periods and types of human literature.

"The home of a retired gentleman, I would say," murmured Captain Quelch. But he kept his hand on a pistol.

"And, it seems, a serious recluse," the Rose added.

Whereupon, as if summoned by their references, suddenly a side door opened with a startling creak and from behind it emerged a gaunt, uncouth figure, its stooped shadow flung upon the books as it extended an unappealing hand to Quelch and announced that it was Count Manfred, Lord of Castle Zion, and that the travellers were welcome to rest and take refreshment, but that they were trespassing and should be aware that they were disturbing one who did not relish human company.

This statement was belied by the happy security and hospitable air of the place, but the pirates said nothing. The hands looked to the sideboard and at Count Manfred's signal helped themselves to drinks. The Count regretted that his servants were at present visiting the mainland, but they would be back at any time. Meanwhile he would be grateful if they respected his need for privacy. "I am a scholar, used to my own company." He spoke in a resonant, gloomy voice which seemed a little cracked at the edges, as if it had been used too much or too little.

The Rose, however, was impatient with this charade, for she recognised her errant relative. "This is simply not your style, Count Manfred. Why dress in rags and tatters and pay such poor attention to personal appearance when this furniture is so lovingly kept? This is a room of a sybarite. You were never that! I suspect that you have no right to be here. I know you for my ancestor, whom I am charged to bury at the Oasis of the Ouled Näil. I beg you, for all our sakes, to end your play-acting, for it is dreadfully unconvincing, and come with me to your long-deserved rest."

At this the creature drew himself up, the deep hollows of his eye-sockets moving with angry lights, and his long-fingered, shaking hands went to his head, as if to protect it from further assault. "Rest?" cried the monster. "Rest?" His laughter was hollow. "In the radium pits? Oh, I have begged for rest so many times! I have yearned for release from this terrible enslavement of life. I have climbed to the peaks of the world's tallest mountains, flung myself into the deepest gorges, given myself up to the wildest torrents, descended into the maelstrom and sunk into the bubbling lava of that same Vesuvius that destroyed my Pompei town-house. Yet all to no avail. Death has been denied me. Rest is unattainable—or seemed so until now. Rest, Rose von Bek, has eluded me for almost two thousand years! I grew reconciled that I was never to know it. I long to be buried in my native soil with the full rites of the church and a tranquil soul reunited with its redeemer in Heaven. I do not deserve some desert pit, where I am never fully dead but consigned to spend eternity amongst the poisons and residues Society would rather forget it ever created! Is that justice? All I ask is for a true end to this. I have to go back to Nuremberg. Blood calls to blood. It is one of our most basic understandings. I am tired of my struggle. I need to go home! *Mein Kampf*! *Mein Kampf*! Is it over at last?"

Captain Quelch showed evident impatience with this self-dramatising rhetoric. "What did you do to my crew, Count Manfred?" he demanded. "What unnatural power did you exert over them to make them bring you here?"

"Power?" The Count of Crete threw back his cadaverous head, cackling his mockery. "Power? What? Am I the Devil? No, I am as human as you, Captain Quelch. The power I had was the power of their stupid superstitious minds. Nothing else. I have no special supernatural skills. One of your boys was curious and tried to open the box. Happily I am possessed of considerable physical strength. I was grateful for my freedom. When they saw me appear on deck the laskars thought Death commanded them. I told them I would take them with me into the Land of Shadows unless they worked hard and got the ship to this island in record time. It is not always visible.

"Very little energy was required to bend those

laskars to my will. It never requires much energy. My appearance and their fear achieves most of what I need. They were terrified that if they slept I would suck their brains and souls out, so they made liberal use of the cocaine each of them had been planning to smuggle into Barcelona.

"As a result, when they got to this island they were thoroughly crazed and absolutely exhausted, falling asleep on their feet. I had grown attached to one or two of them, but I left them all on the schooner, then made my way up here. To my castle." This last was said with a certain defiance.

"It's plain to us that you neither prepared this fire or laid down that book, sir," said the Rose. "This castle is not your work."

He turned aside with a slouching, surly motion of his shoulders. He stared into the fire. "What's that to you, madam? My servants are responsible for this. Now, leave me in peace. Or stay the night, if you wish. But do not expect me to accompany you to the radium cemetery. I intend to return to Hamburg and from there make my way slowly east. I have some old debts to repay. For almost two thousand years I have wandered and I have grown weary. Now, here, I can find honest death...."

"Good Heavens, old boy! You're not..." Quelch found it almost impossible to utter the words, '...suggesting that you are the original Wandering Jew?"

At this the Count drew himself up, his entire horrid frame trembling with deep emotion. He moved his head until his cold eyes glared with something akin to passion into Quelch's own.

"What?" he demanded. "Wandering *what?* You braying fool! You short-lived ape. You make the same obtuse assumptions as all the others!" His pitted features twisted in torment and anger. "Cretin! I have travelled the world for forty lifetimes and more, seeking the one human soul who could save me—or one human being who would believe my story. Almost two thousand years, and I never discovered that one creature. Not one in all the centuries of my agony. None, that is—*until now!*"

"There's no excuse for bad manners, old boy," remonstrated Quelch mildly.

The other pirates looked embarrassed, as if they were regretting leaving the harbour. One of them murmured that he was ready to believe anything after the events of the past few days but feeling the Count's eye upon him spoke up nervously. "And what is that story, sir?"

The creature's hollow sockets burned with recollected agonies and disappointments. "It is a tragic story," he replied. "A tale of terrible events and unjust adventure. I was born on the site of modern Nuremberg, the spiritual capital of the Teutonic people. My name is not Lazarus, but Manfred, and I am not Jewish. True, it is impossible to kill me or fo me to kill myself. True I am doomed to live forever, for failing to give Christ a cup of water on his way to Calvary, but the whole thing was a dreadful mistake. I was employed as an agent for a Greek grain dealer and just happened to be in Jerusalem on the day. I had no direct involvement with any of the proceedings. I was never guilty. Can you not see why I am so obsessed with a sense of injustice? I have endured every kind of insult, every calumny! And much of it because of mistaken identity. No, my friends, it is not the Wandering Jew who stands before you...."

He paused, staring again into the fire as if he saw the flames of Hell there and yearned for them. "I am Manfred the Goth. And I am the Wandering Gentile."

At this Captain Quelch looked sceptical, and even the most gullible pirates were unimpressed. It was left for the Rose to ask the obvious: "Are you suggesting that for all this time the world has been mistaken and that there is no such person as the Wandering Jew?"

He turned on her again, his bony fingers stroking his body as if seeking wounds. "Did I tell you that? Oh, the Wandering Jew exists. He is very much alive. For almost two thousand years I have pursued him, following rumours, myth, folk-tales—I have walked the length and breadth of all the world's continents. I have seen miraculous sights and had thousands of extraordinary experiences. I knew he existed. I believed that as soon as I found him, and if that meeting were witnessed, then I would know rest. I

421

would be freed from the curse and the world would see at last how specifically I had suffered. Almost two millennia—and I never discovered him and was never redeemed. How I begged the God above to release me from my bondage, to bring us together so that the curse would be lifted. All I had to do was prove to another human soul that I was cursed as he was cursed. Then the soul of the Wandering Gentile would be at peace. Now it has come about. My soul can return to the womb of its fatherland, in Nuremberg. I shall go first to Hamburg and travel a little in Bohemia and Poland, concluding my journey in Warsaw perhaps. The route will to a large degree define itself. But I shall die where I was born. It is all I ask."

"I wish you luck, old boy." Captain Quelch was uncomfortable and not sure why. "Well, where's the original occupant of this place, then? You haven't murdered the poor chap, I hope."

The cadaverous wretch again glared, uttering cryptic curses and spitting out his words in a disgusted stream. "*Poor chap*, is it? *Poor chap*, eh? Bah! Save your sympathy for me, my dear sir, not for that *poor chap*! Ugh! Imagine my chagrin when I arrived here only a few hours since and was not challenged. I knew a kind of elation. It was as if I would soon meet my twin soul. I had imagined him suffering as I had suffered, trying to kill himself, standing upon the peaks of midnight mountains in the Himalayas yelling his torment to the skies. I have wandered so painfully, so hopelessly, so needlessly. Have you any notion of what my eyes beheld when I entered this room? Can you imagine the filthy cosiness of the whole sickening scene? I saw him as soon as I opened the door, but he did not at first see me.

"There he sat, in that chair, oblivious to everything but his reading. He lazed in a comfortable smoking jacket, holding a letter from a loved one, his feet on the footstool in front of a blazing fire which sent cheerful shadows round the room, merry as Christmas, beside him on his table a glass of brandy, an opened book, a jar of mints, while the cabinet gramophone you see over there played exquisite Alkan. Could anyone have witnessed such obscenity and not act as I acted? Remember, Captain Quelch, I sought the fellow out for almost two thousand years! I imagined him doing as I did— tramping the solitary trails and rocky roads of an unjust world, forever doomed to seek forgiveness, a fellow sufferer."

"Are you saying that the rightful occupant of this castle actually is the Wandering Jew?" the Rose exclaimed with sudden understanding.

Her relative seemed to approve of her intelligence.

His cold eyes lit with something akin to pleasure. "Exactly!" he said. "*His* name is Lazarus, not mine! He refused Christ a cup of water! He is the true carrier of this curse, not I!"

"What have you done with him?" the Rose wished to know, but the Count dismissed her question with an impatient gesture.

"The creature confessed all this to me not an hour ago! He has been sitting in more or less the same spot, in more or less the same chair, at more or less the same time of day, since the ninth century! He has not wandered at all! He has known nothing but comfort and good-will, the respect and love of his children, grandchildren, great-grandchildren and so on. I demanded to be told how he had suffered and he admitted that he thought he had suffered once, but the suffering was a mere faded memory. It was at about the time of the Diet of Worms, he said, that it occurred to him there was precious little point in wandering, when all common sense suggested taking advantage of the situation and settling down comfortably somewhere to enjoy life as it came. Over the course of centuries his sensible investments made him immensely rich. He married a succession of mortal wives and all his offspring did well in various humanitarian vocations and almost invariably left the world a better place....

"The Jew lived in luxury and security on this island," (Count Manfred continued). "During all those hundreds of years in which I sought him so painfully, he was sedately settled with his books, his companion, his children, protected by the superstitious fear of all sailors who gave his home waters wide berth, refusing to accept that the Isla de Juifes even existed. Occasionally, he told me, he would rescue some shipwrecked maiden who had been ill used by men and found his patient good humour a welcome change.

"The boys, he told me, he usually slaughtered. He

said their blood was particularly efficacious in the preparation of alchemical potions. He was mocking me, of course. He admitted his lies later when, under my close attentions, he became a little more eager to offer me the whole story.... All his nasty little secrets came out in the end. Not such a gay duck, now, Sir Lazarus, eh?"

The Wandering Gentile uttered a chilling laugh, relishing his moment. Then he strode to a tall armoire, all oak and brass, and reached a claw-like hand for the door.

"He is in here now. You may have what's left of him, and welcome...."

CHAPTER TEN
A Mystery Solved—and Another Begun!

And with that (continued Captain Begg) the Count of Crete swept open the door!

After a little hesitation, out staggered a blinking, barefooted old fellow of mild, healthy appearance, who shivered when he saw the Wandering Gentile posturing before him and would not advance further into his room until Manfred had sworn on his honour, and what was left of his putrefying soul, that he would never again use a feather on Herr Lazarus's soles.

"He is a devil!" declared Herr Lazarus. "You have my eternal thanks for this rescue." He was small, plump, neatly bearded.

"Why was he torturing you?" asked Quelch. "Does

he seek your treasure?"

"Treasure? My 'treasure' isn't liquid. These days it is mostly tied up in land. No, he wanted to know my eldest daughter's name. I told him. We've always inspired writers, our family. Still he wouldn't believe that it was indeed the same Rebecca who starred in *Ivanhoe*, the novel. It's my genes. She had a little of my original blood, you see, and went a good seven hundred years before the wrinkles started showing, then she came to live with me. Her gravestone's in the back garden. We were all fond of her. Sometimes I have half-a-dozen relatives staying here. I'm never lonely."

At this last remark the Wandering Gentile uttered a blood-chilling growl and advanced as if to fix his rotting fingers about the throat of the Wandering Jew, who frowned unhappily and stepped back a little.

Several of the pirates, none in his first youth, tried to restrain Count Manfred, but he was far too strong for them. He flung them off, yet did not advance further on Herr Lazarus. Instead he leaned forward, pointing an accusing forefinger. "You old boaster! You complacent dolt! What right had you to discover reconciliation, even of this earthly kind? What right, when I wandered round and round the globe in search of you, only missing this island by a few miles because I had been told it did not really exist and that no ship had ever sighted it! But now, thanks to the Haze, you are exposed.

"Wretch! You deceived the world so cleverly. You

cunningly made use of our honest credulity! How handsomely you profited from our simple Teutonic generosity. Do you know how many times I have circumnavigated this miserable little planet? How many storms I have weathered? How many times I have been swallowed by earthquakes, endured pestilences, pogroms, dungeons? I have been engulfed by volcanic lava at least fifteen times. I have been pursued and attacked through a thousand different wars. I have been hunted by mobs, by angry fathers and husbands, vindictive wives, crazed bed-fellows! I have known no mother's comfort. I have never enjoyed the confidence or advice of a father. I have tasted blood so many, many times—yet have never seen my own long enough for a drop of it to fall upon the ground! Oh, you do not deserve such peace of mind! What a deep injustice is this! How have you earned such rest?"

The Wandering Jew was pouring fresh drinks for his guests. He crossed the Turkish carpet to place a tumbler of brandy in his tormentor's palpitating hand. "I sat down and thought it all out one day," he said reasonably. "There were, after all, a lot worse fates that could befall a Jew than being cursed with eternal life. I decided to go, as they say, with the flow. And here I am. About as contented and comfortable an immortal, I must admit, as any I've heard about! Why blame me? I simply made the best of things."

The Rose told me how the wholesome old man exuded a sense of considerable peace and good will and was clearly content with his lot. She asked him if he did not regret the chance to die. Some would think he was being denied the promise of heaven. Of grace. He disagreed. "This is heaven enough for me," he said.

Again this produced a dramatic response in his rival who lifted up his long pale head and howled.

"Poor devil," interjected Captain Quelch, trying to bring down the emotional temperature a little. "Couldn't you both let bygones be bygones and work together? *Che sera sera*, as the Lombardians have it. Why not shake hands and call it a day? After all, at least one of you can now find his final resting place…" and he looked expectantly at the Wandering Gentile.

He was affronted. "Why address *me* first?" he wanted to know. "Why not that miserable hypocrite who, in a manner typical of his horrid race, has made himself comfortable in circumstances where it was not intended for him to be comfortable!" But he spoke hopelessly, in the tone of one long used to prejudice and rejection.

"Because Captain Quelch understands," said the Jew patiently to the ensemble at large, "that I am in no great hurry to wander anywhere. I am not in torment. I do not long for death et cetera, et cetera. In fact I have found, as far as I know, a perfectly adequate resting place and plan to remain here until the Last Judgement. Not a bad spot to wait out eternity, all in all."

"Tcha!" Again the Wandering Gentile was barely

able to contain his fury. He appealed to the company. "Look at these poor ruined feet of mine! Look at these wretched hands! Look at this torn flesh, this rotting body, these pathetic remains—these rags of clothing— these shreds of skin and shards of bone—these hideous scars! What an ugly creature I have become. Is it any wonder I am avoided, reviled, stoned, driven from the settlements of my fellows, never to know decent human company, placed in a box by my relatives who now seek to dump me in a radium pit! Why should I not hate you, who sits in contentment in your cosy home, drinking Twinings Assam and Ovaltine while wearing cardigans knitted for you by doting descendants?"

The Wandering Jew considered this, then answered reasonably. "My dear sir—you, too, could have enjoyed pretty much the same life as mine. You did not *have* to wander, any more than I. You could have found yourself a little island, perhaps in the Hebrides or in the Indian Ocean, depending upon your taste in climate and so on, invested in a few long-term portfolios to pay for your needs and retired. In your own home you could be at very least decently fed and clothed, and you would not have to endure any insults. None."

"He has a point, old boy," says Captain Quelch. "You seem to be complaining mostly that it was the Jew's idea to make the best of things and not yours. You were simply obsessed with finding him. It seems to me you've wasted your opportunities."

Even the Rose thought this a little insensitive of

him under the circumstances, and it did seem to be the last straw, for the Wandering Gentile flung his brandy glass into the fireplace and let out an enormous roar of frustration and misery. "Oh, damn him forever! Damn him to the deepest pit, the hottest hell!" he cried, gesticulating vigorously with his unnaturally long arms. "I put my own curse upon you, Lazarus. Even when the Last Trump is sounded—*you shall never know death*!"

And with these thrilling words, which left ice in every heart, Manfred, Count of Crete, stormed from the room and was not seen there again. He made his way down the Sacred Trail of Death to the harbour where he was at first mistaken for the long-awaited messenger by Barnaby Slyte, who greeted him warmly and gratefully until the Count entered a pool of silver moonlight and stood glaring up at him from the lower deck.

Which was how, said Captain Begg, the *Scheherazade* came so quickly to be abandoned by the pirates, enabling Count Manfred to take the boat under his own control, aided by two quaking laskars, who had the misfortune to be sharing the bunks of friends aboard.

Almost immediately one of the laskars escaped in the ship's dinghy, and that was how he came eventually to be picked up by me. But I had only a partial story and was not to know the whole truth until much later.

Upon the laskar's urgent instruction I gave the order to pursue the *Scheherazade*, believing that she carried as prisoners Captain Quelch and the Rose....

It was a long chase, through heavy seas, with winter coming out of Russia like a cat out of a dog's home—blind, ferocious and careless of anything that gets in its way—but just off Bilbao we caught up with her and put a shot across her, though she was virtually out of our jurisdiction. She hove to and I took a boarding party over.

The long and the short of it was, we found nothing suspicious about the dhow—no arms, contraband or prisoners. I had been deceived by the laskar or misinformed. It emerged that he had been referring to a different ship altogether. There was certainly nothing we could nail her captain for, unless it was his smell and general appearance which suggested that he was no great enthusiast for bathing. He was a tall, cadaverous individual with a bad head cold who held a heavily scented rag in front of his face most of the time. He had a strong foreign accent which I guessed to be Middle European.

The only thing that was remotely odd about the dhow was in the hold—a long, narrow box roughly wrapped in red velvet. When we opened it we found only some gold and silver cord and a beautiful crucifix which the captain said was all he had left of his family and, he guessed, perhaps his religion, too. It was the badge of a Papal emissary.

There was nothing for it but to share a glass of rum with the captain, who gave his name as Manfred, and let him explain how he had followed Captain Quelch to the Isla de Juifes, which he passed regularly, and had made sure his fellow captain was safely anchored before continuing on his way to Hamburg, where Manfred had some business. He had no idea, he said, why Quelch had decided to visit that jungly rock and suggested I ask him myself.

The old boy's story could not be contradicted, so we decided to escort him on his way for a bit, send in a report and let the matter drop, at least until we knew more.

The last time I saw him was off Le Havre in freak snow, the big flakes boiling around his head as he steered his ship into a storm which was roaring out of Germany as if the *Fimbulwinter* had already defeated the forces of life and we were witnessing the Twilight of the Gods. That was in 1932.

He told me he planned to leave his dhow in Hamburg for a while and then take the train east, via Berlin, with the thought that he would enjoy one last tour of his fatherland before coming home to die in Nuremberg. I assumed his words to be fanciful and that he spoke of retirement. He showed me a book. He said it contained a list of names. All those who were indebted to him, he said. All those who had betrayed his trust in them. Whole families, in some cases. I understood him to be some merchant's steward engaged to collect bad debts through the territories of the Holy Roman Empire.

I watched him go off under full sail. There was rime

like diamonds on his rigging, the canvas gleamed like silver, and snow was thick on his shoulders, royal ermine. His fingers, sticking out of his tattered gloves like picked bones, seemed frozen to the wheel, and his lank, grey hair stuck up in spikes, a halo.

I know now that I was the last Englishman to report an encounter with the Wandering Gentile, whose fame grew in those years, but I have since heard a little more of his story from others. The Gentile's expectations, it appears, were false. He still wanders the world, a ragged scarecrow, his eyes cold as iron, seeking the mysterious Isla de Juifes which, he swears, is protected by a supernatural glamour. The island he says can only be seen by his arch-rival's co-religionists. Moreover he blames climactic shifts for his further inconvenience. As you know, shortly after all this, the Haze vanished completely and our present tranquil age began....

A black-haired listener roused himself from Begg's spell to interrupt. "Not so tranquil if you're in corsair waters, to this day, old boy!"

Captain Begg agreed. "If it were not for the corsairs ours would be a perfect world. But if it were to *remain* a perfect world we might find it necessary, perhaps, to introduce corsairs into it!"

"That sounds like a bit of a paradox," declared a large woman with Pre-Raphaelite hair.

Begg smiled. "If we do not allow for paradoxes, my dears, we're doomed to repeat all our failures again and again. Just like the poor Gentile. Even with the prospect of fulfilment, he did not seem a happy man. And he has clearly learned nothing from his experiences. He repeats them over and over. Just like the poor old Gentile…"

"Has he never revisited the island?" the original speaker wished to know.

"Never," said Begg. "The Rose told me, the last time we met in Sporting Club Square, that nothing has ever changed. For some reason Count Manfred is blind to the island, even when he sails past it close enough to rip that old dhow's keel wide open. But the ship's protected by whatever keeps the poor devil alive and invulnerable, so it is never damaged. Yet the Count is convinced his map is at fault. Or his informants. Or his crew. Whatever small sums he gets he always spends on larger or older or more detailed maps of those waters. And is always, of course, disappointed."

"He never learned the lesson of Lazarus, then?" enquired the Pre-Raphaelite woman.

"Exactly," agreed their narrator. "It was not, I suppose, in his nature to rest."

"And what of Las Cascadas—and Quelch—and the Rose?" the dark man wished to know, waving his empty ballon as if to emphasise his curiosity.

"We live in a new and tranquil age," said Captain Begg. "The last time I returned to Las Cascadas the most urgent talking point was the outrageous price of fish. It's the same almost everywhere, these days."

Then the old seadog paused, as if choosing his words carefully. "Meanwhile, Captain Quelch and the Rose returned to their island stronghold. Which," he concluded with a sigh of considerable relish, "is quite a different story."

EPILOGUE
on the Nature of Miracles

"...quite a different story," repeated Captain Begg, smiling broadly, for he was once again at Las Cascadas, and Don Victor Dust's other guest was the Rose herself. These were in the days when the Haze was already being described as evidence of mass hysteria, "and not for me to tell, my dear."

Don Victor responded to this with his usual shy courtesy. "Well, Countess, is it to remain your secret?"

"There's no secret, your excellency. After our encounter with Herr Lazarus and upon learning the nature of Count Manfred's singular doom, some of the magic left our romance, and we were not to rediscover it until much later. But poor Horace never did get his other quarter-million ryads. What's more, you can imagine what the family thought of me when I had to admit that our ancestor was up and wandering again...."

"And the Lombardians?" asked Captain Begg.

"Something to do with the Pope. My father was a little vague about it. There was no great harm resulted, as far as I could tell."

"A rather prosaic end to a marvellous tale," said

Don Victor. "Or are we to hear of further miracles from the Wandering Jew?"

The Rose was amused. "I asked him much the same question, your excellency, before we left the island. Indeed, I was very direct. I asked the Jew if he *could* work miracles. But he shook his head. 'It seems to me,' he said, 'that legendary miracle-workers are always those who have been driven from the fold under some curse or other and are not generally recognised until after they are dead. Indeed, the fact of their banishment or execution adds to the authority of their legend!' In his experience it often becomes politically useful to revive a myth (if not a memory), and that dangerous psychopath of a generation gone becomes a lovable old uncle or a troubled boy with a heart of gold. The politically involved nun becomes a saint. The saint becomes a demon. And so on. He thought that most miracle-workers found their reputations enhanced by a distance in time and space. 'People do love to dream, don't they?' he said. 'I have no special powers, my dear—merely a little more experience than most. I was always of a placid disposition. They completely misjudged me, you know, from the very beginning of this. I wasn't *refusing* the poor boy a drink! Who could? I suspect he misheard me. I was merely asking him if he preferred lemonade or apple-juice.

"'And thus,' concluded the Wandering Jew with a philosophical shrug, 'thanks to a moment of middle-class insensitivity, I was damned to eternal life. Well, if that's God's idea of justice, I'm making the best of it. For all I know they're still arguing my case somewhere.'"

"He seems eminently sane for one of such bizarre experience," suggested Don Victor. "Did the Jew offer you no special wisdom? No great secret drawn from all his millennia of existence?" Don Victor was a little sceptical of her reticence. "Countess, did he tell you nothing else?"

"Only one thing," said the Rose. "It was perhaps the most startling narrative of them all. About a lustful abbess who, as penance, determined to discover if all trees were God or if there were evil trees as well. There were the familiar ingredients of innocence betrayed, loss, dispersal and festering revenge.... The Jew called it "The Tale of the Wandering Moslem," and *her* story began, apparently, in the Sinai, a few centuries ago...."

But the tale the Rose told was meant only for her listeners and was never to be published.

THE END

THE

David v. Barrett

LEGEND OF POPE JOAN

David V. Barrett has, at various times, made
Kendal Mint Cake, delivered Tetley's beer,
taught English and Religious Education, done
things he can't talk about for GCHQ and
NSA and been a senior editor on a computer
magazine.

He edited the anthology of computer-
related science fiction Digital Dreams
and has written, among others, ten books on
Tarot, Runes, dream interpretation, and
related subjects. His short stories have
appeared in a variety of books and
magazines—and on BBC radio—and he has
reviewed science fiction and fantasy for
many of the "quality" British newspapers and
periodicals. From 1985 to 1989 he edited
Vector, the critical journal of the British

Science Fiction Association, and he from 1992 to 1995 was administrator and chairman for the annual Arthur C. Clarke Award for the best SF novel published in the UK.

"I'm not superstitious in the sense of throwing a black cat over my shoulder if I spill salt," he says, "but I'm very wary of ceremonial magic, particularly anything from the darker side of the Judaeo-Christian tradition (Crowley-like summoning of demons); there's some dangerous stuff there. I have far more time for 'natural magic'; if someone heals my headache I don't ask whether they're an evangelical Christian or a white witch. Healing works—sometimes even at a distance—whatever god or power has been invoked."

Barrett has been fascinated by the legend of Pope Joan since reading Lawrence Durrell's "appallingly written" translation of a nineteenth-century novelization of her story some ten years ago. "As Francis Atterbury says, there have been many attempts to prove or disprove the legend: "Proof" may be found in Joan Morris's Pope John VIII: An English Woman, Alias Pope Joan, and "disproof" in Rosemary and Darroll Pardoe's The Female Pope: The Mystery of Pope Joan. The official Church position today is that the story is fiction, but many official accounts of the popes through the centuries have included her. My story draws heavily on the "facts" of the legend, though the explanation is my own."

But did she really exist? Barrett likes to think so. "And I can see no reason why not," he adds. "After all, female abbots were ordained for centuries and had at least partial episcopal powers. There are also several records of women disguising themselves as men and becoming monks (St. Hildegund is the best-known example)."

Are you sitting comfortably? Then we'll begin....

From The Journal of Medieval Studies, vol. xxxvi, no. 109, p. 47ff.

The opening up of the Vatican Library has made available to historians and theologians a wealth of material incomparable with any previous hoard. By unlocking the doors at last, on the tenth anniversary of his accession, Pope John Paul has not only done something of inestimable worth for the world of scholarship, but has initiated a process which, far more even than the Dead Sea Scrolls and the Nag Hammadi Library, discovered in the 1940s but still largely unpublicized, may shake not only the Roman Catholic Church but Christendom itself to its foundations.

It will take generations for historians and theologians to search and sift and sort the authentic first-hand accounts from the later obfuscatory rewritings of history in which the Pope himself admits the Church has excelled for centuries. Much of the history of the last two thousand years will have to be rewritten as the undercover involvement of the Church in world affairs is by stages revealed. The separation of fact from fiction will be one of the hardest tasks awaiting the scholars: simultaneously fascinating and frustrating.

The story of Pope Joan has been believed and denied for around a thousand years. Numerous essays and books have "proved" both the truth and the falsehood of the tale [see Bibliography below]. I have long been interested in the legend, and when I found "Johanna Anglicus, a Woman" in the vast indices of the Library, I hoped that its veracity would finally be established one way or the other.

But can we believe the account which I present here, one of the first fragments of the Vatican Library to be released to scholars and thus to the world? Most would immediately say not, for reasons which will rapidly become obvious; yet the mass of supporting detail requires that the possibility of its truth not be discounted out of hand.

I attest that what follows is an accurate rendering into modern English of the tenth-century Italian of the original. The text was amongst the personal papers of Pope Sergius III (904-911 C.E.) along with numerous related letters, notes and diary entries, which I detail in the Notes below. From internal evidence and from its prose style [see Notes 5, 6 and 7a], particularly the shifts of tense to heighten the immediacy of emotion, this account appears to be a transcription of Pope Joan's own dramatized oral tale, told by her to her family in or just outside Rome some time in the first few years of the tenth century—probably in either 900 or 904 C.E.

Francis Atterbury, OBE, PhD, D Phil, FRS
Professor of Medieval History
Priory College, Durham

✤

It was a time of tribulation, and more. Everything, which had been going so well, so wonderfully, fell apart, flew apart—and most vexing of all, I can place little of the blame on anyone other than myself.

Maybe Antonio, a little—but only a little. It was my carelessness, not his, that nearly lost us everything.

Oh, I had such power—had priests and princes bowing to me—and lost it through my lusts.

I wished, often then and sometimes even now, that I had never left Germany, that I had never left my family; that gray, rainy country so different from this sweating, plague-infested Rome; that arguing, fighting, loving, supporting family so different from the arguing, fighting, hating, back-stabbing men of God here.

But I was very young, in our years, still just nearer to thirty than to forty. It was my time to travel, to find new experiences on my own, but not for myself only: We always bring back what we have learnt and tell it to each other, that we may all share, may all learn.

Remember this, my children, when you begin to travel.

We were an English family, though we lived in Mainz. One of my fathers, for reasons I didn't understand as a child, was a missionary to the Germans. I was brought up in a house of scholarship. From my childhood I knew myself to be a scholar, rather than a merchant or a farmer; and I knew also that I could not be tied, as several of my mothers were, to the family

home. My birth-mother had left early for her final
Wandering, having brought three healthy litters of
children into this world and then into adulthood; she'd
had enough of fetching and carrying, of cooking and
cleaning, of being a wife among many and a mother of
many.

"Don't let yourself get trapped, as I have been,"
she told me. "I wanted to study, but I ended my travels
too soon and joined this family. A wonderful family—
don't get me wrong—but I have spent too much time
thinking of Us, not enough of Me." She went on, my
mother, a good deal more than that, but it all meant
much the same: She'd been familied too soon, before
learning to be herself.

I must not do the same. She told me, and I knew it
for myself.

I would be a scholar, and there was only one place
for that: the Church. No matter that, like all of us, I
had no belief in God; I have none now and had none
even in that highest position—but then, neither had
many of my predecessors, nor many of my successors, I
am sure. Here in Rome, at the very center of the
Church, there is less faith than anywhere else in
Christendom—and almost no Godliness. It shocked me
when I first arrived here, even though I was well aware
of how dishonest humans are.

I did not wish to join a nunnery; there is too much
devotion there, and—with some exceptions—too little

scholarship. I changed to man's form and joined the Benedictine Abbey at Fulda, near to our home in Mainz.

Why? Because there, I was amongst some of the finest minds in northern Europe. I could learn from them, argue with them, study their work firsthand, read more books than were collected almost anywhere else, except Rome—and here they are collected but not read, not studied. There is no scholarship here; only fighting for position.

I listened and studied and learned, and argued and taught and wrote. And made the beginnings of my reputation.

From there I went to Athens to extend my studies to Greek literature—and there, unknowingly, I took my next fateful step.

Each mistake is greater than the one before, each built on all that has gone before. This one seemed so right, so wonderful, so (if I'd believed in God and an afterlife) heaven-sent.

Danger, danger, danger. Why did I not see? Because I was blinded by that which lights one's life but throws all that one does not wish to see into the shadows. Love.

Love!

Antonio and I met first in a tavern, where as a brother of the order of Benedict no doubt I should not have been; but too many of the brothers knew their scholarship only as a dull, dry thing, unrelated in every way to living. I had to breathe. There in the ancient squares and taverns I found release in conversation with men and women of all sorts and conditions, in rough wine and, from time to time, in women. Some I paid, but most became friends and friendly bedmates.

In a man's body I enjoyed bedplay with women; I would have liked the occasional man, for inside I was still deeply female, but there was too much risk.

In the abbey I could have had a dozen of the brothers; but I would rather have fornicated with a rotting dead pig than touch one of them or have them touch me.

I sensed Antonio across the tavern, just as he sensed me; our eyes touched across the room. I bought a carafe of wine and wandered, as if casually, over to the quiet corner he had moved to.

"Antonio of Verona, known as Brother Andrew of Tours."

"Gerberta, of an English line, known as John of Mainz."

We touched hands shyly, eagerly. *He* knew I was female.

I'd come across many others of our people over the last few years: the odd young traveler like myself, a few older ones on their twilight travels, and families here and there. We'd met, we'd talked, we'd spent evenings together sometimes—but we'd never gotten close. It almost seemed that I could make friends—shallow friends, anyway—more easily amongst humans than my own people.

But Antonio...

From that first meeting there was a power between us, a communication deeper than any I had known before. We were lovers from that first touch between our eyes; and only hours later we became lovers in bed also.

We made love first as two human men, because we couldn't wait to change our forms. And then later, the following morning, we made love again as ourselves, in our true forms.

It was the first time in five years that I had enjoyed the sexual sensations of my female body.

Oh, how easily are we betrayed!

And when I moved from Athens to Rome, Antonio came with me; neither of us even considered that he might not.

Oh, there are times when I wish I believed in God, for then I could cry out in the depths of my despair, "Why, why, oh Lord?"

I taught at the Trivium, in the Greek church attached to the Church of Santa Maria in Cosmedin. I became well liked and well respected for my learning, in that city of influence and ignorance. In time, Leo IV gave me a cardinal's hat. And when his successor, Benedict III, a holy man whom in other circumstances I might have loved, died, I took on the triple tiara. I said no, of course; I claimed I was not worthy; I hid myself in St. Peter's. But the crowd would not hear my protests, and claimed it was God's will.

Oh God, I wish I could believe in you. I could beg for your help, or at the least for your solace; I could take comfort in the promise that you would protect me; I could try to persuade myself that all this is part of some great divine plan, that you know what you are doing, that good will come of it in the end; or I could rail against you for what you have done to me.

But I can only rail against myself, and know that my help cometh only from myself, in whom I despair.

Antonio and I were careless in our loving, just as young lovers should be. It never crossed our minds that I might become pregnant; after all, we had no group marriage, there were only the two of us, and this gave us—this *should* have given us—the sexual freedom that our young people enjoy. Sex for fun, sex for play, sex for excitement, sex for friendship, as well as sex for love. Sex with a glorious variety of partners, experimenting with and enjoying the gifts of our bodies and minds and spirits and emotions, the gifts to give as well as those to receive. Sex without the responsibility of children—that's what group marriages are for.

I should not have become pregnant, not outside a group marriage; but I did. We were stunned, horrified, Antonio as much as I. Then over the weeks and months we grew more used to the idea, began to look forward to it. I had never been a mother and was at the age when I should begin to think about settling down in a marriage group. Maybe my body, fooled by my being with Antonio for three or four years, thought I was in a group marriage...a group of two.

We made plans. The baby was due in June of the year 858, a hot and filthy month when my absence from Rome would be regarded as sensible. We would go to a villa up in the hills, where there would at least be trees to shade us from the blazing sun, and where we would be away from the filth and stench and disease of summer Rome—and from the intrigue, the watching eyes and wagging tongues.

I had brought Antonio with me from Venice as my priest-attendant, and he still attended me as my cardinal deacon and secretary. It was expected that where I went he would go also.

Oh, Antonio! So beautiful, my only love, and you are gone. So beautiful, and so close to me, you turned down propositions almost daily from the fat priests and cardinals and dukes and administrators who jostle for position and power and wealth, who bribe and steal and seduce and kill to raise their social standing by one small degree, to move from one sphere of influence into a competing one, to gain another rich jewel or bag of gold, and all in the name of the God of love.

He wanted none of them; he wanted only me.

And I lose him, I lose him, and our child.

You know the place, some of you: between the Colosseum and the Church of St. Clement. The day was hot, sticky, sweaty, as so much of that summer had been. The air itself seemed diseased. The Rogation Day procession between the Lateran and St. Peter's wound slowly through the streets, priests and cardinals and choirboys before and behind me, a hundred pious nuns walking together in their midst.

My bearers stumbled from time to time, exhausted by the heat. I had tried to cancel the procession, the ceremony, but that body of administrators who actually run this hellish place would not allow it. It was tradition, it was custom, it was law. I, as Pope, had no say in the matter.

My time was near, but not too near: three or four weeks. This was my last compulsory appearance before I could flee this filthy place with Antonio; tomorrow we would go into retreat for the rest of the heat of summer, and I would have our child in peace.

The pain hits me and my waters break forth, together. I'm soaked from my loins down, and spasming; my entire body heaves and thrusts. I scream with the agony. One of my bearers, startled, chooses this moment to stumble; the litter tips and falls, and I with it.

My body reacts to the emergency without my conscious thought; I feel my vagina, closed with a fold of skin beneath my penis, open up and widen, widen suddenly and agonizingly as the baby within pushes itself into the world.

Priests, cardinals, attendants of all sorts, rush to my aid, knowing only that their Pope has fallen and is hurt.

I lie half on the ground, half still in the soaked finery of my litter, my legs wide apart as the thing inside me tears itself from me. And cries.

That tiny infant sound stills the hubbub around me. Choirboys, monks, nuns, priests, cardinals in their sweat-stained robes, all stop, and stand, and turn, and stare. And then they come for me, for me and for my barely born child, with their fear and their hatred, their boots and their fists, kicking and clawing and tearing and stamping....

Three days, now, three days to repair my ripped and ravaged body, but three lifetimes would not be enough to repair my torn heart.

Somehow I crawled away and hid, in rotting piles of rubbish in the shell of a half-broken building only a few minutes away from my scene of degradation and discovery and despair. Hid, until I could stop the bleeding from my own wound, my womb which had betrayed me, and from the cuts and tears and rough grazes and bone-deep bruises from the mob's attack.

And while I healed, I changed my appearance: I made myself a hand's width shorter, I changed my hair from its distinctive copper—a legacy from an Irish forefather—to black, and I made my face rounder and more anonymous. I remained a man; my attackers, the Curia, the entire priesthood, half of Rome for all I knew (though some might secretly admire my presumed audacity)—all would be looking for a woman.

Now I was safe, at least from recognition, though my weak state would make me more prone to the illnesses of the city.

I sought out a small family group I knew, and told them what had happened. They were amazed, but they took me in; though we may fight and squabble amongst ourselves, we will always help each other against human threats, and besides, with my new appearance, there was no danger to them.

Three days, my children, three days and I have heard nothing. My child is gone, Antonio is gone: my baby no doubt torn apart or trampled underfoot, as they tried to do to me; Antonio—I do not know. I cannot believe he has deserted me. He was in the procession, near to me; if he tried to come to my help they may have taken him, beaten him, killed him.

There is little value placed on human life in this festering city, not when it is not one's own. His body may be in the Tiber, with so many others; I have asked the Fantonis, the family who have taken me in, to listen for reports.

I could so easily have been in the Tiber myself.

There have been popes from our people before, three of them, but none lasted longer than my two years, five months and four days. They fared no better than most other popes. Maybe one day it will come that popes are not ripe for assassination; but even a pope's life is cheap when ambition rules.

All of Rome is buzzing with stories of how the Pope gave birth by St. Clement's, and the greater amazement of the Pope being a woman. Such a thing has never been heard! I do not know if it has happened before; it is possible, though there is nothing in our history, and it would have been still more difficult for a human woman.

It was another week before Antonio and I found each other. He too had changed his appearance—he was taller, thinner—but I recognized him at once, and he me. Perhaps it is our scent, that even if subconsciously we can know each other; this is, after all, the main way that we know each other from humans. Perhaps we recognized each other's individual scent across the piazza.

But I prefer to think it was our spirits calling to each other in their love.

You can imagine the joy with which we fell into each other's arms, even those of you too young to know the love between two adults. Each of us had pictured the other dead, trampled and pulled apart, or else captured and tortured and longing for death. (I still hear the screams from the Castel Sant'Angelo in my sleep at night; Antonio will tell you. Those tortured in the name of the God of love know the depths of agony and degradation, if ultimately they know nothing else.)

Each of us had searched that plague-strewn city; each had listened everywhere for rumor, while hoping desperately we would hear none. Each of us had so hardly escaped that we could not imagine the other having also such fortune.

People were beginning to stare, and in a city so leprous with suspicion, that was dangerous. We remembered suddenly that we were both male in appearance. We drew back, looked into each other's eyes, laughed gaily (it was hard, but it was so easy!), and clapped each other on the back like old friends who had not seen each other for a long time.

"I did not even know you were in Rome," Antonio boomed.

"I didn't know you were either," I replied. "My wife, her sister is dying, and so I brought her. And you?"

Antonio looked sly. He glanced around as if to see who might be listening, then lowered his voice—but still kept it loud enough that those nearby, straining, might hear.

"I am here…on business, shall we say. A merchant friend of mine, he told me of a deal I could make…." He let his voice fade away as we walked away across the piazza, through an alley and into the anonymity of a crowded street. Our eavesdroppers, I knew, would smile and shrug; such deals were commonplace, and the reason many came to the city. Some were lucrative, but most came to nothing.

We walked through the crowds, yearning to touch each other, to hug, to hold, even just to say something to show our love for each other, our joy at finding each other.

Antonio led me into a small inn, and to a quiet corner. And it was only when we were seated, with a jug of rough red wine between us, that I thought—suddenly, sickeningly, with overwhelming guilt—of our child.

Antonio saw the change on my face, and reached over, laying his hand on my arm.

"It's all right," he said, "he's safe."

I couldn't speak. My sight went gray, then white, then black. It was some time later when I realized that

Antonio was holding a cold, damp cloth to my forehead and neck.

"It's all right," he said, over and over again. "It's all right."

I sat back, and the dim interior of the inn slowly came into some kind of focus. Antonio gave me my beaker, his hand steadying mine as I raised it and drained it in one long gulp.

"Our son is safe," he said, and my destroyed world, my distraught spirit, were made whole again.

It was only an hour—it seemed a month—before I held our son for the first time. He had beautifully thick dark hair and deep blue eyes, and his tiny fingers closed on mine. His body was human in shape; Antonio told me he was changing from his natural birth appearance to human almost as soon as he was born. Instinctive mimicry: our deepest survival trait. But at birth he had looked like us, unchanged, and his initial appearance, then the flowing of his infantile features as his body adjusted them to human, had compounded the horror of the Pope giving birth. This was a monster, a demon, devil's spawn. Small wonder that the priests and cardinals and other dignitaries and their attendants had tried to kill both him and me.

Antonio had had one moment in which to act, when, horrified by the tiny squirming creature before them. these holy men had turned their attention to a horror they could cope with: myself. He snatched the baby, tearing the cord with his nails, and tucked him into his robes, then let himself be pushed back as others pushed forward to get at me.

He didn't know, he told me as I sat with our son cradled to my still human, still male breast, how he was able to leave me. But I maybe had a chance, however small; the tiny mewling creature had none without his immediate help, his full attention, his love and care and devotion. Apart from safety, our baby needed food, literally in the next few minutes. His first act in life had been to change his appearance, which drained him of every scrap of energy he was born with. If he were not given food, and then safe sleep, straight away, our son would die.

Antonio, my beloved one, my darling husband here, saved our son. Like me, he found friends to take him in, and one, who had recently had a litter of three children, had milk enough to feed our baby as well. It was fortunate in many ways that my first birth, as sometimes happens, was of only one child.

The two families lived at opposite ends of this teeming city, but knew each other well; two of the wives in "Antonio's" family were sisters of two of the husbands in "mine". Together they helped us away from Rome, to a quiet village three days' ride away, and to a quiet farmhouse in the hills above the village.

There, for the next few months, Antonio and I could live as ourselves when we wished, though for the most part we retained our human appearance.

We both preferred his new, leaner look to his old, so he kept it; I reverted to my old appearance, which I had when I was a girl in Mainz, with a little added maturity we both agreed I suited. He was delighted with the new me; he told me now that this was how he had always seen me, deep inside...

...and this is how I have remained ever since, though the lines and wrinkles of added years have given, perhaps, yet more maturity to my looks!

The Church soon chose a new pope, and new scandals quickly replaced my own story as gossip on the streets of Rome. A woman pope giving birth to a demon is not a tale the Church would wish to have remembered.

And now we skip some fifty years to bring us to today. My children, my family, the youngest of you will not remember your oldest brother; he left the home first. But we shall see him next week, with joy.

From his earliest years, your brother Simon showed the same leanings that I had: scholarship, philosophy, human theology. We did not discourage him; his life, his yearnings, were his to follow, not ours to dictate.

He had absorbed everything Antonio and I knew by the time he was twenty. And then he followed much the same route I had done, through the monasteries, before being appointed Bishop of Ostia, then managing to be assigned to Rome to take his cardinal's hat.

And now that we have had six popes in five years,

fighting and deposing and killing each other, all the cardinals have been summoned in conclave at Rome, to try to find a pope who might last a little longer. Some men of the Church wish earnestly for the fighting to be over.

There are two likely candidates for St. Peter's throne, two equally strong men who hate each other, and whose followers battle for supremacy with a passion such as I did not witness even when I lived there.

Your brother is well positioned, and, amazingly for this place, this Church, he has few enemies. Neither of the favorites will allow the other to take the throne without war following. The Church, however stupid it might be at times, has enough sense not to want that.

By next week your brother may be pope, following in his mother's perhaps ill-advised footsteps. He will have his own problems, but there is one he will not share with me. He will not give birth on the Lateran Way.

Whether "Simon" was elected to the throne of St. Peter is difficult to confirm either way; there were several popes of unknown origin (and unknown original name) around this time, none of whom lasted very long. There is, however, no record of a Bishop of Ostia becoming pope (they usually had the privilege of crowning the pope), so it seems more

probable that he was unsuccessful—in which case his life was doubtless considerably longer.

This Journal is not a place for fanciful speculation, let alone for fiction. It must be stressed, however, that this story has immense historical significance, whether it is fact or fiction.

If the story is fiction, its very existence as a contemporary attempt to explain Pope Joan gives credence to her legend; it predates by two centuries what had been the earliest known reference to the woman pope.

If the story is true, it explains at last the legend of Pope Joan, which some have accepted for a thousand years, though to others it has always seemed unbelievable that a woman could have become pope. But it is even more unbelievable that another sentient race, a race of shapeshifters, has throughout history coexisted, undetected, alongside humanity—though it would certainly account for much mythology, folklore and tales of witchcraft.

If, for the sake of argument, such beings have existed in the past, could they still be amongst us today? Such a thought might not, after all, be dismissed as populist foolishness, in the light of some completely unconnected recent research.

It is widely known that when the poet Percy Bysshe Shelley drowned in July 1822, his body was only identified by a copy of Sophocles in one pocket and a copy of Keats in another; conventional wisdom has it that ten days in the *sea and the depredations of hungry fish had rendered his features unrecognizable. His body was hastily buried with quicklime, and later cremated on a pyre on which were poured frankincense, oil and wine.*

I am grateful to Dr. J. A. Cole, Reader in Victorian Studies at York, for drawing to my attention his paper which examines the recently discovered notes of a correspondent for The Times, who had interviewed Lord Byron, Trelawny and others who saw Shelley's body when it was washed ashore. "It had a head, a torso and four limbs," said one witness, "but there was no further resemblance to anything human." Another spoke of his "horror and revulsion at the misshapen and hideously deformed thing lying upon the beach." These descriptions were, of course, suppressed in the published account.

The use of quicklime, as Dr. Cole points out, would hasten the decomposition of the body in an "acceptable" manner, so disguising its original state; the libations are said to be "in accord with ancient custom," though this is not further explained.

Without wishing to establish yet another conspiracy theory—the bane of the historian's life—I have, since translating the Legend of Pope Joan, become aware of many occasions, past and present, when a body has inexplicably been destroyed before a planned post-mortem could occur, and also of a number of occasions, in societies where open-coffin funerals are the norm, when the casket was closed without explanation.

It is dangerous to argue from an absence of data, but if such shape-shifting beings are amongst us, they presumably still wish to conceal their presence.

Francis Atterbury

[Editor's Note:

On behalf of his colleagues, the *Journal* would like to express its regret on learning shortly before this issue went to press of Professor Atterbury's sudden retirement and departure from England. The *Journal* has lost a regular and respected contributor, the academic world has lost a fine mind, and many of us have lost a good friend. We extend our best wishes to him, wherever he has gone.]

GRANDMA AND THE BABKA'S CHRISTMAS GINGER GOOD LUCK/BAD LUCK LESHY

Ken Wisman

With Weird Family Tales, Ken Wisman was responsible for one of last year's most engaging short story collections. The slim volume— just sixty-five pages featuring seven stories—contained more ideas, invention and memorable characters than most books weighing in at ten times its size.

A regular visitor to the pages of the late lamented Pulphouse, Wisman has also had pieces in Fantasy and Science Fiction, Weird Tales, Deathrealm, 2 AM and Eldritch Tales. Three of his stories—"The Finder Keeper," "My Mother's Purse" and the wonderful "In the Heart of the Blue Caboose"—were nominees for the Horror Writers of America's Bram Stoker Award.

462

Born on Manhattan Island, Wisman moved with his parents to New Jersey where he was brought up "in the shadows of the New York skyline." Since then, he has spent time in Europe, Scandinavia and Africa, "hitching rides, sleeping in open fields and woods and picking grapes for quick money." He now lives in the small Massachusetts town of Boxborough, in a condo on the edge of a patch of wooded area with his wife and son, writing technical manuals by day and stories by night. "About the only truly consistent and stabilizing thing in the first half of my life has been the writing," he says.

Several years ago, Wisman had a dream that he was kneeling in front of a grotto formed by an overarching of forsythia bushes. "In the dream," Wisman says, "I reached beneath the bushes and dug in the rich, black soil where I kept finding pennies. I interpreted this as delving into the rich soil of my unconscious to uncover little treasures of creativity—my stories. From that," he adds, "I developed the belief that every time I found a penny lying on the ground I would soon get an idea for a short story. The funny thing is my belief is supported by reality—after finding a penny, I am very often rewarded with a new idea."

The background to Wisman's story for Blue Motel started about nine years ago, when one of his colleagues at the company where he worked would bring in gingerbread houses— of varying shapes and sizes—for Christmas. "Her daughter made them," Wisman explains, "constructed them by hand. I bought one immediately upon seeing it...with its gumdrops and wafers and sugary snow.

"My son, Eric, who was nine months old at the time, was mesmerized by the house. The following year, he recalled it and was pleased when I brought another one home for Christmas. And so it went on until I left that company.

"My biggest pleasure in the gingerbread houses was vicarious, through my son. I guess you can say the story of Grandma Babka, the Leshy and the house of ginger grew out of what I saw in Eric's eyes."

Throw a little more wood on the fire...it's about to get cold.

Christmas began at Thanksgiving.

When we were done with dinner and Father waddled away to sleep the meal off and Mother was busy cleaning, Grandma Babka would call Sister and me into the kitchen to construct the Christmas house of Ginger. From the age of two we helped gather up the implements and necessary ingredients, participating in the tradition each year to our seventh.

That was the year that our story takes place—the year the bad luck came.

"Brother, bring scissors!" Grandma Babka said, whipping us into action. "Sister, fetch spatula and knife!"

Grandma Babka was brusque. And spoke her mind. And did not ask, but barked her orders.

"Sister, eggs! Brother, flour!"

She had the face of a withered monkey with wens and warts and moles with hairs protruding, so that it looked like tiny animals had taken residence on her face.

"Baking pans, Brother! Pastry bag, Sister!"

Once full-bodied and robust, she had shrunken in on herself, and her actions were spare. ("I remove all my water," she once whispered mysteriously to Sister and me. "Like salted fish, it preserve me.")

"Sugar, gumdrops, peppermint sticks, pistachios!"

But Sister and I loved Grandma Babka better than

waking to a snowfall on a schoolday morning. Better than Christmas candy.

When the kitchen was at the proper stage of chaos with flour clouds swirling, pans banging, and cooking implements bouncing on the floor, Grandma Babka announced: "Shuttup!"

Sister and I watched as she went through the ritual of laying out. Like the serving master at a Japanese tea ceremony, she arranged each tool and ingredient according to a rigid and preconceived plan. Then and only then did the construction of the ginger house truly begin.

Now each year Grandma chose a new type of house, so that one year she had a chalet, another a bungalow, still another a Queen Anne with delicate trimming. That year was to be a house from "the old country."

First, she mixed the walls made, of course, of ginger. While these baked she made the icing.

"Cement," she called it.

Which was concocted of egg whites and cream of tartar and confectioner's sugar.

Halfway into the process, Mother came in. She was humming a strange song, and she looked wistfully after Sister and me. She retired without a word.

Then Grandma Babka took out the ginger walls, raising them in her hands with the reverence of a priest raising the host in consecration. The walls went up pasted down on cardboard. The windows went in on either side. (Clear as glass and made of sugar crystals, Sister and I called them our "peeking-in windows.")

When the roof was going up, Father woke and came in.

"Don't keep them up too late," he growled.

He didn't like Grandma Babka much. When she was in the house, his authority was in question. And he didn't believe in her "stupid superstitions."

She ignored Father. She would be ready when she was ready.

Father slunk off to bed.

The decorations went on, each gumdrop heart placed with care, the icing snow with fastidiousness, the sugar-melt icicles with a particular attention to detail. Last on was the door made from a Social Tea Biscuit and put on paper hinges so that it swung in and out.

Then Grandma Babka took a tiny bag hung on a band around her neck. She procured a pinch of blue powder and sprinkled it on the threshold.

The blue powder smelled like fresh milk, sheets dried in sunlight, wind off a lake filled with summer.

"What's it made of?" Sister asked.

"Spring," Grandma answered arcanely.

"Why do you use it?" I asked.

"You think Leshy stupid? Want to stay out winter in cold? Reminds Leshy of warm days in forest." She stood back to admire the cottage—all ginger, and gumdrops, peppermint and icing. "Is remind me old country." A tear squeezed forth from that salt-dried, wizened body. "Must go this year."

Sister and I protested.

"Will see you Christmas," Grandma Babka said. Then she picked up the cottage and carried it out on the back porch that overlooked the forest beyond our house.

It was traditional for Grandma to "read" Sister and me bedtime stories after the ginger house was made—though the hour was past midnight. Our room looked out on the forest and our window was just above the porch. We three kept vigil.

"I read this one," Grandma Babka said, grabbing a book at random. She sat in the rocking chair near the window, and with the book upside down pretended to read.

"Blue moon rise in black sky. Is shine on far fields covered in snow. And now moon opens a blue hole in drifts. Grandma is walking with Sister and Brother and they fall into blue hole through blue light into land called Baboosh."

"Where is Baboosh?" Sister asked.

"Next to Ziloptka," Grandma Babka said annoyedly. "Shuttup now to listen." And she took us into Baboosh, and there we had adventures.

After the story, Grandma Babka rocked. Over her creaking we heard the approach of a train through the morning.

"Is Death-Train," Grandma Babka said.

Sister and I shivered.

"You hear clicketty-clack?"

Sister and I nodded in the dark.

"Is Shmertsh himself snapping fingers to make train go faster. Don't like stay on earth too long."

Grandma Babka said you knew by the sound of the whistle where the train was bound. If it was a wailing like all the mourners that ever mourned, it was bound for Pee-eckwo. If it was a sound like choir boys singing, raising their voices in rejoicing, it was bound for Nyeh-bo.

The last note of the Death-Train trembled like the breath in a lark's breast and was gone. Sister and I fought sleep, drifting in and out of dreams: Grandma Babka rocking across the Milky Way, sprinkling her powder which became blue stars filling empty space.

Between three and four we heard walking across the moon night, the silence of a second hand ticking...

click

    click

        click

...around the ginger house. Then voices—silver bells tinkling in the wind; laughter—pure and brittle like hail against ice.

"They're in."

Grandma Babka rose. She went downstairs, tiptoed out on the porch where she carefully lifted the ginger house. By the time she brought it inside, Sister and I were asleep.

The following day, the ginger house rested on the table in the living room.

It was even more impressive in the daylight. Against the ginger slabs were red pistachio nuts mortared with icing into walls of brick. A layer of Nabisco Shredded Wheat thatched the roof, which in turn was covered with a coating of white icing heaped into drifts. Icicles hung in sugar melts from the eaves.

The barest of wisps of colored smoke curled from the chimney (made of mortared gumballs), the first indication that the Leshy were ensconced inside.

"Pine," Sister said, smelling the smoke.

"Peppermint," I said, sniffing.

And we smelled all the special scents of Christmas—orange sauce and incense, red wine and candle wax, duck and lemon whiskey—until Grandma Babka chased us away.

"Don't bother Good Luck Leshy," she hissed. "If upset could mean—" She left the sentence hanging.

"What?" I asked.

"They move out."

"And?"

"Disaster move in."

We were given a time (at sundown) when it was okay to peek.

And in the particular year (our seventh) of which

we tell, we observed a family of five. It wasn't easy to tell the sex of a Leshy. Each had a beard—the grownups blue ones; the children white. But the family seemed to be comprised of a father, mother, sister, brother, and a tiny grandmother.

A fire burned on their hearth, but not a flame of the ordinary kind. Leshy fire was a bright, sparkling light of changing colors—blue fading gold fading silver—which produced the spiced odors in the chimney.

The Leshy father told a story: "On far field covered with snow is shining big, blue moon. Blue hole opens in snow drifts. Grandma walks with Brother and Sister and falls into hole into Baboosh.

"There they have adventures...."

Sister and I can vouch for the luck we had when the ginger house was occupied by Leshy. Thanksgiving to Christmas (though the ginger house stayed until spring) was especially fortuitous.

Winter was the time Father got promotions and raises. Which meant more gifts and presents. And overall we were in the best of health—while everyone around us caught colds and flus, we went apple-cheeked and healthy.

But this year was to be different.

Three days after Thanksgiving, Grandma Babka was boarding a plane and saying good-bye to Father, Mother, Sister and me.

"Sister, Brother, guard ginger house," she whispered.

We nodded, determined to fulfill our responsibility.

"Disaster," Grandma Babka mouthed and disappeared inside the big plane on her way to the old country.

A week passed. Aunt came over with Uncle and their son, Ricky J.

Ricky J was the kind of boy who was polite and always said "thank you" or "excuse me"—as long as a grown-up was around. But when we were alone he'd get nasty and call us names.

"What about that stupid gingerbread house," Ricky J said when we were alone in the living room. "You got to eat it is all."

He made advances on the ginger house, but when he saw that Sister and I were serious in guarding it, he slunk away.

Before bed, we got Mother to put the house up on the mantel between the clock and candlesticks. And when everyone was asleep, Sister and I snuck down and built the fire in the hearth and stood vigil. But between three and four our eyelids drooped as low as pine branches laden with snow.

We slept.

When we awakened, the fire in the hearth was cold ashes. A ladder stood against the mantel. The gumball chimney was snapped off at the top. Several bites in the snowy roof exposed the shredded wheat. And a missing candy cane in the corner left the cottage leaning precariously.

Sister and I stared at the ginger house with dread. We saw smoke curling from the ruined chimney. And climbing the ladder, we sniffed.

"Sewer water," Sister said.

"Wet dog," I confirmed.

We peeked into the special windows and something with red eyes stared back. Later, Ricky J was found in bed with a stomach ache, his belly filled with a terrible flatulence.

The effects in our house were more gradual.

Instead of the usual joy that went with the weeks before Christmas, a heaviness settled in.

Christmases past, Mother would set up scenes on the windowsill: cotton laid down for snow with a pocket mirror placed for a pond of ice, and little skaters made of lead and brightly lacquered blue and gold. Sister and I would watch these scenes with the hot radiator air rising, smelling of snow and white sheets.

Christmases past, Father would hang lights in strings around the outside windows: the bulbs melting little, blue caves in the drifting snow, warm places we imagined curling up in and falling asleep.

And the tree. Mother said we should dress it like a lady come out to dance: her gown silver, stars on her arms and a string of tiny flames around her waist.

And Grandma Babka's baubles from the old country, made of glass as fragile as an egg. Seven went on our lady. And the sparkle of candleflame reflected on chalets depicted with foot-thick roofs of snow— country scenes from Baboosh and Ziloptka.

And, oh, the hours of adventures, stories forgotten like patterns faded on a quilt, the half-remembered pages of a dream.

But that terrible year, Mother and Father were distracted and cross. They quarreled over the least triviality, avoided each other, refused to do anything until the other apologized.

No lights went up; no windowsill scenes. The house didn't smell of butter cookies cut in the shape of Santas and snowmen. But these were only portents of coming things.

Two weeks before Christmas, Father was fired. He took it hard and grew sullen. One week before Christmas, Mother got sick. First a cold, then a flu with fevers that rose every day. She took to her bed.

Father withdrew into drinking, sitting long hours at the dining table throwing back whiskey to hold back the fear. We could not blame him. It was the Bad Luck Leshy. Day by day the ginger house changed—its roof turned gray, its corners round until it looked like a mushroom cap.

Sister and I peeked in at the window to see a ring of red eyes huddled around a red fire; we heard the whispered stories of Pee-eckwo and Shmertsh and the Death-Train.

Yet, we held on to hope. For Grandma Babka

promised she would be back. Then on Christmas Eve the telegram came. Sister and I answered the door (Mother and Father were that far gone). And it said that Grandma Babka was dead.

And what was Grandma Babka? Just the soul and essence of all our Christmases. She carried the secret of snow in her fingertips, in her eyes the mystery of a candle's luminescence, in her cupped hands the sacred scent of pine.

Thus Christmas crawled into our lives.

Darkness flowed down the chimney, put out the fire, dimmed the lights. Shadows rose in every corner— visions of Mother in the hospital, pale, cold, dead; of Father wandering, found frozen in an alley; of Sister and me orphaned, alone.

We tiptoed into the dining room where Father sat drinking whiskey. The room was dark, and we could see his eyes, like the red glowing eyes of the Bad Luck Leshy.

Then we tiptoed into Mother's room filled with candles. She stared out the window. And the wind whispered.

Doomed.

The whole house was enveloped in a dark flame, and we were to be consumed.

We went to weep in our room.

Sister and I fell into a fitful sleep. But it was between the hours of three and four that we awoke and heard the mournful sound—like babies crying with no one to comfort them, like a mouse caught in an owl's talon.

Sister threw open the window.

I called out her name: "Grandma Babka!" three times.

Shmertsh screeched as the engine ground to a halt. Then we heard the "chuff, chuff, chuff" of his angry impatience.

She came. Gliding through the forest, enveloped in a blue egg of light, up the porch steps and into the house.

Our joy soon dwindled in her ire.

"You failed!" Grandma Babka said.

There was no use in making excuses; we had failed.

"Can we save Mother?" I asked.

"Can we save Father?"

"Is too late." Grandma Babka stared at the ginger house. The round cap roof grew on a sickly stem. Two red eyes peeked from the one remaining window at the top. "Unless—"

"Yes?"

"Answer questions. What is Christmas meaning?"

Sister and I searched through our heads. All the while the fungus expanded before our eyes; the gloom thickened.

Ornaments and snow and Santa, I thought.

475

Roast duck and stockings and peppermint sticks, Sister thought.

"Gifts!" I said.

The mushroom grew a little; stench filled the room.

"Giving!" Sister seconded.

Laughter issued from the window in the mushroom cap.

The blue, plasma egg around Grandma Babka erupted in streaks of lightning that popped like firecrackers. Two blue balls of lightning flew tumbling from her eyes and pinned us with terror.

"What is greatest gift can give?" Grandma Babka roared. She produced a long-bladed knife.

Our thoughts melted together, and we saw Father frozen in the dining room, a drink at his lips, and Mother in the bedroom wasting away.

"Ourselves!" we cried. "Take us instead!"

"Sacrifice," Grandma Babka said. And grabbing our hands, she slashed deftly down our thumbs—nail to knuckle, and held the bleeding fingers over the deadly fungus. Steam hissed off the slippery surface, the mushroom shrank, and inside the Bad Luck Leshy shrieked.

"Blood of innocents," Grandma Babka said.

The toadstool withered down to nothing.

"Is okay now," Grandma Babka said. "Father get job back tomorrow. Mother have miracle recovery."

A mournful wail—like an animal in pain—sounded from the back of the house.

The blue plasma egg that was Grandma Babka bulged toward the door. "Shmertsh impatient."

"Where will you go?" Sister and I asked.

"Made deal with Death. He let me come back; I go with him to bad place."

"Pee-eckwo!" we wailed.

And we tried to hold Grandma Babka, but our arms wrapped around air. She glided through the door.

Sister and I rushed to our room and the window to get a last glimpse. The forest had mysteriously disappeared leaving a far field covered with snow. Bisecting the field were tracks upon which was a black locomotive with two red eyes glaring from the rear. A line of black cars stretched across the horizon.

Grandma Babka glided over the landscape. And as we watched, the moon peeked out from the clouds and opened a blue hole in the snow. Grandma Babka turned one last time to wave farewell, and not seeing the hole, fell in.

And now that Sister and I are grown up and have children, we bake gingerbread houses of our own and tell the story. And sometimes at Christmas when the moon shines on the snowy fields we take our children down to Baboosh and sometimes neighboring Ziloptka where we visit Grandma Babka (who cheated Death), and there we have adventures.

ALL IN THE TELLING

Jeremy Dyson

Jeremy Dyson's claim to fame thus far centers on the fact that Janice Long once played the third single by the "minor league indie" band, Flowers for Agatha (for which Dyson played keyboards), on her Radio One show.

In addition, however, he has had a spell at art college "making bizarre videos," and spent time as a magician, a children's entertainer, a disc jockey and a "sticker-on of whiskey bottle labels," as well as working for Warner Bros. in publicity and marketing. He's also managed to get a degree in philosophy and write his first feature film, Darkness Waiting, which he describes as "a psychological thriller," He currently runs the SF/fantasy/horror department of Waterstone's in Leeds—"Supposedly to pay the bills," he says, "but more accurately to feed my long-time record and CD addiction."

"All in the Telling" is Dyson's first professional short story sale.

"I used to be dangerously superstitious," he recalls, "going as far as inventing my own systems of signs and omens involving the interpretation of random events. 'If the British Gas advert comes on television now, everything is going to be all right,' and 'If the next Smartie's green, I'm going to die...' until my fear began to spiral out of control and rule my life.

"Eventually, I got the better of it: The only lingering remnants are an over-observance of the number of magpies outside my flat and a belief that the numbers five and six are lucky for me."

Settle down now, because Jeremy wants to tell us a story: and he wants to tell it r e a l bad....

"**R**eelax, Meester Fletcher. Ees only a storm." For a moment the dank barroom had become electrically bright. Santini cracked his knuckles and smiled, revealing rotten keyboard teeth. He waved his right arm extravagantly in the air. "Another dreenk for me and my good friend." No one seemed to take much notice.

"Will she be here soon?" Fletcher asked. He didn't want to appear impatient even if he was, for his impatience was bred from fear, not boredom.

"Yes, yes, she weell be here, she weell be here. Dreenk, Meester Fletcher, dreenk." Santini placed his fat heavy hand over Fletcher's and moved it towards the tumbler that lay neglected on the table in front of him. The bourbon, if that was the true nature of the piss-colored fluid in the glass, was almost undrinkable and yet Fletcher raised it to his lips at his companion's request. It seemed unwise not to. "Good, yes…" Santini laughed. His laugh was worse than his smile.

Fletcher had doubted the wisdom of his visit to Mai Li's almost as soon as he had walked in. It was the first time he'd ventured into this part of the city although he had read much about it and heard even more. The laws of this country were strict, but perhaps the authorities were prepared to turn a blind eye to certain businesses. Of course, Fletcher had entertained the idea of visiting many times, but it was Santini's impromptu soliciting in the hotel lounge that had made it happen. That and a few too many Jack Daniels.

He had never spoken to the fat Colombian before tonight, although he had seen him, lurking around various bars, telling extravagant tales in broken English to any foolish ex-patriots lonely or drunk enough to listen. Perhaps this evening, for the first time, Fletcher came into that category.

Santini had importuned and then seduced him as surely as any Latin lover, and the relief that he had promised made the trip across town seem worth a thousand dangers, imagined or real.

However, as the rickshaw rattled through the humid streets and the white faces thinned out to be replaced by their native counterparts, Fletcher's bravado began to evaporate along with the whiskey which transformed itself into a sheen of sweat over his burning face. The lack of street lighting did nothing to boost his confidence. The jolly yellow lanterns strung between poles that he was so used to were now nowhere to be seen; just an occasional bare bulb hanging over an intersection, fizzing and buzzing in the soaking heat.

Fletcher was aware that there were those back home who might consider such a trip exciting—the boys in the Duchess, his bachelor colleagues—but he was not like them. Yet the memory of Santini's promises and the anticipation of their experience were just enough to keep him in his seat.

"When you see thees girl, Meester Fletcher, you

weell fall een love. Een love. She ees called Tai De. She has a face like a china doll. She ees more beautiful than a rose. You will fall een love," Santini reiterated.

Mai Li's had appeared unheralded. In fact it was only the halting of the rickshaw that had indicated their arrival. For some reason, Fletcher had imagined a garish neon sign or a window full of naked flesh. As always, reality was more mundane. A black wooden door with no handle and a flickering white porch lamp marked the entrance. Santini gave a rattle of knocks— that may or may not have been coded—and the door opened.

Upon entering, Fletcher immediately found himself thinking of his one visit to a sex shop many years before. In London, on business. Drunk from a couple of afternoon pints. Stumbling down the stairs past the faded "adults only" sign. A library of multi-colored "continental" magazines. A urinal's worth of men: young, old, faceless, colorless. Shaking hands, sightless eyes. Jostling a place amongst them. Reaching up for a pair of glossy breasts.

The men here were similar: all ages, mostly alone, clinging to anonymity as a shield against shame. They were dotted amongst the ill-lit tables, staring at their drinks.

However it wasn't just the men. There was something in the decor that reminded him of that other "establishment," six thousand miles away on the

Charing Cross Road. Perhaps it was the peeling veneer intended to suggest planks of stripped pine. Perhaps it was the burnt brown carpet or the empty booth next to the bar with its homely little Visa/Mastercard sign. Whatever it was, Fletcher tried to shake off the unwelcome association as their drinks were ordered and they took their seats. If what Santini had said was true, then it wasn't sex they were here for. Mai Li's offered a more exclusive service unavailable elsewhere.

"You have your story ready, Meester Fletcher?" Santini asked, returning from the bar. Fletcher merely nodded. The question seemed so unnecessary. How long had he been waiting? Too many years to count. With each passing season the pressure to narrate grew inside, and yet the opportunity for the tale's narration seemed to recede more and more. How he had come by this story he did not know, but it was there, inside him, like a child sewn into a womb.

"Have you told yours before?" Fletcher asked and Santini laughed his ugly laugh again.

"Oh yes, yes. But weeth each telling it becomes sweeter."

For the first time since entering the place, Fletcher found himself relaxing a little. Perhaps it was Mai Li's appalling bourbon, or perhaps it was the fact that he felt he was with his own kind: these lonely-looking, single men, all with untold tales which they could not release elsewhere. For years he had considered his affliction to be unique, a suffering particular to himself, but in this concealed and alien place it seemed he had found fellow victims, and with them a source of relief.

When Santini first spoke of his experience here, Fletcher was initially surprised but very quickly adjusted to the fact that there were others like him. And it also made sense that in this foreign land, with its ancient and wise culture, there would be those who would understand, those to whom he could unburden himself, those who would heal. That they chose to remain hidden and covert like the affliction itself seemed natural too.

Fletcher had attempted many times to convey his story: sometimes in speech, to lovers, to friends, sometimes in writing on paper, in pen. But the words never actually emerged. They remained both unseen and unheard, coiled together somewhere within.

Tonight, however, things would be different, for beautiful Tai De, with her ancient Oriental skill, would charm them outside, persuade them to slither up through Fletcher's throat and slide over his tongue, until at last they would be revealed to the outside world and he would be free. The story would no longer be exclusively his. Someone else would have heard and understood.

A ripple of activity passed through the otherwise silent bar. Chairs scraped, glasses were put down, throats were cleared. Looking across the dimly lit room,

Fletcher saw that a figure now occupied the wooden booth.

"There. I told you she would come. Go to her, Meester Fletcher. Take your place."

Fletcher's heart began racing as he stood. His legs felt weak beneath him, his mouth dry. Like an inexperienced teenager about to ask the class beauty for a dance, he felt that now, when he most needed them, words might fail him.

Tai De was indeed sublime. For once Santini had not been exaggerating. Her skin seemed impossibly pure and white, her hair incalculably black. Her lips, blood red and wet, were ready to coax and instruct the reluctant fiction from Fletcher's open mouth. And her youth… Although she possessed the body of a woman her face was that of a child's.

"Yes," thought Fletcher as he staggered toward her, adrenaline allowing his confidence to return, "at last I will be able to tell."

Men clamored around the open window. In the light cast from the adjacent bar, Fletcher was able to observe their faces for the first time. Expectant, eager, wide-eyed, they looked not unlike he imagined himself to. A mixture of nationalities, although none of them native, they ranged in age from early twenties to late sixties. In fact, looking closer, the oldest of them could have been nearer seventy. Slack-jawed, slack-skinned, the old man waved a wad of paper money in Tai De's direction, a look of eager anticipation in his eyes. Fletcher wondered if the man had waited all his life for this opportunity.

"Please, please. Can only take one of you." Tai De's voice was as delicate as her face. But her tone was both confident and concerned. Fletcher experienced a flash of anxiety. What if he was to lose this one precious chance? As if in answer to this fear, the old man, utilizing reserves of strength that seemed unfitting for someone of his age, thrust himself forward, forcing his money into Tai De's hand.

"Madame. Moi. Moi." He was like a desperate child.

"Okay. Okay." The girl smiled as she tucked the notes into the silk purse that hung around her neck. Fletcher was enveloped immediately in black despair. He had to return to England in two days. What if he had just seen his only chance disappear, as suddenly as it had presented itself.

"No," he told himself, "that cannot be. I will return."

The other men, presumably experiencing similar feelings, began dispersing gloomily to their tables. He was about to join them when he noticed the mien of horror that had settled over the nameless Frenchman, who stood gazing glassy eyed at Tai De.

"Non, non…j'oublie…j'oublie…." There was a tone of such terror, such hopelessness in the aged voice that Fletcher's first response was one of pity. And then it occurred to him that this man's misfortune was his golden chance.

"Tai De...I know my story...I know it backward." She turned toward him, a faint smile playing across her incandescent face. She unbuttoned her purse and made to hand back the money to her former client. He did not take it; he had no interest. He stood rocking slightly from foot to foot, lost in misery. Observing how much money the Frenchman had given, Fletcher handed her the same as quickly as possible, which she took, her black eyes settling on his.

Stepping forward, Fletcher readied himself to tell his tale. He felt the words bubbling up from that hidden place, deep within, propelled by the accumulated pressure of enforced concealment. The back of his tongue began to press gently on the roof of his mouth, ready to receive the first phoneme cast its way. His lips parted....

"No silly. Not here." Tai De had stepped out from behind the booth placing her tiny hand on Fletcher's forearm. He blushed and looked to the floor, embarrassed at his own naiveté. It hadn't occurred to him that the service would take place in private. "We go up here." She gestured toward a small wooden door behind the bar, decorated with miniature fans.

He followed her up the narrow staircase, lit by one dim bulb, its walls lined with the same familiar wood veneer wallpaper. Cheap perfume hung in the air masking another more unpleasant, unnamable smell beneath.

They reached the cramped landing, which had three doors in each of its walls. Tai De turned to smile at Fletcher as she reached for the one in front of them. She had to force it open, as the wood didn't fit the frame, which seemed to have been knocked together at angles other than ninety degrees.

Fletcher felt his heart beginning to race again. A certain tension had settled at the base of his stomach, but the sensation was not unpleasant. He realized with a thrill that the telling had finally arrived; and not only that, but he would be able to enjoy it. He could relax and take his time. There was no need to hurry the narrative. He could savor the twists and turns of his elaborate little story line and relish its conclusion. And he would also be able to draw pleasure from Tai De's response: watch her react to the gentle subtleties of his plot, derive satisfaction from a smile that he, or rather his story, had placed upon her face.

The room was completely bare apart from a dirty-looking futon stretched across the floor. The fake veneer had spread from outside across the room's walls, its artificiality obvious even under the forty-watt bulb that flickered above them. Tai De reached down and removed her small shoes, before settling down on the unpleasant-looking sheets. She reached for Fletcher, pulling him toward her. She allowed her kimono to fall open a little as she arranged herself, revealing more of her beautiful skin. It made Fletcher forget his surroundings.

"So," she smiled, "you like it here?" Fletcher assumed she was trying to put him at his ease. Playing along he looked around the room. He was surprised and slightly unsettled to see a window in the wall behind Tai De. It seemed to look onto another room.

"It's...not what I'd expected." Was that a figure in the room beyond? There wasn't enough light to be sure. "But then the whole place wasn't what I expected." Tai De nodded, as if she had heard this before. She moved a little closer. Fletcher could smell the sweetness of her breath.

"Shall we lie down?" she asked, flattening herself against the sheets. Fletcher slipped off his espadrilles, quickly adopting Tai De's position. She smiled again as his head joined hers and a sudden wave of joy flooded over him. She looked so understanding, so sweet, so ready to hear him. But something was not right.

Fletcher was concerned about the lurking form behind the glass. He didn't like the feeling of being watched or the sense that his intimacy with Tai De was being compromised in some way.

"Is there..." It was difficult to express his concern. "Is that a person...in there?" He gestured towards the room beyond. Tai De looked over her shoulder. She turned back to Fletcher and smiled. She hadn't answered his question.

Fletcher tried to settle himself down once more. He wanted to recapture the feeling he had experienced, albeit momentarily, that everything was just right. Tai De looked at him, a hint of encouragement in her eyes. Perhaps things wouldn't get any more right than this. He closed his eyes. The feeling welled up once more. His heart began thumping....

"Once there was—" A finger settled firmly against his lips. Fletcher opened his eyes. Tai De smiled like a mother having to deny an indulgent, over-excited child. Her other hand fell to his belt buckle and began loosening it.

"There's no need to speak. Not here," she said softly. Fletcher felt his heartbeat quicken even more. Anticipation flipped over suddenly into anxiety.

"But...my story...?" Tai De looked at him inquisitively for a moment. Then realization settled over her face.

"Silly. That's just..." She searched for the words. "...a cover." The room faded a little. For a moment Fletcher felt that he was no longer there. Suddenly he felt shame: shame at his presence there, shame at his misjudgment, shame at his lack of worldliness. He tried to cover his humiliation with a little laugh.

"Oh. I am naive," he stuttered. Tai De grinned at him, although it was clear she did not understand his words. As she reached down and unbuttoned his fly, Fletcher felt his throat tightening and tears pressing their way into his eyes. He could just about make out a face pressed against the glass of the dark window. Although he was unable to discern its sex, he could see it was smiling.

GREEN

m a r k   m o r r i s

Getting a short story out of Mark Morris is a neat trick…and by that I mean a s h o r t story. Being such a consummately effective tale-spinner has that one drawback: length. Because when Mark tells a tale, he tells it all. Consequently, there aren't too many Mark Morris stories around…so "Green" is something of a collector's item.

His debut novel, the 250,000-word T o a d y—written on the back of an Enterprise Scheme grant—caused something of a stir when it appeared in 1989 by virtue of its stylish mixture of horror and fantasy. The more traditional horror tome, S t i t c h , (just 220,000 words), which followed in 1991, plumbed even darker depths and

492

cemented his reputation. The Immaculate (105,000 words...is the boy running out of steam?), Mark's more gentle third offering, displayed his hand at the ghost story, a sadly much ignored sub-section of the genre. A fourth, The Secret of Anatomy, was released earlier this year and, in hitting the 200,000 mark, the signs are he's got his second wind.

Mark lives with his wife, the artist Nel Whatmore, in Boston Spa, where he divides his non-writing time among watching Doctor Who videos, moaning about Leeds United, providing a rural retreat for fellow writers, making cheese sauces and talking to me on the telephone.

Mark never tempts fate. When he's had a particularly bad day he takes it out on God by calling him names...and then spends hours of contrition apologizing profusely to the Big Guy. "And if I see a single magpie," he adds, "I hold the sighting over until I see a second one...even if it's weeks later or even if it's the first one I saw simply flying back the way it came."

This is a careful man.

"It's a lovely dress, Claire, but I can't possibly accept it."

"Course you can. Think of it as an incentive, something to slim into once the baby's born."

Hilary Sterland gave her sister a rueful smile. "It's not that. It's the color. Bob would do his nut."

Claire rolled her eyes in exasperation and lowered the backless, strapless, emerald-green evening gown she'd been flourishing like a toreador's cape. "Oh God, you're joking. Can't you tell him to stuff it just this once? It's his daft superstition, not yours."

Hilary merely shrugged, apologetic but resigned. Claire bit back her vitriol; she wouldn't have another go at Bob, however much he grated on her, however much she thought he pushed her sister around. She knew that Hilary doted on him. Horses for courses, as their grandmother was wont to say. Claire loved her sister dearly, though it bugged her that she had inherited their mother's blind spot when it came to men.

To put it bluntly, their father had been—and probably still was—a bastard. None of the family had seen hide nor hair of him for twelve years, not since he had run off with that whore from the bakery, who had merely been the latest in a long line of whores. Not that Bob was like that; his disrespect for women took a different form. He saw them as pretty objects— amusing, desirable, but ultimately trivial. Claire was not the first woman he had laughingly referred to as "one of those feminist lesbo-types" because she actually had the temerity to stand up to him, to *dare* to pick holes in his woolly, bigoted world-view. In Claire's opinion, men like Bob needed to dominate women for the simple fact that they were scared of them. His was the classic inferiority complex.

She folded the dress carefully and replaced it in the box, thinking that next time she and Dave were invited round to her sister's for dinner, she'd wear it herself purely to spite Bob. To cool down she made more coffee, and then she and Hilary discussed the topic that had dominated their conversation for the past seven months: the imminent arrival of Hilary's second child.

Claire knew that Hilary was worried because of her age—she was thirty-four—and because she did not know what kind of reaction to expect from Bob and her eleven-year-old son, Kim. The three of them had a comfortable, if somewhat staid, lifestyle; a kind of balance had been established over the years that Hilary was afraid the new baby would comprehensively disrupt. If that happened, the odds were that Hilary would get the blame. When she had first revealed to Bob that she was six weeks pregnant despite her coil, he had tutted and shaken his head in exasperation and told her she was "a silly girl" for allowing it to happen. In the seven months since then his attitude did not seem to have changed. He appeared to regard her pregnancy as some minor, typically female misdemeanor, like putting one of his white shirts into the washing machine with the red duvet and turning it pink, or forgetting to buy cereal at the supermarket. Of the two of them—father and son—it was Kim who had shown Hilary the greater support. However, he was going through a sullen, secretive stage. When he was in the house he spent most of his time in his room playing with his computer games, or stuck in front of the TV, face blank.

"Maybe I should have had an abortion," Hilary sighed, not for the first time.

"Don't you dare say that!" Claire responded. "When you got married you told me you wanted a boy and a girl."

"Yeah, but…" Hilary's voice trailed off. She sighed and linked her hands over her swollen belly as though protecting it from disapproval.

The front door opened, and Kim walked into the lounge, school tie awry, Puma sports bag over his shoulder. "Oh…hi," he said as if surprised to see the two of them there.

"Hello, Kim," said Claire. "How are you?"

"Fine, thanks."

Claire noticed that the boy's hands were stained blue and that he had an orange smudge on his cheek. "Been painting?" she asked.

"What? Uh…yeah." Kim looked guiltily at his hands. "At school." He turned to Hilary. "What's for tea, Mum?"

Despite her pregnancy, Hilary was still expected to run the house and cook all the meals. Suppressing a sigh she said, "How does beefburgers, chips and beans sound?"

Kim shrugged, pulling a face. "Okay, I guess. I'm...er...going upstairs."

"Have you got much homework?"

"Nah...a bit." He left the room.

Hilary sighed as though communicating with her son was an ordeal. "I think my being pregnant embarrasses him," she said, and tried (and failed) to smile.

Claire crossed to her sister, put her arms around her shoulders and gave her a hug. "Hey, come on," she said. "He'll be thrilled when the baby comes and so will Bob, you'll see. This baby will be the best thing ever."

A weak smile filtered across Hilary's face. "Yeah, I know," she said, but she sounded unconvinced.

Bob Sterland rolled back the sleeves of his shirt and looked at his watch. He did it with a flourish, as a magician might do to show he had nothing to hide. Though he did not know it, this was one of the many things that his sister-in-law, Claire Adams, despised him for. Bob, of course, was completely unaware of this habit he had of transforming his most insignificant gesture into an exaggerated, somehow arrogant statement. He looked across the open-plan office that housed the entire workforce—some sixteen in all—of the Starmouth Leisure Services, and he announced loudly, as he did most days, "Soon be hometime, boys and girls."

There were a few mutters of acknowledgment, one or two nodding heads. Most people, however, ignored Bob completely. Mike Travis, whose cluttered desk was directly opposite Bob's, looked up and glared at him. The unspoken statement conveyed by Mike's expression was clear and bright as neon: I knew you were going to say that. I just *knew* it. Why, just this once, couldn't you keep your irritating gob *shut*?

Bob grinned at Mike, naturally oblivious. Then he did something else that never failed to drive Mike silently wild. He inclined his head, made a clicking noise out of the side of his mouth and gave a conspiratorial wink. "Got anything lined up for tonight, Michael?"

Bob was the only person who called him "Michael." He somehow managed to make it sound both pally and belittling. Mike bared his teeth in a snarl that purported to be a grin. "Lined up, Robert?" he said tightly. "I don't know what you mean."

"Oh, I think you do," said Bob heartily. He jerked his elbow, nudging air. "How's that new totty of yours?"

"Barbara's fine." Each syllable was a bullet that Mike wished would penetrate Bob Sterland's crocodile-thick skin.

"I bet she is," agreed Bob. "Nothing like a bit of what you fancy to put some color in your cheeks. Am I right or am I right?"

Mike raised his eyebrows and grunted, wishing as

always that he could pluck up whatever it took to vent the anger that seethed beneath his veneer of equanimity. He knew under ordinary circumstances that he never would. But the Christmas office party on December 16th was only a week away, and Mike was already harboring vague plans of getting blind drunk and telling Bob exactly what he thought of him. Ideally, he'd love to smash the creep's nose all over his leering face, put him in traction for the festive season, but he doubted that things would go that far. To be truthful, he even had doubts as to whether consuming copious amounts of alcohol would finally enable him to speak his mind. It was likely to loosen his stomach before his inhibitions. He stood up abruptly, scooping his bomber jacket from the back of his chair.

"Right, I'm off," he said.

Bob tutted in playful disapproval. "Naughty, naughty. It's only ten to."

"I don't care. I've done my bit for today."

"What's the situation with Ken Dodd?"

Mike was responsible for booking the acts for the summer season. He knew that Bob had asked him the question purely in an attempt to prevent him leaving early. "A bit iffy," he said. "I don't think we'll get him."

Bob contrived an expression of interested concern. "What's the problem?" he asked earnestly.

"Well, would you do Starmouth when you've been offered Blackpool?"

"Starmouth's more refined," Bob said almost sulkily.

"Exactly. Smaller crowds, less money."

Bob sighed, as if Mike had disappointed him in some way. "So what has his manager said exactly?"

"That he'll ring me tomorrow, but I shouldn't start making any plans."

Bob shook his head, tutting like a schoolteacher. "That won't do at all, will it? Would you like me to have a word with him?"

Mike clenched his teeth, felt the band of anger around his temple tighten a further notch. "There's no point," he said tersely, "because I've already spoken to him. At great length. All that could have been done has been."

"That's as may be, Michael, but let's face it, there's no substitute for experience. I think if I could just—"

"Please," Mike blurted, raising his hand. His voice was louder than he had intended. He became aware of faces turning toward him and immediately felt embarrassed.

"Please," he said again, lowering his voice. "Just trust me on this one will you, Bob. I'm quite capable, you know."

Bob spread his palms exaggeratedly, fingers pointing toward the ceiling like a mime artist encountering an invisible wall. "Oh, I don't doubt that, Michael, not for a minute. No, no. I wouldn't dream of casting aspersions. I simply felt a different approach, a separate voice...." He smiled expansively, the good Samaritan ever prepared to aid a struggling colleague.

Mike managed to contort his facial muscles into a fair approximation of a smile. "Thanks, Bob," he said.

"That's very kind of you, but if you don't mind I'll handle it myself."

Bob shrugged like a cartoon Italian. "Okay, okay. It's your funeral. But if Ken slips through the net you're going to have to find an alternative pretty pronto."

"It so happens I've already got one lined up," Mike said smugly.

"Oh, really. Who?"

"Hinge and Brackett."

"But they're a drag act!" exclaimed Bob. "Oh, come on, Michael, you can't be serious!"

"They're very popular."

"But...A drag act?"

"What's that got to do with anything?"

Bob smote his brow. Mike wondered how he could make that crack sound without knocking himself senseless.

"I can't believe you asked me that. Don't get me wrong, I've got nothing against them personally. But...well...it's their following isn't it?"

"I'm sorry, Bob, I'm not with you."

"Their *fannns*," Bob emphasized. "Before we know it, the place'll be crawling with arse bandits."

Mike simply stared at him, unsure whether to laugh or cry, though in truth it was not an unexpected reaction from Bob. He was not exactly a man renowned for his tolerance. Of course, Bob always insisted that he had nothing against *them* personally, he was sure most of *them* simply didn't know any better. *Them*, of course, was an all-embracing term which included

501

racial minorities, homosexuals, feminists, vegetarians, lefties, AIDS sufferers, punks, hippies, men with earrings (who were, by definition, either homosexuals, lefties or punks anyway), Southerners and a fair proportion of women.

Finally Mike managed to squeeze out a laugh. "Don't be daft," he said. "They've had a series on the BBC."

"Ah, but why do you think they're not on the BBC any more? Answer me that one, eh?"

"Oh come off it, Bob. Anyway, I couldn't give a monkey's who their fans are. At least they've got fans. Which means bums on seats."

Bob shook his head. He looked mortified. "Have you no sense of responsibility? Think of the citizens of Starmouth. Think of the children."

"The *children*? Don't you think you're over-reacting slightly?"

"You don't know what these people are *like*, Michael. You don't know what they get up to."

Mike yanked up the zip of his jacket. "I'm going home." He stomped out before Bob could reply.

Bob stared after him for a few moments, shaking his head. Michael was a pleasant enough lad, but misguided, and altogether unsuited to the responsibility of his position. In Bob's opinion the boy had been promoted too early. He was bound to make mistakes, impetuous decisions he would regret later. It was up to his elders and betters to put him right, to keep him on the straight and narrow.

Bob looked around and was satisfied to see that none

of his colleagues were paying him the slightest attention. The majority of them were in the process of finishing up for the day; some had already left.

Casually he stood up and sauntered across to Mike's desk. He tutted at the disorder—papers strewn about, a half-finished mug of cold tea sitting in a pattern of white rings on the wooden surface, biscuit crumbs, a spidery pot plant trailing green fronds among the debris. Really, this was just a reflection of Michael's inability to cope. For goodness sake, the boy still wore jeans to the office! If that wasn't an indication of his attitude, Bob didn't know what was.

He allowed his gaze to wander across the jumble of letters, official memos, scribbled notes. Despite his bluster, Bob was sure that the boy would be grateful for a surreptitious push in the right direction. Ah, there was what he was looking for. Typically, the letter from Ken Dodd's agent was crumpled beneath Michael's pot plant and speckled with soil.

Shaking his head, Bob reached for it. As he did so his hand brushed against the hanging fronds of the plant. Suddenly and shockingly, a searing pain, like a cross between a bee sting and the touch of a red hot poker, sizzled across his skin where the plant had touched it. Bob let out a high-pitched howl and snatched his hand away. As if he'd been infected with a toxin whose effect was deadly and instantaneous, his gorge rose, sweat broke out on his brow, he felt faint. Just before the world swam away from him, he looked at his hand and saw deep grooves carved in the flesh, grooves filled not with blood but with a viscous luminous-green liquid which actually seemed to be *bubbling*. As his knees buckled and the darkness rushed in, Bob thought of his mother's antipathy to the *bad* color, the *unlucky* color, and his own unquestioned inheritance of it. He had never really thought about *why* it was bad until now. But suddenly he knew, he *really* knew. Such a pity he'd found out too late…

Frankly he was surprised to wake up. He came to, feeling sick and dizzy, faces hovering above him like balloons. The muzz of sound sloshing against his eardrums slowly clarified, fragmenting into separate voices. "Is he all right?" "Do you think he had a heart attack?" "Look, he's coming round." "Get back everybody. Give him some air."

Bob struggled to sit up and was aware of hands fluttering down like birds to aid him. Hands, he thought fuzzily, and then with sudden panic remembered his own hands, the green poison that had sizzled like acid in his wounds. He cried out, was aware of the crowd jerking back in unison, like a single entity. He brought his hands up to his face, turned them over and over, but his eyes refused to focus.

"Are you all right, Bob?" asked a tentative voice. A lined, heavily jowled face drifted down to him, came to rest on the tips of his fingers like the sun poised on the horizon.

"My hands," Bob tried to explain. "I must see. I *need* to see."

The flabby features creased in puzzlement. "Your hands? Your hands are fine, dear boy. Nothing wrong there."

Bob closed his eyes, blew air from his mouth, fought to control his senses. He felt hands touching him again, presumably in comfort, but he found them intrusive, unwelcome. "Leave me," he said, shrugging them off. "I'm fine. I'll...I'll...just don't touch me."

The hands fluttered away. After a few moments, Bob felt ready to open his eyes and examine his own hands again. He did so. He turned his hands over and over, but there was not a mark on them. Not a scratch, not a scar, nothing.

He was still the center of attention, still surrounded by alarmed, expectant, concerned faces. A modicum of his old pride began to seep back, and he said brusquely, "Help me up. I need to get up."

Eager volunteers rushed forward and hauled him into a chair. He tried to smile, but it was a shaky effort, not his usual wide, almost savage, grin.

"Thank you," he said. "Thank you very much. I'll be perfectly all right now."

"That was quite a fall you took there, son," said the balding, heavily jowled man.

"What...what happened, Mr. Sterland," asked a young girl with a blond corkscrew perm and wide eyes. "Did you faint?"

Bob bridled. "Of course I didn't faint," he snapped. "I'm not a swooning schoolgirl. No...I...I slipped and hit my head. Must have knocked myself out for a minute or two."

"Hit your head?" said Trevor Dicks, the Parks and Gardens Co-ordinator. "Are you sure? You haven't got a lump or a bruise or anything."

Bob glared at him. "Of course I'm sure. It was *my* head, wasn't it?"

Dicks shrugged and turned away. To Bob's relief the crowd was dispersing a little now. However, some remained, like Bernard Hoyle, the heavily jowled man who always smelled of pipe tobacco and called everyone "My boy" or "My girl."

"Nevertheless," Hoyle was saying, "I think it might be an idea to pop you down the infirmary, get you checked out."

"Oh no," Bob said, "no need for that." He hated hospitals because he hated the idea that anything might be wrong with him.

Bob didn't notice the blond-haired girl—Shirley—had left until she reappeared holding something out to him. "Here, Mr. Sterland, drink this."

Ordinarily Bob would have welcomed Shirley's attentions. The number of times he'd fantasized about sinking his face between those gorgeous tits...But right now all he could do was look with horror at the object she was holding out to him. It was a glass filled with water. A *green* glass filled with water.

"No!" Bob yelled, jumping up and making the chair he'd been sitting in rock backward. Shirley flinched, slopping water onto the floor. A second later she screamed as Bob's arm swept round and dashed the glass from her hand.

The glass sailed across the room and smashed against the wall, causing a spray of water and glass fragments to rain down on Bernard Hoyle's desk. "What the hell...?" Bernard cried, then he too was staggering backward as Bob barged past him.

"Just leave me alone!" Bob shouted. "I've told you I'm fine, I'm bloody fine. Are you all too stupid to understand that?"

He turned and fled from the room, eyes wild, back hunched, panting like an injured animal.

"Bob," asked Hilary tentatively, "are you sure you're all right?"

Immediately after she'd asked the question she wished she hadn't. She quailed at the thunder in Bob's eyes. He drew back his lips and snarled, "Of *course* I'm all right. I've *told* you, haven't I? Now stop fucking going on at me. Leave me alone."

Hilary looked down at her meal, cowed. She opened her mouth, wanting to tell him she was sorry, she was only concerned, but she knew that the sound of her voice would only exacerbate his anger, and so in the end she said nothing.

Very few people saw this side of Bob. To everyone else he was the life and soul, always laughing, always joking. Oh, she knew he could be narrow-minded, opinionated, of course, and she knew that some people found this irksome. But he was generally regarded as harmless, uncomplicated—even her sister, Claire, thought of him in this way, and Claire was closer to Hilary than anyone. It was only Hilary who saw the anger in Bob, the way he brooded sometimes. It was only Hilary who had felt the sharp edge of Bob's tongue, had heard him spew invective like poison. Thankfully his anger never lasted for long, and never spilled over into physical violence. And yet Hilary couldn't help thinking that the propensity was there. The best thing to do, as always, was simply not to antagonize him, not to give the anger a target. With nothing to feed on, it would retreat back into its hole until the next time. And so they sat silently, eating their meal, Hilary stealing no more than the occasional glance at her husband. She wondered what he was brooding about—something at work maybe; he had a very responsible job. She wondered too why he was not eating his peas. But she didn't dare ask.

After the meal, Bob stomped out of the kitchen without a word of thanks, without bothering to offer to wash up. Hilary sighed and eased herself slowly from her seat, her back aching intolerably, the baby like an anvil in her belly. If anything, she should be the angry one. Eight and a half months pregnant, and not once had her husband asked her how she had been today. He had not kissed her, had not even asked where Kim was. She collected up the crockery, scraping his uneaten peas into the flip-top bin.

She was putting the last of the pots away when the doorbell rang. She listened for a moment, wondering if Bob would answer it, but there was no sound from the lounge. "I'll go," she called, and waddled into the hall. When she opened the door and saw the uniformed policeman, her immediate thought was: *Bob's done something. That's why he's so preoccupied. My God, what's he done?*

Then she saw Kim. His face was clenched and pale as if he were readying himself for some ordeal. He was standing behind and to one side of the policeman. A policewoman, almost concealed from view by the policeman's bulk, was lightly holding Kim's left forearm.

"Mrs. Sterland?" the policeman said. He was younger than she had at first thought.

"Yes." She looked at the policeman's face and then at Kim's. "What's happened? What's going on?"

"Mrs. Sterland, your son was caught with three others boys defacing council property earlier this evening."

"Defacing...You mean vandalism?"

"In a sense. He was spray-painting graffiti onto the walls of the Public Conveniences building in Beachside Park."

"Oh, Kim," said Hilary sadly. She looked at her son, but his head was bowed, his gaze fixed firmly on his shoes. "Will he have to go to court?" she asked the policeman.

"That's not for me to say, Mrs. Sterland. We'll let you know of any developments."

The policewoman let go of Kim's arm, and he

shuffled into the house, still refusing to meet his mother's gaze.

"Well...thanks for bringing him home," Hilary said.

"That's all right, Mrs. Sterland, no problem. Goodnight."

"Goodnight," said Hilary. She closed the door.

As soon as she had done so, Kim bolted up the stairs and into his room, slamming the door behind him.

"Well, young man, what have you got to say for yourself?"

Hilary stood, hands on hips, glaring down at the top of her son's head.

Kim was sitting on his bed, hands clasped between his knees. He looked small, huddled and pathetic. Hilary fought down an urge to feel sorry for him, an urge to sit beside him and gather him into her arms. She *wanted* to sit down—the weight in her belly made it feel as though a screw was being slowly tightened at the base of her spine— but she felt that doing so would somehow undermine her authority. In a way she felt more angry at Bob for being in one of his moods than she did at Kim. Bob should be handling stuff like this at this stage in her pregnancy. She could do without all the upset.

"Well?" she said. "I'm waiting."

Kim flinched, his shoulders hunching as though her words were sticks she was using to beat him with. He glanced quickly up at her, his untidy fringe curling darkly over his eyebrows.

He needs a haircut, she thought, and immediately felt guilty for not noticing before now. His hunched shoulders twitched in a shrug, and he murmured something.

"What? I didn't hear you."

"I said I'm sorry."

His voice fractured on the apology. When he next looked up, tears sparkled in his eyes.

That did it. Her resolve melted at once, an ice cube before the raging fire of his misery. She crossed to him, sat beside him, draped an arm across his thin shoulders.

She couldn't remember the last time she had seen him cry. It made him look so child-like, so vulnerable.

"Oh, Kim," she sighed, "why did you do it?"

He answered her question with one of his own. "Are you going to tell Dad?"

She said nothing for a moment. She *ought* to tell Bob, but the thought of doing so just now made her shudder. "I don't know," she said. "Not yet. He's got a lot on his mind at the moment."

A little of the tension seeped from him, and he rested his cheek against her swollen breast. She noticed the hands in his lap smeared with paint, orange and blue and black. Gently she prised his hands apart and turned them over, confronting him with the evidence.

"You know you shouldn't do this sort of thing, don't you? Defacing property…it's as bad as breaking things up. It's senseless. You should know better than this, Kim."

She felt him tense again at her words. "It's not," he muttered.

"Not what?"

"It's not like breaking things up. It's making things better, more colorful. It's art."

"Spraying paint on walls is art?" she said scornfully.

"Yes!" The tears had gone now. He stood up suddenly, moved away from her, turned and faced her so that their positions of a few moments before were reversed. She could see him struggling to express himself, and despite everything, she wanted him to succeed, to convince her. Finally he shook his head and muttered, "You don't understand."

"No I don't. But I want to. I can't condone these things, but I want to know why you did them."

The look he gave her was part suspicion, part eagerness. He stood, apparently undecided for a moment, then seemed to come to a decision and nodded abruptly. "All right," he said. "I'll show you."

He walked back across the room, got down on his hands and knees and rooted under the bed. He dragged out two large books, brushed fluff from their covers, and placed them beside her. Hilary picked up the first book, *Subway Art*, the cover of which showed people standing on the platform of an underground station in New York, about to board a train smothered in breathtakingly psychedelic graffiti. The other book, entitled *Inner-City Dreams*, depicted two boys, one black, one white, wearing baseball caps and shell suits, leaning proudly against a wall that had been transformed into a stunningly colorful space battle.

She began leafing through the books. On each page, colors leaped out at her, a kaleidoscope of images demanding her attention. Kim hovered beside her, watching her face closely, as nervous for her reaction as if the work were his own.

"Where did you get these?" Hilary said, putting down the first book and opening the second.

"I bought them," Kim said. "I saved up my pocket money." When Hilary looked at him, he shrugged and looked embarrassed. "And my dinner money," he admitted.

She decided not to comment on that. She began looking through the second book. After a minute or two, unable to contain himself, Kim said, "Well, what do you think of them?"

"They're…amazing," Hilary admitted. "Are you as good as this?"

"Nah. But I'm not bad. With a bit more practice—"

"Kim," Hilary said warningly.

Kim looked sheepish, knowing he had overstepped the mark. "Sorry, Mum," he said, "but you've got to admit a lot of places do need livening up, don't they? I mean, like that toilet wall in Beachside Park. It's just all covered with names and stuff at the moment, it looks a real mess. We were going to do something really good on it, something that people could look at and…and…"

"Admire?"

"Yeah, admire. Like a real work of art."

Kim looked appealingly at his mother, willing her to understand. Hilary sighed and shook her head.

"I can see what you're getting at Kim," she said, "but don't you see it's not up to you to make that sort of decision? That wall is not your property."

"Yeah, but where can I practice then? I haven't got any property."

"What about if I got you some boards of wood? Like old doors or something?"

"Where from?"

"I don't know. The tip maybe."

Kim pulled a face. "Nah, I need something really big. Hey, what about if I had a wall of the house? I could do some really good pictures. And I could keep painting over them, doing better and better ones."

Hilary almost smiled at the idea of this but managed to suppress it. "I don't think so, Kim," she said. "Your dad would do his nut."

Kim tutted disgustedly. "Well, what about the garage then?"

Hilary raised her eyebrows. "What do *you* think?"

"Aw, it's not fair," Kim said. "I never get to do anything I want."

Hilary was silent for a moment. She felt she ought to be nipping this in the bud right now—it had already got him into trouble with the police, for God's sake! And yet she admired Kim for wanting to brighten up the world, felt almost proud of his need to express himself in this way. He had always liked drawing and painting, and it had been something she had always sought to encourage in him. She would feel a hypocrite if she now condemned him for what he had done.

"Look," she said. "I'll have a think about it. Just promise me you won't spray graffiti on any more public property in the meantime."

Kim set his mouth in a stubborn line, his only response a petulant shrug of the shoulders.

"Promise me, Kim," Hilary said firmly. "I'm trying to be fair with you. I could always tell your dad about this and take away these books."

Kim puffed out his cheeks, expelling air through his pursed lips. "Okay," he acceded, though his voice was low and reluctant. "Okay, I promise."

Bob stared at himself in the bathroom mirror, half expecting to see some evidence of the truth in his face. He had been struggling to grasp the exact nature of that truth since he had woken up on the office floor with his colleagues leaning over him. But it remained veiled in his mind, a bright moon of knowledge wrapped in dark stifling cloud. All that Bob could be sure of was that his superstition, which he had borne almost absently since childhood, had finally been revealed as possessing an authentic and terrible significance. Though exactly what that significance was, what form it would take, Bob did not know.

He stared deep into his own eyes and willed the clouds to shred, for the light of his moon to come blazing through. It was no good. He would have to be patient. But waiting was hard, for he sensed that something was coming, something awful and relentless. All night he had stared unseeingly at the TV screen, trying to recapture that split-second just before he had passed out, when his moon had shone bright and clear. But there were too many distractions; his mind felt dulled by them. Absently he reached for the soap, then glanced down and froze, realizing he had almost fallen straight into a trap.

The soap was green. A pale milky green, it supposedly exuded the scent of fresh pine. Bob's mouth went dry, his stomach clenched and his heart began to pound uncomfortably. Glancing behind him to ensure he was not stepping into any more traps, he edged slowly backward until he felt the cold shock of the metal towel-rail touch his spine. He stood for a moment, staring at the soap, and slowly an idea, an urge almost, formed in his mind. He would try a little experiment, see if he could rip the clouds apart through force. He took three steps forward until he was standing before the sink again. His face in the mirror was pale, jaw muscles clenched into knots of bone. Squeezing his right hand into a fist, he extended his little finger, reached out and touched the soap with its tip.

Instantly his flesh shriveled and peeled back like cellophane exposed to heat. Raging pain hissed up his finger and into his hand, engulfed his wrist and then surged toward his elbow. Bob wrenched his hand away, the pain so bad he could not even cry out. His knees buckled and he collapsed to the floor, his shoulder colliding with the edge of the bath.

Gritting his teeth, blinking furiously, he fought against the emerald darkness that flowed through him, struggled to stop himself losing consciousness. At the same time he prepared himself to receive the truth that he hoped the pain would bring, to capture it before it could slip away. He won his battle against unconsciousness, but the truth eluded him. His thoughts raged bitterly: all this for nothing! His vocal cords were beginning to release involuntary sounds of pain now. He grabbed a damp towel from the edge of the bath and stuffed it into his mouth, biting down hard so that Hilary wouldn't hear.

Green pus was leaking from his finger, bubbling like acid. Fighting against nausea, Bob dragged himself over the edge of the bath and twisted the cold tap. Water spattered on enamel. Bob thrust his hand into it and held it there. A minute or so later, the pain eased enough for him to spit the towel from his mouth. He pulled his hand from the water and examined it.

It was completely healed.

The moon was green, bloated, like rotting fruit. It filled the sky, casting its Halloween light onto slate roofs and tarmacked roads.

Bob stood at his bedroom window staring out, like a child watching the skies for Santa Claus. But it was no benign presence he was waiting for. It was evil...and he was afraid.

As he watched, something fell from the moon—a drool of light, pulsing in the center like a heart. The moon convulsed as it gave birth. The green skin of its light shivered on the earth, cold and reptilian. The speck of light fell from the moon, tumbled toward the horizon, a falling star, destined surely to become a cinder in the earth's atmosphere or to shatter like glass on the planet's surface. But no. The light fell slowly, sedately, and though he was far away and couldn't possibly have known, Bob *did* know that the light was in control and aware not only of the world toward which it fell but of *him*, Bob Sterland, and of his knowledge of its coming.

With a final flash it disappeared behind the horizon, burning the sky with green fire. As the glow faded, darkness seemed to rise and swallow the moon, plunging the earth into the blackest midnight. Bob knew it would not be long now. He could feel the threat of it, the promise of its evil, crawling on his skin like electricity.

Sure enough, moments later, the green light reappeared, a thin line of it which expanded along the horizon. Then, slowly and relentlessly, it began to sweep across the earth, moving toward him, devouring as it came.

Bob had never known such terror, yet he did not vacate his place by the window, he did not run, he did not cry out. The light came closer. Now it was three streets away...Now two...Now one....

And suddenly here it was, sidling around the chimneys, across the roofs, filling the gaps between houses on the other side of the street.

And still Bob did not move. He felt paralyzed, bound to the spot. The light seeped across the road, turning cars to lumps of corroded metal, felling street lamps. It edged onto the pavement on his side of the street, just a yard from his garden gate. Now Bob could see it sizzling at the edges like an egg in hot fat. The flagstones of the pavement became porridge at its touch. It extended tendrils, touched his garden gate, which instantly began to smolder and within seconds was a charred ruin. The tendrils reformed, became one fat tentacle of light which surged up his garden path. Just a few feet away from the house itself, directly beneath his window, it halted, quivered for a moment, then reared up like an angry cobra.

As Bob watched, the light transformed into the shape of a man. Limbs sprouted from the central column; above that a neck and head flowed from the shimmering flux like clay molding itself. The form was basic but powerful. An umbilicus of light trailed from the center of its back, linking it with its greater mass. The light-man took two strides forward and placed its palms flat on the walls of the house. The brick began to hiss like escaping gas: Smoke curled between the man's blazing green fingers.

Like a mountaineer without support, the green man began to scale the wall. Bob watched as it climbed toward him, leaving smoking blackened brick in its wake. When its head was just a few feet beneath the window it stopped, trembling on its perch like a spider.

Slowly, with a sound like fire, it raised its head so that Bob could see its face....

He was torn from the dream so violently that he felt he'd left bits of himself behind, shreds of flesh and cloth clinging to the barbed-wire fence of sleep. He was bleeding inside, could taste it at the back of his throat, feel the pain of his wounds in his heart. "It's coming!" he was shouting at the darkness. "It's coming! It's coming! It's coming!"

Beside him, Hilary, belly huge, jerked awake. "What?" she blurted in a voice thick with sleep. "What's the matter? Bob, what's wrong?"

Bob was hunched up, pressed against the headboard, knees drawn up to his chin, arms wrapped protectively around himself. "It's coming," he repeated in a voice that was hoarse and afraid.

"What is?" snapped Hilary, in no mood for vagaries. "Bob, what is?"

Bob turned to her, and his eyes were wide, the pupils almost lost in the gleaming whites. "Something," he hissed.

Over the course of the next two weeks, Bob Sterland's work colleagues noticed a marked change in him. Gone were the expansive gestures, the domineering manner of the old Bob, and in their stead came a man who was subdued, covert, nervous, watchful.

Some people welcomed this sudden change of character, and hence failed to question it, whereas others found that this new Bob, for entirely different reasons, unsettled them more than ever. Mike Travis, for instance, had been merely irritated, and occasionally infuriated, with the old Bob—but this new one was even worse. Though he kept himself to himself much of the time, Mike felt constantly on edge.

Office rumors as to what had precipitated this change grew rife. Bernard Hoyle believed it was caused by Bob's hitting his head on the desk when he'd fallen recently; others whispered of marital problems. A few propounded with fearful relish the notion that Bob had some terminal illness—cancer or a brain tumor or perhaps even AIDS; the least melodramatic wondered whether someone "high up" had had "a quiet word" with Bob about "his attitude," because "let's face it, he gets up enough people's noses."

What unsettled Mike Travis most of all was not so much the fact that Bob was always looking around as if afraid someone was out to get him, nor even the way he flinched when the telephone rang or someone called his name. No, the thing that *really* made Mike's flesh creep was the fact that Bob Sterland had taken to wearing gloves.

They were gray gloves, very tight-fitting, and made of some soft material like felt. And since that day when Bob had fainted or knocked himself out or whatever he had done (Mike had not been there so could rely only on hearsay), he had worn them constantly.

On a number of occasions Mike had almost asked Bob about his gloves but had always chickened out at the last minute. Though they seemed sinister

521

(connotations of criminals not wishing to leave fingerprints), there was probably some perfectly innocent explanation for them. Perhaps Bob had something wrong with his hands—eczema, for example—and needed to keep them covered. That would kind of fit in with his personality change too, wouldn't it? Wasn't eczema often a result of stress? Mike tried hard to convince himself that Bob's undoubted problems were home-based and ordinary, either financial or marital, but it didn't quite ring true. Bob's reactions were too extreme. He acted more like a man who'd been threatened by the Mafia than one who fought with his wife.

At least Bob's behavior rescued Mike from having to speak his mind at the Christmas party, because for the first time in the four years since Mike had been with the Leisure Services, Bob simply didn't turn up. Normally he was there, quaffing the free alcohol and chatting up anything in a skirt, but this year he slunk out of the office at five o'clock and failed to reappear.

Another advantage from Mike's point of view was that he was able to work without interference. He finally booked Hinge and Brackett with not even so much as a disapproving glance from Bob.

Nevertheless, no matter how much he tried, he could not relish this new-found impunity.

Despite all this general unease, however, there was really only one *truly* disturbing and significant event throughout these two weeks leading up to Christmas, and that was right at the end, when Shirley brought some mistletoe into the office. It was December 23rd, and Shirley was tipsy. Unlike some of the office staff— Mike, for instance, who had to oversee the start of this year's panto on Boxing Day—she was about to start a ten-day holiday and had begun celebrating already.

There was a festive mood in the office that afternoon, not least because a light snow had started to fall outside. The office was bright with cards and decorations, someone had brought in a tape of Christmas carols which was playing softly in the background, and Elsie Marsden who was responsible for The Evergreen Club (Entertainment for the Over 80s) had been handing out her legendary mince pies which Mike proclaimed quite truthfully to be the best he'd ever tasted.

Shirley's boisterous and meandering return from an extended lunch break was, therefore, received in the right spirit. No one objected as she tumbled onto laps, brandishing her mistletoe, and greasily smothered the menfolk with lipstick. When Mike's turn came he laughed along with the others and hoped that he wasn't blushing *too* strongly. As Shirley clambered unsteadily off him, he caught a glimpse of Bob sitting rigidly behind his desk, watching Shirley's antics with an expression of wariness and hostility. Bob's teeth were showing in a near-snarl, his gray-gloved hands were gripping the edge of his desk as if the room had begun to tip and he was trying to stop himself from falling. Mike felt a thrill strong enough to be termed fear, and he thought, "Surely not. Surely even Shirl's not *that* drunk?"

But she was. Apparently oblivious to the way Bob was uncoiling in his seat like a panther preparing to spring, Shirley advanced upon him, giggling. "Come on, Bobby, your turn," she said. She held up the mistletoe as though to lash him with it.

Mike saw Bob's face turn bestial, saw him pounce across the desk, arms outstretched, and he tried to yell a warning, but was too late. "*Getawayfromme!*" Bob screeched at the same instant as his gloved fists slammed into Shirley just above her breasts.

An expression of almost comic surprise appeared on her face, then her legs shot from under her and she fell backward, landing heavily and unceremoniously on her bottom. Mike felt his desk vibrate as her blond head made sickening contact with it. Horror and fury rose within him. He leaped up, knocking his chair backward, and advanced on Bob, hands curling into fists.

"What the bloody hell did you do that for?" he shouted, and then added with feeling, "You bloody nutcase!"

Bob was backing away, crouched over like an animal. When he screamed, "Leave me alone!" spit flew out of his mouth.

Other people were shouting at Bob, but Mike was so enraged that he barely heard them. He glanced down at Shirley. She looked dazed but not unconscious, and thankfully there appeared to be no blood.

"What's wrong with you?" Mike yelled. "You're bloody unhinged! You should be put in a loony bin!"

Bob was still backing away, hands clenching and unclenching. He glanced behind him, and then with an abrupt change of direction, leaped forward, screaming.

Mike was so surprised that he didn't even have time to defend himself. He thought afterward that Bob must have done what he did to catch him off guard, but at the time he'd seemed genuinely terrified. But there was nothing behind Bob to frighten him as far as Mike could see: just a low filing cabinet with the two-foot-high office Christmas tree sitting atop it. He hardly saw Bob's gloved fist lash out before it impacted with his nose. More shocked than anything, Mike fell onto one knee like a suitor about to propose. The pain was clean and sharp.

As his blood began to patter on the floor and Shirley sat up, rubbing her head, Bob whirled and made his exit.

"I'll get you next time," Mike thought dazedly, "just see if I don't."

But he never saw Bob Sterland again.

"Come on, Hilary, I'm your sister. I can *tell* when something's wrong."

Hilary gazed down into her teacup as if she'd found something interesting among the tea-leaves. "No," she mumbled, "it's nothing really, I'm okay."

Claire sighed. "Is it the baby?" she persisted. "Is that what's worrying you?"

Hilary's hand crept to the dome of her stomach and caressed it absently. "No, no," she said a little irritably, "the baby's fine."

"Well, what then?" said Claire.

Hilary scowled. "I've told you, it's nothing."

"Yes it is, and I'm not leaving until you tell me. For God's sake, Hil, the baby's due any day. You can do without any sort of upset at a time like this."

"What would you know about it?" Hilary snapped, and then immediately regretted her words. She saw Claire's face fall. An ectopic pregnancy at the age of eighteen meant that Claire could never have children.

"Oh God, Clarry, I'm sorry. I didn't mean it like that."

Claire's voice was small, hurt. "I know I'm bossy, but it's only because I'm concerned about you."

"I know, Clarry, I know. I'm so sorry." Hilary picked up her tea cup, swirled the dregs around and put it down again. As if to herself she said, "It's Bob."

"Bob," repeated Claire, and immediately felt her hackles rise. She fought to keep her anger under control. "He hasn't been hassling you over this again, has he?"

"Oh no," said Hilary, "nothing like that. It's just that...well...he's been acting very strange lately."

So what's new? thought Claire but didn't say so. Instead she asked, "How do you mean—strange?"

"Well, you know how he usually is? Quite sort of..."

(*A pain in the arse*, thought Claire)

"...outgoing?"

Claire nodded.

"Well, these last couple of weeks he's been very...quiet. Moody. Sort of introverted. I daren't ask him what's wrong because he just gets annoyed. And he's been...doing strange things as well."

"Oh yeah?" said Claire warily.

"Mmm. Like for instance..." Hilary swept a hand around the room. "Do you notice anything different in here?"

Claire looked around. She *had* noticed something as soon as she'd come in, but had been unable to put her finger on it. "Yes," she said suddenly. "It looks...sort of bare. Like there's something missing."

"My plants," said Hilary. "Bob burnt them all."

"*He did what?*"

"He said they were all infected with something. He took them out into the back yard and put them in a pile and burnt them."

"Didn't you try and stop him?"

"I...I protested, but he went mad. You don't know what he's been like to live with these past couple of weeks, Claire. It's not been easy."

Claire shook her head. "The bastard. And just when you need support too. You should have given me a ring."

Hilary shrugged. "There's been other things too."

"Like what?"

"I don't know. Strange things. *Really* strange

things." She paused for a moment as if struggling to find words to describe complex ideas. At last she said, "He refuses to step on the lawn. He says that the grass is infected too and will have to come up. And the other night, when Kim asked him when he was going to fetch the Christmas tree, Bob looked absolutely horrified and said, 'We're not having one this year.' When Kim and I both started to protest, he completely flew off the handle and made Kim cry. He won't have holly or mistletoe in the house, and he even refused to let me get the Christmas decorations out.

"Also there are some foods he won't eat any more, like salad and vegetables and apples. He says they make him sick. What else?... Oh yes. He's started wearing gloves when he goes out. It's as if...I don't know...as if he thinks the whole world's infected with some disease that he's going to catch."

Claire shook her head worriedly. "He sounds like he's going off his trolley, Hil. I think you ought to tell someone."

"I'm telling you."

"No, I mean a doctor or something. Bob sounds like he needs help."

Now it was Hilary's turn to look worried. "Oh no," she said, "I'm sure it's not as bad as that. He's just under a lot of strain at the moment."

"*He's* under a lot of strain? You're the pregnant one."

"All the same...It'll probably just blow over. Bob can get a bit obsessive sometimes."

Claire sighed. "Has he said anything about how he's feeling? Have you tried talking to him about it?"

"Not really," admitted Hilary. "He just loses his temper all the time. He's not sleeping very well. He keeps having bad dreams."

"What kind of dreams? Does he talk about them?"

"Not really. He shouts out sometimes, though. He seems to think that something is coming to get him."

"Bloody hell," said Claire, shaking her head. "Sounds like serious paranoia. Something's got to be done, Sis. You can't be dealing with this now."

"No," Hilary admitted, and then abruptly she burst into tears.

Claire moved across and comforted her as best she could. She felt worried for her sister and the baby, and angry at Bob. Though mental illness was nobody's fault, she couldn't help thinking that this was just bloody typical of the man.

"Look," she said, "why don't you bring Kim and come and spend Christmas with me and Dave? We'll look after you."

Hilary shook her head firmly, then blew her nose. "No," she said. "Bob needs me. He's going through a difficult patch, that's all. I can't abandon him."

"I'm not suggesting you abandon him, I'm just talking about the next few days until the baby's born. You really need to relax, Hil, to be pampered a little bit."

"All the same," said Hilary. She shrugged, sighed. "I'll stay here. I'll be okay."

"God, you're bloody stubborn," Claire said, not without affection. Often she felt like the elder sister. "You will call me, though, won't you, if you need anything? Anything at all?"

"Yes," sighed Hilary.

"Promise?"

"Yes."

"You'd better mean that," Claire warned, "or there'll be trouble."

Hilary smiled tiredly, then looked up as they both heard the front door open and close. "Kim?" Hilary called. "Is that you?"

"Yeah, Mum."

"Come here a minute, will you? Say hello to your Aunt Claire."

There was silence for a moment, then they both heard Kim's dragging footsteps. He appeared in the doorway wearing a gray and turquoise sweatshirt, hands stuffed into his jeans pockets.

"Hi, Aunty Claire," he said dutifully.

Claire felt a little hurt but tried not to show it. There was a time when Kim would have been excited to see her, would have demanded her constant attention. When he'd been six, Kim had said, "When I grow up, I'm going to marry you, Aunty Claire." Now, though, he seemed to regard her visits as an intrusion. On the occasions when she'd broached the subject with Hilary, her sister had assured her, "It's just a phase. He's like that with everybody nowadays."

Smiling brightly, Claire said, "Hi, Kim, how's it going?"

"Okay," Kim said. He had stopped just inside the door and was rocking back and forth on his heels as though readying himself for a quick getaway.

"I've got something for you," Claire said.

"Oh yeah?"

"Yes. But you're not to open it until Christmas, okay?"

Kim glanced at his mother with an expression that seemed to say, "Christmas? What Christmas?" He shrugged as if he couldn't care less. "Okay."

Claire reached into the plastic Sainsbury's bag she'd brought with her and lifted out a box wrapped in silver and red-striped paper. "Ta da!" she proclaimed and held it out to him.

Kim simply stood where he was, making no move to enter the room and take the box from her. He looked decidedly uncomfortable.

"Well?" Hilary said. "What do you say?"

"Uh, yeah. Thanks," said Kim, and started to edge backward out of the room.

"Kim!" exclaimed Hilary. "Don't be so rude. Aren't you going to accept Aunty Claire's present?"

Kim seemed actually to consider the question—Claire felt sure he was about to say "No"—then his shoulders slumped and he seemed to brace himself for some ordeal. He slunk into the room, hands still stuffed in his pockets, and positioned himself very deliberately with his back to Hilary. Only then did he remove his right hand from his pocket and reach out to take the brightly wrapped package. Claire saw that his hand was stained with green and yellow paint. She glanced up at Kim and saw an appeal in his eyes.

"Kim." Hilary's stern voice spoke from behind him. Claire saw Kim flinch, his face scrunching up in anticipation of trouble.

"Yeah, Mum," Kim said.

"Show me your hands."

"What for?"

"I'm not stupid, Kim. Show me your hands."

Kim closed his eyes briefly, then opened them again. He turned, dragged his hands reluctantly from his pockets and held them out to his mother.

Hilary stared at them for a long moment, glancing from one to the other, face cemented with anger. "You've been at it again, haven't you?" she said. "And after you promised me you wouldn't."

"It's not what you think, Mum," Kim said.

"Isn't it?" she snapped.

"No." Kim frowned. His voice became whiny but defiant. "Phil Wallace's granddad has got a big wall that we practice on."

"Oh, really?" said Hilary in clear disbelief.

"Yes. You can ring him if you don't believe me. I'll give you his number."

"If it's all so innocent, why were you being so secretive?"

"Because I knew you'd be like this. You don't really like me spray-painting at all."

"That's not true."

"Yes it is. You said you'd sort something out for me, but you haven't done anything."

"I've had a lot to think about, Kim."

"Yeah, same as always. What do you have to have a stupid baby for anyway?"

He stormed out of the room, slamming the door behind him.

Claire looked at Hilary's stricken face and asked gently, "What was all that about?"

Bob pulled up at the traffic lights and sat there, staring straight ahead, gloved hands fidgeting on the steering wheel. He knew they wouldn't be following him—they didn't have to, they were already everywhere—but he kept glancing in his rear-view mirror nonetheless.

They'd almost got him back there in the office. For a while now he knew they'd been planning something, surrounding him with all those awful things. With Christmas nearly here the world had become a minefield. He'd never realized before quite how pervasive the influence of that evil color was. Glancing to his right he shuddered at the shop window displays—there were lurid imitation fir trees, cut-out representations of holly and bells with green bows, green lettering spelling out the words MERRY CHRISTMAS.

The sight of it all, all that green, was beginning to hurt his eyes and he looked away, concentrating on the snow-dusted road ahead. That was another way in which they were out to get him. Over the past couple of days, the color had actually started to make his eyes prickle like hay fever; if he stared at it for too long he got a headache. This meant that he couldn't be as watchful as he would have liked. Slowly but surely the color was building up its power, undermining his own defenses. Bob felt sure that soon it would launch its final, most devastating attack. It was a nightmare. Only he knew of the threat, the terrible build-up of evil, and yet alone he was helpless.

As he sat, waiting for the lights to change—to green, of course (a further example of how deeply the roots of the evil had embedded themselves)—Bob heard the roar of an engine approaching from behind. He was waiting to turn right on a dual carriageway. He glanced to his left as a car pulled up alongside him. Immediately he went rigid, his hands tightening on the steering wheel, puppyish whimpering slipping from between his whitened lips. The faint squeaking of his windscreen wipers as they swept the snow aside was like the sound of his own mind as its hinges strained and buckled.

The car beside him was big and American, with a bonnet you could play football on and fenders like barricades. It had shark-like fins curving above the tail-light clusters, and a soft-topped roof which had been rolled back like a giant concertina. What terrified Bob Sterland was the car's color—its bodywork was a bright lime-green, its interior well-padded olive-green leather—and its occupants. Driving the car was a female chauffeur in green shades and green livery, whilst standing up in the back was a green Father Christmas, complete with green suit, green skin and a green beard.

Father Christmas leaned toward him, grinning wolfishly, and Bob saw that he had green teeth. "Hello, Bobby," he said. "Merry Christmas. Ho Ho Ho." Saliva like snake venom drooled into his beard; Bob saw the hair sizzle and char, saw little spirals of green smoke rise and disperse in the cold air. Snow did not settle on this apparition, nor on the chauffeuse, nor even on the car itself.

Father Christmas blinked, and when his eyes opened a split-second later they were no longer human. They were grape-green, with black vertical slits for pupils.

Though Bob had his car windows rolled up, he could hear Father Christmas' voice clearly, as if the creature was speaking inside his head. "It's coming, Bobby. It's near," Father Christmas hissed.

Bob felt his paralysis snap like a frayed rope. He screamed, released the handbrake, slammed the car into gear and floored the accelerator. Horns blared, cars swerved, the screams of Christmas shoppers tore the seasonal atmosphere apart.

Bob saw a wall of screeching metal rearing up to meet him.

Then all became confusion, pain…and darkness.

Later, after she, Hilary and Kim had visited Bob in the

hospital, Claire found herself wondering whether her sister's husband had tried to commit suicide. It would be just like him to choose a method whereby other people could get hurt too. Thankfully, no one had been killed or even seriously injured. Even Bob's injuries, though ugly, were superficial—cuts and bruises, whiplash and a cracked rib. He was to be kept in overnight for observation and then discharged the next day, Christmas Eve. Claire was aware she knew too little of the situation to seriously contemplate whether Bob had been trying to end his life, and yet the thought nagged her nevertheless.

Not that she would ever share it with Hilary. Her sister had been shaken enough by what had happened. And if anything, their visit to the hospital had made things even worse. Not only was Bob's face a mess, but his mind was too.

Hilary, of course, had told her all about Bob's peculiar behavior these past few weeks, and yet Claire was shocked by the extent to which he had changed. When they had first entered the ward, he had been hunched up like an old man, hands squeezed tightly into fists and drawn up under his chin, eyes darting everywhere. The moment he saw them he had grown agitated. As soon as they got close enough to hear, he leaned over as far as his injuries and the white surgical collar encircling his neck would allow. "Please," he had croaked, "you've got to get me out of here."

Their reassurances had fallen on deaf ears. Gazing into space, seeming at times oblivious to their presence, Bob had kept moaning about "needing my gloves," and "that thing in the corner," which he claimed was "out to get me."

Only Kim had seemed unfazed by Bob's behavior. He had squinted at "that thing in the corner" and then back at his father. In a matter-of-fact voice he had said, "Don't be silly, Dad. It's just a Christmas tree."

When they left, Bob was frowning and muttering to himself, and Hilary was more upset than ever. Claire wondered whether the accident was to blame for Bob's scrambled thoughts, or whether this was simply the extent to which his mind had now deteriorated.

It was one-fifteen on Christmas Eve morning. Claire was lying on Hilary's narrow camp-bed in the half-finished nursery, staring at the darkness writhing on the ceiling like bacteria. She knew this wasn't really her problem, that Hilary had to make her own decisions, and yet she felt nervous tension chewing at her stomach, felt her mind turning the situation over and over in its search for answers.

Her instinct was to advise Hilary to jettison Bob, to get him out of her life, but as a solution it was neither practical nor compassionate. God knew why, but her sister loved the man. And right now Bob needed all the love and help and support he could get. He couldn't simply be discarded, thrown away like a faulty toy.

And yet...Hilary had the baby to consider. That, surely, had to be her first priority. It was a pity Bob couldn't simply be put on hold for a while, thrust into deep-freeze and thawed out when a more opportune moment arose.

That was the trouble with life, she thought. Like a bad comedy, the timing was always lousy and the laughter was tinged with despair. No amount of strategy or planning could ever change that. The thing to do was simply to muddle through, to rely on instinct and fate, and to salvage what you could.

She drifted to sleep with the matter still unresolved, with questions, problems circling around and around in her head. She dreamed of planets orbiting the heavens. It was her task to keep them grinding slowly, remorselessly on. She moaned, tossing and turning. The duvet slid to the floor like a melting bank of snow. When she awoke it was with a start, her eyes popping open. Though her limbs ached, she felt alert, wide-awake. It was quiet, yet she knew that *something* had woken her.

"Claaiiirrre." The supplication was feeble, racked with tiredness and pain. Immediately Claire's heart began to thump so loudly that she could hear the blood roaring in her ears. Barefoot, dressed in one of her sister's billowing nightshirts, she jumped up and ran across the landing into Hilary's room. Hilary was a heaving mound in the darkness. When Claire switched the light on, the first thing she saw was her sister's open mouth trying to draw breath.

"Hil, what's wrong?"

"Where've you been? I've been calling for ages." Before Claire could even say "Asleep," Hilary jabbered,

"Phone for an ambulance. I need an ambulance."

Claire wanted to ask questions but all she said was, "Right," and ran out of the room. Halfway down the stairs she almost slipped; her reflexes and the strength of her grip on the banister prevented her falling headlong. As she dialed 999 she drew two long breaths and muttered, "Calm...calm..." over and over. With the ambulance on the way she felt better, her head clearer. She switched the hall and landing lights on and ran nimbly up the stairs.

Ten minutes later, when the ambulance arrived, Hilary was downstairs on the settee with her dressing gown on and her overnight bag, which had been packed and re-packed over the course of the past ten days, by her side. The ambulance men were kind and calm; one of them smelled of coffee and peppermints. Claire saw Hilary into the ambulance, deposited Kim with Hilary's sleepy but accommodating next-door neighbor, hastily dragged on some clothes and followed in the car.

"Mr. Sterland? Mr. Sterland?"

The voice, booming and distorted, slipped like a razor into the sac of Bob's dreams and slit it open. Bob clawed his way out, shaking and whimpering. Behind him, formless horrors lurched and stirred sluggishly, forerunners of the greater horror from which there would be no escape. Bob rubbed the afterbirth of sleep from his eyes and goggled up at his rescuer. A round-faced nurse with scraped-back hair and a pimply forehead was smiling down at him. Bob reached out, his hand inadvertently clutching her breast. "It's almost here," he said. "It's so close."

Her smile faltering only slightly, the nurse gently disengaged his hand and helped him sit up. "Don't you worry, Mr. Sterland," she said, "you're safe now. You've been dreaming is all."

Her voice, a soothing Irish brogue, reassured most patients, but Bob was suffering from more than post-accident trauma.

"No," he urged, "you don't understand. Nobody understands but me."

The nurse sat by his side, enclosed his clenched left fist between the cool softness of both her hands. "Now then, Mr. Sterland," she said, a trace of firmness creeping into her voice, "Would you just hush up a minute. Don't you want to hear the good news I've brought you?"

Bob looked at her as if she were mad. "Good news?" he repeated.

"That's right." She paused a moment, a smile playing on her lips. Then she told him, "Your wife gave birth to a healthy baby girl at seven o'clock this morning."

Bob didn't say anything. He just stared at the nurse, a look of incredulity on his face. At last, as if it were a word he'd never heard before, he muttered, "A baby?"

"That's right," the nurse said, disappointed by his reaction. "You have a daughter, Mr. Sterland. Aren't you pleased?"

"Pleased," repeated Bob bleakly. How could anyone, ever again, be *pleased* about anything? Maybe once, in another life, he might have been pleased...But now...he shook his head...the idea was almost obscene.

"Come on," the nurse said briskly, strong arms wrapping themselves around his back, shoulder supporting his injured neck. "Maybe *seeing* your little girl will clear your head a bit."

She got him into a wheelchair and began to push him from the ward. As they neared the double doors, Bob pointed at the Christmas tree standing to one side of them and said in a panicked voice, "Don't take me near that. Keep it away from me."

The nurse shook her head but obliged. Anything to keep the peace. She knew from experience that a whack on the head could do the queerest things to a person's reason. On the short journey to Maternity, Bob flinched from the most innocuous objects—plants, a trolley draped with a green cloth, a poster with a crocodile on it. Once he screamed when a chubby black lady wearing a green overcoat walked by, scaring the poor woman half to death. The nurse, whose name was Maeve Fenton, wondered if this was such a good idea. But she knew Mrs. Sterland had been asking for her husband. And besides, you couldn't keep a father away from his own child when the sight of her might help bring him to his senses.

In Maternity they were directed down a corridor to a row of blue doors. Hilary was in room number six.

They halted outside, and Maeve helped Bob to his feet. The room would be poky and cluttered enough, she knew, without Bob's wheelchair taking up more space. "Now then, Mr. Sterland, lean on me." Maeve pushed the door open and the two of them awkwardly entered the room.

It was a drab room, almost colorless, the half-drawn curtains adding to the gloom. It was a far cry from the idealized images of frothy fiction: a radiant mother cuddling a rosy baby, everywhere sunny and spotless and riotous with flowers. Hilary was in bed, her belly still large. She looked pale and exhausted, her fringe a limp sweaty curtain. Whenever she moved, her face creased in pain. On the side of the bed nearer the door, Claire and Kim sat on tatty metal-framed chairs with blue plastic seats.

"Hello," said Maeve shyly as the three of them looked up. "I've brought a visitor to see you."

"Bob!" Hilary's voice was a half-sob of relief and joy. "Oh, Bob, it's so good to see you."

Bob said nothing, simply looked at Hilary as if bemused by the whole situation. He glanced back at Maeve, seeking guidance. She applied pressure to the small of his back, the merest suggestion of a push. Pointing to what looked like a plastic fish tank on the other side of the bed, she said, "Don't you want to see your daughter, Mr. Sterland? You'll be able to make it okay if you hold on to the bed."

Bob glanced quickly round the room as though searching for booby traps and then dutifully obeyed.

As he edged his way round the bed, using it to steady his bruised legs, his family watched him. Hilary was nodding in unconscious approval, Claire was scowling slightly and Kim's expression was unreadable. Kim it was, however, who spoke first. "She's brill, Dad. You'll really like her."

Bob reached the fish tank and peered into it. A tiny red thing in a nappy lay there, a scrap of humanity, its fists clenched and its mouth clamped in a grimace. Its eyes seemed to bulge behind closed eyelids as though too big for its head. The hair on its head was black and spiky. It looked, thought Bob, like a skinned chimpanzee.

He looked up to see his wife smiling blissfully at him. "Well, what do you think?" she said softly. "Isn't she beautiful?"

Beautiful. The word was an arrow in Bob's heart. What was the point of beauty any more? "Yes," he mumbled and looked back down at the crib. The baby moaned and wriggled, then opened its eyes and looked at him.

The attack took Bob so by surprise that he couldn't even scream. As the paralysis set in, he cursed himself for not realizing. This was why he had been chosen. He had *known* it was coming and yet he had been blind to its methods, its true nature. He stared down with abhorrence at this...*thing* that purported to be his daughter. To think, that he could possibly have fathered this! He felt the green light that shone from its eyes driving him to his knees. "Bob," he heard someone calling from far away. "Bob! Bob! Bob!" He wanted to scream at them, to warn them that this was the vessel, the gateway, through which the evil would be unleashed. But the green light swamped his brain and bludgeoned him into unconsciousness.

If it had been any other time of year, Hilary might have stayed in the hospital for a couple of days. However, she couldn't face the thought of spending Christmas in that dire little room, and so, just twelve hours after giving birth, she was being helped through her own front door by Claire. Kim brought up the rear, holding his new sister as if she were bone china. Hilary thought it wonderful the way he had taken to the baby, especially in light of his previous comments.

"Ow," she complained. Whenever she moved too suddenly, her stitched-up flesh informed her of the fact in a loud and piercing voice.

"Are you okay, Mum?" Kim asked anxiously.

Hilary managed a tired smile. "Yes, darling, I'm fine. Just a bit sore, that's all."

The house was cold, though not unwelcoming. Whilst Kim fetched the carry-cot from upstairs, Claire made tea. They installed the baby in the front room, then the three of them sat around the fire, talking quietly.

"I still think you should come and spend Christmas with me and Dave," said Claire. "Honestly, we'd love to have you. It wouldn't be any trouble."

"Yes it would," said Hilary. "Sleepless nights, nappy-changing, constant feeds. Your place is too small for that not to be intrusive."

Claire wafted a hand dismissively. The emerald-green evening gown, which she had offered to Hilary a few weeks before, and which she was now wearing in readiness for a meal out with Dave, shimmered like lizard-skin. "None of that matters," she said.

"I'm sure that's not what Dave thinks."

"Is that why you won't come? You think Dave wouldn't like it?"

Hilary sipped her tea and shook her head. "No, no, not really. I just...I want to be here, at home. I'll be fine. I've got Kim to look after me."

Kim nodded. He looked honored and a little surprised to be thought capable of such a responsibility. "Yeah," he said, "I'll look after Mum."

"I know you will," said Claire. She raised her hands palm upward in defeat. "All right. I can see I'm not going to persuade you."

"No," said Hilary, smiling, "you're not."

"But at least allow me a compromise?"

Hilary sighed, good-humoredly and exaggeratedly. "Go on."

"Let me and Dave come round here tomorrow, say about noon, and cook you Christmas dinner?"

Hilary looked at Kim. He was nodding eagerly, eyes wide and bright. It was as if the birth of the baby had somehow changed him back to the boy he had once been, sapped his sullen rebelliousness. She was realistic enough to know that it probably wouldn't last. Best to enjoy it while she could.

"Okay, okay," she said. "You've twisted my arm."

"Great," said Claire. "This is going to be an excellent Christmas."

"Mm," said Hilary. She looked at her new daughter and smiled wistfully.

Kim was sitting by the carry-cot, fascinated by the way the baby's tiny hand gripped his index finger. He glanced up and noticed his mother's expression.

"You okay, Mum?"

"What? Oh yes. I was just thinking…I wish your dad could be here, sharing all this."

Claire took a large gulp of tea and turned to look out of the window. Neither she nor Kim said anything.

If she had been a split-second earlier, Claire would have seen a bruised, black-eyed face on the other side of the glass, staring back at her. As soon as her head began to turn, however, the figure stepped back from the window, concealing itself in the shadows.

"Gone? Well, where's he gone to?"

Nurse Fenton squirmed under Sister Leach's accusatory glare. "I don't know, Sister. I've had a look round for him, but I can't find him anywhere."

The two of them looked down at Bob Sterland's empty bed. The cupboard beside the bed, which had contained a neatly folded change of clothes brought to the hospital by his wife, was now yawning emptily.

"Perhaps he's gone home," Nurse Fenton suggested.

"His wife's just had a baby. Maybe he wants to spend Christmas with the family."

"But he was in no state to go home, was he?"

Nurse Fenton shrugged. "It was more his mental state than his physical state that Dr. Singh was worried about. I think he just wanted to keep him in for observation for another day or two."

Sister Leach puffed out her cheeks in exasperation. "Well, I don't suppose there's a great deal we can do about it now. This is not a prison, after all, and with the Christmas Eve revelers due in at any minute we haven't got time to hunt for wayward patients."

"Shall I give his wife a ring, see if he's arrived home?"

"Only if you've got a minute. I know I won't have."

She waddled off, puffing, having made that last comment sound admonishing. Nurse Fenton stuck her tongue out at Sister's back. If she was quick she could call the Sterlands now...but just then Mrs. Laverton in Bed 4 began feebly to request her assistance. "Maybe later," she thought, but she was still thinking the same thing at three o'clock in the morning when the demands for her attention finally began to abate. She felt guilty, but not as guilty as she would feel in three days time when she read about Bob Sterland in the *Starmouth Gazette*. Despite telling herself it was not her fault, she would be unable to help feeling at least partly responsible for the terrible things he had done.

When the knock came on the front door, Kim was

sprawled on the settee, watching *The Terminator* on BBC2. It was now ten o'clock. At nine-thirty, Aunty Claire's boyfriend, Dave, had rung, and Kim had heard his tinny voice over the telephone demanding, "Are we going for this meal or what?" Though Aunty Claire had assured Dave she would be home in ten minutes, she had stuck around for at least another twenty, fussing over Mum and the baby, making sure they were all right and had everything they needed. Kim thought that Mum was quite relieved when Aunty Claire finally left. She told Kim she was tired, and that she was going to take the baby upstairs and lie down for a while.

Kim was quite disappointed to have his new sister taken away from him, but he just nodded and said, "Okay." Though *The Terminator* was a film he had been wanting to see for ages (Phil Wallace had seen it on video and had described it as "totally excellent"), Kim found he was having trouble concentrating on the action. He kept thinking how momentous this day had been, how amazing it was to have a little sister. The spectacle of Arnold Schwarzenegger slaughtering the entire clientele of a night-club with a machine-gun seemed petty and unreal.

He did not mind, therefore, dragging himself off the settee to answer the front door. He wondered who'd be calling at this time of night. He was reaching out for the handle before he realized it might be the police. He'd lied to his mum about Phil's granddad's garage wall; what in fact had resulted in him having green and yellow hands had been the painting of a dragon

:hat he, Phil and Rod had been doing on the back wall
of the primary school. He rubbed his hands together
now fruitlessly; it would be a few days yet before the
evidence began to fade. He ought to be more careful,
use methods other than his hands to block off color.
He'd heard of being caught red-handed but this was
ridiculous.

Sidling up to the door, he put his eye to the peep-
hole. The image on the other side startled him at first.
It looked like a deformed vicar with a vast white collar.
The figure blinked and swayed as though drunk. Kim
suddenly realized, not entirely joyfully, that it was his
father.

He unlocked the door and pulled it open. His father
immediately snapped alert, though seemed to look
straight through Kim as if he wasn't there. His swollen
lips opened then closed; his bruised and battered face
made his expression inscrutable. Kim had the sneaking
suspicion that his father didn't recognize him. "Dad,
hi," he said as a prompt.

His father didn't reply. He swayed to the right,
brought his hands up to the door frame to steady
himself, and suddenly Kim noticed something that sent
a cold spasm of shock through his stomach. His father's
hands were covered with fresh blood. Kim looked
beyond his father and caught the barest glimpse of
something green and shimmering sprawled in the front
garden, half concealed by the hedge. Then his father
was pushing him back as he forced his way into the
house, slamming the door behind him.

549

Kim backed away, disbelief pounding into his skull like nails. "Aunty Claire?" he tried to say, but his mouth was so dry it felt glued shut. His father moved methodically, unconcernedly, like a machine. He twisted the key in the front door, then pulled it from its slot and pocketed it. Kim just stood there, rooted by shock, as his father strode past him and into the kitchen.

When he heard his father yanking open drawers, making cutlery rattle, he began to tremble. As though in slow motion, feeling sick inside, he drifted over to the telephone. He reached for the receiver with fingers that felt nerveless as sausages. Then he heard a sound behind him and whirled round.

Bob had reappeared noiselessly and was now standing less than six feet away, holding the largest carving knife the Sterlands owned loosely in his right hand. Kim looked into his eyes and saw no warmth, no reason, saw only empty cold whirlpools, sucking everything that made sense into a formless black void where nothing worked.

"Dad," Kim mouthed. The word that emerged was less than a whisper. "Dad, what are you doing?"

Bob's cold, dead gaze focused on Kim, then flickered slowly down to the boy's hands. When he saw the paint on them his face became instantly, terrifyingly, bestial.

"Dad, no!" Kim screeched as his father lunged for him. He jumped back, saw the knife slice through the place where his head had been a split-second before, then he turned and fled.

With a howl, Bob launched himself in pursuit. Kim screamed so hard he tasted blood in his throat. Dad had suddenly become his every video nightmare rolled into one: Freddy Krueger, Jason Voorhees, Michael Myers. Kim glimpsed the flash of the knife as it arced toward him, and panic enabled him to put on an extra spurt of speed. If Bob had not been hampered by his injuries he would have caught his son easily. Kim screeched "*Muuuummmmm!*" and leaped at the stairs.

He bounded up them two, three at a time. His mother suddenly appeared on the landing just above him, clutching the baby, looking pale, confused, frightened.

"Kim, what's the matter?" she said. Kim glanced at her and saw her eyes widen as she looked behind him. "*Bob, no!*" she screamed.

It was that glance which probably saved Kim's life. He threw himself forward onto the top step and rolled over. The knife thudded into the stair carpet, barely an inch from Kim's thigh. As his father loomed over him, Kim kicked out with his legs, a panic-reflex. His right foot smashed into the center of his dad's face. Though Bob's head snapped back, blood spurting from re-opened wounds, Kim felt as though he'd kicked an iron post.

Bob pinwheeled his arms, but he couldn't keep his balance. Kim closed his eyes as his father fell backward down the stairs. His body sounded as though someone was destroying the banisters with a sledgehammer. His mother was screaming, and Kim wished she'd stop. She'd deafen the baby, or terrify her, or both.

He opened his eyes and saw his father sprawled motionless in a star shape at the bottom of the stairs. Using arms that felt shaky as old age, Kim hauled himself onto the landing and tried to stand up. His leg hurt terribly; when he put weight on it, it flared in agony, making him cry out. His mother was quieting a little now, clutching the baby to her. The baby was blinking and mewling, wriggling a little in her arms.

"We've got to get help," Kim said. "You stay here, I'll ring the police." Holding onto the banister, he began to limp down the stairs.

Hilary shot out an arm and grabbed her son's wrist. "What are you doing?" she demanded. "You can't go down there. What if he wakes up?"

"The phone's down there," Kim said. "I don't think he'll wake up, Mum. I'll take this just in case."

He curled his hand around the handle of the knife that was embedded in the stair carpet and tugged, but the knife wouldn't come free. Kim shuddered at the force his father must have used to drive it so deep.

"There's a phone in the bedroom," Hilary said. "Why don't you use that one?"

Kim looked at her. His mind was so scrambled with panic that he'd forgotten about that. He nodded and hauled himself back up the stairs. Led by his mother he limped toward her bedroom at the end of the landing. Just before entering he glanced down at his father's body. It was still motionless, limbs so splayed that it resembled a mannequin more than a human being.

When he entered the bedroom, his mother was standing by the telephone on the bedside table as though keeping guard. Unbelievably, the baby had fallen asleep again. Kim's bad leg was making him feel sick. He dropped onto the bed gratefully and snatched the receiver from its cradle. His finger had already dialed two 9s before he realized. He held the receiver away from him and looked at it incredulously, as if it had changed into a carrot before his eyes.

"It's dead," he said, looking up at his mother. "Dad must have cut the wires before he came in."

"Oh no." Hilary's body seemed to sag. She rocked the baby as if it needed comforting. "What are we going to do?"

Kim was just as scared as Hilary, but his fear was forcing his mind to work, to race through alternatives. He crossed to the window and peered out. All that confronted him was a sheer brick wall, a twenty-foot drop on to a crazy-paving path. He felt despair rising in him and gulped it down like nasty medicine. There was only one thing to do: sneak down the stairs, step over his father's body and escape via the back door in the kitchen. He outlined his plan briefly to his mum. She didn't like it, but she had to agree. There was simply no alternative.

Kim led the way back to the landing, senses alert. The house was quiet, apart from the squealing roar of a car chase caged within the TV. Kim crossed the landing and peered over the banister. Instantly a wave of terror, awful and absolute, coursed through him. He managed to turn his head and look at his mother. He tried to speak but his brain, his vocal cords, his entire head felt locked in ice.

"What is it?" Her voice rose in panic with each syllable, her son's fear infecting her. She stumbled forward, face creasing at the razor of pain between her legs. She looked over the banister.

"Oh God," she whispered.

Bob was gone. Where he had lain were only bits of broken banister and a smeary pool of blood in the shape of Africa. Kim looked around and saw that the knife which had been embedded in the stairs was gone too. He tried to force his mind to work, to decide on the best course of action. For now he and his mum had a clear run at the stairs. Could they risk it? Or was Dad lying in wait for them somewhere along the way?

Kim leaned over the banister as far as he could, craning his neck. He could not see his father anywhere. Maybe he had gone away, or even passed out again. Certainly there was nothing to be gained from waiting here. He explained this to his mum. She looked terrified, but nodded. They began to creep along the landing, both wincing at their own separate hurts. Kim winced too every time the floorboards creaked. In the quiet house, the tiny sounds of bending wood were like the bellowing blares of a klaxon.

They were over halfway along the landing, only a few feet from the head of the stairs, when the door at the end of the landing crashed open. It was the bathroom door. Framed there was a monster that resembled Bob Sterland barely at all. Its face was a glistening mask of gore, its hair standing up in clotted spikes. Its eyes were black and dead like a shark's, its bared teeth slick with a pink froth of blood and saliva. Its shirt-front was a bib of red; dangling in its right hand, pointing at the floor, was the carving knife. It took a shaky step forward, and its hand came up until the knife was level with its face.

"Bob." Hilary's voice was a pleading cat's mew. "Please, Bob. Please."

Bob took another step forward, then another. Deliberate. Slow. Robotic. He blinked blood from his eyes, swayed as if about to collapse. Then he recovered and took another step closer. He was no more than eight feet away.

Kim tugged at his mother's arm. "Come on, Mum, in here." He pulled her, limping, into his own bedroom and slammed the door. There was no escape, not really, but they couldn't just stand there and wait to be butchered. Hilary was wailing now, great racking sobs convulsing her body. In her arms the baby slept, oblivious.

In the split-second before his father opened the door, Kim looked around for a weapon and couldn't find one. And then the handle jerked, the door swung back, and there he was, the mad slasher from a thousand drive-in movies come true. Hilary screamed. The baby woke up and began to cry. Kim positioned himself before his mother, and the two of them began to back away.

Kim knew there was nowhere to go. Once they reached the wall that was it. He was so scared he couldn't even scream or cry. His father advanced unsteadily. His surgical collar, streaked with blood, resembled a carapace of exposed bone, the suggestion of a protective exo-skeleton like the thing in *Alien*. His dad's face was so mashed and covered in blood that individual features were almost indiscernible. He was not even showing his teeth any more, which made it look as though his mouth was gone.

Kim was just building up the courage to fly at his father, make a suicidal attempt to wrestle the knife from him, when his bad leg caught the sharp edge of the bed-frame. The pain was so severe it was like being hamstrung. He howled, his knee buckled, and he fell on to his backside. Fresh pain flared at the base of his spine. Hilary screamed again as Bob made a gurgling sound of triumph and loped toward Kim's sprawled body.

Frantically, Kim tried to crawl under his bed, but the space was too tight and there was too much debris under there. His hand closed around something metal. He drew it out. It was one of his spray-paint cans. Desperately he hurled it at his father. Bob barely flinched as the can rebounded off his shoulder. Kim drew out another can, this one heavier, almost full. He was about to throw it when a better idea struck him.

He pointed it at his Dad's face and pressed down hard on the spray-head.

A filmy jet of bright green paint leaped from the nozzle. It mingled with the blood on Bob's face, making him more hideous than ever. He looked like a zombie now, a car crash victim come alive, rot sliding down his face with the seepage from open wounds. Kim gritted his teeth and sprayed the paint directly into his father's eyes. Bob screamed and reeled back, like Frankenstein's monster scorched with flame.

As Bob staggered about the room, Kim dragged himself painfully to his feet. His mum had fallen silent and was simply staring at his dad with wide-open eyes. Her mouth was open too, locked in a still-born scream. The baby in her arms was struggling, uncomfortable in its mother's overtight grip.

"Come on, Mum," Kim said, "let's go now." He took her arm, the muscles of which were rigid as a bodybuilder's. When he pulled at her, her eyes flickered and focused on him. Shuffling, face blank, she allowed herself to be led.

Bob was crouched on the floor, hands working at his eyes, trying to rub the stinging blindness away. The knife was by his side. Kim darted forward and snatched it up. He propelled his mother out of the room as fast as their injuries would allow, closing the door behind them. It was only when they were out of the house and Kim had pulled the kitchen door shut behind them, that he finally allowed himself to cry.

❦

Bob saw the moon first, a slice of light that penetrated the black burning of his vision. But it was not a good light. It was sickly and evil, green as decay. His eyes still smarted, weeping tears, but little by little the world was coming back to him. As it did so he knew he had lost, and he wished he had been blinded after all. The evil was everywhere, crawling over every surface. Bob held up his hands and saw they were thick with it, sticky and burning like fire. His heart was racing in his chest, threatening to burst, each rapid pump a stab of pain. He blundered to his feet, head spinning, knowing that the poison was already raging through his system.

He had lost. *Lost.* The notion was almost too colossal to accept. As he rose, his reflection rose too, in a mirror across the room, confronting him.

"No," Bob murmured, "no." Something flexed inside him, the last of his control, and then suddenly, shockingly, broke. "No!" he screamed. "*Noooooo!*" He ran full-tilt at the mirror and hurled himself toward it head-first.

The din of shattering glass was accompanied by a hot, pure pain that Bob almost reveled in. He was hoping it would be the last pain, the end pain, but it subsided all too quickly. His shattered thoughts swam like confused fish in his mind. His vision was a boiling kaleidoscope of green and red. Something glinted. Light. A promise of salvation.

Bob snatched at the light, swept it up. It was a

triangle of glass. Ignoring the jagged edges, the slivers that cut through his skin and embedded themselves in the soft meat of his palm, he began to hack at his face, trying to remove the mask of evil. It was no good. The evil had sunk deep, like water into a sponge; even now he could feel it working its way to his core. If it took over his soul then he too was lost, would be in thrall to it forever.

Squirming, he hauled himself across the carpet of broken glass to the window. The evil moon leered at him, taunting him with its victory. Bob shook his head, moaning his defiance. He raised his arm, hand flopping onto the bar that secured the window, trying to lift it. Pain screamed in every muscle, the evil trying to dominate him. Bob felt something give, and the window swung open. A freezing wind swept in, stinking of decay.

With a gargantuan effort Bob hauled himself on to the windowsill. The world was careering, spinning round and round, but Bob held on, refusing to be disoriented. His upper body was out of the window now. He kicked his legs, and suddenly he was falling. As the wind rushed past, the rags of his blindness were torn away and all at once he could see clearly. He screamed, but the trap was sprung, there was no going back.

The green man, waiting below, raised its arms to catch him.

ALSO EDITED BY PETER CROWTHER

JOURNEY INTO THE MOST MYSTERIOUS
AND MYSTICAL STRUCTURES OF HISTORY
AND OUR IMAGINATION...

AN ANTHOLOGY OF SHORT STORIES
WHICH EXPLORES FORCES, PEOPLE AND
THINGS BETTER LEFT FORGOTTEN.

HORROR
HARDCOVER ANTHOLOGY
WITH DUST JACKET
ISBN 1-56504-905-5
WW04905/13005
$19.99 US/$27.99 CAN

EDITED BY EDWARD E. KRAMER AND PETER CROWTHER

PRAISE FOR *TOMBS*

"THE STANDARD OF CRAFTSMANSHIP AND IMAGINATION IS HIGH. SPLENDIDLY
ECLECTIC...WITH A REASSURING HUMOROUS STREAK."
    KIRKUS REVIEWS

"THIS IS AN AGREEABLE GRAB BAG OF CLAUSTROPHOBIC, MORTIFYING PLEASURES."
    PUBLISHERS WEEKLY

"YOU KNOW WHAT TO EXPECT FROM AN ANTHOLOGY WITH A TITLE LIKE TOMBS—
RIGHT?
WRONG! THE 22 ORIGINAL STORIES HERE RANGE THROUGH HORROR TO FANTASY, SF,
AND CONTEMPORARY HIGH-TECH, AND FROM THE WILDEST HUMOR TO THE STARKEST
TRAGEDY. THERE'S SOMETHING HERE FOR NEARLY EVERY TASTE. IN ALL A MOST
IMPRESSIVE GATHERING. COME SEE FOR YOURSELF!"
    LOCUS
    FAREN MILLER

CONTAINS STORIES BY MICHAEL MOORCOCK, NEIL GAIMAN MICHAEL BISHOP, LARRY
BOND, BEN BOVA, NANCY A. COLLINS, JOE R. LANSDALE, KATHE KOJA, STORM
CONSTANTINE, ROBERT HOLDSTOCK, AND OTHERS.

PAPERBACK AVAILABLE JUNE 1996